HUNT
FOR DARK
INFINITY

*This book is dedicated to my siblings: Michael, Lisa,
David, Paul, and Sarah.
Thanks for making life fun and adventurous.
I just wish you had shared more of the Dashner
good-looking genes. I love you guys.*

THE
13TH REALITY

HUNT FOR DARK INFINITY

Sweet Cherry Publishing Limited
Unit 36, Vulcan House,
Vulcan Road,
Leicester, LE5 3EF,
United Kingdom

Originally published in the USA in 2008 by Aladdin,
an imprint of Simon and Schuster's publishing division.
First published in the UK in 2018 by Sweet Cherry Publishing

Hunt for Dark Infinity ISBN: 978-1-78226-404-0

www.sweetcherrypublishing.com
Printed and bound by Replika Press Pvt Ltd.

THE ILLNESS

The boy stared at his world gone mad.

The wintry, white face of the mountain housing the End of the Road Insane Asylum towered behind him, its forever-frozen peak lost in the grey clouds blanketing the sky. Before him, the boy saw the last person of his village succumb to the claws of insanity.

The man was filthy, barely clothed, scraped from head to toe. He thrashed about in the muddy grass of what used to be the village common, clutching at things above him that were not there. The man's eyes flared, wide and white, as if he saw ghosts swarming in for the haunt. He screamed now and then, a raw rasp that revealed the condition of his ruined throat. Then, spurred by something unseen, the man got up and sprinted away, stumbling and getting back up again, running wildly, arms flailing.

The boy finally tore his eyes away, tears streaming as he looked back towards the icy mountain. A lot of the crazies were already there, filling the asylum to capacity – prospective inmates had been turned away for a week now, left to wander the streets and fight others who were as mad as they were.

The boy had not eaten in two days. He'd not slept in three, at least not peacefully. He'd stopped grieving for his parents and brother and started worrying about how to survive, how to live. He tried not to think–

You are mine, now.

The boy jumped, looking around for the source of the voice. Someone had spoken to him, as clear a sound as he'd ever heard. But no one was there.

There's no need to be alarmed. The Darkin Project will be fully functional soon. Until then, survive. This is an automatic recording. Goodbye for now.

The boy spun in a tight circle, searching his surroundings. He saw only the burnt ruins of his village – weeds, dust, rubbish. A rat skittered across the ruined road. Someone was screaming, but it was very far away.

The boy was alone.

The voice was in his head. It had begun.

PART I

THE UNWANTED
WINK

The Two Faces of Reginald Chu

Mr. Chu hated his first name. It was evil. Crazy, perhaps, for an adult to think such a thing – especially a science teacher – but as he walked down the dark, deserted street, he felt the truth of it like a forty-pound weight in his gut. He'd felt it since childhood – an odd uneasiness every time someone called his name. A black pit in his belly, like rotting food that wouldn't digest.

'Mr. Chu!'

The sharp ring of the woman's voice slicing through the air startled him out of his thoughts. His breath froze somewhere inside his lungs, sticking to the surface, making him cough until he could breathe again.

He looked up, relieved to see it was only Mrs. Tennison poking her frilly head out a high window, no doubt spying on her neighbours. Her hair was pulled into dozens of tight curlers, her face covered in a disgusting paste that looked like green frosting.

Mr. Chu drew another deep, calming breath, embarrassed he'd been jolted so easily. 'Hi, Mrs. Tennison,' he called up to her. 'Nice night, huh?'

'Yeah, she said in an unsure voice, as if suspecting him of trouble. 'Why, uh, why are you out so late? And so far away from your house? Maybe you'd like to, uh, come up for a cup of tea?' She did something with her face that Mr. Chu suspected was supposed to be a tempting smile, but looked more like a demented clown with bad gas.

Mr. Chu shuddered. He'd rather share a cup of oil sludge with Jack the Ripper than spend one minute in Mrs. Tennison's home, listening to her incessant jabbering about town gossip.

'Oh, better not – just walking off some stress,' he finally said. 'Enjoying the night air.' He turned to walk away, glad to have his back to her.

'Well, be careful!' she yelled after him. 'Been reports of thugs in the town square, mobbin' and stealin' and such.'

'Don't worry,' he replied without looking back. 'I'll keep an eye out.'

He quickened his step, turned a corner, and relaxed into a nice and easy gait. His thoughts settled back to the strange fear he had of his own first name. The name he avoided whenever possible. The reason he always introduced himself as 'Mr. Chu' to everyone he met.

Having taught science at Jackson Middle School in Deer Park, Washington, for more than twenty years, he'd hardly ever been called anything *but* Mr. Chu. Single and childless, his parents long dead, and separated from his brothers and sisters by thousands of miles, he had no one to call him anything more intimate than those two lonely, icy words. Even the other teachers mostly hailed him by his formal title, as if they dared not befriend him. As if they were afraid of him.

But it was better than the alternative. Better than hearing the word he despised.

Reginald.

Wiping sweat from his brow, he thought back to an incident several months earlier when a fellow teacher had uttered aloud the rarely heard *Reginald* when poking her head into his classroom for a question. A student had stayed after school that day, and the look that had swept over the boy's face upon hearing Mr. Chu's first name had been a haunted, disturbed expression, as if the kid thought Mr. Chu stole children from their beds and sold them to slave traders.

The look had hurt Mr. Chu. Deeply. That cowering wince of fear had solidified what he had considered until then to be an irrational whim – the childish, lingering superstition that his name was indeed evil. The knowledge had always been there, hidden within him like a dormant seed, waiting only for a spark of life.

The student had been Atticus "Tick" Higginbottom, his favourite in two decades of teaching. The boy had unbelievable smarts, a keen understanding of the workings of the world, a maturity far beyond his almost fourteen years. Mr. Chu felt an uncanny connection to Tick – an excitement to tutor him and guide him to bigger and better things in the fascinating fields of science. But the look on that fateful day had crushed Mr. Chu's heart, tipping him over a precipice onto a steep and slippery slope of depression and self-loathing.

It made no sense for a man grounded in the hard science of his profession to be so profoundly affected by such a simple event. It was an elusive thing, hard to reconcile with the immovable theorems and hypotheses that orbited his mind like rigid satellites. A name, a word, a look, an expression. Simple things, yet somehow life-changing.

Now, as he walked home in the darkness of night, the new school year only a few days away, the air around him mirrored his deepest feelings and unsettling thoughts. Instead of cooling off, it seemed to get hotter. The suffocating heat stilted his breathing despite the sun having gone to bed hours earlier. Since Mrs. Tennison's intrusion, neither people nor breeze had stirred in the late hour. The muted thumps of his trainers were the only sound accompanying him on this now habitual midnight walk, when sleep eluded him. He turned onto the small lane leading to the town cemetery – a shortcut to his home – a creepy but somehow exhilarating path.

It had been a long summer – weeks of huddling under the burning lamp in his study, scouring the pages of every science magazine and journal to which he could possibly subscribe. He'd channelled his growing self-pity into an unprecedented thirst for knowledge, his brain soaking it up like a monstrous, alien sponge. Oh, how he'd enjoyed every single minute of his obsessive study binge. It kept him sane, helped him–

Mr. Chu faltered, almost stumbled, when he realised a man stood just outside the stone archway of the cemetery, arms folded across his chest, silhouetted against the pale light of a streetlamp in the distance. He seemed to have appeared from nowhere, as Mr. Chu had detected no movement prior to noticing the stranger. Like a black cardboard cutout, the figure didn't move, staring with unseen eyes, sending a wave of prickly goosebumps down Mr. Chu's arms.

He recovered his wits and continued walking, refusing to show fear. Why was he so jumpy tonight? He had no reason to think this man was a thug, despite Mrs. Tennison's absurd warning. Even if the still figure, standing there like a statue, *was* a bad guy, it would do no good to act afraid. All the same, Mr. Chu slyly changed his course to cross the lane, knowing the small, wooded area between here and the town square would provide cover if he needed to run and hide.

Quit being ridiculous, he chided himself. However, he kept the mysterious shadow of the man in the corner of his vision.

Mr. Chu had just reached the gravel-strewn side of the road when his late-night visitor spoke – a slippery, soft-spoken whisper that nevertheless carried like clanging cowbells through the deep silence of the night.

'Where do you think *you're* going?'

Bitter mockery filled the voice, and Mr. Chu stopped walking, falling through the thin ice of apprehension straight into an abyss of outright terror, something he had never truly felt before. It turned his stomach, squeezed it, sending sour, rotten juices through his body; he wanted to bend over and throw up.

Another man stepped out of the woods to his right. At the same moment, a finger tapped him from behind on his right shoulder. Shrieking, Mr. Chu spun around, his fear igniting into panic.

This time, he saw a face – a shadowed mug of hard angles, rigid with anger. Mr. Chu saw a flicker of movement, then a flash of blue light. An explosion of heat and electricity came from everywhere at once, knocking him to the ground in a twitching heap. He cried out as pain lanced through his body, tendrils of lightning coursing along his skin. With a whimper, he looked up and saw the person holding out a long device that still crackled with static electricity.

'Wow, you look just like him,' the nameless face said.

☼

Reginald Chu, founder and CEO of Chu Industries, stood within his massive laboratory, studying the latest test results from the ten-storey-tall Darkin Project as he awaited word on the abduction of his Alterant from Reality Prime. It amused him to know the science teacher would be brought to the same building in which he himself stood – a dangerous prospect at best, certain death at worst. Mixing with alternate versions of yourself from other Realities was like playing dentist with a cobra.

Which is why his employees had been given strict instructions to never bring the *other* Reginald Chu within five hundred feet of the *real* Reginald Chu (the one who mattered most in the universe anyway). They'd lock the lookalike away in a maximum-security cell deep in the lower chambers of the artificial mountain of glass that was Chu Industries until they needed the captive to serve his dual purpose in being kidnapped.

Dual purpose. Reginald took a deep breath, loving the smells of electronics and burnt oil that assaulted his senses. He reflected on the plan he'd set into place once the information had poured in from his network of spies in the other Realities. They had brought news of intriguing developments with massive potential consequences – especially the bit about the boy named Atticus Higginbottom.

If Reginald was not the most supreme example of rational intelligence ever embodied in a human being – and he most certainly *was* – he would have doubted the truth of what he'd heard and had verified by countless sources. It seemed impossible on the face of it – something from a storybook told to dirty urchins in an orphanage before they went to bed. Tales of magic and power, of an unspeakable ability in the manipulation of the most central force in the universe: Chi'karda. A human Barrier Wand, perhaps.

But Reginald knew the mystery could be explained, all within the complex but perfectly understood realm of science. Still, the idea thrilled him. The boy had no idea what was at stake – he had something Reginald Chu wanted, and nothing in the world could be more dangerous than that.

Reginald walked over to the airlift that would ascend along the surface of the tall project device. He allowed his retina to be scanned, then stepped onto the small metal square of the hovervator. He pressed the button for the uppermost level. As the low whine of the lift kicked in, pushing him towards the false sky of the ridiculously large chamber, he heard the slightest beep from the nanophone nestled deep within the skin of his ear.

'Yes?' he said in a sharp clip, annoyed at being disturbed even though he'd *told* them to do so as soon as they returned. The microscopic particles of the device he'd invented took care of all communication needs with no effort on his part.

'We have him,' the soft voice of Benson replied, echoing in Reginald's mind as though from a long-dead spirit. Benson had been the lead on the mission to Reality Prime.

'Good. Is he harmed? Did you raid his house, gather his ... *things?*' The airlift came to a stop with a soft bump. Reginald stepped onto the metal-grid catwalk encircling his grandest scientific experiment to date. From here, all he could see was the shiny golden surface of the enormous cylinder, dozens of feet wide, reflecting back a distorted image of his face that made him look monstrous.

'Everything went exactly as planned,' Benson said. 'No blips.'

Reginald stabbed a finger in the air even though he knew Benson couldn't see him. 'Don't you dare bring that sorry excuse for a Chu near me – not even close. There's no guarantee who'd flip into the Nonex. I want him locked away–'

'Done,' Benson barked.

Reginald frowned at his underling's tone and interruption. He took note to watch Benson closely in case his lapse in judgement developed into something more akin to insubordination or treachery.

'Bring his belongings to me and ready him for the Darkin injection.'

'Yes, sir. Right away, sir.' Reginald's nanophone registered a faint quiver in Benson's voice.

Ah-ha, Reginald thought. Benson had realised his mistake and was trying to make up for it with exaggerated respect. *Stupid man.*

'As soon as we inject him,' Reginald said, 'we can begin phase two. You've checked and rechecked that the others are still together?'

'Yes, sir. All three of them, together for another two days. School starts after the weekend.'

'You're *sure?*' Reginald didn't want to waste any more time away from his project than he must.

'Seen them with my own eyes,' Benson said, the slightest hint of condescension in his voice. 'They'll have no reason to suspect anything. Your plan is flawless.'

Reginald laughed, a curt chortle that ended abruptly.

'You always know what to say, Benson. A diplomat of diplomats – though one not afraid to squeeze a man's throat until he sputters his last cough. A perfect combination.'

'Thank you, sir.'

'Call me when you're ready.' Reginald blinked hard, the preprogrammed signal to end his call with the synthesised sound of an old-fashioned phone slamming into its cradle.

Clasping his hands behind his back, Reginald continued pacing around the wide arc of the Darkin Project, his carnival-mirror reflection bobbing up and down in the polished, cold metal. He loved doing this, loved the feeling he got when the words that lay imprinted in large, black letters appeared on the other side. He slowed for dramatic effect, running his left hand lightly across the indentation of the first letter. A few more steps and he stopped, turning slowly towards the cylinder to look at the two words for the thousandth time – the thrill of it never ceased to amaze him.

Two words, spanning the length of his outstretched arms. Two words, black on gold. Two words that would change the Realities forever.

Dark Infinity.

SPAGHETTI

'Dude, that stuff smells like feet.'

Tick Higginbottom stifled a laugh, knowing his friend Paul's brave statement would bring down the wrath of Sofia Pacini, who was hard at work kneading a big ball of dough in the Higginbottoms' kitchen. Tick loved watching the two of them go at each other. He adjusted the red-and-black scarf around his neck, loosening it to let more air in, and settled back to enjoy the show.

'What?' Sofia said, using her pinky to push a strand of black hair behind her ear – the rest of her fingers were covered with flour and yellow goop. '*What* smells like feet?'

Paul pointed at the kitchen counter, where a mass of raw pasta dough rested like a bulbous alien growth. '*That* – the famous Pacini spaghetti recipe. If I wasn't helping you make it, I'd swear my Uncle Bobby had just walked in with his shoes off.' He looked over at Tick and squinted his eyes in disgust, waving his hand in front of his nose. 'That guy's feet sweat like you wouldn't believe – they smell like boiled cabbage.'

Sofia turned towards Paul and grabbed his shirt

with both hands, obviously not concerned about how dirty they were. 'One more word, Rogers. One more, and I'll shove this dough down your throat. You'd probably choke and save Master George the trouble of firing your skinny Realitant hide. Plus, it's the feta cheese that stinks, not the dough.'

'Whatever it is, I'll eat it,' Paul said. 'Just hurry – I'm starving.'

Sofia let go and turned back to her work. 'You Americans – all you want is fast food. We still have to make the sauce while the pasta dries.'

'Tick,' Paul groaned, 'can't we just make some hot dogs?'

'Grab some potato chips out of the pantry,' Tick said, pointing. 'I'm waiting for the world-famous Pacini spaghetti.'

More than six months ago, Sofia had won a bet to visit Tick. Since her family had more money than most movie stars, she not only paid for her trip from Italy, but she also paid for Paul to come from Florida at the same time. Tick had looked forward to the visit all summer, thinking every day about his friends and their crazy experience in the Thirteenth Reality where they'd all been lucky to escape alive. Although this was only the second time the three of them had been together, they were already friends for life, not to mention members of a very important group – the Realitants.

'All right,' Sofia said. 'Time to get busy. Help me spin out the strands.' She grabbed a small wad of dough and showed them how to shape it into a long, slender rope. Like soldiers following orders, Tick and Paul got to work while Sofia started on the sauce, chopping ingredients and pouring one thing after another into a huge metal pot.

'So is Master George going to call us or what?' Paul said. After stealing Mistress Jane's Barrier Wand, they'd been assured from their leader that it wouldn't be long before the Realitants would gather again.

'It's been almost three stinkin' months,' Tick replied. 'I check the mailbox every day.'

Sofia snorted and shook her head. 'He can track people all over the world using nanolocators, but he still sends messages in crumpled old envelopes.' She measured a teaspoon of something orange and dropped it in the pot. 'You'd think the old man could figure out how to use email.'

'Chill, Miss Italy,' Paul said, holding up a long strand of dough and swinging it back and forth, grinning like it was the grandest form of entertainment in the world. 'It's so he can't be tracked down by all the bad guys. Don't you ever watch TV?'

Tick spoke up before Sofia could reply – he was hungry and didn't want any more delays from his friends' bickering. 'I just hope he's figured out how we winked out of the Thirteenth with a broken Barrier Wand.'

'How?' Paul asked. 'I'll tell you how. You're a regular Houdini – all you need is a cape and one of those funky black hats.'

'And a wand,' Sofia said as she began stirring her cauldron of blood-red sauce.

'He had a wand,' Paul said. 'It was just broken.'

Tick's spirits dampened a bit, his heart heavy at remembering the terror of that moment when the Barrier Wand hadn't worked, when he'd pushed the button over and over again as hordes of screaming, sharp-toothed fangen rushed at them. Any reminder that such monsters existed in the world – or worlds – was enough to make a spaghetti feast not quite as appealing.

'He made it work somehow,' Sofia said, nodding at Tick as she stirred. 'Magic Boy himself.'

Tick did his best to smile, but it didn't last.

☼

Two hours later, the homemade meal passed Sofia's inspection – barely. She kept insisting the sauce needed to simmer the rest of the day to taste perfect, but finally gave in to the impatient hunger groans of Paul and Tick. *It was worth every minute,* Tick thought as he shovelled in the food, not caring that he'd already spilled sauce on his scarf once and his shirt twice. He felt much better about things now that he wasn't starving.

'I'm not gonna lie to ya,' Paul said through a huge bite, a vampire-like drip of red sauce streaked on his chin. 'This is the best thing I've eaten in my entire life.'

Sofia sat back in her chair, pressing a hand to her heart. 'Did you, Paul Rogers from Florida – King Smarty Pants himself – just say something nice to me?'

'Yes, ma'am, I did. And I meant every word of it. Dee-lish.'

'It's really good,' Tick chimed in. 'I'll never doubt you again about your family's claim to fame.'

Several moments passed, everyone too busy eating to talk. Sofia slurped her spaghetti, sounding like a renegade octopus trying to climb a slippery metal pole. Tick almost made a joke, but didn't want to waste any breath when there were still spaghetti on his plate.

Paul wiped a big swathe of sauce from his plate with a piece of garlic bread and shoved the whole thing in his mouth. 'Man,' he mumbled as he chewed, 'I can't wait to visit more Realities so I can check out the ladies.'

Tick almost choked on a laugh. 'Yeah, right. You'd be lucky to get a date with Rutger's little sister.' Tick's friend Rutger was an incredibly short and fat man from the Eleventh Reality. And full of pranks.

Paul shrugged. 'As long as she's not quite so ... bowling-ballish, I'm cool with that. Paul ain't picky.'

'Good thing, too,' Sofia said. 'No girl I know would give you a second glance.'

'Oh, yeah? And why's that?'

Sofia put down her fork and looked him square in the eyes, her face set in matter-of-fact stone. 'Your ears are crooked.'

'Excuse me?'

'Your. Ears. Are. Crooked.' Sofia emphasised each word as if Paul spoke a foreign language, then folded her arms and raised her eyebrows.

'My ears are crooked,' Paul repeated, deadpan.

'Yes.'

'My ears are *not* crooked.'

'Yes, they are.'

'No, they're not.'

'Crooked.'

Paul reached up and felt both of his ears, rubbing them between his thumbs and forefingers. 'What does that even mean? How could they be crooked?'

Sofia pointed at Paul's face. 'Your left ear is almost half an inch lower than your right one. It looks ridiculous.'

'No way.' Paul looked to Tick for help. 'No way.'

Tick leaned forward, studying Paul's face. 'Sorry, big guy. Crooked as bad lumber.'

'Where's a mirror?' Paul half-yelled, standing up and running for the bathroom. A few seconds later, his shriek echoed down the hall: 'Tick! My ears are crooked!'

Tick and Sofia looked at each other and burst out laughing.

A dejected Paul came slouching down the hall; he pulled back his chair and collapsed onto the table. Then he held up a finger, like he had a brilliant idea. 'Fine, but I have beautiful toenails – here, let me show you–'

'*No!*' Sofia and Tick shouted together.

Thankfully, the low rumble of the garage door opening saved the day. Tick's family was home.

✿

'Well, if it's not my three favourite heroes in the world,' Tick's dad said as he stumbled through the door, both arms full of packages and bags – new school clothes, by the looks of it. 'How'd the spaghetti experiment go? Smells great.' Tick knew what his dad was really thinking: *Give me some. Now!* The guy loved to eat, and his big belly showed it.

'The way these boys ate,' Sofia said, 'I'd say it went pretty well.'

Paul moaned with pleasure, rubbing his belly. 'Yes, sir, Mr. Higginbottom. The chef is a tyrant, but she can cook like you wouldn't believe.'

'Best I've ever had,' Tick agreed, just as his mom entered from the garage. 'Oh, sorry, Mom. Yours is good too.'

'It's okay, Atticus,' Mom said as she set a couple of bags down on the counter. 'I'd hope a young woman from a family well-known for their spaghetti would be able to beat mine any day.'

Dad shook his head. 'I don't know. You sure do know how to add spices to that ragu sauce.'

'Very funny,' Mom replied.

Newly driving Lisa and newly turned five-year-old Kayla came through next, both holding bags of their own.

'Whoa, Mom,' Tick said. 'How much stuff did you buy?'

'Enough to keep three kids clothed for a year.' She pointed a finger at Tick. 'No growing until next summer. That's an order.'

'Did you kill anyone driving to the shopping centre, sis?' Tick asked.

Lisa gave him a mock evil stare. 'Just one old lady – and I hit her on purpose.'

'Wow,' Paul said. 'Sounds like–'

A sudden *crack* from upstairs interrupted him; a booming sound of splitting, shattering wood shook the entire house. A plate fell from the counter and broke on the floor. Kayla shrieked and ran to her mom.

'What the–?' Dad said, already on the move out of the kitchen and down the hall, everyone following behind him. As his dad bounded up the stairs as quickly as he could move his big body, Tick anxiously looked around him to see what had caused the commotion.

Through a swirling cloud of dust and debris, Tick could see a large, silvery metal tube with a sharp, tapered end jutting from the wall outside Tick's room, splinters of ripped wood holding it in place. It looked as if it had been shot from a cannon; a dud bomb lodged in the drywall.

'What on *earth* ?' Mom said in a shaky voice, putting a hand on her husband's arm.

Dad had no answer; Tick hurried past him to his bedroom door and opened it, expecting to see a disaster area – broken windows, a gaping hole in the side of the house. *Something*. But his breath caught in his throat when he saw no damage at all – not a crack or tear in the ceiling, the windows, or the walls. His room was in perfect shape. The only thing out of place was the other end of the metal tube, which stuck out of the wall to his left. It also had a tapered end.

Tick poked his head back into the hallway, examined the ceiling. No damage there, either. Everyone looked as perplexed as he felt.

Dad leaned forward and studied the strange object. 'Where'd that thing come from? And how in the *world* did it get stuck in our wall?'

SOMETHING ODD IS HAPPENING

Tick stepped forward; everyone else seemed frozen to the floor in amazement by the sudden and violent appearance of the strange metal tube. Dad stood there and shook his head, muttering under his breath.

Tick reached up, his hand slowing as he approached the sharp end of the cylinder sticking out into the hall.

His mom yelped. 'Careful! Maybe we shouldn't touch it.'

'It's fine, Mom,' Tick replied. 'There's gotta be some reason it was sent here.'

'Yeah,' Paul said, 'like, maybe to kill the state of Washington once you trigger its thermonuclear reactor inside.'

Ignoring Paul, Tick tested the side of the object with a quick tap to see if the metal was hot. Feeling only hard coolness, he wrapped his hand around the tube and yanked as hard as he could. With a high-pitched groaning squeal, it gave way and slipped out of the splintered hole. Finding it to be quite light, Tick bounced the three-foot-long cylinder in both hands as he turned to show it to everyone else.

'But what is it?' Sofia asked.

'Here, son,' Dad said, sticking his chest out as if to show he was the brave one who should examine the cylinder. 'Let me check it out in case it explodes or something.'

'You're so brave, sweetie,' Mom said, rubbing her husband's shoulder with affection.

'Yeah,' he mumbled back. 'A regular Iron Man.'

Tick handed the tube to his dad, who took it, turning it this way and that in front of his face, examining it with squinted eyes. He peered down its length as if he were aiming a sniper's rifle.

'Having inspected this object fully,' Dad finally said, 'I hereby declare it to be nothing but a solid metal rod.'

Tick cleared his throat, having just noticed something as his dad tilted the tube just right. 'Well, um, there *is* a seam circling the middle.'

'Huh?' Dad lifted the thing until it was an inch from his eyeballs, then squinted again. 'Oh. Yeah. You're right.' With both hands, he gripped the ends of the rod, right before they tapered to sharp points, and pulled in opposite directions.

With a metallic scrape, the object split into two pieces. As soon as it did, a smaller tube fell to the floor, a flash of white that bounced once, rolled, then came to a stop by Sofia's feet.

Sofia snapped it up and quickly unrolled the piece of paper. Her eyes quickly scanned the contents, then she looked up with a wide grin on her face.

'It's a message. From Master George.'

☼

They went back downstairs, the group huddled around Sofia as she sat in a chair at the kitchen table. Tick wiggled his way to be closest to her, looking down at the typed message as Sofia read it aloud.

Dear Fellow Realitants,

I hope this day finds you all warm and happy. If so, enjoy it. Dark times are upon us, and I fear we must gather as soon as possible.

Something odd is happening within the Realities. Something unnatural, indeed. Sinister forces are about, and I have my suspicions as to the source. And no, it is not Mistress Jane. I shan't write about it any further; you will be briefed during our meeting.

On the twenty-second of August, please report to the nearest cemetery at your earliest convenience, whereupon I will wink you to headquarters straight away, based upon your nanolocator reading.

Now I really must be going, as poor Rutger appears to have hung his malodorous socks in front of the cooler vent, creating quite a smell, I assure you. Wish me luck in finding a can of powerful air freshener.

Most sincerely,

Master George

P.S. Muffintops sends her warmest regards.

P.P.S. Please attach the Spinner to a blank wall and observe carefully to learn about entropy and fragmentation.

'Spinner?' Paul asked. 'What's he talking about?'

'The twenty-second? That's only two days away,' Tick's mom whispered, her voice not hiding the sudden dismay at the possibility of her son running off again.

Tick's initial excitement at hearing from Master George quickly faded into a sickly pang in his gut. He had dreaded this moment in many ways, knowing he'd be summoned again, leaving his poor mom to worry about him. Even though she'd been convinced of the truth about the Realities, Tick knew that when the day actually came for him to leave again, she'd throw a fit.

Like any good mother.

'Mom ...' Tick said, but no other words filled his mouth.

His dad reached over and squeezed Tick's shoulder, then shook his head ever so slightly when they made eye contact.

'Honey,' Dad said, 'let's go for a drive and talk a bit. Lisa, Kayla, you come with us – we'll get some ice cream.'

'But I want to hear–' Lisa protested, but Dad cut her off.

'Just come on. In the car. Let's go.'

Tick didn't completely understand what his dad was doing. He had insisted all summer that he believed in Tick and in his responsibilities as a Realitant, and that he would do whatever it took to support him and make sure nothing got in his way. But now, in the moment, Tick couldn't believe his dad was going to leave them to discuss the message and its meaning alone.

He was treating Tick like an adult, and Tick wasn't sure he liked that as much as he thought he would.

As his parents left for the garage, half-dragging Kayla and Lisa, Mom staring at the floor with dead eyes, Tick tried to push aside the swirling, conflicting emotions he felt about involving his family with the Realitant stuff. He wished he could somehow separate them into two different worlds, independent and unaware of the other. But he couldn't. And he was a Realitant Second Class with people depending on him. He pulled out a chair and sat next to Sofia; Paul did the same.

'So, what do you think?' Paul asked.

Sofia threw her arms up. 'What's there to think? Instead of flying back to our homes, we're going to the cemetery with Tick.'

'But my ticket is for tomorrow night,' Paul said. 'Just because your parents don't give a–'

He stopped, looking quickly at the floor. Tick groaned on the inside. The more they got to know Sofia, the more they realised her parents didn't seem to care too much about what she did. This time they'd even let her come without her fancy butler, Frupey. But the verdict was still out as to *why* they didn't care; Sofia refused to talk about it.

'Go home if you want,' she said with a sneer. 'They have dead people in Florida, too, don't they? Find a cemetery there.'

'Ah, man,' Paul said as he dropped his head into his hands with a groan. 'You have no idea how hard it was to explain this stuff to my family. I don't know if I can go through that again.'

'Fine. Then quit.'

'Oh, give me a break. I didn't say squat about quitting.'

'It's gonna be hard for all of us,' Tick interjected. 'We just need to make them understand.'

'Easy for you to say,' Paul said. 'I swear your dad is the single coolest person that's ever breathed.'

'Maybe. But none of us can quit. Ever.'

Paul leaned back in his chair, crossing his arms in anger. 'Dude, quit preachin'. Paul Rogers is not gonna quit. I was just saying, man, it's gonna be killer telling my old lady I'm running off again.'

The full load of spaghetti in Tick's stomach was starting to churn. 'Our parents just have to trust us. That's all there is to it.'

'Yeah,' Paul agreed in a murmur.

'Okay, you know what?' Sofia said, her voice laced with annoyance. 'You guys are getting on my nerves. We just got a letter from Master George – which we've been waiting for all summer – and you both are sitting here moping like you just found out you have two hours to live.' She stood up and started walking towards the stairs. 'Let's go look at the tube again to see if we can figure out what M.G. meant by *Spinner*.'

When neither Tick nor Paul moved a muscle, Sofia turned and cleared her throat loudly. 'Come on.' She paused. 'I promise I'll be nice.' Another pause. 'Please.'

Paul looked at Tick, as surprised as if he'd just seen an extra arm bloom from Sofia's shoulder. Tick shrugged.

'Now!' Sofia yelled.

Paul and Tick jumped from the table, stumbling over each other as they followed her up the stairs.

Sofia picked up the broken metal tube and started shaking the two pieces towards the floor of the hallway. A small object fell out of one end and clinked when it hit the carpet. Paul reached it first, holding the odd thing up for everyone to see.

'What *is* it?' he whispered as he studied it.

Tick took it from him to get a better look. It was a two-inch wide, red plastic suction cup. Attached to the back of the cup was a thin, silvery metal rod bent at a ninety-degree angle. The L-shaped rod was about the size of Tick's index finger. Tick clasped the cup in one hand, then flicked the tip of the rod with his finger. The small rod spun so fast the metal became a circular blur of silver.

Sofia flicked the rod again, watching it twirl. 'Spinner. Master George is *so* brilliant when he names things.'

'I wonder if it's from Chu Industries,' Tick said. 'Does it say that anywhere?'

Sofia stopped the spinning rod and looked closer. 'I don't see anything.'

'What do you think it does?' Paul asked.

Tick pointed back down the stairs. 'Master George said to attach it to a blank wall – let's try the one in the dining room.'

'Let's go,' Sofia said, already on the move.

4

THE WRETCHED BOY

The Spinner's suction cup stuck to the middle of the wall with a simple push; the bent end of the "L" pointed towards the floor and swayed back and forth until it finally came to a rest.

'What now?' Tick asked.

'Spin it,' Paul said.

Sofia leaned forward and flicked the rod to make it spin, then stepped back. Without a word, the three of them quickly moved all the way to the other side of the room, pressing against the wall to watch. You couldn't be too careful when it came to gadgets sent from Master George.

Strangely, the spinning metal rod didn't slow at all, instead going so fast it appeared as a perfect circle of shimmering silver. A slight hum filled the room, like the soft sound of a ceiling fan. After several seconds, Tick's eyes started to water as they tried to focus on something. Anything. Then the Spinner changed.

A red light flared from the tip of the metal rod, instantly creating a much larger circle that took up most of the wall, a hazy, flat disc of redness. Sofia gasped; Paul let out his usual, 'Dude.' Tick could only stare.

'How's it making a perfect circle?' Paul asked.

Sofia answered. 'It must be shooting out some kind of scaled laser.'

'Ooh, like a lightsaber,' Paul said.

'But–' Tick stopped.

The red colour faded from the projected, spinning disc, replaced by a large image of Master George, dressed in his dark suit, standing in front of a fireplace, staring out at them. He caressed Muffintops the cat in his arms. The picture quality was perfect – as good as any movie – it was just ... *round*.

'My fondest greetings to the three of you,' Master George said. The sound of his voice seemed to come from everywhere at once, though slightly warbled. Tick couldn't help but wonder what kind of speaker could have such power and still be so small – they certainly hadn't noticed anything when they studied the Spinner a few minutes earlier.

Master George held out a hand. 'Don't attempt to reply – I assure you it will be a waste of your breath. This is only a recording, you see. Quite nice, don't you think? The Spinner comes in handy when you get a bit depressed and want to watch an old black-and-white. It's one of my favourite things. Although, it's a bit difficult to use when you're in a forest – particularly when you're being chased by wolves ...'

Tick exchanged a look with Sofia, both of them trying to hold in a laugh.

'Oh, dear, I've already gone off on a tangent,' Master George said, clearing his throat and growing very serious. 'My apologies. There is a *point,* you see, to my sending you this Spinner. I must show you footage of something very frightening – something

34

you must see and prepare yourselves to study with the greatest vigour. I want you to remember two words – *entropy* and *fragmentation*. These two things serve as our greatest challenge when studying the Realities; they are also the source of much heartache.'

Master George paused, looking past the camera or whatever was recording him. 'Rutger, please put *down* that pastry – get ready to cut to the footage you filmed in the fragmenting Reality.' Master George focused back on Tick and the others. 'No wonder I constantly find sticky goo on my camera. Now, I want you to watch closely. We have no sound, as Rutger had to get in and out very quickly and almost ruined the film entirely. I will narrate as you observe.'

The image on the circular screen changed. All three of them sucked in a quick breath when they saw *Tick* huddled next to a tree, shivering, his terrified eyes darting back and forth, looking all around him.

Tick swallowed. He was filthy in the film, his clothes ripped to shreds. Wind tore at his shaggy hair, and his bare feet were covered with grime. Of course, it couldn't be him – it had to be someone who just *looked* like him. It had to be ...

Master George's narration cut off his thoughts. 'Master Atticus, this trembling wretch is one of your Alterants – created last year when you made the choice to follow the Twelve Clues and solve my mystery. A branching reality was created in which you *didn't* make that brave choice, and here you see the result.'

Tick felt like everything around him disappeared, his eyes riveted to the image of himself on the screen, his heart aching for the boy there. *How can that be me?*

he thought. *Is it me? It can't be me.* Confusion swirled in his mind like poisonous gas.

'This is a terrible thing,' Master George continued. 'One of our goals as Realitants is to prevent this type of fragmenting event from happening. In a very twisted way, this boy *is* you, Atticus. He has your mind and heart, your goodness and courage. And he doesn't deserve the fate that's come upon him. Watch closely.'

The trees around the Alterant Tick started to shake; the brisk wind picked up even more, tearing at Tick's pitiful, filthy clothes. There was no sound, but Tick saw the boy scream, hugging his arms around himself tighter. Above his head, the wood of the tree *vibrated,* then broke apart into a million tiny pieces, swept away by the wild wind. The other Tick screamed again, scooting away until he hit another tree. An instant later that one liquefied into a horrific brown goo, splashing all over the Alterant. Another scream, as if the tree burned him.

The real Tick watched in horror at what happened next.

The boy on the screen started to *dissolve.*

The Entropy of Fragmentation

The image flashed to black. Master George reappeared, his ruddy face creased and frowning. 'I'm very sorry you had to see that.'

Tick felt his back pressed against the wall, felt the slime of sweat on his palms. The movie had stopped before getting too bad, but he'd seen enough. The boy's skin and hair and clothes – all dissipating into a million pieces, breaking apart, dissolving, whipped away by the wind.

That was me, he thought. *That was* me.

'Now listen closely,' Master George said. 'You may already have heard the term *entropy* in your studies. It describes the natural ... urge of the universe to destroy itself, to cease to exist, to *deconstruct.* All things – no matter what, no matter how strong – will eventually erode into nothingness, into chaos. It is an unchangeable law. All things fade away. This is called entropy.'

Master George looked down at Muffintops, petting her as she purred. 'The process of entropy can take a few years or billions of years. Think about your bodies. When you die, your flesh and bone will slowly turn to dust. A towering mountain can stand for millions of years before it slowly but surely breaks down. Nothing can stop the inevitable – entropy wins. Always.'

'What does this have to do with–' Paul began to ask, obviously forgetting they were watching a recording. Master George kept talking.

'Here is the disturbing part. The Thirteen Realities we know about are solid and permanent. But *fragmented* Realities are not – we've told you before how unstable they are, and how they eventually fade away or destroy themselves. Now you know the reason – an extreme heightening and acceleration of entropy. And I mean *extreme*. It almost becomes a living entity, devouring everything in its path, as you just witnessed. Once fragmented, a Reality doesn't last long – and its final moments are pure terror for the poor chaps living there. It is an awful thing.'

Master George took a deep breath. 'We don't understand all of it. There's much to learn, much to discuss. It's time the three of you started your Realitant studies, and this is the first lesson of many. And most importantly, I wanted you to see first-hand the severe consequences of your choices. If you'd lacked the courage to pass my tests, perhaps ... well, it is a very deep and complicated situation. But we must stop the fragmenting. Even though we will never feel the pain and terror of those temporary Alterants, it's very real to them, if only briefly. Makes it hard for me to sleep at night.'

Muffintops jumped out of his arms and disappeared off screen. 'Very well, thank you for watching. There are many other mysteries to discuss – like the odd properties of *soulikens* and the Barrier Haunce. All in good time. We'll look forward to the gathering of Realitants. Until then, remember your courage, my good friends. Goodbye for now.'

Master George smiled at the camera for a few seconds, saying nothing. His eyes flickered to the side, as if he were uncomfortable. Finally, he mumbled something out of the side of his mouth. 'Turn the camera *off*, Rutger.'

The screen went black, then red, then silver. The hum of the Spinner died out as the metal rod slowly came to a standstill. All the while, no one said anything.

'What was *that*?' Sofia finally asked.

Tick ignored her, pushing past and walking out of the dining room. The spaghetti churned inside his stomach, and he didn't know how much longer he could last before throwing up. A throbbing ache raged behind his eyeballs.

'Tick?' Paul asked from behind.

'I don't wanna talk about it,' was all Tick could get out.

He barely said a word the rest of the evening, ignoring his friends and family equally. The image of that boy on the screen – of *himself* – screaming and then dissolving...

How could he ever get that out of his head?

He went to bed early that night while everyone else watched a movie downstairs.

☼

The next morning, Tick, Paul, and Sofia decided to get out of the house and talk over things – maybe do some research at the library. Tick felt a little better on waking up; every time the disturbing image of his fragmenting Alterant popped in his head, he tried to picture Muffintops. After another excellent Lorena Higginbottom breakfast of eggs and fried potatoes, the three of them headed out.

They stayed mostly silent until they reached the long road that led from Tick's neighbourhood to the town square of Deer Park. The rising sun kept the east side of the street in shade, the towering evergreens and oak trees of the forest providing relief from the late summer heat.

The humidity had dipped considerably in the last couple of days, giving the air a hot but pleasant feel. Birds and crickets sang their songs in the woods; somewhere in the distance a lawnmower cranked up.

'Man, feels good out here,' Paul said, bending over to pick up a rock. He threw it deep into the woods; it cracked against a tree.

'You guys need to come to Italy sometime,' Sofia said. 'In the summer, we can go up to the Alps and cool off. Best place in the world.'

'No argument here,' Paul replied. 'Florida downright stinks this time of year. You go outside for two seconds and presto – sweaty armpits.'

'Lovely,' Sofia said.

Tick only half-listened to the conversation, staring into the woods as they walked. They neared the spot where so much had happened a few months ago – meeting Mothball, the sign from Rutger about the midnight meeting on the porch, getting clues from the two of them, screaming in desperation after Kayla had burned his original letter from Master George. It all seemed like a dream now.

'–to Tick, Earth to Tick.' Paul had stopped, snapping his fingers in the air.

'Oh, sorry,' Tick said. 'Just daydreaming.'

Sofia sighed. 'Better than listening to Paul drone on, trust me.'

'Miss Italy, be nice to me. I might have to save you on our next mission.'

'I better update my will.'

'Hilarious.'

'I know.'

The Muffintops distraction trick wasn't working so well for Tick as they walked. *That kid. That poor kid.* The whole concept of Alterants was confusing – especially when you threw in the whole thing about fragmented Realities. What was the difference between the Tick they'd seen in Rutger's film, Tick himself, and the Ticks that existed in the stabilised Thirteen Realities? It made his head hurt thinking about it.

'What do you guys think of all that entropy stuff?' he asked, kicking at a pebble on the road and watching it skitter across the pavement.

'I remember studying it in science,' Sofia said. 'Seems crazy that it could be accelerated like that and just ... eat away at the world.'

'It's freaky, dude,' Paul said. 'I mean, if I decide to turn left instead of right up here, am I gonna create a nasty Reality where I get eaten alive by monster air? That ain't right.'

'It's weird that–'

Sofia never finished her sentence, cut off by a loud yelp in the woods to their right, followed by the sudden, rushing sound of crunching leaves and breaking twigs. Someone, or some *thing,* was running towards them through the trees.

Tick and the others froze, staring towards the sounds, which grew louder as the whatever-it-was came closer. *Crick-crash, crick-crash.* Another yelp, this time more of a short scream, echoed off the towering trunks and leafy canopy.

'What *is* that?' Paul asked.

'Maybe we shouldn't stick around to find out,' Tick offered. Every nerve in his body had just lit up with warning flames.

Before anyone could respond, a man burst through a wall of thick foliage fronting two large trees, hurling himself forward until he lost his balance and fell onto the steep slope that led up to the road. As soon as the skinny, dark-haired man hit the ground, he scrambled to his hands and feet and started clawing his way towards them. With growing dread, Tick stared at the stranger's tattered clothes and bloody splotches on his shirt.

Just a few feet away, the man finally reached the road and stood up, lifting his head enough to be seen clearly for the first time. Dishevelled, dirty hair framed an olive-skinned face covered with terrible scratches and terror alive in his eyes.

Tick sucked in a huge gulp of air, half-relieved and half-shocked.

It was Mr. Chu, his science teacher.

6

INTENSE PAIN

'Mr. Chu!' Tick yelled, running forward to help his favourite teacher, who looked ready to collapse. Sofia moved to assist, both of them grabbing an arm of Mr. Chu and lowering him to the shoulder of the road. The poor man crumpled into a ball, great heaves of breath making his chest rise and fall as his eyes darted between Tick, Sofia, and Paul. A leather satchel was slung over Mr. Chu's shoulders with a thin strap, its bulky, sharp-angled contents clanking when it hit the ground.

'What happened?' Tick asked, fighting the panic he felt. *What if he's dying? Did someone out there attack him?* He couldn't help but look up at the trees, which suddenly seemed dark and ominous.

'Atticus ...' Mr. Chu said with a dry rasp.

Tick knelt on one knee, lowering his head until he was close to Mr. Chu's face. 'What happened to you, Mr. Chu?'

'Atticus ... I barely escaped ...' A racking cough exploded from his lungs, shaking his entire body.

'Escaped?' Tick repeated. 'From what?'

Sofia and Paul knelt right behind the teacher, both of them looking at Tick with wide, confused eyes. So far, a car had yet to pass by the woods, and Tick hoped one did soon so they could ask for help.

'From...' Mr. Chu whispered, starting to gain control of his breath. 'From ... a very bad man. Looks like me. *Is* me.'

Tick exchanged a puzzled look with his friends. He'd never seen his teacher like this, or heard him say such crazy things. He'd never seen *anyone* act like this. An idea hit him. 'Do either one of you have a cell phone?'

Mr. Chu's hand shot out and grabbed Tick's shirt, pulling him closer with surprising force. 'No!' he yelled, a sharpness narrowing his eyes with a clarity that hadn't been there moments earlier. 'Help me back into the woods – we need to hide.'

'Mr. Chu, I don't–'

'Just help me!'

With a grunt and another dry, loud cough, Mr. Chu pushed himself back into a sitting position, then held up his hands. Tick and Paul lifted the miserable man to his feet and wrapped his arms around their shoulders. Then, half-carrying, half-dragging Mr. Chu, the three of them stumbled down the small slope and entered the woods, Sofia right behind.

They made their way past a few smaller trees and then rounded a massive, towering oak, finally finding a secluded patch of ivy-strewn forest floor with enough room for all of them to sit. Specks of sunlight littered the ground, the call of birds in the air far too cheerful for the situation. The smells of pine and earth and wood were strong – scents that Tick loved but for some reason made him uneasy at that moment.

They settled into a circle, facing each other. Mr. Chu appeared to be gaining his strength back with every passing minute, though his hands shook with apparent fear; a small drip of drool crawled down his chin. No one said a word, a silent understanding hanging in the air that Mr. Chu would tell them what was going on when he was good and ready.

'It was terrible,' he finally whispered, barely audible.

'*What* was?' Sofia asked. Tick cringed; it seemed like a really bad time for her usual impatience.

Mr. Chu continued to stare at the ground in front of him. 'These men ... with some kind of electricity weapon, kidnapped me and took me to a place that was like the barracks of a battleship – metallic and cold. They ... did things to me ... Unspeakable things.' He stopped talking.

'Who were they?' Tick asked. His mind couldn't settle on any possible reason someone might want to take Mr. Chu, who was one of the nicest people Tick knew.

'It was ... *him*.' Mr. Chu squeezed his eyes closed as if in pain.

'Him?' Paul asked. 'Who's *him*?'

'The other me. The bad me.'

Tick felt his breath catch in his throat. An Alterant Mr. Chu?

Tick looked at Sofia; she mouthed the word *psycho*. A storm of anger surged inside Tick. His face flushed hot, and for the first time since he'd known her, he wanted to scream in fury at Sofia. This was one of his favourite people she was talking about. He was just about to say something nasty when Mr. Chu unexpectedly shot up from the ground to his feet.

'Did you hear that?' he whispered, twisting and turning, searching the surrounding forest.

Tick stood, as did Paul and Sofia, the three of them looking for any sign of what had alarmed the teacher.

'Did you hear that?' Mr. Chu repeated.

'No,' Tick answered. 'What was it?'

'Something's out there. What was I thinking? What was I *thinking?!*' Yelling the last word, Mr. Chu knelt down beside his leather satchel and opened it up, rummaging inside before pulling out three strange objects. 'They followed me here. How could I be such an idiot?'

As Mr. Chu got back to his feet, Tick finally heard it. Coming from deeper in the woods, it sounded like hundreds of spinning circular saws, sharp and shrill, accompanied by the horrible crunching and breaking of trees, as if King Kong himself were trampling through the forest with the world's largest electric razor buzzing at full speed.

'What the heck is that?' Paul asked, a look of alarm spreading across his face that Tick thought must surely mirror his own.

Sofia took a few steps towards the sound, rising onto her tiptoes and tilting her head as if that would help her hear better. 'That doesn't sound good,' she finally said. Paul rolled his eyes and stomped his foot, clearly impatient to be away from this place. Tick felt a thick veil of creepiness hanging over him.

'They let me go ... they let me go,' Mr. Chu murmured, handling the objects he'd pulled from his bag. Tick got a good look at them for the first time, but had no clue what they were. All he could see were a bunch of cloth straps and pieces of dull metal.

'They let me go ... They knew I'd come to you. I'm such an idiot! Atticus, I'm so sorry.'

Something was wrong about the whole situation, and Tick knew it wasn't just the rush of ominous sounds that were growing louder by the second, filling the air with horrible screeches of metal and the splintering crack of wood. Nor was it just the overall strangeness of Mr. Chu's sudden appearance. Something was *wrong*, out of place – but Tick couldn't pinpoint it exactly.

'Shouldn't we get out of here?' Paul said.

'Won't do any good,' Mr. Chu replied, stepping close to Tick. He stretched out one of the things in his hands, two strips of cloth attached to a circular ring of metal in the middle. 'Until we get these on you, they'll follow you wherever you go, until you're dead.'

Mr. Chu grabbed Tick's right arm and started wrapping the cloth strips around his bicep. Tick was so stunned by the odd situation that he didn't move or resist. In a matter of seconds, Mr. Chu had snapped the metal ring around Tick's elbow, and wrapped the attached strips of cloth, like sticky gauze, in candy-cane fashion down the length of his entire arm.

'What ... what are you doing? What is this thing?' A sick, uneasy feeling spread through Tick and he started to sweat.

'Yeah, what is that?' Sofia asked.

'You all have to put them on,' Mr. Chu answered. But when he stepped towards Sofia, she swiped his arms away and held up her fists. 'You aren't touching me, you crazy old man.'

The sounds – the spinning saws, the crunching and crashing of trees, a mechanical roar that sounded like something out of an old sci-fi movie – it was all coming very close, very fast. Though Tick couldn't see anything yet, he could *feel* whatever was approaching, as if it were pushing the very air away as it rushed through the woods.

Mr. Chu tried again to wrap his gadget around Sofia's arm, but she swatted him away, then actually swung a fist at his face, barely missing. 'I said, stay away!' she screamed at him.

Mr. Chu turned towards Tick, his face intense. 'Atticus, I've known you and your family for a long time. I taught your sister, I taught you. We're friends, are we not?'

'Yeah.' Tick looked at Sofia, then Paul. His head swam in confusion. How could this be happening? Why did he feel so ... *wrong*? Was this a dream?

'They'll be here in seconds. If we put these devices on our arms, they won't see us. Do you hear me?'

Tick didn't say anything.

'Just wink us away again!' Paul said. 'You can do it, Tick. Concentrate and wink us away. Forget this dude.'

'Give me a break,' Tick said. 'I have no clue how I did that.'

'Just try,' Sofia said in a calm voice, as if she were trying to talk someone out of jumping off a skyscraper.

Tick barely heard her over the mechanical chorus of horrible sounds.

'Atticus!' Mr. Chu yelled. 'We have only seconds left! They ... are going ... to eat us ... alive!' He pointed towards the sounds with every pause, his voice filled with fire.

'Just do it!' Tick finally said. 'Sofia, just let him do it!'

'Tick, you expect me to trust this nut–'

'Just do it!'

Completely surprising Tick, she obeyed with a huff, sticking her arm out to Mr. Chu. He quickly wrapped the second device on her arm, just as he'd done with Tick. Nearby, a thunderous, ear-splitting crack of wood was followed by the sound of a tree crashing to the forest floor. The mechanical sounds whirred and buzzed, roaring like monstrous robots.

Mr. Chu worked feverishly, wrapping the third and final ... whatever it was ... on Paul's right arm, who protested the entire time that this was crazy and stupid and that they should *run*.

'What about you?' Tick asked Mr. Chu.

His teacher pulled out a small, rectangular object from his pocket that looked like a TV remote control. He looked down at it as his finger searched for one of the many buttons scattered in rows across its front side. Then he looked up at Tick.

'Don't worry about me,' he said. He held up the small remote device and pushed the button.

In that instant, a pain like nothing Tick had ever experienced or thought possible lanced through his body from head to toe, and the world spun away, leaving him in darkness and agony.

MASTER GEORGE'S
INTERVIEW ROOM

Sato was bored out of his mind.

The Big Meeting wasn't for another couple of days, but Realitants had been arriving at the Grand Canyon Centre from all over the world – well, *worlds* – since last week. And George made Sato sit with every last one of them, sometimes for hours, asking them questions, gathering information on their assigned areas, looking for clues on the strange happenings in the Realities. As if the long, tedious interviews weren't enough, Sato then had to compile everything into very specifically outlined reports for George's later analysis.

As Mothball would've said, it was driving Sato batty.

A lot had changed in the last few months – since the day in the Thirteenth Reality when everything he'd thought and felt for years had been turned upside down. The pain of losing his parents hadn't faded – it never would – but the anger and drive for vengeance he'd fostered and groomed for so long had been …

altered, forged into an entirely different sword. In many ways, Sato thought that was a bad thing, not a good thing. He felt more lost than ever, floating in a pool of confusion and misdirection. The sword wasn't as sharp as it used to be.

Tick had done this to him. Tick had changed everything, forever.

And Sato didn't know how he felt about that.

A knock at the door snapped him to attention. He realised he'd been staring at a small smudge on the wall to the right of his desk. At the moment, Sato felt for all the world like he and the dirty spot shared a lot in common.

Though he already knew the answer, Sato asked anyway. 'Who is it?'

'It's me – who else?' replied the muffled voice of Rutger. 'Do you really have to keep the door closed? My poor knuckles are getting bruised from knocking every time.'

Yeah, right, Sato thought. *You've got enough cushion on those hands to protect you from a sledgehammer.* 'Hold on.'

Sato quickly gathered his latest notes and reports and filed them away in his desk drawers. Though he'd acted the part of a trusting friend to Rutger for weeks, he still had his doubts about the short, fat man. *Anyone can be a spy.*

He stood up and walked over to the wooden door, slightly warped from a small leak that had crept through the tons of solid rock above them. He unlocked the door and yanked it open, jerking it harder than necessary.

Sato looked forward with a glazed expression, then left and right, as if searching for someone. Finally, he slowly lowered his gaze until he met Rutger's eyes. 'Oh, it's you. Down there.'

'Very funny, very funny.' Rutger's short, round body barely fit in the hallway. He took in a deep breath, inflating himself even larger than he'd been a second earlier. 'At least it was funny the *first* hundred times. Come on. Our next visitor has arrived.'

Grumbling inside – no, *screaming* inside – Sato stepped into the hall, turned and closed the door, and then locked it. Without a word to Rutger, he walked towards the welcoming room at a brisk pace, knowing the poor little man could never keep up on his tiny legs. When Rutger yelled, 'Wait up!' from behind, the briefest hint of a smile flashed across Sato's face before he swiped it away with his trademark scowl.

☼

'Ah, Master Sato!' George said, his usual jovial self, when Sato entered the room. Even though it was August, large flames licked and spat at the air inside the stone fireplace, warming the room to an uncomfortable level. A couple of nice leather couches hugged the walls; an armchair was set at the perfect angle for someone to sit by the fire and read a book. But at the moment, the only other two people in the room were standing next to the small window that overlooked the canyon river far below.

George stood to the right of the window, dressed in his Tuesday Suit, which only varied from his Monday Suit in that it was a very dark blue instead of a very dark black. One of his hands was outstretched towards Sato, the other towards the stranger standing to the left of the window. 'Sato, I would like you to meet a very dear friend of mine, Quinton Hallenhaffer.'

The man bowed his head in greeting, and Sato couldn't believe the guy could take himself seriously. He wore a twisty turban on his head made up of no fewer than ten different colours, all of them bright and swirling in a whirlpool pattern so that it looked like Mr. Hallenhaffer had ribbons for hair and had been caught in a tornado. The rest of his clothes were no different – a loose robe with dozens of colours splashed about with no definite pattern, purple gloves, and red shoes that appeared to be made out of wood.

Sato gave a curt nod. 'I'm ready for the debriefing.'

George's face flushed redder than usual. 'Er, yes, Sato – though I think we could show our guest a little more, er, courtesy ...'

'Oh, it's all right, George,' Quinton said, waving at the air as if to swat away gnats. He had a trilling, lilting voice, like he couldn't decide whether to sing or talk. 'The boy obviously means business, which is what we need in the new Realitants, don't you think?'

'Yes, indeed,' George replied, giving the slightest frown of disapproval. 'If Sato is anything, he is straight to the point.' George clapped his hands once. 'Very well, then. I'll leave you two alone. Quinton, please fill Sato in on any information you may have gathered since we last met. I have other things to attend to.'

After George left the room, Sato sat down on one of the couches, gesturing for Mr. Hallenhaffer to sit across from him on the other couch. Once settled, Sato asked the question he'd been asking first ever since the fourth such interview, when a common theme had become evident.

'Are people going insane in your Reality? Lots of people?'

✲

Rutger was spouting off at the mouth before Mothball could say one word upon entering the kitchen. 'I tell you, that boy is an insolent, inconsiderate, rude–'

'Calm yerself, little man,' Mothball muttered, grabbing the milk bottle from the fridge. ''Eard enough of yer gripin' for one day, I 'ave. We all know he's a bit rude, no need yappin' off about it one second more.'

'A *bit* rude?' Rutger sat at the large table, munching on something that looked suspiciously like Mothball's cheesecake leftovers from the night before. 'A *bit? That's like saying you're a bit tall.'

'Well, I am, now, ain't I?' Mothball pulled out a chair and sat beside her oldest friend, pulling the plate away from him. 'Pardon me, but I don't quite remember givin' ya the go ahead on eatin' me hard-earned sweets.'

'Sorry,' Rutger said, head bowed in shame. 'You know I get ... kinda hungry sometimes.'

'Ya reckon so, do ya?' Mothball let out a laugh. 'That there's like saying Sato is a bit rude.'

'Touché,' Rutger muttered.

A long pause followed. Mothball had enjoyed seeing her fellow Realitants come to the Centre over the last few days – many of them she hadn't seen in years – though the reunions were somewhat bittersweet. The reason for the gathering was not a good thing. People going bonkers everywhere, Chi'karda getting loopy here and there. Something very strange was happening.

'Can't wait to see Tick and the others again,' Rutger said.

Mothball couldn't stop a huge smile from spreading across her face at the mention of the boy, Atticus. 'I hear ya, there. Goin' to give 'im a big 'ug, I will. Paul and Sofia, too.'

'I just wish it were under better circumstances.' Rutger sat back in his chair, hands resting on his round belly. 'All this time we spent worrying about Mistress Jane and the Thirteenth, and then this comes along. Nasty stuff.'

Mothball thought back to several weeks earlier, when the first sign of the craziness showed up in the form of a madwoman running through the streets of downtown New York City in the Twelfth. The resident Realitant had witnessed it firsthand, and thought nothing of it until the woman started screaming, 'I can't get it out of my head! I can't get it out of my head!' and then *disappeared,* winking away to some unknown destination. Thinking on it gave Mothball the creeps.

''Tis gettin' worse,' she said. 'From what I 'ear, there's a fragmented Reality that's gone good and batty through and through, every last one of 'em. A literal madhouse.'

Rutger huffed. 'I heard there's a town in the Sixth where every last person is acting like a cat, crawling around, purring, fighting over milk. Can you imagine how *disturbing* that must be?'

Just then, Master George entered the kitchen, his golden Barrier Wand – its dials and switches set to who-knew-what – clasped in his right hand like a walking cane, and Muffintops right at his ankles.

55

Mothball had the odd thought that she hoped the little tabby cat hadn't heard the bit about the people-kitties in the Sixth. Could be quite traumatising for the poor thing.

'Having a bit of a snack, are we?' Master George said as he joined them at the table. 'I must admit, I'm quite hungry myself.' He looked around the kitchen as if some food might magically appear in front of him.

'Did you get the letter delivered to Tick okay?' Rutger asked.

Master George blushed, fidgeting with the Wand. 'Why, er, yes, yes, it arrived just fine, I believe. Though I might have miscalculated a bit on the exact delivery location.'

'Miscalculated?' Mothball repeated.

'Why, er, well ... I may have sent it a little ... to the ... *left,* if you will.'

'The left?' Rutger asked.

Master George slammed his hand on the table. 'Fine! I put the blasted thing right in the middle of their wall! And yes, I'm quite embarrassed.'

'Ya could've sliced someone's ruddy head off,' Mothball said.

'I'm quite aware of that, thank you very much.' Master George looked angry, but it quickly flashed into a smile and a snicker. 'I imagine it gave them a jolly good fright, don't you?'

'I bet you did it on purpose,' Rutger said. 'I know I would have.'

'But they got it?' Mothball asked.

'Yes, yes, they got it. I hope they'll forgive me the debt of mending their wall, however.' Master George cleared his throat, then his face grew serious again.

'I'm afraid we have tough times ahead, my friends. This ... problem is growing, and we haven't the slightest clue as to its source. If I could, I would begin our meeting this very instant. But, alas, not everyone will be here until the appointed time.'

'What do you have planned for Tick and his friends?' Rutger asked.

Master George put the Barrier Wand on the table and absently rolled it back and forth. 'Well, the most essential matter is to figure out Master Tick's odd ability to manipulate the Chi'karda. Perhaps we can use it to our advantage in this dreadful mess.'

'Figured out where yer gonna send 'em yet?' Mothball asked.

'Oh, yes, indeed I have.'

Mothball and Rutger waited, expecting their boss to tell them the plan. But he stayed silent, staring at an empty spot on the other side of the kitchen.

'And ...' Rutger prodded.

Master George finally looked up, focused on Rutger, then Mothball. 'My dear friends, I'm afraid my plans for them are quite ... hazardous.'

'Hazardous?' Mothball repeated.

Master George nodded. 'I daresay I hardly expect all three of them to survive.'

8

GUILTY

Tick's eyes flickered, then opened.

Though shaded by trees, the faint forest light looked like atomic explosions, blistering his eyeballs with pain, making him squeeze his eyelids shut once more. He groaned, every inch of his body feeling like someone had mistaken him for a human piñata. He hurt. He hurt *bad*.

To his right, he heard movement – the rustling of leaves, moaning. Tick brought his hands up to his face, wincing as the movement sent shock waves of pain coursing through his body again. He froze until it died down, then rubbed his eyes. He finally opened them again, and the light didn't seem nearly as bad.

Carefully, delicately, he pushed himself into a sitting position.

Darkness had crept into the forest, more and more insects revealing their presence in a growing chorus of mating calls. Paul sat with his arms folded, leaning against a nearby tree, his face set in a grimace. Sofia was curled up in a ball several feet to Paul's right, still moaning, leaves sticking to her clothes as if she'd been rolling around in them since morning. The strange devices Mr. Chu had attached to them were gone.

Surprisingly, Tick felt the pain sliding away, feeling better by the second. Pushing against the ground, he got his feet under him and stood up. Though sore, he no longer felt the pinpricks and bruises he'd suffered from just moments earlier. It was as if someone had injected him with two shots of morphine.

'Dude, what *happened?*' Paul said through a groan, stretching his arms out before him.

Tick stepped over to Sofia, who seemed to be regaining her strength as well. She rolled onto her back, blinked up at Tick, then held up an arm; Tick helped her to her feet.

'Is that guy still your favourite teacher?' she asked, brushing leaves off her clothes. 'He's a real joy to be around, that's for sure.'

'I ... I don't know what–' Tick stopped in mid-sentence, staring at something over Sofia's shoulder.

He squinted to see through the dim twilight, then squeezed his eyes shut and opened them again. 'What the heck is *that?*'

'What?' Sofia and Paul asked in unison, turning to look in the same direction as Tick.

Without answering, Tick walked towards the oddity that loomed over them just a few dozen feet away.

'Whoa,' he heard Paul say from behind him.

Deeper into the forest, several trees had *melted* into a twisting, gnarled, monstrous-looking mass of wood that was as tall and thick as a house. Several other trees had been lifted out of the ground, their roots sticking out like naked fingers, clods of dirt swaying back and forth. Tick could only stare, disbelieving his own eyes. It looked like some giant magician had grabbed dozens of trees, transformed them into liquid wood, and then smashed them together, twisting and squeezing all of it into a deformed, hideous shape.

Sofia gasped, then pointed to a section of the wood-blob near the ground. 'Is that what I think it is? Oh!' She covered her face with her hands and turned around, her body visibly shuddering.

'What?' Paul asked, stepping closer to take a look. Tick joined him, and immediately saw the source of her disgust.

Somehow *twisted* into the wood was the body of a deer. Three legs poked out of the main trunk; its face was half-sunk into the wood, the one visible eye somehow displaying the fear it must have felt at the last second before death.

'That's downright creepy,' Paul whispered.

✿

By the time they reached Tick's house, almost all of the intense pain they'd felt had disappeared, leaving only a weary soreness. Tick, like Paul and Sofia, had hardly said a word on the walk back, trying to figure out which had been more disturbing – the agonising pain or the deformed super-tree with the dead deer sticking out of it.

'Could this day have been any weirder?' Paul asked as they walked up the porch steps to Tick's house.

'Maybe if we'd grown bunny ears,' Sofia replied. Paul let out a bitter laugh.

They walked in to the wonderful smells of dinner, all of them pausing to take a deep breath. Tick was starving. He couldn't tell what his mom had cooked, but he had a feeling she'd felt the need to prove to Sofia that *she* could cook, too.

'So are we gonna tell your parents what just happened?' Paul whispered.

Tick thought a minute. 'Maybe later. My poor mom's worried enough as it is. No harm, no foul, right?'

'Yeah,' Sofia agreed. 'Let's just stay in the house and stare at each other until it's time to go meet Master George.'

'Sounds good,' Tick said. 'Hopefully we can stay out of trouble for one more day.'

They walked into the kitchen.

☼

Mistress Jane felt discouraged.

She sat next to the large stone window of her apartment in the Lemon Fortress, closing her eyes every time the soft, warm breeze filled with the sweet smell of wildflowers blew up from the meadows below. The day was beautiful, the slightest hint in the air that autumn lay just around the corner. Everything was perfect.

And yet, a stinging sadness tempered all of it.

It had been four months since her Barrier Wand had been stolen, trapping her inside the Thirteenth Reality. At the time, she'd been so intrigued by the Realitants' ability to wink away with a broken Wand, and its potential implications for her, that she'd got straight to work – studying, experimenting, *building*. There was a lot about the mysterious power of Chi'karda she'd not yet discovered, and the little group's seemingly miraculous disappearance had led her to change her thinking. She had already made some exciting discoveries.

However, at the moment, she was very frustrated.

For one thing, her efforts to build a new Barrier Wand had hit a major snag. Frazier Gunn, the leader on the project, couldn't find one of the key elements for the wire that would transmit the Chi'karda from its Drive packet to the body of the Wand. The needed material was a complicated alloy of several rare metals, and one of them was proving impossible to find within the Thirteenth. Frazier had grown noticeably irritable, obviously realising the potential consequences if he failed in this project. His room for error with Jane had grown very thin.

But all of this was secondary to what troubled her most.

She was starting to feel *guilty*.

She couldn't remember when it started, or when it had grown to such a staggering weight on her heart. But now, every minute of the day, all she could think about was how evil she had become. When had it come to this? *How* had it come to this? In the beginning, all she'd ever wanted was to make the world a better place, to improve life for all her fellow human beings. It was to fulfil those lofty and noble goals that she'd joined the Realitants years ago, devoting her life to studying the Realities. Though she'd never voiced her intentions, she'd planned from the first day to seek out those things in other Realities that would lead to her ultimate goal.

A Utopia. A perfect world. A haven for all people, where pain and sorrow would cease to exist. Where everyone could be happy.

That was all she'd wanted. That was all she *still* wanted.

And yet, here she was, a fierce and cruel ruler of an entire world, using its mutated powers to create horrific armies of creatures, to repress those who opposed her, to destroy those who dared to fight back. She was a despicable, disgusting person. A terribly *unhappy* person.

But she couldn't change. Not now. She knew that as clearly as she'd recognised what she had become. It was too late for change. Her plans were in full motion, and if it took her full cruelty and reprehensible reputation to win the battle, then so be it.

She realised what that meant. She was willing to sacrifice her own dignity, her own reputation, her own … soul. In the end, though, the worlds would thank her. In the end, everyone would be better off. In the end, life would be perfect.

She looked to her right just in time to see her latest servant-girl, Doofus, stumble through the door and drop a tray, dishes clattering all over the floor.

The timing couldn't have been worse. Jane's *mood* couldn't have been worse.

She threw her hand forward, unleashing a burst of the mutated Chi'karda. Doofus shot into the air and slammed high against the stone wall, pinned near the ceiling by the invisible force. Choking sounds filled the room as the poor girl kicked at the air, her heels thumping the wall.

'How dare you enter without knocking, you pathetic slob.' Jane's voice remained calm and cool, belying the rage and guilt she felt within. With a quick wave of her hand, she made Doofus spring away from the wall and fly across the room. Screams burst from the girl's throat as the chokehold was released. They quickly faded when the servant shot through the open window and plummeted towards her death far below.

'I'm tired of coming up with names for these people,' Jane grumbled to herself.

She stood up, took one last look at the beauty of her fortress grounds, then went back to work. There was much to be done.

A Major Rule
Violation

On the morning of August the twenty-second, Tick
and his friends barely said a word during breakfast
with his family, scared to death that somehow they'd
slip up and say something about the incident in the
forest. They were having enough trouble already with
his mom – she kept insisting Dad should go with them,
that they should demand Master George allow Edgar
to be a Realitant or they would all quit.

Tick hated seeing how much his mom worried. She'd
never looked so distressed and unhappy. Seeing his
mom sobbing uncontrollably was just about enough
to rip Tick's heart into two pieces. But he knew they
had no choice, and he also knew his dad would figure
out a way to console her after they were gone.

Luckily, Dad was firmly on their side, though he,
too, often failed to hide the worries and concerns
inflicted on his own heart.

After stuffing food and clothes into their backpacks,
and after a terribly tearful goodbye with Tick's family,

the three Realitants set off for the cemetery near the town square of Deer Park. Tick thought it was a little surreal, like his parents had packed him off to summer camp instead of to another reality.

'Man, your mom *really* loves you, dude,' Paul said, adjusting his backpack.

'Yeah, I guess,' Tick replied.

'You *guess?*' Sofia said. 'My parents are just glad to get me out of the house. "Yes, sweetie, run along to your adventures. Don't forget to brush your teeth!"'

Paul kicked a loose rock on the road. 'You know my strategy – ask for forgiveness when I get back.'

Tick didn't respond, unable to get the look on his mom's face out of his head.

They walked in silence the rest of the way to the cemetery.

☼

'So good to see you!' George said for the hundredth time that morning. He reached out to shake the hand of William Schmidt, an old man from the Third Reality who Sato thought looked like someone three steps from death's door. Sato stifled a yawn, wondering why George always made him do stuff like this with him.

They stood at the entrance to the large assembly hall, a wide auditorium cut into the stone with a stage in the front and a tinted window at the back overlooking the Grand Canyon. Sato knew they'd somehow camouflaged the windows in the complex, but it still seemed like a foolish thing. He could only imagine the news explosion that would happen if they were discovered.

The Big Meeting wasn't scheduled to begin for another ninety minutes, but the Realitants had been pouring in for hours, wanting to meet and greet and speculate. Sato had never met such strange and diverse people in all his life, and couldn't help but feel amazed at the sheer effort of maintaining such an organisation. A slender woman with flaming red hair entered the assembly hall next, enough make-up on her face to hide a dozen boils. She smiled as George shook her hand, then focused on Sato, nodding her head.

'Is this one of the new recruits?' she asked, her high voice filled with a creepy sweetness.

'Why, yes, yes, he is,' George replied, his voice loud and prideful. 'Young Sato here has proven himself quite valuable in the last few months. A real worker, eh, Sato?'

Sato shook the lady's hand. 'Nice to meet you.' He wanted to add, *Would you mind killing me, please? I'm bored.*

'My name is Priscilla Persephone,' the redhead replied in her slightly disturbing, shrill voice. 'I've heard great things about your mission to obtain Mistress Jane's Barrier Wand. Good to know Master George can trust such ... important duties to someone so young, instead of depending on veterans like myself.'

Priscilla gave George a hard stare, then walked off to grab a glass of orange juice and a pastry.

George mumbled something under his breath; it sounded like he'd used the words *ugly hag* and *yapping dog.*

'What did you say?' Sato asked.

George waved at the air. 'Oh, nothing, Master Sato, nothing at all.'

The next person George greeted was a younger, much prettier woman named Nancy Zeppelin. Her golden hair and brilliant blue eyes made her look like she'd just stepped off a Paris fashion runway. Sato didn't realise he was staring until George nudged him with an elbow.

'Oh, um, my name is Sato,' he said, feeling his face grow warm.

'Nice to meet you. Congratulations on joining the–'

Before she could finish, Rutger rushed into the auditorium, yelling George's name, waddling like a fat duck trying to catch its ducklings before they crossed a busy road.

'Goodness gracious me,' George said, trying to calm the short man. 'What is it, Rutger?'

Rutger spoke in short bursts, sucking in gasps of air between words. 'Tick ... and the others ... their nanolocators ... everything seems normal ... at the cemetery ... but it won't work ...'

George reached down and grasped Rutger by the shoulders. 'Take a deep breath, man, then explain yourself.'

Rutger did as he was told, closing his eyes briefly before opening them again. But when he spoke, it came out just like before. 'I don't understand ... all their readings ... normal ... no malfunctions, no blips ... but the Wand won't wink them in. They're standing there ... waiting! It won't work!'

George tapped his lips, looking down at Sato then at the mingling Realitants gathered in the assembly hall. His eyes seemed afire with concern. 'Oh, dear.'

'What's going on?' Sato asked.

'Unfortunately, I think I know *exactly* what's going on.' George started walking towards the stage, his steps brisk.

Sato looked down at Rutger. 'Do you?'

Rutger shook his head, his face so lined and creased that Sato worried he'd drop dead of a heart attack. He was about to say something when George's voice boomed across the room, echoing off the walls. Sato turned to see George standing at a microphone on the stage.

'My fellow Realitants,' he announced. 'This meeting must start immediately. Please, find anyone lingering in the halls, bring them here, and take your seats.'

'What's wrong?' someone yelled from the audience.

George paused before answering. 'We've had a violation of Rule Number 462.'

☼

Tick fidgeted, rocking back and forth on his feet, wiping his sweaty hands on his trousers. Sofia stood to his left, Paul to his right. The sun made its way towards the top of the sky, beating down on the cemetery with a ruthless heat. Tick hoped Master George would wink them away to a nice, cool place; he couldn't wait to tell him about the bizarre incident in the woods with Mr. Chu. They'd seen no sign of him since, and several calls to the school had only hit the answering machine.

'Come on, already,' Paul muttered, looking up at the cloudless blue sky as if he expected Master George to float down in a balloon and pick them up. He cupped his hands around his mouth and shouted to the air, 'Yo! We're ready! Wink us, man!'

'Maybe he will once you quit acting like an idiot,' Sofia said.

'At least I'm *acting,*' Paul replied.

Sofia pulled back to punch him for his troubles when the screeching sound of a car slamming on its brakes in front of the cemetery entrance made them look in that direction. Tick's heart skipped a beat when he realised it was his mom. She was already out the door and past the stone archway, running at full speed.

'Mom!' Tick yelled. 'What are you doing?'

'Atticus, don't leave yet!' she said, looking ridiculous as her arms pumped back and forth. Tick realised that he'd never, not once, seen his mother run before.

'What's wrong?' he asked, lowering his voice now that she'd almost reached them, only twenty feet away.

'I have to tell you something – I have to tell you before you go.' She slowed, then stopped, sucking in air. 'It's very important.'

Tick was so relieved she wasn't going to prevent him from leaving, he failed to realise how odd it was that she'd raced here to tell him ... what?

'You okay?' he asked. 'What is it?'

Having regained her breath, she began talking. 'I should've told you this years ago – at the least, I should've told you four months ago. I–'

But Tick didn't hear the rest of her sentence. Instead, in that instant, he and his friends were winked away to a very strange place.

A VERY STRANGE PLACE

Tick got his wish in one regard – the place was cold.
Beyond that, he couldn't find one positive thing
about it.

They stood on a cracked stone road, small pools of
stagnant water filling the gaps. The smoggy air reeked
of things burnt – oil, rubber, tar. Metal structures lined
the long street on both sides, towering over them,
black and dirty. Tick first thought they were buildings
of some kind, but that notion quickly evaporated.
They were more like sculptures, the dark and twisted
vision of some maniac artist.

'Man,' Paul whispered, 'it's like Gotham City.' In
some spots, wide, arching pieces rose fifty feet in
the air, ending in a jagged, ripped edge as if some
enormous monster had ripped the top off with its
teeth. In other places, huge, towering cylinders – some
taller than New York City skyscrapers – ascended to
the sky until they disappeared into the menacing,
storm-heavy clouds. Squat, deformed lumps sat in the
nooks and crannies, like weathered statues of ancient
Greek gods. Hideous carvings of animals, worse than
the ugliest gargoyle Tick had ever seen balancing on

the outer walls of a cathedral, lay strewn about like stray dogs, frozen in place by a rainstorm of molten metal. Random triangles and pentagons hung oddly from various structures, seeming to defy the laws of physics.

All of it, everything in sight, was made out of a dark grey metal that dully reflected the scant light filtering through the clouds above. And there was no variation – the bizarre structures and sculptures lay everywhere, in every direction, as far as Tick could see.

One word seemed to describe the place better than anything else: dreary.

'Where are we?' Sofia asked, slowly turning in a circle, just as Tick and Paul were.

Good question, Tick thought. He didn't know if he was looking forward to any locals showing up to answer it.

'What kind of people would *live* here?' he asked, trying to shake the worry of his mom and her undelivered message.

'People who like to gouge their eyes out, obviously,' Paul said. 'This has to be the ugliest place I've ever seen.'

'They ever heard of flowers?' Sofia said. 'Maybe a splash of colour here and there?'

'Do you think we're in one of the Thirteen Realities?' Tick asked. 'One we haven't heard of yet?'

'Where else could we be?' Paul answered. 'Does this look like something in Reality Prime to you?'

'I don't know – maybe these are ruins or something.'

Paul coughed. 'Uh ... don't think so, big guy. Pretty sure we would've heard about a place this weird.'

'What could've led to something like this?' Sofia asked, sliding her hand along the flat side of a large, boxy structure, big spheres bubbling out the side of it like pimples. 'How could they be so different from us?'

Tick stepped towards one of the cylindrical towers, following Sofia's lead and touching the black metal. It was as cold and hard as it looked.

A faint buzzing sound filled the air. At first, Tick panicked because it reminded him of the Gnat Rat and its mechanical hornets that had attacked him in his bedroom the previous fall. But an instant after the droning began, a burst of light to the left caught his attention.

Near a large circle of metal, jutting up from the ground like a half-buried flying saucer, sparks of brilliant white light popped and flashed, igniting into existence only to disappear a second later, like the brief flames shooting off a welding machine. The sparks seemed random at first, exploding all over the place, high and low in the air, across an area dozens of feet wide, reflecting off the metal circle in dull smears of colour. But then the strangest thing happened.

The sparks began to form words.

Tick thought his mind was playing tricks, the constant flashing of lights wreaking havoc on his vision. But soon it became obvious as large letters of bright, streaky light appeared, hanging in the air, flashing and dancing but remaining solid enough to read. In a matter of seconds, a wall of words flickered before them, as big as a movie screen.

Tick swallowed his awe and confusion, reading the words as quickly as possible, scared they might disappear at any second:

INSIDE THE WORDS OF THE WORDS INSIDE,
THERE LIES A SECRET TO UNHIDE.
A PLACE THERE IS WHERE YOU MUST GO,
TO MEET THE SEVEN, FRIEND OR FOE.

OF COURSE, AN ORDER THERE MUST BE,
TO HILL AND ROCK AND STONE AND TREE.
OF WORLDS ABOVE AND WORLDS BELOW,
OF WORLDS WITH WATER, FIRE, SNOW.
OF WORLDS THAT LIVE IN FEAR AND DOUBT,
OF WORLDS WITHIN AND WORLDS WITHOUT.
THE PATH BEGINS WHERE DARK IS CLEAR,
WHERE SHORT IS TALL AND FAR IS NEAR,
ALL THIS YOU MUST IGNORE AND HATE,
FOR YOU TO FIND THE WANTED FATE,
THERE LIES A SECRET TO UNHIDE,
INSIDE THE WORDS OF THE WORDS INSIDE.

Tick read it three times, his eyes wide. He had no clue what the words meant, but they mesmerised him, held him captivated. He felt just like when he'd first read the original invitation from Master George.

Master George!

'You've gotta be kidding me,' Tick said, surprised at how loud his voice sounded, echoing off the world of metal around them. He looked over at his friends.

'What?' Paul asked without returning the glance. He still stared at the poem, which shimmered as brightly as ever, his lips forming the strange words silently. Sofia was doing the same thing a couple of feet from him.

Tick returned to the poem, quickly rereading it. 'I can't believe Master George is messing around with riddles and clues again. I thought we'd proved ourselves already.'

'How do you know it's from Master George?' Paul asked.

'Hmmm,' Sofia said. 'Maybe because he told us to go to the cemetery then winked us here? I know it's a little complicated for–'

A loud, electric *crack* cut her off, followed by a series of hissing sizzles. The letters of the poem quickly sparkled and flashed before disappearing altogether, the wispy, streaming trails of smoke the only sign they'd ever been there. Without any wind, the smoke lingered, slowly coalescing and melding into one hazy glob.

Just when everything seemed utterly silent, another loud crack of electricity made Tick jump, one last explosion of light igniting on the ground a few feet in front of Sofia. It was gone as quickly as it had come, and in its place stood a small metal box, a tiny latch on the front.

Paul got there first, dropping to his knees and reaching out for the box.

'Wait!' Sofia said.

Paul's hands froze in midair; he looked over his shoulder. 'Why? This is obviously from Master George, right? You just said I was an idiot for doubting it.'

'Well ... yeah, I guess. Just ... I don't know, be careful.'

'Open it,' Tick urged. 'We're lucky he didn't wink it into one of our skulls.'

Paul reached out again and flipped up the latch, then carefully lifted the lid open. He leaned forward and looked down into the small space of the container; Tick and Sofia stood behind him, looking over his shoulder.

Inside, there lay only a small piece of paper. Stiff, white paper – cardstock.

'Definitely M.G.'s MO,' Paul said as he picked up the message. He held it up in the scant light for everyone to see.

In the same typed writing of the Twelve Clues from their first adventure with Master George, the paper contained the exact poem, word for word, that they'd just seen floating in the air like the world's most sophisticated fireworks. Paul flipped the paper over and read another mysterious clue:

```
Miss Graham is the key. Repeat: you
must find Anna.
```

'Man, he's getting all fancy on us,' Paul said, standing up. 'Why use all the Christmas lights if he was gonna send us this anyway?'

'Guess he wanted to show off,' Sofia said, taking the message from Paul. She sat down on the stone-paved road and read through the poem again.

Tick folded his arms and shivered, looking up at the sky. There was no sign of the sun, but it seemed to have grown a little darker since they'd arrived. The temperature had dropped too, and for the first time in months, he felt justified wearing his scarf. He wrapped it a little tighter, then walked over to sit on a small metal cube next to the road.

'Hurry up and figure it out, Sofia,' he said, before letting out a huge yawn. 'I don't really wanna hang out here much longer.'

'You could help, ya know,' she mumbled, still studying the paper.

Actually Tick was doing just that, reviewing the

poem in his mind's eye; without meaning to, he'd memorised it. But he didn't know what to look for or try to solve. The riddle seemed to have only one purpose – to confuse its reader.

Paul yawned and stretched. 'Man, I can't just sit here. Let's get moving.'

'Where to?' Tick asked, looking down one length of the endless road, then the other. The heavy clouds had sunk to the ground, as if seeking warmth and companionship. The only things Tick could see were the countless heaps and angles of dark metal, covered in a mist that grew thicker by the minute. Tick shivered again.

'I don't know, dude,' Paul said. 'That way.' He pointed to his left, then changed his mind, pointing in the other direction. 'Nah, that way.'

Sofia stood, shaking her head; she seemed as frustrated as Tick about the riddle. 'Sounds good to me. Let's go.' Without waiting for a response, she started walking down the cracked and pitted road.

☼

Thirty minutes later, nothing had changed except for the air around them, which continued to grow thicker with wet, heavy mist. The world of metal was almost lost in darkness. Obscure, creepy shapes appeared and disappeared, all sharp angles and looming curves. The burnt smells intensified, as if the kids were approaching a huge factory or rubbish tip.

Tick officially hated the place, his panic growing at the thought that maybe they'd be stuck here, that they'd have to *sleep* here. If the stupid riddle was their only way out ...

He kept running through it in his mind, trying to recall the methods he'd used to solve the original Twelve Clues. Those had seemed so easy in comparison, almost childish. Magic words, thumping the ground with your foot, figuring out a day and a time. Compared to that, this new one seemed like advanced calculus.

For some reason, the lines "All this you must ignore and hate, for you to find the wanted fate" kept returning to his mind. Something told him that was the key to figuring everything out.

They approached a wide, thick span of metal arching across the road – rusty, linked chains of varying lengths hanging down every couple of feet. The chains swayed slightly despite the lack of wind. That gave Tick the creeps more than anything else, and he quickened his pace until the odd structure was way behind them.

'Spooked?' Paul asked. His voice was muffled, swallowed up in the mist.

'Yeah,' Tick answered. 'You're not?'

'Maybe.'

'Oh, please,' Sofia said. 'If it weren't for me being here, you two would be running around bawling your eyes out. Just keep moving.'

'Miss Italy, you're probably right, but do you have to be so annoying?'

They walked for another couple of hours, but nothing changed. The path only led to more of the same – mounds of dark metal and looming, odd shapes. Tick finally couldn't take it any more; his feet hurt and his stomach rumbled with hunger.

'We need to eat,' he said. 'And sleep.'

'Amen,' Paul agreed.

Sofia didn't say anything, but she almost collapsed to the ground, sighing as she leaned back against a black wall and pulled out a granola bar and a bottle of water from her backpack. Tick sat across the road from her, diving into his own food.

'How can I possibly sleep here?' Paul asked as he bit into an energy bar. 'I don't have my feather pillow.'

Tick half-laughed, but he already felt his eyes drooping, despite sitting up. Feeling like he'd been drugged, he leaned over and lay on his side, pulling his backpack under his head for a pillow. He fell asleep instantly.

✿

Two days passed, though the only way Tick knew for sure was by looking at his watch and noticing the subtle changes in the darkness of the sky. Tick's anxiety and panic faded into a dull indifference as they trudged along the endless path, finding nothing. For all he knew, they were walking in circles because everything looked so similar.

They grew quiet as they walked, discouragement acting as a gag in their throats.

On the morning of their third day in the miserable place, Tick finished off his measly breakfast of a chocolate bar, half a bottle of water, and a stale piece of bread – he was almost out of food. As he stood and put on his backpack, Paul gave him an ugly look.

'Dude, where are you going?' he said through a yawn. 'I'm barely awake – what's the rush?'

'There has to be something we're missing,' Tick replied. 'I think we need to get off this stupid road and climb up one of these structures. Try to get inside one of them.'

'Tick's right,' Sofia said, getting to her feet as well. 'This road isn't leading us anywhere except in a big circle – everything looks familiar.'

'It *all* looks the same to me.' Paul stretched, then stood up. 'Fine, whatever. It's not like I wanna retire and live on this road some day. Maybe we could try to climb–'

A loud, crashing sound to their right cut him off.

All three of them froze, waiting, listening.

A metallic *clang* rang out from behind a jutting rectangle of metal, followed by a scrape, then the grunt of a man. Tick heard the shuffling of feet, then a cough. Although he knew someone was approaching the road, about to appear at any second, he couldn't move. After almost three days of complete boredom, hearing the presence of another human being was like finding an alien in his backyard.

A man of medium height and enormous build stepped around the corner of the metal obstacle, limping slightly. He had tangled, red hair and a scruffy beard; he wore a plaid red flannel shirt, dirty denim overalls, and heavy work boots. Tick was half-surprised the guy didn't have a huge axe slung over his shoulder.

When the man noticed Tick and the others, he stopped and stared at them with wide eyes. After a long, awkward pause, he spoke, his voice as scratchy as his beard.

'Well, butter my grits,' he said with a heavy Southern accent. 'What you chirrun doin' up in here?'

Tick didn't say anything, not sure why he felt so

odd. Maybe it was the absurdity of seeing a lumberjack in a world made of metal. Sofia saved the situation.

'We're, uh, kind of lost,' she said.

'Lost?' the man repeated, leaning back and putting his large hands in the pockets of his overalls. 'How you reckon on gettin' lost up here on da roofens?'

Tick blinked, unsure if the guy was still speaking English.

'Um, pardon me?' Paul said, clearing his throat. 'Didn't quite catch what you just said.'

The man squinted, looking at each of them in turn, as if doing some deep thinking and analysis. Finally he said, 'Ya'll look as twittered as a hound dawg at a tea party. Whatcha lookin' fer?'

Tick felt it was his turn. 'Sir, we're, uh, like my friend said – we're lost. We're not familiar with this … place. Where are we? Where are all the houses and buildings and people?'

The man folded his arms, a smile spreading across his face; he had a huge gap between his two front teeth.

'Boy, you must be dumber 'an roadkill in maths class. You hear what I'm sayin'?'

Tick shook his head, trying to look as confused as possible – which wasn't hard.

The man stepped forward. 'Boy, you is standin' on the Roofens.' He pointed down to the ground with exaggerated enthusiasm. 'All the people is down *there*.'

11

BELOW THE ROOFENS

Tick looked at his feet, almost expecting to see little fairies running around to avoid being squished. But of course all he saw were his shoes and a thin crack on the stone road.

'Down there?' he asked.

The man made a noise somewhere deep in his throat, a cross between a cough and the clearing of phlegm. 'I reckon that's what I said, ain't it? Who in the guppy-guts are you people?'

Tick fumbled for words, glad Sofia spoke up first. 'We're just up here exploring, that's all. Of course we know what the Roofens are and that we're *standing* on them.' She gave Tick an annoyed look. 'That we're *on top* of the buildings.'

'Ain't usin' dem brains a'yorn too much up here, wanderin' 'round like three hillbillies lookin' for moonshine. No, ma'am, ain't too smart.' The man leaned over and spat something dark and disgusting on the road.

'My name's Sofia, and this is my friend, Tick.' She gestured with her thumb. 'And this is Paul. To tell you the truth, we *are* really lost, and kind of hungry and cold.'

'Mmm-hmm,' the man said with a grunt, eyeing Sofia up and down as if checking for ticks. 'Come along, then. Ol' Sally'll take right good care of ya.'

Paul spoke for the first time since the appearance of the strange man. 'Is Sally your wife?'

The man laughed, a guffaw that hit the mist with a dull thump. 'My wife? Boy, I ain't got me no wife. You're lookin' at him.'

Tick was confused. 'What do you mean?'

'Boy, what you mean, what I mean?'

'He *means,* what do you *mean?*' Sofia said, her voice returning to its normal arrogance.

The lumberjack threw his arms up in the air. 'Feel like I'm talkin' to kai-yotes who done got their ears chopped off. I'm tellin' ya that yer *lookin'* at Sally, and you best not say a word about it.'

'*Your* name is Sally?' Tick asked.

'Sally T. Jones, at yer service.' He bowed, sweeping his arms wide, then righting himself. His face had reddened from the blood rushing to his head; it matched his beard. 'Named after my grandpappy, who was named after his grandpappy. See, Sally's short for Sallivent, a name older than expired dirt, ya hear?'

'We hear,' Sofia said. 'You have a woman's name.'

Tick elbowed his friend. 'Be nice,' he whispered.

'I like it,' Paul said. 'Beats the heck out of being named Princess or Barbie, right?'

Sally gave Paul a confused look. 'I'll eat my own dandruff if you ain't the strangest group of chirrun I ever done seen.'

'What's a chirrun?' Tick asked.

Sally squinted in disbelief. '*Chirrun*. Ya know – you's a kid, a child. More than one of ya – *chirrun*.'

'I think he means *children,*' Sofia said.

Sally took a step to the side, then motioned around the back of the metal block. 'You kids wanna come back with me? Get ya sumthin' to fill dem tummies?'

'Where'd you come from?' Paul asked, leaning to get a look around the metal wall. 'Is there seriously a whole city under us? Under these roofs?'

'Like I said, boy, we standin' on the Roofens. Probably done shaved purtin' near six months off your life stayin' out chere for so long. Dis dirty air'll eat yer innards quicker than a beaver on balsa wood.'

'What's wrong with the air?' Tick asked.

Sally did his funny squint again. 'I reckon you folks ain't lyin' when you says yer lost. These parts 'bout as polluted as my granny's toenails. Why do you think they built dem cities under all this here metal?'

'Why'd you come up here, then?' Sofia asked.

Sally paused, his eyes darting back and forth. 'I, uh, well, ya see, the thing is ...' He scratched his beard. 'See, I done heard yer little twitter feet up on my ceilin' there, so I come up to do some investigatin'. Yep, that's what I reckon, far as I recall.'

Tick exchanged a baffled look with Sofia and Paul. It didn't take a genius to realise they'd already caught Sally in his first lie.

'Well,' Tick said, 'we need a minute to talk about what we're gonna do.'

'Go on, then,' Sally said. 'I ain't got a mind to bother dem there bid'ness and matter, such as it were.'

'Huh?' Paul asked.

Tick quickly grabbed his friend by the shoulders and turned him away from Sally, pulling him into a huddle with Sofia.

'So what do we do?' Tick whispered.

'That guy's something else, ain't he?' Paul asked. 'I can barely understand a word he says.'

'I'm already getting used to it,' Sofia said. 'If you ignore every third word or so, it makes perfect sense.'

'But what do we *do?*' Tick insisted.

'What else?' Paul said. 'Go with this dude and get something to eat.'

'How do we know he's safe?' Tick asked.

'Dude, get off the sissy train. There are three of us and one of him.'

'He seems perfectly harmless,' Sofia said. 'I vote we go with him. We can't walk around up here for the rest of our lives.'

'Plus,' Paul said, 'he said this air's really polluted. I'm not real cool on the whole lung cancer thing. Let's do it.'

Sofia nodded. 'I'm dying to see what's down there.'

Tick thought for a second. He felt uneasy, but he knew it was because their lives had gone flat-out crazy the last couple of days. Sally was definitely holding something back, and that made Tick nervous, but Paul was right – they had him outnumbered.

'All right,' he whispered, then turned to Sally. 'Sir, we really appreciate the offer to go to your house. We're really hungry, and, uh, lost.'

Sally smiled and rubbed his belly. 'I ain't said nothing about goin' to my house. But I know a restaurant's got some good eatin'. Come on, den.' He waved his arm in a beckoning gesture as he turned and walked back the way he'd come.

Tick, Sofia, and Paul paused. But then they followed.

✾

Sally led them through a small trapdoor and down a very long and steep set of wooden stairs, which looked out of place amidst all the surrounding metal. The way was dark and hot, humid and reeking of something rotten. Tick felt more nervous by the second, worried they were walking into a trap, but he didn't know what else to do. Where could they go? Who could they trust?

For now, Sally was their only friend in the world.

This world, anyway.

They reached the bottom of the stairs and proceeded down a long hallway, their surroundings remaining unchanged. A faint light from ahead revealed black water seeping down the wooden walls. A rat scurried by Tick's foot; he barely stopped himself from crying out like the startled maid in an old cartoon.

Sally finally stopped next to a warped door of splintered wood, an iron handle barely hanging on. 'Prepare dem hearts a'yorn,' he said. 'This place ain't like none such you ever saw.' He pushed the door, and everyone watched as it swung outwards, creaking loudly.

'Follow Uncle Sally and you chirrun might live another day or two.' He stepped through the doorway.

Sofia went first, then Paul, then Tick. For the next several minutes, Tick felt as if his brain might explode from taking in the completely alien place.

Stretching before them, below them, above them, was an endless world of chaos. Long rows of roughly cobbled pathways ran in every direction, with no pattern or regularity. Shops and inns and pubs crowded close on all sides. Hundreds of people bustled about. Dirty, ripped awnings hung over the places of business, wooden signs dangling from chains. On these signs were printed the only means of distinguishing one building from another – their names carved and painted onto the wood. Places called such things as The Axeman's Guild and The Darkhorse Inn and The Sordid Swine.

Some of the pathways were actually bridges, and Tick could see the levels below, overlapping and seemingly built on top of each other. The same was true above them, balconies and bridges spanning every direction, up and up and up until Tick saw the black roof that covered everything. The ceiling was filled with small rectangles of fluorescent lights, half of which were flickering or burned out altogether.

It was the universe's worst shopping centre.

Paul leaned over and whispered to Tick, 'Dude, check these people out.'

Tick focused on the occupants of the enormous indoor town. Most of them slumped along, barely speaking to each other, many with hunched shoulders or an odd limp. Black seemed to be the colour of choice for their clothes, everyone wearing drab and dirty garments with rips and tears aplenty. The people's faces were dirty too, with dishevelled, greasy hair. The only spots of colour were an occasional red scarf or green shawl or yellow vest, worn by those who seemed to walk with a little more confidence than the others.

And the smell – it was like a dumping ground, a foul, putrid stench that made Tick gag reflexively every few seconds until he grew somewhat used to it.

'Sally,' Sofia coughed, 'I think we were better off on the Roofens.'

'Quit yer poutin' and come on,' Sally replied, shuffling off to the right.

Tick and the others followed, dodging through the lazy crowd of sullen, black-clad residents, who seemed to be marching towards their destinations with no purpose whatsoever. Tick didn't see one person smiling. For that matter, none of them showed emotion at all – not a sneer, not a grimace, not a frown to be found.

'We've gotta get out of here,' Tick whispered, scared to offend anyone around him but feeling a surge of panic well up inside him. He didn't know how much longer he could last in this horrible place. 'We need to solve that riddle, quick.'

'No kidding,' Paul said. 'I've just about had my fill of Happy Town.'

'It's not just that,' Tick said, still speaking quietly. 'Something's not right here – it's not safe.'

Sally moved them to the side of their current path, next to a small iron table outside a restaurant called The Stinky Stew.

'Have'n yerselves a seat on dem cheers.' He pointed to the four crooked wooden chairs surrounding the table. 'I'll be back with some eats.'

As their guide entered the restaurant, a rusty bell ringing with the movement of the door, Tick and the others pulled out the chairs and sat down. Tick eyeballed the people walking by, looking for potential trouble. Seeing nothing but the unchanging mass of zombie-like shoppers, he said to Sofia, 'Get the riddle out.'

Sofia did, putting the paper on the table in front of her. Tick and Paul scooted their chairs across the uneven stones of the floor until they could see the words of the long poem.

```
Inside the words of the words inside,
   There lies a secret to unhide.
 A place there is where you must go,
 To meet the Seven, friend or foe …
```

Tick read through the whole thing, then sat back in his chair, racking his brain. The poem seemed to offer no direction, nothing specific to grasp on to. At least the Twelve Clues had made it pretty clear that he was to figure out a date, a time, the magic words. This was a bunch of poetic nonsense.

Sofia flipped the page over where the second note was printed. 'Who are Anna and Miss Graham?'

Paul leaned onto his elbows, resting them on the table. 'Do you think it's the same person?'

'Maybe,' Sofia replied. 'We should start asking around here – see if anyone's heard of her.'

'That's the only thing I can think of,' Paul said.

He stood up, almost knocking his chair backwards. 'What are you doing?' Tick asked.

'Asking around, dude.' He reached out and tapped the arm of the first stranger to walk by, an older woman in a filthy black dress, her grey hair sprawled across her shoulders in greasy strings. 'Excuse me, ma'am, do you know who Anna Graham is?'

The old lady recoiled, barely casting a glance at Paul before quickening her step to get away. He didn't give up, tapping the next person, then the next, then the next, each time repeating his question. And the response was the same each time – a flinch, as if the name frightened them.

'Dudes, we don't have leprosy, ya know?' Paul called out. Cupping his hands together, he shouted in an even louder voice, 'Does anyone here know Miss Anna Graham?' The sounds of shuffling feet were all he got in return.

Sitting down with a huff, Paul shook his head. 'This is ridiculous. What's wrong with these people?' Tick's thoughts had wandered slightly. Something about Anna's name bothered him, tickled something in the back of his mind. *Miss Graham. Anna. Anna Graham.*

'This phrase has to be the key,' Sofia said suddenly, pointing at the lines near the end of the poem: 'All this you must ignore and hate, for you to find the wanted fate.'

'Yeah, I thought the same thing,' Tick said.

'Maybe it means–' Sofia began, but stopped when Sally came bustling outside, clanging the door against the wall with his elbows as he balanced several plates and bowls heaped with steaming food.

'As promised,' he said, setting the meal on the table. He almost dropped one plate onto the ground, but Paul caught it and pushed it to safety. 'Grab yer grub and eat. I'm as hungry as a one-legged possum caught in a dang ol' bear trap.'

Sally sat down in the remaining chair and picked up his food with his hands; there wasn't a utensil in sight. Tick couldn't believe how delicious everything looked – chicken legs thick with meat, slabs of beef, celery and carrots, chunks of bread, sausages. It was so unexpectedly appetising; he'd half-expected Sally to bring out a bin full of fly-infested rubbish.

Paul was the first to join in, then Sofia, both of them grabbing a roasted drumstick and chowing down.

'This ain't bad,' Paul said with a full mouth, throwing his manners out the window. 'Tastes a little stale and smoky, but it's pretty good.'

Tick reached over and grabbed his own piece of chicken and a roll. Paul was right – it tasted a little old, even a little dirty, but it was like Thanksgiving dinner all the same – and Tick was starving. No one said a word as they munched and chewed and chomped their way through every last morsel of food.

Tick had just sat back, rubbing his belly in satisfaction, when a young boy in a dark suit stepped up to their table and cleared his throat. His dirty blonde hair framed a face smeared with grime, and his eyes were wide, as if he were scared to death.

'Whatcha want?' Sally asked, wiping his mouth on his sleeve. 'What's yer bid'ness, son?'

The boy swallowed, rocking back and forth on his feet, glancing over his shoulder now and again. But he said nothing.

'Got some dadgum cotton in dem ears, son?' Sally asked. 'I say, what's yer bid'ness?'

The boy's arm slowly raised, his index finger extended. One by one, he pointed at the four people sitting at the table. Then he spoke in a weak, high-pitched voice full of fear.

'The Master ... told me to ... he said ... he said you'll all be dead in five minutes.'

LONG, SPINDLY LEGS

All four of them stood up in the same instant. This time Paul's chair did fall over with a rattling clang.

'What kinda nonsense you talkin'?' Sally asked. The boy looked up at him, his face growing impossibly paler; then he turned and ran, disappearing in the dense crowd of mulling citizens.

'What was *that*?' Paul said.

'The riddle,' Tick said, leaning over and twisting the paper from Master George towards him. 'We have to solve the riddle. Now.'

'Yeah, that'll be extra easy knowing we're about to die,' Paul said.

'Quit whining and think,' Sofia said, joining Tick to study the poem.

Tick tried to focus, reading the words through and then closing his eyes, letting them float through his mind, sorting them out. He thought of the lady's name, Miss Anna Graham ...

Sofia spoke up, breaking his concentration. 'The part about ignoring everything else – it must mean the two lines after it are all that matters – the last two lines. The rest of it seems like nonsense anyway ...

but ... "There lies a secret to unhide ..."'

'"*Inside the words of the words inside,*"' Tick finished for her.

'What is *that?*' Paul said, his neck bent back as he looked up at the ceiling.

Tick ignored him, staring at the last two lines of the poem as if doing so would make them rearrange themselves. Rearrange ...

Paul slapped Tick on the shoulder, then Sofia, who was also ignoring him. 'Guys, cut the poetry lesson for a second and *look.*' He pointed upwards.

Far above, odd shapes crawled across the black roof, defying gravity and blotting out the sputtering lights as they moved around. Impossible to make out clearly, the ... *things* were squat and round with several long, angled limbs that moved up and down rapidly, bending and unbending as they scuttled about. They looked like big spiders, but *false* somehow – artificial. As if their legs were made out of ...

'Bless my mama's hanky – what *are* those buggins?' Sally asked.

One of the creatures jumped from the roof and landed on the closest balcony with a metallic clank. As it flew through the air, its awkward limbs flailing, Tick noticed a flash of steel. Another creature followed its companion, then another, then another. By the time the leader had jumped down to the next balcony, the dozen or so others had reached the first one. Balcony to balcony, down they came.

Straight for Tick's group.

'This is gonna be trouble,' Paul said.

A sharp pain built behind Tick's eyes, his mind spinning in all kinds of directions. He knew these mechanical spiders must be like the Gnat Rat or the Tingle Wraith, things sent by Master George to test them. At least he *hoped* they were from Master George.

' "Inside the words of the words inside," ' Sofia said in a burst, her eyes widening in revelation. ' "Inside the *words* of the words inside!" '

The spider-things were two levels away, close enough for Tick to make out their features. The long, spindly legs were jointed metal, supporting a round ball of steel with all kinds of devices jutting from its body – spinning blades and sharp knives. The clanking and clicking and whirring of the horrible creatures made Tick's insides boil.

Sofia grabbed Tick's arm. '*The words inside.* Those three words are the main part of the riddle!'

The answer hit Tick like a catapulted stone. Anna Graham. Rearranging. Tick had always loved the puzzles in the Sunday paper, everything from Sudoku to number pyramids, but one game had always been a favourite ...

Anna Graham.

'Anagram!' he yelled, probably looking insane to his friends because of the huge smile that spread across his face. The clanking sounds of the oncoming metal spiders grew louder.

'Yeah, but who is she?' Paul asked. 'How do we find her?'

'No, no,' Tick said. 'Not a name – a thing. An anagram.'

'What the heck is an anagram?' Paul asked, stealing a glance at the creatures, now only seconds away from reaching them.

Sofia answered. 'It's when the letters of a word or phrase are rearranged to spell something else.'

'Yeah,' Tick said. 'Whatever we're looking for must be an anagram of "*the words inside.*"'

'Yes!' Sofia yelled.

But their joy was short-lived. The first spider landed on their table with a horrible crash.

☼

The boy named Henry ran, bumping into people, bouncing off them, falling to the ground, getting back up – running, always running. He'd hardly said one word to a stranger his whole life, living in fear of the metaspides and their all-seeing eye. They were always there, waiting, watching.

But he'd done his job. He'd said the words, delivered the message. In doing so, he'd made enough money to buy medicine for his mom for another six months. He knew the docs were overcharging him, but he had no choice. He didn't want his mom to die.

The creepy man who'd offered him the job stood in the same spot, lurking inside an alcove between two pubs. The man had paid him half the money beforehand, promising the other half when the deed was done. Henry walked up to him and held out his shaking hand. When they made eye contact, he couldn't help but take a step backwards.

The man looked at the boy with fierce eyes, his brow tensed in anger, his dark hair hanging in his face. A long pause followed, filled with the sounds of the metaspides launching an attack behind him.

'You did it, then?' the man said. 'You think you deserve some money, do you?'

'Y-y-yes, sir,' Henry replied.

'So you do, boy. You deserve every penny. I'm a businessman, you know, and I've never faltered on a deal in my life.' He reached out and tousled Henry's hair. 'It's why I am who I am. Where do you think the metaspides came from, anyway?'

Henry shrugged, wishing with all his heart he could get away from this strange, scary man.

The tall stranger reached into his pocket and pulled out several bills, which he placed in Henry's hand. 'Take this, boy, and use it wisely.'

'Yes, sir,' Henry said, turning to run.

The man grabbed his shoulder, gripping tightly. 'Grow up smart, boy. Grow up smart, and one day you may work for me.' The man leaned in and whispered into Henry's ear. 'For Reginald Chu, the greatest mind in all the Realities.'

Henry squirmed out of the man's clutches and ran. He ran and ran until he collapsed into his sick mother's arms.

✸

For an instant, Paul couldn't make himself move. He stared down in horror at Tick, who was lying on the ground, the weird metal spider thing on top of him. Its eight segmented legs of steel pinned each of Tick's limbs while a pair of slicing blades popped out of its silver belly and headed for his friend's head. Somehow, in the midst of all this, Paul noticed words printed on the back of the spider's round body:

METASPIDE

MANUFACTURED BY CHU INDUSTRIES

Just like the Gnat Rat.

He snapped himself out of his daze and grabbed the closest chair. Picking it up by the back, he swung it as hard as he could and smashed it into the creature, sending it flying off Tick and clanking along the paved stones of the pathway. Tick scrambled to his feet and joined Paul. Sofia and Sally were right next to them, staring at the thing Paul had just whacked.

The metaspide righted itself, turning to look at the group, though it had no eyes as far as Paul could tell. The thing's buddies had dropped down to the same level of the indoor shopping centre and joined their leader in a pack, as if readying for a charge. Most of the darkly dressed people had fled the scene, somehow finding the spirit to move quickly when vicious robot spiders came calling. A few stragglers pressed their backs against the walls of the buildings, looking on in terror. The place had become eerily silent.

'I just can't buy that Master George is doing this,' Sofia said.

'You chirrun ain't tellin' me the whole truth!' Sally said.

Paul tried to calm his heavy breathing. He knew the only way to get out of this was to solve that stupid riddle. An anagram of "the words inside." He quickly started visualising options in his head, other words those letters could spell: *sword ... died ... snow ... wine ... news ... odd ...*

It was easy to come up with individual words, but using every last letter – and only those letters – was really hard without a pen and paper.

'What are they waiting for?' Sofia said.

The metaspides stood in a line, at least a dozen of them, their bodies turning and nodding, clicking and clacking, buzzing endlessly. They seemed to be communicating, deciding what to do next. It didn't make Paul feel very good thinking that those things were smart enough to call plays, like in football.

'I don't know,' Tick said. 'Sally, where can we go? Where do you live?'

Sally grunted. 'Ain't be leadin' them buggers to my place, no how.'

'Is there a place to hide?' Sofia asked.

'Mayhaps if we go into one of dem there stores or such.' Sally pointed to nowhere in particular.

This triggered a thought in Paul's head. Maybe they were supposed to figure out the *name* of a place, and go there. Maybe they'd be winked away if they made it.

'Look at all the signs,' he said. 'I bet one of them is an anagram of "the words inside".'

Tick's eyes lit up in agreement. 'You're right! Every little place here has a sign out front. That has to be it!'

An abrupt whirring sound made them all return their attention to the metaspides. The creatures had started to move, slowly spreading out in an obvious attempt to surround Paul and his friends.

'We need to split up,' Paul said. 'Run around, level to level, look at every sign. It'll be easy to find the right one. Just keep saying "the words inside" over and over in your head.'

'What do we do if we find it?' Tick asked.

'Scream like bloody murder. We'll come to you.'

The metaspides had formed a semicircle, still moving slowly, closing their trap. Every few seconds, on each creature, a spinning saw would pop out, or twin blades would scissor shut with a snap. They were like gang members taunting their opponent.

'Are you in?' Paul asked Sally.

'Ain't got much choice, I reckon. Fine friends you chirrun turned out to be.'

Sofia spoke, her voice steady. 'We need to go. *Now*.'

Paul quickly pointed out directions of who should go where. 'Okay ... ready ... *Go!*'

Paul shot down a pathway to the left, having to run in between two of the robots. They snapped at him, but he slipped through easily. Sprinting, he made it thirty or forty feet before something became very obvious. He turned, baffled.

None of the metaspides were behind him.

They'd all gone after Tick. Every single one of them.

FLYING METAL

Tick looked over his shoulder when he got to the end of the bridge, shocked to see all of the creatures following him. He caught a quick glance of Paul standing in the distance, staring.

'I'll keep them busy – you just find the place!' Tick yelled. 'Find it!'

He turned and set off running again, winding his way down another cobbled path and then down an alleyway, then back onto a wider, main road. The clicking sounds of his pursuers' metallic feet sounded like a typist overdosed on caffeine. Tick looked up at the signs of the various establishments as he passed by.

Tanaka's Feet Barn … The Hapless Butcher … Ted's Cups and Bowls … The Shack Shop … Mister Johnny's Store …

None of them came close to matching an anagram for "the words inside".

He came to an intersection and hesitated too long deciding which way to go. One of the spider robots caught up with him and jumped on his back, some kind of clamping device shooting out and gripping his neck. Tick shouted out in pain and fell down. He twisted to see his attacker, but could barely move. Two more spiders grabbed his arms, another two grabbed his legs, pinching him viciously.

Tick squirmed and kicked. The rising panic thumped his heart, blurred his vision. He heard metallic snaps and whirring, like the sounds of a futuristic torture device. Something sharp sliced across the length of his back; something pointy stabbed into his left calf. Tick could do nothing but scream as the heat of rage filled him.

A new sound filled the air – something like sizzling bacon or bubbling acid, but a hundred times louder. This was followed by a booming *warp,* the sound of crumpling, twisting metal. Something knocked the spiders off Tick with a ringing clank. Their sharp legs ripped new wounds where they'd been clutching him. Pain lanced through him and all over his body. Groaning in agony, he flipped onto his back.

Above him, the indoor world had gone berserk.

※

Sofia found it near the very spot from which they'd entered the underground complex.

The Sordid Swine.

The rickety sign swung crookedly on a single chain above the entrance to a squat, brick building. Sofia thought it looked like a seedy gambling hall. Etched into the wood, the three words grabbed her attention; her eyes locked in.

It wasn't obvious at first glance, but the phrase had no letters that immediately ruled it out. In a matter of seconds, she'd worked through it. The Sordid Swine was definitely an anagram for 'the words inside,' letter for letter, rearranged.

She turned to face the way she'd come, ready to yell out that she'd found it, but faltered. In the distance, in the direction Tick had run, she saw something impossible. After all, they were *indoors*.

But there, a couple hundred yards away, countless pieces of debris swirled and flew through the air.

It looked like a tornado.

�֍

Paul heard it before he saw it. Crumpling metal, banging, clanking, a roaring wind – it all sounded like the world was coming to an end. He rounded a corner shop and saw a spinning mass of debris up ahead, mostly made up of chunks of metal and wood, some large and some small. As he watched, a long, steel beam hit the rail of an upper balcony then windmilled, smashing through a barber shop window.

'Paul!'

He turned to see Sofia just a couple of paths over, running towards him.

'Tick's over there!' he yelled. Without waiting, he took off, crossing a cobbled path, heading for the same bridge he'd seen Tick cross a short time ago.

'Wait!' she called out, but he ignored her. He knew Tick might be caught in the middle of the weird tornado – of course, he didn't know how he could help if that were the case, but he ran on anyway, making it halfway across the bridge before he stumbled to a stop.

Tick lay on the ground up ahead, bruised and bloody, staring up into the twister that spun right above him, railings and pipes and poles and sheets of metal flying through the air in a circle. He looked to be in the exact centre of the steel storm, the buildings and walls around him ripped to shreds as they provided fuel for the impossible tornado. Nearby, several crumpled metaspides twitched and sparked. One of them had most of its body torn off and another had partially melted, two limbs and a chunk of its torso reduced to a pile of silvery goop.

'What the heck?' Paul said, just as Sofia caught up with him, almost knocking him forward. 'We've gotta grab him!' she said.

'I know, but how?' He turned towards her. 'You got some body armour I don't know about?'

'Look!' she said, pointing at Tick. Their friend was crawling towards them.

✿

Tick didn't understand how this could be happening. Above him, solid metal objects ripped in half, dissolved, and reformed. Everything around him had gone nuts, breaking apart and spinning in the air above him, only to melt together into new shapes. The clank of stuff crashing into each other mixed with the roaring wind, sounding like freight trains were playing bumper cars.

And he'd had enough.

He crawled towards Paul and Sofia, thankful that the raging twister was several feet above him. Worried it might drop at any moment, or that one of the hundreds of pieces of debris would fly at him and skewer him, he scrambled on his hands and knees as fast as possible. When he reached what seemed to be the edge of the twister, he pushed himself to his feet and sprinted across the bridge to his friends.

'What's going on?' Paul asked, staring over Tick's shoulder at the chaos.

Tick turned to see it from this angle. The twisting body of debris contracted into a thin column, spinning faster the tighter it got. The destruction sounded like a loud swarm of bees, the small bits forming a tall, black cloud. Seconds later the mass fell towards the ground, where it landed in a lump, a twisted structure of metal, a hideous pile with several crooked steel beams sticking out. Then everything grew quiet.

'How did that just happen?' Sofia said in a dead voice.

'Yeah,' Tick agreed. 'Could this place get any freakier?' He immediately regretted the question, superstition telling him the answer was *yes* – just because he'd asked.

'I found the place,' Sofia said, turning from the pile of metal junk. 'A perfect anagram. It's called–'

A loud clank cut her off, followed by the horrible screech of scraping metal. On the other side of the pile, a large door slid upwards, revealing a wall of darkness behind it. A shape appeared, stepping into the light. It was huge and silver and spherical, eight massive legs of jointed steel protruding from its body.

The word *Metaspide* was spelled across it in large, black letters.

The clicking, clacking, buzzing monster was twenty times the size of its little brothers. With clumsy, yet strangely graceful movements, it started walking towards them.

'Come on,' Sofia said, grabbing both Tick's and Paul's arms and dragging them after her.

Tick cried out and pulled his arm away, wincing from the cuts on his body as he sprinted after Paul and Sofia. They reached an intersection; Sofia hesitated, trying to remember which way to go.

'This way,' she said, pointing to the left.

Before they took a step, another booming *clank!* rang out behind them, the loudest so far, like the sound of a horrible car wreck. Tick couldn't help himself – he turned to look. The huge, clunky spider had jumped across the large gap, clearing the bridge in one leap. It crashed and rolled, smashing into a whole row of shops, obliterating them entirely. A second later, it sprang back onto its thin legs and started after them.

'Run!' Paul yelled.

Sofia took off on the path, followed by Paul, then Tick. The crashing and banging and clanking of the pursuing metallic monster filled the air like a lightning storm. The ground shook with the booming footsteps of the giant spider, joined by the sounds of breaking glass and splintering wood. Tick knew that if it kept gaining speed and strength, they'd be smashed to bits in less than a minute.

'How far is it?' he yelled to Sofia as they turned a corner and ran up a narrow set of stone stairs. They reached a wide alleyway and kept running. The smash of shattered buildings thundered from behind as the monster forced its way after them, destroying everything in its path.

'We're almost there!' Sofia answered.

They rounded the next corner to see Sally running straight towards them, covered in dirt, his face lit up with fear. 'Dadgum world's endin'!' he screamed. Then his eyes rose up to look over them, his mouth falling open. 'How'd it get so big?'

Sofia grabbed Sally by the arm as she ran past. 'Just come on!'

He stumbled until he got his feet set and joined the escape.

Tick saw it before Sofia pointed. A crooked sign indicating The Sordid Swine, swinging on a single pathetic chain. The clanging sounds of pursuit were getting closer and closer.

Paul passed Sofia, ripping the wooden door of the shop open. All four of them stumbled across the threshold and into The Sordid Swine without so much as a peek behind them, afraid that looking would somehow allow the metal monster to gain ground. Sally was last, slamming the door shut, leaving them in almost complete darkness. A shaft of pale light from a small window gave the musty room a haunted glow. The place was empty except for a crooked wooden chair in the corner.

'What now?' Sofia whispered.

Before anyone could answer, something smashed into the wall from the other side, shaking the room and sending a cascade of debris rattling down the brick walls. The group instinctively ran across the room to get as far away from the door as possible, pressing their backs against the brick wall. The giant metaspide slammed into the wall again, then again. A hinge broke, rattling to the floor. Light seeped through the broken door.

'What are we supposed to do now!' Sofia yelled.

Another crash rattled the door – half of it broke apart and tumbled to the ground. The spider was too big to fit through the hole, but a nasty-looking piece of steel came shooting in, sharp as a blade on one edge, swiping around like a cat trying to get a mouse out of its hole. It was nowhere close to them. Yet.

'Tick,' Paul said, 'sure'd be nice for you to use those nifty superhuman winking powers right about now.'

'Would you shut up – I don't know how I did that!' Tick yelled back, sick of everyone expecting him to be the stinkin' Wizard of Oz. He wished he hadn't said it as soon as it came out.

'Whoa,' Paul said, looking hurt. 'Sorry, dude.'

'Guess we were wrong about the anagram thing,' Sofia said.

'No, we weren't,' Tick said, pushing aside his regret at yelling at Paul. 'There has to be something. *Think.*' The huge metaspide slammed into the door again, making the hole bigger. Several bricks clattered across the ground. Its blade-arm swiped a little closer, only a few feet away.

'You chirrun better get me on out dis chere mess,' Sally said. 'Ain't too particular 'bout how ya'll do it, neither.' He grimaced as the metal arm swung close enough to stir his hair as it passed.

'The only thing in here is that stupid chair,' Paul said. The rickety thing sat in the corner, looking like a sad punishment place for a naughty child.

'Well,' Tick said, 'then maybe we're supposed to do something with it.' He felt defensive, like his inability to recreate the winking trick he'd pulled off in the Thirteenth Reality made him responsible for figuring out another solution.

'What can we do with a *chair*?' Paul retorted.

'I don't know!' Tick snapped back. The room shook

again with another ram from the spider. An alarming chunk of the entrance crumbled to the ground, the hole getting wider. A second metal arm squeezed through, two rough blades attached at the end, snapping together like alligator jaws.

'Boys!' Sofia said. Tick was shocked to see her smiling. 'You're so busy thinking, you forgot to use your brains.'

With a smirk, she darted over to the corner, ignoring the steel blade of death that sliced through the air a few inches from her shoulder. Then she sat down on the chair.

The second her bottom touched the warped wood of the seat, she disappeared.

The Council on Things That Matter

Tick felt like an idiot. Sofia was right; sometimes they thought *too* much.

He grabbed Paul by the shoulders and pushed him towards the chair, following right behind. 'Hurry!' A blade whipped past his left shoulder, slicing his shirt.

Paul reached back and shoved Tick against the bricks. 'Careful, dude. Inch along the wall.'

Sally stood next to the chair, looking confused as he glanced back and forth between the chair and Tick. Paul and Tick scooted along the wall until they reached the corner.

'Sit down, Sally!' Paul yelled. 'Don't worry, it'll take you somewhere safe.'

Sally didn't reply but leaned towards Tick's ear until Tick could feel Sally's beard scratching his cheek.

'What are you doing?' Tick asked, feeling uncomfortable. 'You need to tell me something?'

'Just lookin' at yer dadgum ear, boy.'

Before Tick could stop him, Sally reached up and rammed his pinky finger into Tick's ear canal. Tick stumbled backwards into Paul's arms, a sharp pain exploding inside his head like an eardrum had just ruptured. The pain went away as soon as it had come, and Paul helped him back to his feet.

'What'd you do that for?' Tick yelled at Sally, glaring at the man who'd seemed completely harmless until that very moment.

'Weep to yer mama, boy, not me.'

Sally sat down on the chair, not bothering to hide the grin on his face. He shrugged his shoulders as if to say, *Sorry, can't help myself,* and disappeared.

'What in the world was that all about?' Paul asked.

'No idea,' Tick replied. 'But we've gotta get out of here.'

'You first,' Paul said.

Tick wanted to argue, act brave, be the last one out. Then he realised that'd be the stupidest thing in the world and hurried to sit on the chair. Every second they wasted meant the spider was that much closer.

He had just enough time to see the entire front of the building collapse in a swirl of dust and flashes of metal before everything around him turned bright.

☼

Sofia stood on a slippery slope of rust-coloured sand, squinting in the brilliant sunlight at the small, iron chair that stood rigid on top of the dune as if held in place by magic. She'd stood up and got away from it the second she'd winked there, not wanting someone else to come through and squish her.

Tick showed up a minute later, an instantaneous appearance that shocked her even though she'd been expecting it. There was no effect – no smoke, no sound. One moment the chair was empty. The next, it wasn't. Tick's face looked like he'd just bungee jumped off the world's tallest bridge.

'What took you so long? Hurry. Get up,' Sofia said, slipping in the sand as she stepped forward to help him, sliding down the steep dune. The hot sand seemed to find its way through every teeny hole of her clothes and scratch at her skin.

Tick didn't answer, but stood up and was making his way down the loose sand to Sofia when Paul appeared, a small cut on his right cheek.

'Dang thing got me,' he said, wiping the blood away with his fingers. 'Couple more seconds and I'd be ...'

He trailed off, looking around him with huge eyes.

With her friends safe, Sofia finally had a chance to take a good look at their surroundings as well.

They stood in the middle of an enormous desert, an endless sea of dunes stretching for miles in every direction. The white-hot sun blazed down so the distant horizons shimmered in a wavering haze. The only thing breaking the monotony of sand was a large, shiny pipeline about half a mile away. The tube of opaque glass sat above ground, at least twenty feet in diameter, and ran from one direction to the other for as far as Sofia could see.

'Where are we?' Paul asked. 'And what *is* that?' He motioned to the giant pipe.

'Looks like a huge straw,' Tick said. 'Maybe a giant sand monster dropped it.'

Sofia ignored them and started walking towards the glass structure. Her heart hammered in her chest, a rise of panic as she thought about their situation.

They'd just barely escaped a horrible metal spider and now they were stuck in the middle of a scorching desert. Anger at Master George rose in her as well. *How can he waste our time with this? What if we'd been killed?* But deep inside, she didn't think it was him. Something had gone wrong.

'Wait!' Paul called from behind her. 'Where's Sally?'

Sofia stopped. She'd completely forgotten about the odd man. She turned and said, 'Maybe he didn't want to follow us.'

Paul was standing on the dune next to the chair, looking around. 'No way – he winked away before we did.'

'Yeah,' Tick said, also searching. 'He went right after you.'

Sofia felt a disorienting chill in her gut. 'Well … he never showed up here. I've been watching the chair since I winked in.'

Paul stumbled through the soft sand to stand next to Sofia; Tick joined them as well. Both of the boys had baffled looks on their faces, still glancing at the chair now and then as if expecting Sally to show up.

'You're *sure* he didn't wink in?' Paul asked.

Sofia rolled her eyes. 'Yes, I'm sure. Where would he possibly hide?'

'Dude,' Paul whispered, and that one word summed up how they all felt.

'What could've happened to him?' Tick asked. 'Why would *we* wink here and not him? And what was up with him poking me in the ear?' He rubbed at the side of his head.

'What?' Sofia asked.

'Right before he winked away,' Tick explained, 'he acted all weird and slammed his finger into my ear. It hurt, too. Then he sat down and disappeared.'

'He slammed his finger into your *ear*?' Sofia repeated. 'While a giant spider monster was trying to kill you?' It was such a bizarre thing, she couldn't believe she'd heard him correctly.

Tick shrugged. 'Don't ask me – maybe he went crazy from the panic.'

'What if he's in trouble?' Paul asked. 'I like him – we need to help him. Even if he did try to stab you in the brain.'

Sofia felt the same sadness at Sally's disappearance. He'd been so humble and sincere; there was just something likable about him. But she also knew that standing there waiting on a nice sunburn wouldn't help anybody.

'Not much we can do,' she said. 'Someone must've sent us here for a reason. Let's go check out that glass thing.' She pointed at the tube that looked like a giant crystal worm stretching into the distant horizon.

'What if Sally shows up and we're not here?' Paul said.

'He's an adult,' Tick said. 'He can take care of himself or come find us. I agree with Sofia – we should see what that thing is.'

Sofia started walking again. 'Come on, then.'

Paul and Tick joined her, all of them marching as best they could up and down the slippery, hot dunes.

✿

Master George sat at the head of a long, wooden table, looking around at the few people he'd asked to join him in this special Council on Things That Matter. His last guest had yet to appear, and Master George hoped he would arrive soon. It had been a near thing, winking him away as fast as he had. A large fire roared in the hearth at his back, but it wasn't enough to rid him of the chill that iced his heart. Things were going badly. Very badly. He reached down and petted Muffintops, who purred and rubbed her back against his leg.

Most of the other Realitants had left the Grand Canyon complex already, carrying out various orders and missions agreed upon by the larger meeting earlier. That was good. Things would be said here that not everyone should hear.

Mothball sat to his left and Rutger to his right, balanced precariously on his booster seat. To Rutger's right was Sato, looking as bored as ever, ready to take notes. Then came Nancy Zeppelin, wrapping and rewrapping a long string of her golden hair around a finger; William Schmidt, his ancient face pulled down into a frown that made him look like the Grim Reaper; Katrina Kay, her buzz-cut hair framing a pretty face with eager eyes; Priscilla Persephone, invited only because Master George knew he had offended her enough already (oh, how he hated that snooty smirk on her face, and her *hair* – it was orange, for heaven's sake). Finally, next to Mothball on his left, sat Jimmy "The Voice" Porter. His nickname was sadly ironic now because the poor man's tongue had been ripped out by a slinkbeast in the Mountains of Sorrow in the Twelfth Reality.

'Very well,' Master George said. 'I think it's time we begin.'

'Yes, *let's*,' Priscilla said in her annoying, lilting voice. 'We've only been waiting on you. Wasting valuable time, no doubt.'

Rutger shifted forward in his seat, a slight rolling motion that brought his arms and hands to rest on the table. 'Priscilla, why don't you open up a can of shut the—'

George quickly interrupted his loyal friend. 'Yes, Priscilla, I appreciate your patience.' He wanted to add that perhaps she'd like to take on a mission to the icy wastelands of the Third Reality, but refrained. 'We have much to talk about, indeed.'

'Wasting time,' Rutger mumbled under his breath. 'I'll show you ...' The rest was too low to hear, but Master George thought he caught the words *rat fink*.

'First things first,' Mothball said. 'Methinks we best be talkin' 'bout Master Tick and his friends.'

Master George agreed. 'Yes, yes, quite right, Mothball. Based on the evidence, I have no doubt that someone has violated Rule Number 462 and taken hostage the nanolocators implanted in our dear young friends from Reality Prime. We can track their general location, but nothing more — and even that signal is weak. We have tried repeatedly to wink them here, but they have remained out of our reach. This act violates no less than three Articles of Principles established by the First Realitant Symposium of 1972. It is outrageous, despicable, irresponsible, reprehensible—'

'We get the point,' Rutger said.

Master George slammed his hand on the table. 'Yes! I hope you do, Master Rutger, because this is very serious indeed. Not only can we not wink in our most important recruits in years, but we have a renegade out there capable of such things as hijacking a nanolocator! The technology for such an act–'

'It has to be him,' Nancy Zeppelin interrupted quietly. 'Has to be.'

A long moment of silence passed, broken only by the crackling fire. Master George closed his eyes. No one in the room doubted who the culprit could be. But if Reginald Chu had finally decided to use his significant technological powers to branch out and cause trouble in other Realities, then they were all in for a great deal of trouble. Until today, they'd all hoped, perhaps foolishly, that Chu would be happy ruling his own world with an iron fist.

'Yes, Nancy,' Master George finally said, opening his eyes and sighing. 'We should all be quite nervous that Reginald Chu would stoop to such a thing. He obviously has plans for our new friends.'

William Schmidt cleared his throat, a wet, gurgling hack that made Master George wince. Then the old man spoke in his ghost-soft voice. 'Chu's spies must have learned of Higginbottom's mysterious winking ability. Chu would do anything to have him under his control.'

'For all we know,' Katrina said, 'Tick is strapped on a laboratory bed as we speak, his brain being examined for anomalies.'

Master George held up a hand, wanting the terrible talk to stop. 'We must keep our minds on solutions, my dear associates. Solutions. And we mustn't give up hope. Master Atticus is a special boy, as are his friends, and their recovery is our number-one priority.'

'What about all the people going crazy everywhere?' Priscilla asked. 'That should alarm us a little bit more than a few missing brats.'

Mothball stood up – Master George reached out too late to stop her. She towered over everyone, her suddenly angry glare focused on Priscilla. 'One more nasty word about them three children, and I'll lop off yer 'ead, I will. That's a promise.'

'Yeah,' Rutger chimed in. 'And I'll bite your kneecaps.'

'Please, let's all remain calm,' Master George said. 'Mothball, please be seated. I appreciate your concern for Atticus and his friends. Priscilla hasn't met them, of course, so let's give her time to appreciate their importance.'

Mothball sat, not taking her eyes off Priscilla, whose suddenly pale face made her look like she might never speak again.

'Now, er, we do need to talk of this matter,' Master George continued. 'Sato here has put together a summary of his interviews, and the reports of people going insane are numerous, indeed. Something is very wrong, and it's spreading throughout the Realities at an alarming rate. Almost like a–'

'Disease,' Nancy Zeppelin said. 'Like a disease.'

Master George paused, studying the beautiful woman as he thought about what she said. She didn't look back, staring at the table in front of her with a blank expression.

'Yes,' he finally said. 'Yes, quite like a disease, actually. The pattern shows it spreading from a fragmented Reality – all cases link back to it eventually, with no exception. It is *exactly* like a disease or a virus.'

'Need a sample, then. One of the crazies,' Mothball said.

Before Master George could reply, an urgent knock rapped at the closed door from the hallway. Finally. Perhaps now they would have some answers. He stood up. 'Mothball–'

The door opened before she could do anything. A wave of relief washed through Master George as he saw one of his oldest friends enter the room, though he looked like he'd just taken a bath in a pile of dirt – his overalls were *filthy*.

'Master Sally,' George said, smiling.

Sally grinned through his thick, red beard. 'It was harder 'an findin' a tick on a grizzly bear, but I did it.'

'Did what?' Rutger asked, shocked.

'I found dem kids a'yorn.'

PART 2

THE BEAST IN THE GLASS

NICE MISTRESS JANE

Frazier Gunn was worried about his boss.

As he walked up the winding stone staircase of Mistress Jane's tower, enjoying the smell of burning pitch from the torches ensconced on the hard granite walls, he wondered which version of her would answer the door. The flickering, spitting flames cast haunted shadows that seemed alive, hiding and reappearing like dark wraiths. A team of seven servants maintained the torches throughout the Lemon Fortress, even though Jane probably could have lit the place using only her growing abilities in the mutated Chi'karda.

But she had her own way of doing things, and that was that.

Frazier felt a trickle of sweat slide down his right temple as he passed the halfway point. He'd been sick the last few days, unable to keep any food down, and he felt the effect of his illness now. He almost paused to rest, but his pride wouldn't let him. He kept moving up the staircase, step by step.

His thoughts slid back to Jane's recent mood swings – episodes of inexplicable kindness mixed in with the usual displays of anger and violence. He'd witnessed with his own eyes several of the bizarre occurrences. Just the other day, he'd almost swallowed his own tongue when he saw his boss help her servant Brainless clean up a broken dish Jane had slammed against the wall. The child's face had paled during the incident, sure it was a trap, but when they finished, Jane apologised for losing her temper, dismissed her with a wave, and went back to work.

Frazier would've been less surprised to see a duck-billed platypus knock on his door and ask for tea.

Rumours of other surprising acts had spread through the castle like flames through a heat-wilted cornfield. Stories of kind words, apologies, thank yous, compliments. Tales of Jane using her special powers to help servants lift heavy objects. It was crazy. Frazier had known this evil woman for years, and he couldn't reconcile in his brain how it could be the same person. And yet, interspersed among these un-Jane-like anomalies, there were many moments where she exploded in rage, sometimes worse than ever before.

The whole thing was fishy, and in an odd way, Frazier longed for the days when Jane acted the tyrant every minute of every day. At least then he'd known what to expect.

He finally reached the top step, pausing to take three long breaths to calm his heart. He wiped the sweat from his face, not wanting Jane to see him so weak. After a very long minute, he finally crossed the stone landing and knocked on her wooden door.

It disappeared in a swipe from left to right, as if it had slid into the stone. It was only a trick, however, a manipulation of Chi'karda. Jane loved using her power for such trivial things, always opening her doors in creative and unexpected ways. One time she'd simply made it explode outwards in a spray of dagger-like splinters, permanently scarring the poor sap delivering her mail.

Jane stood there, dressed in a simple yellow gown, her feet and hands bare. Her emerald eyes shone, almost glowing like green embers. Something was off, though. For a second, Frazier couldn't figure out why she looked so odd, but then it hit him.

Jane had a layer of stubble growing across her head, tiny black sprouts of hair. Never – not once since he'd first met her so long ago – had Frazier ever seen so much as one hair on her head. She'd always insisted on baldness for some mysterious reason. Frazier balked and looked towards the floor, almost as if he'd caught her unawares coming out of the bath.

'Good morning, Mistress,' he said, keeping his eyes down. 'I've come to report the latest on the Barrier Wand, and to, uh, report some interesting news.'

'Frazier, dear Frazier,' Jane said, her voice soft. 'Please, come in.'

He looked up to see she had moved aside, gesturing towards her large, yellow velvet couch, beside which a fresh fire burned in the comforting hearth, its bricks freshly painted her favourite colour. Clearing his throat, using every ounce of his will to avoid a single glance at her head, Frazier stepped past her and took a seat, sinking into the wonderfully comfortable cushions.

Mistress Jane sat next to him on his right, crossing her legs so that she faced him only a foot away. The fire reflected in her bright eyes, seeming to ignite them into some odd, molten metal. Frazier didn't like this. No, he didn't like this one bit.

'Frazier,' Jane said, reaching out to caress his arm, just once, before clasping her hands in her lap. 'I know people are talking about me – about my ... change.'

Frazier cleared his throat, faked a cough, hoping to buy time. He didn't know how to respond to this. 'Um, yes, Mistress, the servants have said some very ... um, nice things about you. They are, of course, very grateful when you, uh, show them kindness.' He stopped; every word that came out of his mouth sounded worse than the one before it.

'*Kindness?*' she said with a disgusted tone, as if the word were a highly contagious disease. 'That's the best they can come up with? *That's* how they honour my attempts to elevate my leadership skills?'

'Well,' he said, doing his best to speak clearly without stuttering. 'No, I meant, well, I just meant they're noticing your efforts, saying many *different* words – all very glowing words, actually. Your esteem has skyrocketed in their eyes. In, uh, mine, too.'

Jane folded her arms, glaring directly into Frazier's eyes. 'Do you think I'm stupid, Frazier?'

She's going to kill me, he thought. *Right now, after all these years, she's going to kill me because she's finally gone completely and totally insane.*

'Stupid?' he repeated. 'Of course I don't think you're stupid.'

Jane leaned over and whispered in his ear. 'Then don't *speak* to me like I'm stupid.'

She sat back looking at the fire, her face expressionless. After several seconds, Frazier followed her gaze and caught his breath.

Several burning logs had floated up into the air and out of the main hearth, hovering above a rug made from the skin of a scallywag beast. Sparks and hot cinders fell from the logs, igniting several long hairs of the soft fur, which flared and died out quickly. A mess of white ash flew up from the fireplace, swirling around the flames in midair in fancy patterns, spelling words and making faces. Frazier felt a familiar icy fear in his gut, thinking of such power in the hands of a woman as unstable as Mistress Jane.

With a hiss and crackle, the whole show collapsed back into the fireplace. In seconds, it looked like the fire hadn't been disturbed at all.

'Now,' Jane said, folding her arms and returning her focus to Frazier. 'I know people are worried that my attempts to change are insincere. If anything, they seem *more* frightened of me than ever. Correct?'

Frazier nodded, not daring to say a word.

'This doesn't bother me. Not in the least. I've been ... *unwise* in some of my leadership methods. Perhaps even cruel. I know it will take time – a long time – to change.' Jane shifted in her seat, looking towards the window on the other side of the room, muted light from the cloudy day spilling through onto her bed. 'All I ever wanted was to make things better, Frazier. That's all I still want. If I need to adapt how I rule things, then so be it.'

She turned her neck, looking once again at Frazier, her eyes narrowed. 'But we *will* take over the Realities. We *will* spread the goodness and power of the Chi'karda from the Thirteenth Reality to the others. And in the end, we will make the universe a better place for all. This, I promise you.'

Frazier nodded again, throwing all the sincerity he could into his expression. Jane's words, filled with passion, had moved him greatly. He remembered why he had followed this woman for so many years, despite the constant danger. He remembered ... and felt ashamed of the many times he'd hoped to topple her and take over.

'Mistress Jane,' he said. 'I ... I ... I don't know what to–'

'Say nothing,' she snapped, a sudden thunderclap shaking the room. It was a trick she performed often. 'You've earned yourself back into my full graces. You're my most loyal servant. You will be beside me, always. Nothing else needs to be said.'

A long pause followed, thoughts churning inside Frazier's mind. *How do I act now? What do I say?* His fear of Jane hadn't diminished in the least – if anything, it had grown stronger.

Thankfully, Jane got back to business. 'You said you had an update on the Barrier Wand and some interesting news. Well, get on with–' She paused, forcing a smile. 'Please, report.'

Frazier leaned forward, grunting as he pulled himself out of the soft cushions, and put his elbows on his knees. 'They've found a place in a small mountain range about five hundred miles away – they've spotted signs of ore. It looks encouraging. The Diggers are hunting as we speak. As soon as they find a deposit, I'll let you know.'

'Once they do,' Jane said, 'we should need only two or three more weeks.'

'That's right. The metal is the last thing we need to reconstruct the Wand.'

Something floated up from a shelf near the bed, flying through the air and landing with a thump in

Jane's outreached palm. She held it out for Frazier to see – a complex bundle of wires, pipework, gears, and nanochips – the Chi'karda Drive she'd removed from her previous Barrier Wand. The one Atticus Higginbottom had stolen.

'What's the other news?' Jane asked.

Frazier shifted uncomfortably. His news was very strange, and he worried about her reaction. 'Well, some of our hunters discovered an interesting ... thing.' He paused, unsure how to proceed.

'A *thing?*' Jane repeated. 'Your descriptive skills are less than apt, Frazier.'

'Sorry.' He rubbed his hands together. 'I guess I'll just say it how it is.'

'Brilliant idea.'

Frazier tried to laugh, but it came out as a snort. 'Way out in the Forest of Plague, near the spot of the old battleground, they found a place where hundreds of trees have been cut down. Each stump is perfectly flat, as if the trees had been cut with a laser or something.'

Jane tilted her head, obviously intrigued. 'Interesting. I can't think of anyone ...'

When she trailed off, looking at the fire, Frazier continued. 'Right, no one in our Reality has that kind of technology. But, um, that's not the weird part. Not even close.'

That caught Jane's attention; her eyebrows rose.

'The trees ...' Frazier said.

'Did someone take them? Did they burn them? That area has enormous trees – some taller than the fortress.'

Frazier shook his head. 'I know, which makes the next part really bizarre. I couldn't tell what had

126

happened until I flew on the back of a fangen and looked down from above.'

'What do you mean?' Jane asked.

'Somehow, whoever cut those trees down ... *arranged* them on the ground so they spelled out words.'

'Spelled out words?' Jane repeated. 'With *trees?*'

'Yes. They formed letters out of the tree trunks. Really big trees that made really big words.' He laughed at himself but stopped abruptly.

'What did they say?' Jane asked, not smiling.

Frazier braced himself, knowing he had no choice but to repeat the mysterious message word for word.

'It said, "Mistress Jane, you are a coward. Come and find me."'

16

TUNNEL OF GLASS

Tick slid his hand along the warm, hard glass of the big tube as he walked beside it in disbelief at the sheer height of the structure. It rose at least twenty feet above him, maybe more, and appeared to be a perfect cylinder. The bottom third was buried underneath the shifting sands of the desert. The glass was clear, but so thick he couldn't tell what lay inside the big pipe; he could only see distorted images of varying colour.

'Okay,' Paul said. 'I've seen some strange stuff since hanging out with you two, but this might beat all.' He stepped back and spread his arms wide, looking up at the curved glass. 'What could this thing possibly be?'

Sofia squatted on the ground, digging through the sand to see if the structure changed at all underneath. 'Looks like it just keeps curving in a perfect circle. Maybe if we dug all the way to the bottom we'd figure something out.'

'Do I look like a shovel to you?' Paul asked.

'Well ... actually, you kind of do,' Sofia said. 'You look like a shovel with crooked ears.'

Tick ignored them, walking along with his hand pressed against the glass, hoping for some change or sign of what they were supposed to do next. Sweat soaked his clothes, the sun beating down on them as if trying to cook them for dinner. He could feel his skin beginning to burn – especially his neck. In all the chaos with the giant spider robot monster, he'd lost his scarf.

What is this thing? he thought as he studied the glass structure. Master George – if it really had been him – must have sent them here for a reason, and a clue or riddle must be hidden somewhere. He kept walking.

'Yo, where you going?' Paul called out.

Tick turned to look, surprised at how far he'd walked – at least a hundred feet. 'I don't know!' he yelled. 'Trying to find a clue!'

He stopped, squinting to examine the endless tube as it stretched into the horizon, diminishing in a shimmering haze of heat in the distance. Nothing appeared to break the consistency of the smooth glass – no ladders, no doors, no connected buildings. He finally gave up and walked back to his friends, both of whom were digging in the sand.

'See anything?' he asked.

'No,' Sofia answered. She sat back on her heels, letting out a big sigh. 'Seems like a perfect cylinder. A really big one.'

Before he could reply, a deep humming sound filled the air, a short burst lasting only a few seconds, but so loud it made the glass vibrate. *Or maybe it was the other way around,* Tick thought. Maybe the glass had shaken and *made* the sound.

Sofia and Paul jumped to their feet and moved next to Tick.

'Please tell me you guys heard that,' Paul said.

'Yeah,' Tick said, almost in a whisper. He thought he might've seen something from the corner of his eye – a slight movement in the glass to their left. 'Something happened when it made that sound – I didn't really get a good look.' He pointed to where he thought he'd seen the anomaly and walked closer; the others joined him.

'What do you mean?' Sofia asked.

'I don't know. I thought I saw something move across the glass, a shadow inside or water pouring down it.'

Paul reached out and ran his hand along the curved wall. 'Serious?'

'Yeah, positive.'

'Let's wait to see if it happens again,' Sofia said.

Tick folded his arms, staring at the tube. No one said a word, silently hoping for a clue as to what they should do next.

A minute went by. Then another. Then several. Half an hour passed and nothing happened. Tick felt so uncomfortable from the sweat drenching his clothes and the sticky salt on his face and the burning in his skin and the sand in his shoes–

VRRMMMMM!

The sound boomed out again for five or six seconds, and this time, they all saw it. Right where Paul had touched earlier, a section of glass slid down, as if it were simply melting open, creating a rectangular hole the size of a typical door. Inside, filling the entire cylinder, something huge and dark zoomed past like a train, going at an incredible speed. Tick couldn't see any details, scarcely believing that whatever it was could move at such a velocity.

The train thing was gone as soon as it had come, and the glass melted upwards, closing the door and reforming until not a single blemish or mark revealed it had ever been there.

'Whoa,' Paul said.

'This must be a tunnel for some kind of bullet train,' Sofia said. She gingerly reached out to where the doorway had appeared, then tapped the glass with her fingertip and pulled away. 'It's not any hotter than the rest of the tube.'

'We're obviously supposed to go inside,' Tick said.

'And get smashed by that thing?' Paul said. 'Wasn't much room for a nice stroll in there if that train comes flying by again.'

Sofia turned towards the two of them so they stood in a small circle, facing each other. 'Tick's right. It can't be a coincidence that we showed up here next to this big tunnel, right where a door opens up. We have to go inside.'

Paul shook his head. 'Well, I'm not too keen on the idea of getting run over by a monster train. That door seems to open only every half-hour or so and it only stayed open a few seconds. Jumping in there sounds like the worst idea I've ever heard.'

'There has to be a path and a railing, right?' Tick said. 'Even if it's small. Any subway in the world has a walkway, doesn't it? For people to make repairs and stuff?'

Paul shrugged. 'Maybe, but it sure seemed to me like that thing was right next to the glass.'

'Yeah, it was,' Sofia agreed. 'But what else are we going to do? Sit out here in the sun and bake to death? There's no sign of anything for miles and miles except that stupid chair – I guess we could try sitting on it again, but–'

'We have to go in *there*,' Tick interrupted, nodding towards the tube, knowing he was right.

Paul held out his hands in surrender. 'All right, all right, all right. Look, here's what we'll do. We sit here and wait for the door to open again. When it does, we'll peek in and see what we see – all while making sure we don't let anything slice our heads off or smash our faces in. Ya know, just for kicks. Like I've said before, we wouldn't want to mess up this pretty face of mine or you *know* the ladies would be devastated.'

Sofia groaned.

'That works for me,' Tick said. 'If this door opens every half-hour or whatever, we don't need to rush it. Next time, let's just lean in real quick and take a look around. Hopefully there'll be a walkway with a railing. If not, we'll decide what to do from there.'

'Deal,' Paul said.

'Who's going to poke their head in?' Sofia asked.

'All of us – it looks big enough,' Tick said. 'Sofia, you look left. Paul, you look straight ahead. I'll look to the right – and make sure you look *down,* too. Get in line and let's get ready. Who knows when it'll open next.'

They lined up in the order Tick had indicated and stood just inches from the invisible door in the shiny curved glass. The seconds dragged into minutes as Tick stared at his distorted reflection, trying to stay focused so he could lean forward the instant things changed. The sun had moved farther west, but it still shone down with ruthless heat.

'What if the door closes before we pull out?' Paul said after what seemed like an hour of waiting.

Tick rolled his shoulders, surprised at how stiff his muscles were, tensed as he kept himself prepared to move. His injuries from the metaspides still stung as well. 'Just count to three inside your head then pull back. It stayed open at least–'

The humming sound cut him off.

Tick tried not to blink as he stared at the unbelievable sight of the doorway opening. Like liquid silver, the glass melted and disappeared into itself, dropping in a straight line until a perfect rectangle once again revealed the inside of the tube.

'Now!' Tick said, but the other two were already leaning forward with him.

Everything felt different – the *vrrmmmmm* sound wasn't as loud and nothing shook. Even as Tick's head passed through the opening, he could see that no train or anything else was close by. Mentally counting to three, he stared across the tube and took it all in, hoping his friends were doing the same.

He saw no sign of rails or anything else to indicate train tracks. There wasn't even a sunken floor running along the bottom. The inside of the structure looked much like the outside, a long tunnel of smooth glass almost completely unblemished by objects. It was much darker inside, the sunlight filtering into dark shades of blue and purple as it passed through. Here and there, small, odd-shaped formations of glass jutted into the tunnel. Tick had no idea what they were for.

Tick felt someone tugging on his shirt. He snapped back to his senses and jerked himself out of the tube. A second later, the humming sound returned as the glass magically formed upwards, a gravity-defying sheet of molten crystal, and sealed off the doorway.

'Dang, Tick!' Paul said. 'Weren't you the one who said count to *three?*'

'Sorry – I just ... I guess I lost track of time.'

'How do you lose track of three seconds?' Sofia said.

'Yeah, man – one more second and you'd have been running around here without a head.'

Tick ignored them, still fascinated by the inside of the tunnel. 'So what did you guys see?'

'Glass,' Paul said. 'A bunch of glass.'

'Me, too,' Sofia agreed.

Tick frowned, having hoped they would have seen something different. 'No sign of a walkway or anything?'

Paul shook his head. 'Just smooth glass with little things sticking out here and there – no idea what those were.'

Sofia nodded. 'Below us the glass just curved towards the bottom in the middle then started back up again. It's just a big glass tunnel. That's it.'

Tick folded his arms and leaned back against the tube – a few feet away from the doorway, just in case. 'What was that thing we saw zing past last time?' He wondered if maybe they'd gone to a Reality with extremely advanced technology, some form of travel they couldn't even comprehend.

Sofia seemed to be on the same wavelength. 'Maybe it's some kind of futuristic invention – a train that slides through the tube at lightning speeds. Maybe this is a special kind of glass mixed with a metal we don't know about and super-magnetised. Maybe.'

'Man, that sounded smart,' Paul said as he joined Tick, leaning against the tube.

Sofia put her hands on her hips and stared at them, as if picking out a criminal from a police lineup. 'Okay, so what do we do?'

A long pause answered her. Tick finally broke the silence. 'We go in.'

'Now, wait a minute—' Paul began.

'He's right, Paul,' Sofia said. 'What else can we do? We go in and let the door close behind us. Someone is testing our bravery. If we're willing to just stand out here and roast to death, what good are we as Realitants?'

'What good are we if we get smashed by a big old train?' Paul retorted.

'Courage,' Sofia said. 'Master George expects us to be brave.'

'He also expects us to be smart.'

'How about this?' Tick interjected. He stepped away from the tube. 'We'll wait until the door opens *and* we don't feel the big vibration of the train-thing. The door opens every half-hour, but maybe the train only comes by at certain intervals. We've been here for at least three hours and we've only felt the vibration of the train twice.'

'I'm in,' Sofia said quickly.

They both looked at Paul, who took a long moment to think. 'Fine – but only if there's no doubt the train isn't coming.'

'Sweet,' Tick said. 'Line up again.'

They did, and time seemed to move slower than ever. When the door opened next, it was accompanied by the violent vibration of the travelling machine. Tick caught a blurry glimpse of the dark shape as it zipped past.

'See,' Sofia said. 'It's totally obvious when the train is coming. We can probably go in next time. If we don't see or find anything in thirty minutes, we'll just come back out.'

Again, the waiting game. Tick felt like the heat and the boredom were slowly driving his mind crazy. His stomach ached for food. He thought of his family, picturing each one in turn. Kayla, finally reading and loving every minute of it. Lisa, getting better at the piano and yapping on the phone constantly. His mom, the best cook he'd ever known – though old Aunt Mabel in Alaska was a close second. Finally, he pictured his dad: big belly, funny hair, gigantic smashed nose and all. Thinking of them made him feel a little better, but his heart panged with sadness as well.

What if this time, he didn't make it back to them? His attention came back to the hot desert and big tube when he heard the humming sound again, this time much quieter with no vibrations. The glass doorway melted open, and no one said a word. Together, the three of them jumped through the hole and into the tunnel.

As they slid to the curved bottom of the huge cylinder, Tick heard the swishing sound of the door closing shut behind them.

STREAMS OF FIRE

Tick was surprised at how the glass felt on the inside – cool, but hard as steel. The light came from everywhere and nowhere at once, a muted glow that made Paul's and Sofia's skin look purple. Glimmering shapes skittered along the interior surface of the tunnel, like reflections from a swimming pool. As Tick stood, he thought he might slip on the shiny surface, but the material had plenty of friction – it was almost sticky.

'What's that smell?' Paul said, taking a big sniff with a wrinkled nose.

Tick took a deep breath. 'Ooh, that does stink.' The air smelled like the chemicals in a portable toilet.

Tick walked as far as he could up the curved side of the tunnel, almost making it to the part where it was completely vertical. He saw a round bubble of glass, about three inches tall, bulging out from the wall. Scared to touch it, he leaned forward and took a closer look. A freaky distortion of his own image stared back at him, but nothing else.

'You're gonna break your neck,' Sofia said. 'Come back down, and let's figure out what we need to do.'

Tick scooted down on his rear end, then stood back up. 'Maybe we should just start walking.'

'Which way?' Sofia asked.

'Whoa, whoa, whoa,' Paul said. 'It was a borderline eight on the dumb-guy scale to come in here in the first place. If we start trottin' off away from this door, we'd be complete idiots. Did you forget about that really big train that goes really fast?'

'Maybe we could stand to the side and jump onto it when it flies by,' Tick suggested.

Paul and Sofia both looked at him with blank faces. Then Paul said, 'Dude, you just hit number one on the Top Ten List of Dumbest Ideas Ever Spoken Aloud.'

Tick shrugged. 'Maybe. Got any better ideas?'

'Yeah, let's stand here and hope Santa Claus shows up to tell us what to do.'

'Oh, would you two–' Sofia began.

'Shhh!' Tick said. He thought he'd heard something.

'What?'

'Just be quiet for a sec.' He stilled his body, perked his ears. There it was. A very quiet beeping sound, like a car alarm honking from miles away. 'Do you hear that?'

'No,' Paul answered.

'Yeah, I hear it,' Sofia said. 'Sounds like it's far away but I can't tell from which direction.' She looked down one end of the tunnel, then turned to the other. 'That way?'

Tick shook his head, still straining his ears. 'No, it sounds like it's coming from outside the tunnel. Or below us, maybe.'

'Do you people have Superman hearing or something?' Paul said, throwing his arms up in frustration. 'I don't hear a dang – hey, what's that?' He pointed towards the ceiling.

Tick followed the line of direction, at first not seeing what Paul was pointing towards. Then he spotted it – a blinking red light.

'That looks like a button,' Sofia said.

Tick squinted to get a better look and agreed. 'It's definitely a button. With some words next to it, on a sticker.' The ceiling was about twenty feet above them, just far enough that Tick couldn't make out the words.

'If you can read that, you *are* Superman,' Paul said.

'I can't. But I bet we're supposed to push that button.'

'You think?' Paul frowned. 'Master George built this entire gigantic tube thing just to test us to see if we could push a button?'

'I don't know,' Tick muttered, feeling confused and discouraged.

After a long pause, all of them staring up at the flashing button, Sofia spoke up. 'Maybe if we stood on each other's shoulders, we could reach it.'

'On each *other's* shoulders?' Paul asked. 'What does that mean?'

'Well ... you're probably the strongest, though that isn't saying much.' She looked Tick up and down, weighing him with her eyes. 'I'll get on Tick's shoulders, then you lift both of us up.'

Paul flexed his arms, showing off his not-so-impressive biceps. 'I might have some guns, Miss Italy, but that sounds ridiculous.'

'Let's just try it,' Tick urged. 'Show us you're a man.'

Paul laughed. 'You two are crazy. But whatever, I'm game.'

Tick got down on his knees and let Sofia crawl onto his shoulders, wrapping her legs around his neck so that her feet dangled over his chest. As Paul helped him stand up, Tick thought the blood vessels in his brain might burst from the effort. He couldn't help but groan out loud as he struggled to balance with Sofia on top of him. He opened his mouth to say something, but Paul held a finger to his lips.

'Don't say anything,' he said. 'Nothing. No matter what you say, you'd be calling her fat. So just zip it.'

'You're not so dumb, after all,' Sofia said from above.

Tick braced his feet and finally steadied himself. 'How in the world are you going to lift both of us?'

'I surf, man. My legs could lift an elephant.' He looked up at Sofia. 'Not that I'm saying you weigh as much as an–'

'Just get on with it,' Sofia said, kicking out at Paul.

Paul smiled at Tick, then walked behind him. 'All right, dude. Let's do this thing.'

Tick shuffled his feet apart and soon felt Paul grabbing him by the thighs and lifting with his shoulders. To his complete amazement, he rose slowly into the air.

Paul screamed out words as he struggled to stand. 'Good ... gracious ... mercy ... mama ... you people ... are *FAT!*'

The three of them swayed slightly as Paul fought to keep his balance and strength. Tick's stomach turned; he couldn't believe what was happening. *I've been zapped into a Saturday morning cartoon.*

'I can't reach it!' Sofia yelled from above. 'I'd have to *stand* on Tick's shoulders!'

'Then *do it!*' Paul screamed from below. 'Hurry!'
Sofia lifted her right foot and wedged it between Tick's neck and shoulder, grabbing his head with both hands and pulling his hair.

'Ow!' he yelled.

Sofia ignored him and tried pushing down and lifting her other leg up to his left shoulder. That's when everything came apart and they fell on the ground in a chaotic heap of arms and legs.

After they'd finally squirmed away from the pile and stood again, the three of them stared at each other, panting with red faces.

'You're right,' Tick said between breaths. 'That was ridiculous.'

'I don't think my body will ever heal,' Paul said through a wince.

Sofia stared up at the button with a grin. 'Well, at least I got a closer look at the words on that sticker.'

'Really?' Tick asked, his hope rising. 'What did it say?'

Sofia let out a discouraged sigh. 'Two words: *Push me.*"'

✿

Sato lay on his back, staring at the ceiling. He'd focused so long on a bear-shaped shadow caused by the pale moonlight seeping through his window that it seemed to be moving, growing smaller and larger as if breathing. He knew it was only a trick of his eyes, but it still gave him the creeps.

He'd dreaded going to sleep lately because of an old dream that had come back to haunt him. He had no idea why it had returned in recent days, causing him to jerk awake every night, a sheen of sweat covering his whole body. Actually, it wasn't a dream at all – it was a memory.

The memory of his parents' murder.

What a day that had been, almost eight years ago. A terrible, frightening, horrible, horrible day. Master George had been there. Mistress Jane had been there, too. Others as well, but for some reason he couldn't remember their faces. But he'd never forget the way the old man had looked that day, or his closest ally – the woman dressed in yellow. He'd never forget. Sato would never, ever forget.

He closed his eyes, knowing the dream would come but giving in to exhaustion, hoping the memory might strengthen his hopes for revenge. Revenge on Mistress Jane. Revenge ...

'Yama-kun, come meet our guests!' his mother called from downstairs. She'd always called him that. It meant Little Mountain.

Six-year-old Sato stepped out of his room and slowly walked down the stairs, not wanting to meet a bunch of strangers. While preparing for the big dinner, his father had called them "Realitants" as if any person in the world should know what that meant.

Realitants. A strange word, especially for a six-year-old. But after witnessing what Sato saw that night, the word burned a place in his mind, never to be lost. Realitants. In years to come, he'd end up thinking the word every day, sometimes repeating it aloud as he looked in the mirror. Realitants. The word came to mean evil and death to him, and he made a pact to one day rid the world of them.

He'd known so little back then.

He entered the front room, where several people sat on the leather couches and fancy armchairs, sipping ocha

*tea and speaking with each other as if discussing the
weather or the latest sumo tournament. Most of them were
unrecognisable, their faces a blur. The only ones he saw
clearly were the slightly chubby man in the suit – Master
George – and the beautiful but chilling bald woman,
Mistress Jane. They sat together on the couch, mumbling
something he couldn't quite hear.*

*It was the image of those two sitting side by side on the
couch that stayed in his memory more than anything else.
It was that image that many years later would make him
distrust Master George with a passion. At least for a time.*

*Without warning, the room grew silent, and everyone
turned to look at Sato.*

*'I'd like you all to meet my son,' his father said, gripping
Sato's shoulders from behind and squeezing. His mother
joined them, pulling Sato's hand into hers.*

The dream froze for a moment, as if paused on
television. It always did at this exact point, and Sato
knew why. Although he was nervous at meeting
strangers, uncomfortable in his nice clothes, perhaps
even hungry at the time, it would be the last time Sato
ever felt the comforting touch of his parents. The last
time he ever felt safe and protected.

That moment with his parents would be the last
time Sato ever felt happy.

The dream continued playing out.

*Mistress Jane stood, then Master George and the rest.
Each of them stepped forward around the great, round
coffee table and shook Sato's little hand. George knelt on
the ground, a big smile creasing his face.*

*'Goodness gracious me,' the old man said. 'I can see it
in the boy's eyes. The passion, the hunger, the intelligence.
A splendid Realitant he'll make, Master Sato' – he looked*

up at Sato's father – 'a splendid Realitant, indeed. We'll begin the testing shortly.'

Mistress Jane was next, also kneeling before Yama-kun. Though her smile shone and her face was pretty, even then, Sato felt that something was wrong with her.

'Yes,' she said. Sato almost expected her to cackle like an evil old witch. 'A smart child by the looks of it.' She leaned forward to whisper in Sato's ear, so quiet only he could hear her. 'But whose side will you fight for? Everything is about to change, little boy.'

Mistress Jane stood. 'This is as good a time as any,' she announced, turning slowly as she spoke so everyone could see her face. 'My team has discovered a new Reality – a stable one. It's solid enough to officially call it a branch.'

'Really?' George shouted. 'That's delightful, simply delightful!'

Jane looked down at Sato, who returned her glare. She rolled her eyes and stuck out her tongue, as if disgusted by George's enthusiasm.

'The Thirteenth Reality,' she continued, not taking her eyes off Sato, 'has … unusual qualities. We've explored it extensively, realised its potential.'

'Why didn't you tell us before?' Sato's father asked, his voice laced with anger. 'If you've been exploring it this long–'

'The Chi'karda there,' Jane said, ignoring the interruption, 'is different. More powerful. More potent. It's mutated into something quite extraordinary. We may finally have the secret to finding our Utopian Reality. If this place isn't it, the power in the Thirteenth will help us make it ourselves.'

No one spoke for a long time; a few people exchanged nervous glances.

'Why all the sad faces?' Jane asked. 'Haven't you trusted me all these years? Don't you still trust me?'

'Not if you break the rules,' Sato's mother said. 'How can we trust you if you break the rules and hide things from us?'

'This calls for an immediate Discretionary Council,' Sato's father said. 'George, you know it does. I demand you call in the Haunce, this instant.'

George stood. 'Now, Master Sato, let's not be hasty—'

That was the line. Those seven words would stick in young Sato's mind, making it even harder for him to trust the man in the future, when his own recruiting call came. That was the line, because after George said it, not another word was spoken by him before Sato's parents were dead.

'I don't have time for this,' Jane said. 'I thought this might be the reaction, so I brought along something to show you all how important this discovery is. For all of us. For the Realities. For humanity.'

'Stop,' Sato's father said. 'Stop this instant. I demand it.'

'You ... demand it?' she replied, her lip curled ever so slightly. 'You demand it?'

'Yes,' Sato's mother answered for her husband. 'You're scaring us. This doesn't feel right.'

Mistress Jane smiled then, an image Sato would never forget. The smile held no humour, no joy, no kindness. It was an evil smile.

The next moment, the windows erupted, blowing inwards with a shower of tinkling glass shards. Shouts of pain surrounded him as streams of fire poured in from outside, streaking spurts of lava that whisked around the room like flying eels of flame.

The dream always grew dim at that moment, the memory fading into horror. He remembered his father's comforting grip on his shoulders disappearing, his mother's hand letting go of his own. He remembered intense heat. He remembered people running around, their clothes on fire. He remembered Jane vanishing into thin air. He remembered crying, turning to find his parents, wanting to run away.

But then, like always, he saw one last thing in the dream before it ended. One last image that would haunt him forever. His mother and father, lying on the ground, side by side.

Screaming. Burning.

Dying.

Sato woke up.

A Very Scary
Proposition

'Okay, it's my turn,' Sofia said as she took off her right shoe. 'You guys couldn't poke yourselves in your own eyeball.'

Tick wanted to argue, but didn't have much evidence to the contrary. He and Paul had been trying to hit the button with a shoe for at least ten minutes, their only reward being smacked in the head a couple of times as the shoes fell back down.

'"Poke yourselves in your own eyeball"?' Paul said. 'Never heard that one before.'

Sofia ignored him, planting her feet and staring up at the button with intense concentration, swinging the shoe up and down with both hands as she readied herself. Finally, she swung hard upwards and let the shoe fly. It missed by three feet.

Paul snickered. 'Ooh, so close. Hate to break it to you, but you throw like a girl.'

Uh-oh, Tick thought.

Sofia bent down to pick up her shoe, then bounced

it up and down in her right hand like a baseball. 'What did you say?'

Paul folded his arms. 'I said, you throw like a girl.'

'Huh,' Sofia grunted, staring down at her shoe.

Then she reared back and threw it straight for Paul's face, smacking him square on the nose.

He grabbed his face with both hands, jumping up and down. 'That hurt, man!' he shouted. But a second later, he started laughing. 'Ah, Tick, it was worth it to see Miss Italy mad. Her face looks like her daddy's spaghetti sauce.'

This time Sofia punched Paul in the arm with a loud thump. 'You want some more?' she asked.

Paul rubbed the spot. 'Dang, woman, I give up. How'd you get so mean, anyway?'

Tick was loving every minute of the exchange, but he knew they had to push that button. He felt something – a pressure in his chest – that told him they'd better get serious quick.

'You lovebirds cut it out,' he said. 'Start throwing.' They tried for another five minutes, dodging each other's shoes and scrambling around to pick up their own. Sofia finally hit the bullseye.

When her shoe connected, a quiet click echoed off the round glass of the tunnel and the blinking light stopped, turning off completely. All three of them stared, waiting for something amazing to happen. Nothing did. Tick rubbed his sunburned neck, sore from craning it upwards for so long.

'Great,' he said. 'Just great.'

Sofia huffed and looked down. Tick noticed her body tense, her eyes widen. She stared at the floor, transfixed, as if hypnotised. Tick quickly followed her gaze. He couldn't stop the gasp before it escaped his mouth.

On the very bottom of the tunnel, at their feet, a perfect red square had formed on the glass, about five feet on each side, as if a neon light were glowing right beneath them. In the middle of that square, several lines of words appeared like text on a computer screen, black on white.

'Guess we *were* supposed to push the button,' Paul said.

Tick fell to his knees and scooted around until the words were right side up. It was another poem – a pretty long one. He started reading.

You pushed the button; it called the beast.
It moves real fast; it likes to feast.
You can stop it once, but cannot twice,
It's the only way to save your life.
How to do it, you may ask;
This will not be an easy task.
Your mind will beg of you to quit,
But if you do, your mind will split.
On this very spot you'll stand;
You will die if I see you've ran.
I'm testing strength and will and trust.
Move one inch, and die you must.
Do not step outside the square.
No matter what – don't you dare.
When this is over, you will see
A grand reward for trusting me.

'Dude,' Paul breathed. 'There's no way Master George is behind all this.'

Sofia sat down next to the poem. 'For the first time in my life, I think I agree with you. He said in the letter we were going to a gathering, not doing more tests.'

Tick read through the poem again, feeling very uneasy. Paul and Sofia were right – this was getting weird. Even though Master George had sent the Gnat Rat and the Tingle Wraith after them during their initial recruiting test, this seemed too sinister for the jolly old man. It felt dark and threatening.

'This isn't even a riddle,' Tick said, standing up.

'What do you mean?' Sofia asked.

Tick pointed down the long tunnel in the direction from which he thought the train thing had come the first time they'd seen it blur past. 'There's nothing to solve. We have to stand inside this square no matter what happens. No matter what ... *comes.*'

He couldn't get over the sick feeling in his gut. Something felt wrong, like he'd left a fat wallet full of money on a city park bench. Or probably how his mom would feel if she realised she'd left the oven on, right after taking off in the aeroplane to go visit Grandma. The world seemed twisted, off balance.

After a long pause, Sofia spoke up in a confident voice. 'It doesn't matter.'

'What doesn't matter?' Tick and Paul said at the same time.

Sofia shrugged. 'If it's Master George – which I doubt – we need to do what the poem says. If it's not him, we *still* need to do what it says. We'll be really tempted to leave the square, but we can't. Then, at the last second, whoever it is will wink us away. Poof, nice and easy – just like the chair thing.'

'How do we know for sure we'll get winked?' Tick asked, even though the answer had just clicked in his head.

'If somebody else is doing this,' Sofia said, 'they could obviously just kill us if they wanted to. Why would they go through this whole ordeal to get rid of us? If anything, now we have even more pressure to pass these tests.' She shook her fists and screamed in frustration. 'This is so stupid! Stupid, stupid, stupid!'

'Way to sum it up intelligently,' Paul muttered.

When she gave him a cold stare, he threw his hands up. 'Hey, I agree with you!'

'Wait,' Tick said, shushing them, holding a hand out. He felt a slight tremor beneath his feet, a small vibration with no sound.

'It's coming, dude,' Paul said. 'It's coming!'

The shaking grew stronger, almost visible now; Paul and Sofia seemed to jiggle up and down. Tick had never been in an earthquake, but he knew this must be what it felt like.

'What do we do, man, what do we do?' Paul was looking left and right as if trying to decide which direction to run.

Sofia reached out and grabbed Paul by the shirt, jerking him towards her until their faces were only inches apart. 'We stand in this square, Rogers, you hear me? We stand in this square!'

At once, they all looked down at their feet. Tick had to shuffle a foot closer to the others to be inside the red-lined boundary.

'She's right,' he said as Sofia let go of Paul. 'No matter what, we have to stay in the square.'

The tunnel trembled violently; Tick had to spread his feet a little and hold out his arms to maintain his balance. A sound grew in the distance, a low rumble of thunder. Whatever it was – the poem had called it a beast – was coming from the direction Tick had thought it would. He narrowed his eyes and stared that way, though nothing had appeared yet in the distance.

'This is crazy, man,' Paul said. 'Are you guys *sure* about this?'

'Yes,' Tick said, not breaking his concentration. He thought he could see something dark, far down the tunnel.

'My brain wants me to run,' Paul insisted.

This time, Tick did turn, pointing at the poem still printed on the ground. 'The message said we'd think that. Don't move.' He looked back down the tunnel. There was definitely something dark way down there, growing larger, bit by bit.

'I'm watching you, Rogers,' Sofia said, almost shouting as the rumbling and shaking increased. 'We're going to wink away. No one's going to kill us!'

'Fine! Quit treating me like a baby.'

Tick strained his eyes as the dark shape grew bigger. Something about its movement made him think it was *twisting* – corkscrewing through the tunnel like a rollercoaster.

'What *is* that thing?' he said, though the roar had grown so loud he knew no one could hear him. He braced himself, knowing it would be easier if he didn't look, didn't see it coming. But his curiosity was too strong.

Then the air around them suddenly brightened, flashing a blinding white.

'Look!' Paul shouted from behind him.

Tick turned to see sand dunes and sunlight through a gaping hole in the side of the tunnel.

The door had opened.

THE TRAIN THING

A shot of elation and relief surged through Tick's nerves, like he'd been rescued from a burning building. There it was, their escape! He even took a step towards it before reason pulled his thoughts back to reality. Sofia grabbed his arm.

'No!' she screamed.

'I know!' he answered, looking down at his feet. His toes were within inches of the red line. The world around them shook and roared, as if they were in a small building pummelled by a tornado. The wind had picked up, rustling their hair and clothes.

Paul stared at the open door, his eyes glazed over. 'Don't even think about it!' Sofia shouted at him. 'No matter what, remember? If we run, we die!'

Paul snapped out of his daze, looked at Tick. 'Dude, it's right there!'

'Whoever it is, they're just tempting us!' Tick yelled. He moved as close to Paul as he could, then pulled Sofia in. 'Link arms!' He could barely hear his own voice.

Sofia obeyed immediately, but Paul hesitated, the wind ripping at his shirt.

'Do it!' Tick yelled.

Paul's face sank into a frown as he wrapped his arm around Sofia's elbow, then his other around Tick's. All this time, the door remained open, staying open far longer than it ever had before. *This was all planned out,* Tick thought. *But by who?*

From the way they stood, only Sofia faced the onrushing nightmare, her face set in cold fear, eyes wide, mouth in a tight line. The air swirled around them, making them sway dangerously close to the line. Tick thought Sofia's hair might simply fly off at any second. And the noise. The *noise.* Like screaming brakes and revved jet engines and pounding hammers and hissing steam – a chorus of terrible sounds that pierced Tick's ears with sharp pain.

Finally, as if giving in to some inevitable fate, he twisted his neck to look behind him.

The thing was very close now, dark and hideous, spinning upside down and right side up again, corkscrewing as it sped towards them, faster and faster. Tick squinted, thinking the panic must have scrambled his brain – what he was looking at didn't make any sense. The poem had been more accurate than he'd thought.

The train was not a train at all. It wasn't a car, truck, or plane. It wasn't even a spaceship. The thing thundering towards them at unbelievable speeds was an *animal.* The biggest, strangest, ugliest beast Tick had ever seen.

'What ...' he said, trailing off, knowing his friends couldn't hear him. Nothing made sense any more. Nothing.

As the beast got closer, Tick felt the fear in him swell, burning like fire, surging through his veins, hurting him.

The animal had at least a dozen sets of thick, muscled legs, almost a blur as they churned back and forth to move the creature in its twisting pattern. Its huge head spun but, impossibly, didn't turn as quickly as the rest of its body, as if the legs were on springs or gears. Dark, scaly skin covered a hideous head, spikes and stunted bones sticking out in random places, enormous teeth jutting from its mouth.

As it approached within half a mile, then quarter of a mile, Tick felt more scared than ever before, despite the things he'd been through. His mind couldn't come up with any possible explanation why a gigantic glass tube would exist in the middle of the desert, made for a terrible beast to run through at ridiculous speeds. Confusion and fear mingled together inside his brain, squeezing his thoughts until his head pounded with a drumming pain.

Wink us away, he thought. *Time's almost up, wink us away. Wink us away. WINK US AWAY!* The wind, the noise – the horrible noise. *What is making that stupid noise?* He thought he heard a scream, maybe two. Maybe it was him.

When the beast was only fifty feet away, growling and snapping its jaws and twisting and pumping its powerful legs, bulleting towards them, everything went crazy.

For the slightest of moments, a hush swallowed the area, the noise ending in an abrupt clap of empty silence. Then a booming, deep toll, like millions of huge bells and French horns playing at once, rang out, drowning out all other sound. Tick let go of Paul and Sofia and clapped his hands over his ears. The volume became unbearable; the ache in his head became a splitting pain behind his eyes.

The entire tunnel rocked upwards and crashed back to the ground, sending a web of cracks shooting in all directions, spreading like a branching tree with the sound of ice breaking over a frozen lake. Tick crashed to the ground, his knees buckling from the impact. Paul fell on top of him, then Sofia.

Somehow Tick got out the words, 'Stay in the box!'

In both directions, the tunnel started *warping* – impossible waves rippling in the glass up and down its length. The massive beast had stopped a few feet away, its many legs coming to a rest on the bottom of the tube. Its head swivelled around at the chaos as if it were as frightened as the humans. The deep, vibrating horn-like sound continued to boom through the air.

Tick and the others scrambled to the centre of the square and clasped arms around each other, huddled on top of the still-glowing words of the poem. Everything shook, much worse than before. The glass rippled and cracked; the tunnel bounced in places like a writhing worm. The beast let out a roar, its huge mouth opening to show dozens of teeth; saliva flew everywhere. Still, the sound of it was nothing compared to the clanging, ear-piercing toll of the mysterious bells.

'What's happening?' Sofia shouted. Tick barely heard her and had no answer.

The creature moved towards them, anger ignited in its black eyes that looked through a hooded brow of horns and scales. Almost on top of them, it roared again, this time louder. The air reeked of something foul and rotten.

'Stay in the box!' Tick shouted again. *Wink us away. Wink us away. WINK US AWAY!*

The beast lunged at them, its legs catapulting it into the air. Its outermost horn came within inches of Tick's face when something suddenly slammed the whole creature away from them and against the wall of the tunnel to their right, where the door still stood open – though it was way too small for the beast. The glass exploded outwards, the huge animal crashing through and into a steep desert dune.

As it landed, sending up a massive spray of sand, large sections of the tunnel began melting into liquid, forming huge flying globs that looked like molten silver as they moved through the air. More and more of them appeared, completely destroying the tunnel except for the small spot on which Tick and the others stood. All at once, the melted glass hurtled towards the monster, engulfing the beast completely. The liquid hardened back into glass, tinkling and crackling.

As quickly as it had started, everything stopped. Tick sat next to Paul and Sofia, all of them squeezing each other, gasping to catch their breath. Only a few dozen feet away stood a horrific sculpture of glass, twisted and bent, parts of the poor animal's body sticking out here and there. One large horn jutted from the front, pointing at them as if it had all been their fault. No one said a word. They had stayed in the square.

They had done what they were supposed to, despite everything.

A few seconds later, someone winked them away to another Reality.

An Invitation

Mistress Jane walked through the darkening woods, enjoying the smells of the forest and fresh air more than she thought she would. She'd rarely ventured out of the Lemon Fortress since losing her Barrier Wand to the Realitants, too busy working and planning. Too busy thinking.

A bird cawed in the distance, a shriek that sounded like someone being tortured. She faltered a moment, then stepped over a log and continued walking. *There you go again,* she thought. *You can take anything and see the worst in it.* Why couldn't she just hear the sound of a bird and appreciate the beauty in it – the joy of nature? When had she become so dark and morbid? How had it got this bad?

She closed her eyes and took a deep breath, loving the strong scent of pine. Such simple things used to please her, make her happy. Until her mission to find the Utopian Reality consumed her and turned her into what she'd become. Someone feared and hated. When it came down to it, Jane didn't like herself very much. Not one bit.

She reached a sudden break in the trees, the place

Frazier had described to her. He'd wanted to come with her, insisted on it with more bravery than usual. Jane had finally ordered him to clean the kitchens for being obstinate. If anyone could take care of themselves in the Thirteenth Reality, it was Mistress Jane.

The sun had fallen behind the line of trees on the other side of the huge clearing, a random twinkle shining through the leaves as she kept walking. She'd believed Frazier's report, but she still felt a thrill of shock at seeing it for herself.

The gap in the forest was at least quarter of a mile in diameter, almost perfectly circular. She saw no signs or tracks of heavy machinery that had mowed down hundreds of trees overnight. She saw only a few footprints, and they looked to be those of the hunters and Frazier's investigating party.

Who did this? And how?

As she neared the centre of the clearing, she tried to come up with possibilities. It certainly wasn't a natural phenomenon – especially considering the felled tree trunks spelled out words in massive letters. From this low vantage point, she couldn't make out the words, of course, only a general sense of the individual letters – even though they were almost too big to recognise. But she had no doubt as to what it said, trusting Frazier implicitly.

Mistress Jane, you are a coward. Come and find me.

She continued on, knowing exactly where she wanted to end up. The message had a hidden meaning, a literal clue. *Come and find* me. That's exactly what she was doing, counting on her growing powers to help her if she ran into any trouble.

She made it to the other side of the clearing, her arms and legs weary from crossing over – and sometimes *climbing* over – the many logs. She could have levitated herself, flown to her destination without another thought, but she was enjoying the nostalgic effort of physical exertion. Finally, in the centre of where she estimated the word "me" was spelled out, she stopped.

'Here I am,' she said, not stooping so low as to shout; she had her dignity to preserve. 'We're near enough to the old battleground and its thick Chi'karda. Wink in and be done with it.'

A few minutes passed in silence. Jane grew restless far quicker than she expected, and stilled herself to be sure her emotions didn't show. She would not utter another word or move another muscle, no matter how long the mystery person made her wait.

Ten more minutes went by, the cloudless sky growing ever darker, a deep blue slowly bleeding to purple. Then, with no fanfare or smoke, a man appeared ten feet in front of her. Dressed in a pinstripe suit, he had dark hair and olive skin. He was tall and almost handsome, but not quite. His arms were clasped behind his back, perhaps holding something, hiding it from her. Though she'd never met him, she knew his name immediately. After all, just a few months ago she'd tried unsuccessfully to arrange a meeting with him.

Reginald Chu, perhaps the most dangerous man in the Realities.

But surely he couldn't possibly know her powers in the Chi'karda were growing enough to match his technological gadgetry. *Why is he here?*

'Hello, *Mistress* Jane,' Chu said, mocking her title. 'We finally meet, several months later than you had hoped.'

'You got my note, then?' she asked.

'I did.' He paused, not moving, staring at her. 'I waited for you in the park, but you never showed up. You wasted time that was not yours to waste.'

It took every ounce of willpower for Jane to remain calm, to not lash out and whip this man with one of the fallen logs. She could do it, and the man spoke to her as if she were inferior. *No,* she told herself. *He's here for a reason.*

'My apologies, Mister—'

'Call me Reginald,' he snapped. 'Never call me Mr. Chu. Never.'

Jane bowed her head ever so slightly. 'My apologies ... Reginald. I had a proposition for you, a good one, but the Realitants stole my Wand, trapping me here. I'll soon have another one built.'

Chu moved his arms from behind his back to reveal what he'd been hiding – a brand new Barrier Wand, its golden surface sparkling despite the diminishing light, seven dials and switches running along its length.

He hefted the three-foot-long device in his left hand, holding it out to her as a gift. Then he dropped one end of it towards the ground and leaned on it like a cane. 'I've had spies here since the week you stood me up. I know a lot about you. I also know about this Reality and its twisted version of Chi'karda.'

It took considerable effort for Jane not to look at the Wand, staring Chu in the face instead. 'I'm glad you know how to do your research.'

'That's not all I found. You're missing one of the metals. It'll be months before you can extract enough from the ore you've discovered.' He nodded towards the Wand at his feet. 'So I've brought you a new Wand to save you the trouble.'

Jane folded her arms. 'At what price?'

Chu broke into a smile, something Jane would never have expected to see on such a man. 'I can see you're as wise as I hoped. Nothing, of course, is free. Especially in my Reality.'

'Tales of your business skills are widespread, I assure you.' She wanted to add, *And your ruthlessness and greed are likewise well-known.*

'That's good to know.'

She expected him to say more, but he grew silent, keeping his gaze locked with hers. *Oh, I do not like this man.* 'Your price?' she asked again.

'I've developed something that will completely change the Realities. It's a new invention–'

'What is it?' Jane asked, trying to assert some authority, show her impatience.

Chu paused, his face pulling tight, his eyes narrowing. 'Listen to me, *Mistress*. Never interrupt me. You will stand there and listen to my proposition and you will not utter a word until I am finished. Do you understand? Indicate with a nod of your head.'

Jane felt her face fill with blood, heat up, and burn. A small sound escaped from somewhere in the back of her throat, a mortifying squeak. At that moment, she swore to herself that when this man died, he would be looking at her smiling face. The only thing staying her hand from unleashing her powers was curiosity. Intense curiosity.

She nodded.

'Good.' He pulled up the Barrier Wand and held it

in front of him, parallel to the ground. 'My project is called Dark Infinity, a tool that artificially creates massive amounts of Chi'karda – far stronger than anything you've encountered here. It's more powerful than all of my previous accomplishments combined. However, there is still one missing piece.'

Jane almost asked him what, but stopped just in time. Her curiosity burned like an itch.

'It's so strong that I can't control it alone,' he continued. 'I need another person, someone of proven strength, someone extraordinary. I've studied and searched every Reality, every region. I have narrowed it down to only two people. I don't fully understand yet what sets these two apart, but I do know that one of them will do. And I only need ... one.'

He paused, and Jane was dying to speak. She didn't know what she had expected, but it was certainly nothing like this.

Chu continued. 'One of the two is you. Your powers here do not exist solely because of the mutated Chi'karda in this place. Otherwise, everyone would be able to do what you do. There is something extraordinary about you, and I do not say that lightly.'

Who is the other? she screamed inside her head, completely ignoring the compliment.

'You might be wondering about your competition,' Chu said, smiling. 'And here is the proposition. It's very simple. I'm currently sending the other person through a series of tests. If he passes them and ends up where he's supposed to, he will win the honour of standing by my side as we rule the Realities. Meaning, of course, you lose and will be disposed of.' He paused. 'You may speak now.'

'I … I'm not sure I completely understand,' Jane mumbled, hating herself for appearing so weak. Chu had said she could be "disposed of" like a sickly fly. *How dare he?* And yet, she felt uneasy. 'How do I win?'

Chu walked forward, holding out the Barrier Wand and gesturing for her to take it. She grasped the golden rod with its dials and switches eagerly, like a child grabbing for sweets. It was cold and hard in her hands.

'Like I said,' Chu continued, 'it's very easy. If the boy makes it to me, you lose. If he doesn't, you win. Only one of you will survive in the end – only one of you will be worthy to serve with me in controlling Dark Infinity. That's it.'

'That's it?' she repeated, her courage returning. 'Nothing else?'

Chu nodded. 'You've been given your test, and I assure you, it's not a simple task. You must kill Atticus Higginbottom.'

AN ELEVATOR IN STONE

'Come on,' Mothball said, stopping for the tenth time to allow Rutger to catch up. 'You're slower than a sloth with no legs, you are.'

Truth be told, Mothball appreciated resting for a spell. It was blazing hot in the Arizona desert, and she was hauling a big load of logs she'd gathered from the riverside. Carried down by the Colorado River, stray wood often lodged in one particular bend, and Master George had to have his fires, didn't he?

Rutger, sucking in every breath, his face the colour of boiled cherries, stopped and craned his neck to look up at her. He was like a big ball rolling backwards, pivoting on little legs. The man looked absolutely exhausted.

'Can't ... really run when I'm ... carrying all of this ... wood ... now can I?' he managed to get out between breathing spells.

Mothball glanced at Rutger's short arms, holding all of two sticks – one of them barely more than a twig. 'Yeah, I'm quite shocked you haven't called someone on the telephone to announce you've broken the world's record for stick-luggin'.'

'It probably is a record for someone from the Eleventh.' Rutger nodded towards the door hidden in the canyon crevice, about forty yards away. The two of them stood at the bottom of the Grand Canyon, its majestic red walls of stone towering over them, reaching so far to the sky they couldn't see their tops. Having finished gathering firewood, they were making their way back to the elevator shaft entrance.

'I reckon Sofia would call you a *flimp* right about now,' Mothball said as she resumed walking towards the hidden crevice.

'It's *wimp,* you tall sack of bones, and if she did call me that, she'd pay the price.'

'Oh, really?' Mothball called over her shoulder. 'And wha' exactly would you do? Sit on her toesies? Bite her shins, perhaps?'

'I'd do whatever it took to teach the young lady some proper manners, that's what.'

Mothball made it to the small crack of a cave that led to the elevator and dropped her stack of logs onto the ground. She reached her arms to the sky in a long, satisfying stretch. When Rutger finally waddled over and dropped his pathetic two sticks onto the pile, he put his hands on his waist and took deep gulps of air, as if he'd just completed a marathon.

'Congratulations,' Mothball said. 'You're the first tiny fat man to haul two twigs across a weed-scattered spit of sand. Right proud of yourself, I reckon?'

Rutger looked up at her and grinned. 'Push the button, or it'll be *your* shins that get bitten.'

Mothball's booming laugh escaped before she could stop it. She looked around to make sure no stray hikers were around to hear it. 'Quit makin' me laugh, ya little ball of bread dough. Get us in trouble, ya will.'

She stepped through the thin crevice and pushed a button that looked like the nub of a rock. She heard the rumble of machinery and pulleys from deep within the mountain, then the low whine of the descending elevator. She groaned, having expected the doors to pop right open since they'd just exited an hour ago and no one else should've used it.

'Blimey, who called up the ruddy thing?' she said as she stepped out of the cave and back into the sunlight. 'Probably that rascal Sally, playin' one of 'is jokes.'

'Oh, calm yourself,' Rutger said, his face finally returning to its normal colour. Sweat poured down his face, however, and his hair was matted and wet. 'It only takes a couple of minutes. Master George has Sally too busy to mess with jokes anyway.'

'I'll bet ya tonight's dessert that when the door pops open, Sally'll be there with a trick up his sleeve.' Rutger looked up at her, his face creased in concern. 'D-d-dessert?' he asked, as if she'd just suggested wagering the man's life savings. 'Let's not get foolish, Mothball.'

'Then you'll take it?' she asked, folding her arms and peering down her nose at him.

Rutger hesitated, fidgeting as he rocked back and forth on his tiny feet. 'Um, no, I think you might be right on this one.' He cleared his throat. 'Probably, um, going to throw a bucket of water on us. That silly lumberjack.'

Mothball shook her head, pretending to be disgusted. 'You'd throw your own mum in the sewer for a dessert, you would. You can 'ave mine – s'long as you give me some of your bread and jam. Quite tasty stuff, that is.'

Rutger rubbed his chin, deep in thought. After a few seconds, he said, 'No, I like the bread and jam, too. Let's just stick with our own portions. Deal?'

Mothball reached down and patted him on the head. 'You're a good man, you are. A bit short for my likin', but a good man indeed.'

'Oh, stop – look, it's here.'

A few feet inside the crevice, a rock wall slid to the side, revealing the lighted cube of the elevator, its walls made of fake wood panels. Master George stood inside, dressed in his usual dark suit, arms clasped behind his back.

Mothball's surprise quickly turned to concern. 'What's wrong?' she asked.

'Oh, nothing, nothing,' he said, breaking into a smile that was obviously forced. 'Just wanted to come down and get a bit of fresh air.'

He stepped out of the elevator and squeezed past the narrow walls of the cave and into the open canyon. He took a deep breath, then let it out in a satisfied sigh.

'Simply beautiful, don't you think?' he asked, turning back to look at them. 'I really should come out here more often. Good for the heart, I'm quite sure.'

Mothball rolled her eyes at Rutger. 'Out with it, Master George. Somethin's botherin' ya.'

Master George tried to look startled, an expression that for some reason reminded Mothball of a frightened chicken. Then his face wilted into a frown, and he huffed.

'Goodness gracious me,' he said. 'I can't get anything past you two.'

'That's a good thing,' Rutger said. 'What's going on?'

Master George put his hands behind his back again and paced in a wide circle for a full minute. Mothball knew better than to interrupt him. He finally stopped and looked at both of them in turn.

'I've just read through Sato's final report of his interviews, and it concerns me greatly. He's made conclusions with which I can't disagree, and given me a proposal, in private, that frightens me to no end.'

'You have our full attention,' Rutger said. Mothball nodded.

Master George continued. 'I've known all along that Reginald Chu was behind the strange things happening throughout some of the Realities. There've been whispers that he has a new invention, something terrible – something abominable. And I no longer have any doubt it's directly related to the people who are going insane. I'm quite sure of it.'

'What is this invention?' Rutger asked.

Master George paused. 'Let's go back up to the complex. I'd like Sato and Sally to join our discussion. We've much to talk about.'

Mothball, troubled, bent over to pick up her large pile of logs, wet from soaking in the river; she grimaced at how filthy they were after lying in the dirt.

'Could you take mine, too?' Rutger pleaded. 'It's hard enough for me to fit through this ridiculous cave as it is.'

'Don't know if I can handle your twigs,' Mothball muttered. 'Might tip me over.'

Rutger happily picked them up, then threw them on top of the stack bundled in her arms. One end smacked her in the nose.

'Blimey, that hurt! Go on with ya, get in the ruddy lift.'

Master George had already entered the well-hidden elevator, waiting with arms folded and slightly shaking his head, as if observing the antics of misbehaving children. 'Please, would you two *hurry?*'

Rutger sucked in a huge breath, trying to shrink his tummy, then ran forward into the dark slice of air between the two vertical walls of the cave. He made it two feet before he came to an abrupt halt; his legs dangled below him, his body lodged in place.

'Help!' he cried out, like a monster was coming to eat him.

Mothball snorted as she held in a laugh. With glee, she balanced herself, lifted one leg, cocked it, then kicked Rutger in the rear end as hard as she could. As he tumbled forward into the elevator, he managed to say, 'Thank you!'

Mothball stepped into the lift and pushed the *up* button.

✿

Buzz.

Sato looked up from his bed where he'd been reading through his reports again. The intercom had rung for him. He put his papers aside, swung his legs off the bed and onto the floor, then reached over to hit the button on the wall.

'Yes?' he shouted.

'Ow, do you have to answer so loud?' It was Rutger, his voice a hollow echo of itself.

'Sorry. What do you want?'

'We're meeting in the conference room in ten minutes. I'll be providing refreshments, so snap-snap!' *Click.*

Sato put his elbows on his knees and rubbed his face with both hands. The nightmare of his parents' death had seemed more vivid lately, the horrific images floating in his thoughts for hours after waking up. They hung in his mind like dirty, tattered curtains blocking out the sunlight. He shook his head and bent over to put his shoes on.

'Another meeting,' he mumbled. 'Joy.'

A few minutes later, he slid into a cushy chair around the conference table, reaching out to grab a Chocolate-Chip-Peanut Butter-Butterscotch-Pecan-Walnut-Macadamia-Coconut Delight, one of Rutger's specialties. The little man always said the name in full, despite its length. No one in the complex cared what they were called because they tasted delicious.

Everyone else was already seated: Mothball and Rutger to his right, Master George across from him, Sally to his left. They were the only Realitants at the Grand Canyon Centre at the moment – the others had gone off with various duties and assignments.

'Sorry to bother you, Sato,' George said. 'I know you wanted some time for a bit of relaxing after we spoke earlier, but I felt this gathering couldn't wait.'

'No problem,' Sato muttered. He'd tried so hard to improve his mood lately, but the recent spate of dreams had quashed his efforts. The world seemed bleak and grim – the only thing that gave him reprieve was trying to figure out the mystery of the crazy people.

George rested his clasped hands on the table in front of him. 'First, let's summarise where we are at the moment. Thanks to our good man Sally, here' – he gave a nod to the lumberjack, who seemed lost in thought, his thumb picking suspiciously at his nose– 'for putting the Earwig Transponder inside Tick so we could track him better and scramble Chu's eavesdropping capabilities. For as long as I shall live, I shan't forgive that man for his violation of Rule Number 462 on those poor kids. Hijacking a nanolocator ... it's evil, I tell you!'

George's hands squeezed together as his face reddened. 'But the milk's in the kitty litter, as my mum was fond of saying – no use weeping and wailing. With the transponder in Tick's ear, we'll have much more information.' He cleared his throat. 'For example, we know they've just had a bizarre incident in the Tenth Reality, but we're not quite sure what happened.'

Rutger slammed his hand on the table. 'Don't tell me that wretch stuck them in the Grinder Beast's training tunnels?'

Sato leaned forward at this question – the words "Grinder Beast" would pique anyone's attention.

George nodded. 'Indeed. I must say, I was rather tempted to go rescue them, but I didn't want to ruin our chances at getting on the inside of Chu's plans. I believe we all agree that Chu would not put them in total danger – not yet, anyway. It appears he's running them through some sort of test, and I can't imagine he'd waste their potential by letting one of the Grinders kill them so easily. They serve us best as spies – albeit unknowing spies – at the moment.'

'That's a big risk on your part, it is,' Mothball said,

the most accusatory thing Sato had ever heard her say to George. The tall woman loved those kids like her own children. Sato felt a little jealous; she didn't seem to care so much for him.

'That's neither here nor there,' George responded. 'I was right to wait. They've been winked to the Sixth by Chu, where they seem to be safe and sound for the time being.'

'What was that you said about a bizarre incident?' Sato asked.

'I can't say for sure. There was a surge in Chi'karda in that area, some kind of great disturbance that caused a Ripple Quake in one of the fragmented Realities. If I had to guess, I'd say Chu destroyed one of the training tunnels in order to wink them out. That glass is particularly resistant to Barrier Wands.'

'But how would he do that?' Rutger asked.

'Well ... that brings us to our next item of discussion.' George looked over at Sato. 'Based on the information Sato has gathered, combined with the evidence of our spies and the disturbances we've seen this past summer, I believe Chu has built some sort of superweapon that contains more simulated Chi'karda power than anything ever built previously. I believe it's responsible for some of the odd things happening to Tick and the others, as well as for spreading the plague of insanity.'

Everyone turned to look at Sato, as if he would follow this up with a brilliant statement supporting George's theory.

'Everything points to that,' he said, unable to think of anything else. George had said it better than he ever could.

'We can dig more into the details later in the meeting,' George continued, 'but I want to put something on the table now before we say another word. It's rare that I must give an assignment as terribly important as the one I'm about to ask of Sato.'

Sato's mind had been drifting, and he wasn't sure he'd heard correctly. 'What was that? An assignment?'

'Yes, a mission of sorts.'

Sato swallowed. He felt as if the temperature in the room had risen twenty degrees. 'You want *me* to ...' He had mentioned the possibility of sending someone to gather samples, but he'd never guessed the old man would choose *him*.

'I can think of no better Realitant for this than you, Sato. You have stealth and wit about you. Plus, no one will suspect someone so young, and if you do get in a bind, I trust your ability to get out of it.'

'Wait, wait, wait,' Rutger said, squirming on his booster seat. 'What mission are you talking about?'

George paused before answering. 'Sato and I are positive the explanation for people going crazy is some type of plague – literally. And we're quite sure it's linked to Chu's superweapon. I want to send Sato into the area most infected with this plague and obtain a blood sample from one of the victims. Until we understand the disease, we won't know how to fight it.'

Sato barely heard George's words, as if they were coming down a long, dark tunnel. George wanted to send *him*. What if ... what if he *caught* the plague?

He was perfectly willing to face danger in his quest to avenge his parents' death, but the prospect of a nasty disease that made you crazy sickened him. Frightened him.

'Are you up to it?' Mothball asked, reaching over and patting Sato's arm.

'Huh? What?' he said.

'Are you up to it, I said.'

Sato looked around at the others in the room. Several beads of sweat finally let go and slid down his temples. He hadn't expected *this*.

'I ... uh ...' In that moment, the image of his parents burning popped into his head, and his fear hardened into concrete resolve.

'I'll do it,' he said, trying his best to keep his voice firm. 'I'll be fine.'

Sally stood up, folding his arms across his broad chest. 'I reckon I'll go wid the young fella.'

George shook his head. 'No, Sally. I have an entirely different mission for you.'

LOTS OF LEFT TURNS

They'd been walking for hours.

This new Reality seemed the most normal of any Tick had visited so far. Aside from a few oddities, it wasn't much different from his hometown in Reality Prime. One of those differences was the style of the buildings and the clothes of the citizens. It was slight, but everything here seemed a little more elaborate, a little fancier. Many businesses had huge fountains in front, with complex displays of shooting water, and the mouldings on the houses had carved pictures of animals and trees. The men wore fancy dark suits and greased back their hair, and the women wore dresses with white gloves pulled clear past their elbows. Also, an eerie, operatic soprano voice sang from speakers throughout the town. Another odd thing: the place appeared to only have left turns – at least off the road on which they currently walked.

'Dude, what's up with this?' Paul said, pointing to his right, where a thick forest of tall trees loomed like an ominous wall. 'Look at all that land out there. Why aren't they building on it?'

'Who cares?' Sofia said, annoyance creeping back

into her voice. 'Maybe they're a bunch of idiots.'

Tick understood her mood. Even though the weather was pleasant here – partly cloudy sky, soft breeze, warm but not hot – he felt like they were going nowhere fast. Not to mention the sick feeling he still had from almost being trampled by a raging monster inside a gigantic glass straw.

Paul yawned. 'Just seems a little weird that there's this huge town to our left, but nothing at all to our right. We should open a real estate office.'

Sofia ignored him. 'Well, our plan to stay on this road isn't working. I say we go into the city.'

'Me too,' Tick agreed. 'Everything is starting to look the same – I swear I saw that exact building a couple of hours ago.'

He pointed to a tall office complex made of dark granite with shiny, black windows that sparkled as if inlaid with gold.

'Whoa,' Paul said, stopping.

'What?' Tick and Sofia asked at the same time.

'That building doesn't just look familiar – it *is* the same one we saw earlier. I'm positive. Man, this road is a ginormous circle that goes *around* the city. No wonder we're not getting anywhere.'

'That explains all the left turns,' Tick added.

'I thought we were all supposed to be smart,' Sofia said. 'It took us *how* long to figure this out?'

'Come on,' Paul said. 'Let's go into the town and find a sweet old lady who's willing to feed some starving kids.'

Right on cue, Tick's stomach rumbled with hunger. 'Hope our money works here.'

'I doubt it, but we can try,' Paul said.

At the next road, they turned left, the wall of trees now at their backs.

☼

Reginald looked down at the weaselly little hotel owner of Circle City, rocking between his two feet, fidgeting with the buttons on his fancy red vest. Chu was astonished that someone could show so much weakness in front of another grown man. His name was Phillip, and he couldn't be more than five feet tall, fat, with streaks of black hair pasted in greasy lines across his obviously bald head.

Ah, yes. The comb-over. Delightful. Reginald swore that if he ever went bald, he'd simply invent a way to make his hair grow back. *Hmm,* he thought. *I can't believe I haven't done that yet …*

'What do I get out of all this?' Phillip said, his voice sounding to Reginald like a talking rat high on helium. 'And how do I find the kids?'

'They're in the city. Three young teenagers – two Caucasians: a boy with brown hair, a girl with black hair, and a dark-skinned boy who's a full foot taller than you and ten times as handsome. They'll be wandering around, obviously lost, smelling like a bag of three-week-old tuna – the brats haven't showered in days.'

Frankly, Reginald was annoyed that Atticus still had the other two kids with him. He'd hoped they'd have been killed by now, but they seemed as determined as their powerful friend. No matter. That was the beauty of the test – there were no rules, not really. If Atticus made it to the end, he made it to the end. Even if he had the help of friends and the Realitants.

Realitants. What a waste of human DNA.

'All right,' Phillip said. 'I'll send out my boys to find them, bring them here, offer them rooms, as you said.'

'And feed them. They'll be here at least a week, probably longer. I want the boy – I mean, I want *all* of them – well-rested and strong for what lies ahead. I will pay you double your rates, plus a bonus.'

'What kind of bonus?' The hotel owner tried his very best to display an expression of professional hardball on his face, but it looked more like a fat squirrel eyeing an acorn.

Reginald stifled a laugh. 'The value of one week's worth of rent for all your rooms.'

Phillip choked, his eyes wide with the prospect of such a sum for doing almost nothing. 'I'll have to think about–'

'Shut up and take the deal,' Reginald said.

Phillip nodded, his face flushed red. 'Okay, it's a deal. I'll have them here, safe and sound, by tonight.'

'Good.' Reginald reached into his pocket and pulled out two sealed envelopes, then handed them over. 'The thick one is half your money, including the bonus, plus money for the kids to spend. You'll get the rest of your portion when they ... disappear.'

'And this other one?' The hotel owner held up the thin envelope.

'I want you to deliver that to them at precisely six o'clock. If you can't get them to the hotel before then, wait until morning to deliver it. I don't care if it's a.m. or p.m., just give it to them at *six* o'clock.'

Phillip's eyes squinched up in confusion.

'Don't ask any more questions,' Reginald said. 'Just do as I say and enjoy the money.'

After giving Phillip a few more instructions, Reginald turned and walked away, enjoying himself and his clever ways even more than usual.

☼

'All right,' Paul said as they passed a small group of kids playing a version of football with a square ball. 'I've known for a while that *you* guys stink, but now I can smell *myself*. I don't care if it's in one of those fancy fountains – I need to get clean.'

Tick lifted up his arm and smelled his armpit. 'We do stink. Dude.'

'I don't,' Sofia said. 'But I'm starving.'

'I'm glad you think you smell so nice,' Paul said, stopping to study Sofia up and down. 'What's your secret?'

Sofia halted as well, folding her arms and returning the stare. 'I don't sweat.'

'You don't sweat?' Paul looked over at Tick. 'She doesn't sweat, Tick. Now I've heard everything.' He continued walking towards the centre of town, shaking his head.

Nothing much had changed since they'd left the border road and headed deeper into the city. The buildings had got a little bigger with fewer pillars and less frilly decoration. Apartments and condos had replaced the extravagant neighbourhood homes. The sun had sunk lower in the sky, the darkened glow of twilight fast approaching. None of the people they passed paid them much mind, despite their dirty clothes and haggard appearance. Everyone seemed extremely busy – all made-up and pressed clean.

'Look up there,' Sofia said, pointing straight ahead.

Less than quarter of a mile ahead of them, twelve roads came together like spokes of a wheel, intersecting in a huge open-air shopping centre where hundreds of people milled about. Tick realised something, and he couldn't believe he hadn't noticed it before. 'Where are all the cars?' he asked.

Sofia and Paul stopped, as if stunned by the simple question.

Paul snapped his fingers. 'I knew something was missing. We haven't seen a single car.'

'That doesn't make sense,' Sofia said. 'There's nothing primitive about this place. If anything, it seems a little more advanced than our reality.'

'Ah, dude,' Paul said. 'What if they beam around like in *Star Trek?*'

Sofia snorted. 'I'll be sure to ask Dark Gator if I see him.'

Paul burst out laughing; Tick held his laugh in, pressing his mouth closed.

'What?' Sofia said.

'What did you call him?' Paul asked.

'Dark Gator.'

'Man, oh, man, you are too good to be true, Miss Italy, too good to be true.' Still chuckling, he walked towards all the people. 'I think I see a restaurant up there. Let's check it out.'

Sofia looked at Tick, her eyebrows raised.

'It's Darth *Vader,*' he whispered. 'And he's from *Star Wars,* not *Star Trek.*'

'Well, they both sound stupid,' she concluded, then followed Paul.

The shopping centre was a collection of all sorts of shops and eateries, surround by a broad expanse of inlaid bricks. The three of them stopped to see which restaurant looked most appetising – assuming, of course, they accepted Reality Prime money. Tick's hopes were rising, because this place had some of the same fast-food chains as back home – their logos were just slightly different.

'Ooh, look–' Tick started to say, but a man stopped him by pulling on his elbow. Tick looked behind him to see a short, fidgety man with the worst comb-over Tick had ever seen.

'Excuse me,' the man said, his face breaking into a smile that would have looked more natural on a rattlesnake. 'Is your name, er, Atticus Higginbottom?'

Tick didn't know what he'd expected the man to say, but his mouth dropped open and his heart started thumping.

'Um,' he said, looking over at his friends to see if they'd heard. By the stunned looks on their faces, he figured they had. He turned back to the man. 'Yeah, I'm Tick, I mean, Atticus.'

'That's great, real great,' the man said, more relieved than happy. 'Someone named, um, Mothball asked me to find you and offer you rooms in my hotel, The Stroke of Midnight Inn. My name is Phillip, and I'm happy to accommodate you.'

Then he bowed. He actually bowed.

Tick felt immediately suspicious, and it only took a second for him to see his friends felt the same.

'Mothball sent you?' Sofia asked.

'Why didn't she come herself?' Paul added. Phillip pulled his head back, looking like a startled – albeit pudgy – chicken. 'I don't know – why would I make something like that up?'

'What does she look like?' Tick asked.

The man didn't hesitate. 'She's very tall – the tallest person I've ever laid eyes on. Black hair, thin, not very … well, what I mean to say is … well, she's a bit homely, to be honest.'

'A-plus on that quiz,' Paul muttered, and Tick felt himself relax a little.

'She said you'd be staying here for a week or so,' Phillip continued. 'She paid me in advance and asked me to provide you three meals a day, plus whatever else you might need.'

The prospect of a nice hotel room, a hot shower, and all the food he could eat sounded to Tick like the single best idea in the history of best ideas.

'Good enough for me,' Paul said. 'Where do we go?'

'Wait a minute,' Sofia said, holding out her hand. 'There has to be something else. There's no message, no reason, nothing? I don't like this.'

'Actually,' Phillip said, 'she did leave you an envelope. It's sealed, so of course I don't know its contents. Oddly enough, she asked me to give it to you at exactly six o'clock.' He looked at his watch. 'Um, tomorrow morning.'

Tick looked at his own watch – it was just past six-thirty. 'Sounds pretty legit to me. I actually feel a ton better – like maybe Master George is behind all of this after all.'

'Yeah,' Paul agreed. 'Let's go eat.'

Sofia didn't answer at first, her eyes distant as she thought it over. 'Where's the hotel?' she finally asked.

'Right this way,' Phillip said, stepping aside and sweeping his arm wide. 'If you'll follow me, it's on the edge of town. In fact, I've reserved rooms for you with a great view.'

As Phillip led the group north along the road, Paul asked, 'A view of what?'

'The forest, of course,' Phillip said without missing a step. 'If you look out your window after dark, you might see the glowing monkeys.'

Tick waited for the man to laugh, but the only one who did was Paul. Tick almost asked if he'd been serious, but with everyone else silent, he felt stupid for even thinking it. Of course the guy was kidding. Wasn't he?

THE TIME RIDDLE

The hotel was like something out of Hollywood. Big pillars, stamped gold everywhere, doormen in green velvet coats running around, treating their guests like royalty. A huge sign hung above the entrance with *The Stroke of Midnight Inn* written in fancy script. Inside, everything sparkled and shone, and not a person in sight had a grimace or the slightest hint of a frown. Plush red carpet blanketed the floors and grand staircase, over which an enormous chandelier hung with hundreds of crystalline lights.

I've died and gone to heaven, Tick thought.

He knew Paul must feel the same, but Sofia would surely find something to complain about, having come from such a rich family.

Phillip led them to the fourth floor – walking up the stairs, the poor man sucked in huge gasps of breath with every step – and down a long hallway to their rooms. When Paul asked him why they hadn't used the elevator, Phillip responded with a baffled look, as if he'd never heard of such a thing.

Phillip opened up a room with an old-fashioned key. Tick was surprised since he'd only ever seen the magnetic-stripe key card at hotels. The room was filled with normal hotel things: a king-sized bed, a small refrigerator, a couch, a desk, and a bathroom. The only difference was that the items were ten times nicer than the stuff in hotels Tick had been in when his family travelled.

'There are three rooms in all,' Phillip announced, passing out keys accordingly. 'There's a menu on the desk for you to order food from the restaurant. Please be reasonable, but make sure you feed yourself nicely. Is there anything–'

'Where's the TV?' Paul asked.

Phillip gave him that same bewildered look, his brow crunched up into dozens of wrinkles. 'A TV? What's that?'

'Television. You know – movies, shows, commercials, *television?*'

'Sorry, I don't know what you're talking about.'

Tick looked at the light on the wall, which Phillip had turned on when they'd entered the room. They obviously had electricity here, but seemed to be missing a lot of other things common to Reality Prime.

As if reading his mind, Sofia asked, 'Where are all the cars?'

Phillip put his hands in his pockets, his confused look morphing into suspicion. 'Cars have been banned for at least twenty years.'

'Banned?' Tick asked. 'Why?'

'And how do you get around?' Paul asked before Phillip could respond.

The hotel man shook his head, looking at his three guests in turn. 'When that ... when Mothball made me this deal, I didn't realise she'd be sending such odd people. Where are you kids from?'

'Florida,' Paul answered. 'Well, originally from California—'

Sofia cut him off. 'It doesn't matter. But we're curious about the cars. Where we come from, they still use them.'

'The darn things were polluting us to death,' Phillip said, still appearing uneasy as he rocked back and forth on his feet. 'So they banned them, made towns where everything was in walking distance. If you want to visit another town, you take the Underground Railroad – named after the lady who escaped the slave drivers a long time ago – the one who became president, Harrietta Tubben.'

Tick and Sofia exchanged baffled looks.

'So you've got trains, underground?' Paul asked.

'Fastest ones in the world,' Phillip answered, eyeing the door. 'If there's nothing else ...'

'Thanks for letting us stay here,' Tick said, liking the idea of seeing Phillip leave and finally ordering some food. 'Don't forget to bring us that message from Mothball.'

'I won't, I won't,' the man assured them, already backing out the door into the hallway. 'Order a nice dinner and get some rest.'

Tick closed the door before the last word made it all the way out of Phillip's mouth.

'Well,' Sofia said, 'this place is just like home compared to the last Reality – desert, glass tunnel, raging beast.'

'All I care about right now is food,' Paul said. He'd already picked up the phone to call room service.

※

Later that night, his stomach stuffed with roasted duck and asparagus (they didn't have pizza or hamburgers in this place), fully showered and clean, Tick lay in his bed and stared at the ceiling. Every ounce of his body begged for sleep, his mind deadened with exhaustion. And yet, he remained awake.

Man, I have a weird life.

He'd lost track of how long they'd been gone – it seemed like a month, but he knew it was only a few days, maybe a week at most. He knew his mom and dad were back home, worry eating at them like ferrets trapped in their gut, trying to stay chipper for Lisa and Kayla. Tick wished he could send them a message, talk to them somehow. Just to let them know he was okay.

A hard knock at his door made him jump. Crumpling up the sheets in his bed, he wiggled into a sitting position, his back pressed against the wall. He stared at the small space under the door, where two small shadows marked someone's feet.

'Who is it?' he called out, embarrassed at how shaky his voice sounded to his own ears.

'It's me, sleepyhead,' Paul replied, the words muffled through the wood.

Tick sighed with relief as he threw the covers aside. He hurried over and opened the door. Sofia was behind Paul, her eyes puffy with sleep. Each of them wore fancy-looking flannel pyjamas provided by the hotel, and Sofia's looked about three sizes too big.

'What's going on?' Tick asked.

'Dude, have you looked out the window?' Paul stepped into the room, pushing past Tick.

'Um, no.' Tick stepped aside to let Sofia in, then closed the door. He flicked on the light, but Paul quickly waved his hand at him.

'No, dude, turn it off!'

Tick did as he was told, grumbling a little. All he wanted right now was to be left alone and sleep for days. He felt so tired and his body hurt like he had the flu. The only light in the room was a mysterious panel on the wall that shone a dull yellow. Something about it gave Tick the creeps.

Paul leaned next to the window, carefully pulling aside the curtains to peek through the corner, as if spying on someone in the car park. Tick faltered as he joined Paul – this place didn't have a car park.

'What are you looking at?' Tick asked.

Sofia knelt at the other end of the window, lifting that corner of the curtains to peer out. The two of them looked ridiculous.

'Santy Claus,' Paul whispered. 'What do you *think* we're looking at?'

'I don't know – that's why I asked.'

Sofia turned towards Tick, the disgusted look on her face barely discernible in the faint light. 'The glowing monkeys.'

'Oh, yeah!' Tick couldn't believe he'd not even looked – a sign that his brain had gone to sleep even though his body had refused. He squatted on the floor between his friends and slowly lifted the bottom of the curtain to take a peek.

Outside, the dark forest stood like a fortress wall, massive trees silhouetted by the pale moonlight seeping through the thick clouds above. The city behind the hotel had a surprising lack of night-time lights, making Tick feel like they were in a cabin deep in the wilderness. And there in the woods, radiant and eerie and constantly in motion, dozens of creepy glowing shapes moved about the trees.

'Those don't look like monkeys,' Tick whispered. When he'd heard the word *glowing*, he'd imagined his old skeleton Halloween decoration back home, which appeared as a whitish-yellowish blur in the darkness. But this light was much different. This light was bright and stark and reddish, and the creatures looked a lot bigger than monkeys. 'They look more like ... radioactive bears.'

'Yeah,' Paul whispered back. 'Demon bears.'

'Why are you guys whispering?' Sofia said, so loud that both Tick and Paul quickly shushed her. 'What? You think those things will come and eat us? I'm pretty sure the hotel would've gone out of business if their customers were routinely eaten by monkeys whenever they spoke louder than a whisper.'

'I don't know,' Paul said, still in a low voice. 'Just seems like you should whisper when spying on monstrous, glowing creatures. So be quiet.'

'Pansy,' Sofia muttered, returning to the window.

Paul reached over and elbowed Tick. 'Did you teach her that word?'

'No.'

'She's getting way too American – makes me uncomfortable.'

Sofia tsked. 'I love it when you guys talk about me as if I can't hear you.'

'What do you think those things are?' Tick asked, trying to steer the conversation in a different direction before Paul ended up getting punched again.

'I bet it has something to do with the ban on cars,' Sofia said. 'Something really weird happened here. Maybe it affected the animals. Maybe they *are* radioactive.'

'Remind me not to go on a walk out there tomorrow after breakfast,' Paul said.

Tick let the curtain fall into place and leaned back against the bed. 'That's enough monkey-watching for me. Phillip's bringing us that message from Mothball in just a few hours. We need some sleep.'

'How can you sleep with psycho-radioactive-gorilla-bears playing outside your window?' Paul asked, his nose seemingly glued to the glass.

'I think I'll manage. Get out.'

Surprisingly, Sofia grumbled more than Paul did as Tick kicked them out of his room.

✿

The next morning, Phillip didn't pound the door nearly as hard as Paul had done just a few hours earlier. At first, the light tapping came in the form of a woodpecker in Tick's dream, one where he sat in the backyard laughing while his dad jumped about trying to put out flames on the barbecue. It happened every time the man made hamburgers, which is why Tick always made sure he had a front-row seat.

A woodpecker had never been there, however, and even in his dream, Tick knew something was wrong. When it kept knocking and pecking and tapping, he somehow pulled himself out of sleep. With groggy eyes and cottonmouth, he got out of bed and stumbled to the door, sad that the dream had been interrupted.

Phillip wore the exact same clothes as he had yesterday, still rocking back and forth on his feet. He handed over a yellow envelope – one that looked very familiar to Tick, who snatched it without meaning to.

'Sorry,' he said. 'Just eager to read it.'

'Are you finding your stay pleasant?' Phillip asked, no emotion or sincerity in his voice whatsoever.

'Yes, we really appreciate it,' Tick said, unable to take his eyes off the envelope, which bore no marking or writing. When he finally looked up, Phillip had already begun walking down the hall towards the stairs.

Thoughts of the odd man quickly evaporated as Tick hurried to knock on Paul's door. It took three tries, but Paul finally answered, rubbing his eyes. 'Come on,' Tick urged, heading next door to Sofia's room.

He'd just held up his hand to knock when the door flew open, Sofia waiting there – fully dressed in her newly provided clothes and looking surprisingly pretty. 'Did you get the note?'

Tick held up the envelope.

'Then get in here and let's open it,' she said, stepping aside and almost comically jerking her head towards the inside.

Tick entered and sat in the desk chair, with Paul looking over his right shoulder, Sofia his left. With slightly trembling hands, Tick opened the envelope and pulled out a piece of white cardstock paper. With the others following along, he read the typed words out loud:

This place is nice, but not quite heaven.
You must start on the hour of seven
Add six hours then take away three,
Then add ten more and do it with glee.
Let one week of time go by,
Sit and rest and eat and sigh.
Then twenty-two hours less three plus two,
At that time decide what to do.
It does not matter; I do not care.
Just make sure your feet find air.

'It's easy,' Sofia said.

'Yeah, too easy,' Paul agreed. 'Which means we're in deep trouble.'

Tick shook his head. 'It'll be easy to figure out the time, but there's nothing that tells us what to do *at* that time.'

'Yowza,' Paul said, then whistled. 'You're dead on. What are we supposed to do at five in the afternoon one week from tomorrow?'

Tick jerked his head around to look up at Paul. 'You already figured it out?'

'I told you it was easy.' He slapped Tick on the shoulder. 'Don't worry, little dude, not everyone can be as brilliant as the Paulmeister.'

Sofia snorted. 'I figured it out, too, Einstein.'

Tick quickly ran through the riddle in his head. Sure enough – 5:00 pm, one week from tomorrow.

'A whole week?' he said. 'What are we supposed to do until then?'

'I'll tell you what we do,' Paul said, flopping onto the small couch and sticking his feet up on the armrest. 'What my grandpa calls a little R and R.'

Sofia walked over and slapped Paul's feet to the floor, almost knocking his whole body off the couch.

'If you ever did that in my house, my butler would chop off one of your toes.' She sat next to him, ignoring his stuck-out tongue. 'It does sound good to relax for a while, but we'd better start thinking hard about what's hidden in that message.'

'Yeah,' Tick said. 'What happens if five o'clock rolls around and we don't do what we're supposed to?'

His only answer was a very long silence.

An Insane Mission

Sato adjusted the straps on his backpack, pulling them tight so they wouldn't rub blisters on his skin. It was heavy, Mothball and Rutger having gone overboard as usual to make sure he had everything he needed.

'What did you put in here?' he asked. They stood by the window overlooking the Grand Canyon, the early streams of sunrise reflecting off the sheer stone walls with a reddish glow. 'Some bricks in case I need to build a house?'

Mothball laughed. 'Methinks you've a sense of humour after all, Sato.' She reached down and tousled the hair on Rutger's head. 'Almost as funny as this one, 'ere.'

Rutger huffed. 'He only seems funny because he's the world's biggest grouch. Anything slightly different pops out of his mouth, and everyone laughs like he's Bojinkles the Clown.'

'Who?' Sato asked.

Rutger slapped his hands to his face. 'Who? *Who?*' He stomped his right foot. 'Don't tell me you haven't heard of Bojinkles! Oh, how he made me chuckle when I'd read him in the funny parcels as a kid ...'

His voice wandered off as he stared at something through the window, seemingly lost in childhood memories. Sato and Mothball exchanged a look, both of them stifling a laugh.

Just then, George entered the room, his face flushed like he'd been running a race. He held a Barrier Wand in one hand, so sparkly and shiny it appeared brand-new.

'Ah!' he said. 'Looks like Master Sato is all set and ready to go.'

George stepped in front of Sato, inspecting him like he was a soldier going off to war. Sato still felt confused inside, his mind and heart full of swirling, haunted images and feelings. He'd grown to trust George and the others, had grown to accept his role as a Realitant. He'd especially solidified his resolve to avenge the murder of his parents.

And yet … for so many years, the man before him had represented all the terrible things in his life.

George had been there that day. Why hadn't he saved his parents?

'Ready as I'll ever be,' Sato said, momentarily closing his eyes to squeeze away his ill thoughts.

'Splendid,' George said, taking a step back so he could look at the three of them. 'Our dear friend Sally is off, too. He, er, didn't want to say goodbye because of, er, well, you know – what we did to his hair to disguise him. The old chap's surprisingly vain about his looks after all.'

'Well, I *do* know how he feels,' Rutger said, smoothing his black hair.

George turned to Sato, his face serious, squinting as if he couldn't quite focus on Sato's face. 'Are you *certain* about this?'

'I'm doing this for my parents.'

George nodded absent-mindedly. 'Yes, yes, indeed. Your bravery would make them proud.'

Sato fumed inside. He wanted to scream at the old man, blame him for their deaths. But he stayed silent, channelling his thoughts into the task at hand.

'The needle and vials are in the outer pocket of your pack,' Rutger said. 'They're bubble-wrapped for protection, but please be careful. You have only a couple of extras.'

George grunted, but Sato wasn't sure what that meant. 'We want you to get in and get out. You'll be winking to the original Reality, the ... *host* Reality where all of this nonsense began. It's not one of the major branches, and it's fragmenting as we speak. Still not sure of the event that was so powerful as to make them completely unstable.' He shook his head. 'I need not remind you of the necessity of caution.'

'In and out,' Sato said, staring at the wall in front of him. An old picture of Muffintops hung there, a close-up from when she was a kitten, licking something that looked suspiciously like George's foot. 'The first crazy person I meet. No problem.'

Rutger cleared his throat. 'It might not be *that* easy. Most people won't let you walk up and stick a needle in them.'

''Specially the crazies,' Mothball added.

'Then I'll use the ... thing you gave me.' Sato jerked his head towards the top of his backpack.

'Only as a last resort,' George said, holding up a finger. 'A last resort.'

Sato shrugged. 'Last resort. What does it matter – they're all crazy.'

'It matters because we're trying to *save* them, find a cure,' George answered.

'But it's a fragmented Reality,' Sato countered. 'Again, what does it matter?'

George shook his head. 'It's not our place to determine the value of their lives, Master Sato. They're people, just like you and me.'

'Chances are one of 'em *is* you, actually,' Mothball said with a quick snort of a laugh. When no one responded, she continued, 'His Alterant. Get it?'

'Yes, Mothball, we got it,' Rutger muttered as he shot a look at Sato as if to say, *just humour her.* 'Good one, very funny.'

As for Sato, his head spun; it was impossible to wrap his rational mind around the confusing facts of how the multiverse functioned. 'I'm ready. Wink me away.'

George held up the Barrier Wand in both hands. 'You'll appear on the stone outcropping of a mountain; it's soaked in Chi'karda, for reasons we don't know. Return there when you've obtained the blood sample. Rutger will have his eyes glued to the command console and will wink you back the instant you're ready. Your nanolocator is in good working condition.'

'Okay,' Sato said, taking a deep breath as he reached out and clasped his hands around the bottom of the golden cylinder. *Just do it before I change my mind.*

'Best of lu–' Mothball started to say, but she was cut off with the click of the Wand ignition button.

Sato winked away.

☼

'Mmm, this rabbit food ain't so bad,' Paul mumbled through a bite of fancy salad – walnuts and pears scattered over dark green leaves.

They sat at a table in the hotel restaurant, the last gloomy glow of sunset painting the large windows a sleepy amber. They'd spent most of the day walking, making three complete trips around the main road that circled the town – aptly named Circle City. They saw nothing new – more buildings, more nicely-dressed people, more glittering fountains, more eerie opera music – as they discussed the riddle and the possible hidden meaning behind it between long bouts of silence.

'This Reality must not have an Italy,' Sofia said. 'Nothing on the menu even comes close to real food.'

Tick nodded, too busy eating to say anything.

He'd ordered something he couldn't pronounce but which looked and tasted like pork chops, and he was loving every bite. Sofia, stubborn as usual, hadn't even ordered yet, still staring at the menu like an impossible homework problem.

'Just get the chicken stuff,' Paul said, wiping his mouth. 'They eat chicken in Italy, don't they?'

'Well ...' Sofia said, her eyes focusing on one item. 'This one does have some kind of cheese on it.'

'Really?' Paul said, leaning over to take a look at where her finger pointed. 'Chicken and cheese. I'm getting that next time.'

Tick stopped listening to them, having noticed a strange man enter the restaurant, looking about as if he were lost. He was heavily built, head shaved bald, and dressed in a suit as fancy as any Tick had ever seen worn by Master George. The man's eyes finally fell on Tick and his friends, and he started walking directly for them, stumbling twice in his polished new shoes.

'Uh-oh,' Tick whispered. When Paul and Sofia looked at him, he nodded towards the stranger.

'Who's that guy?' Paul asked. Tick only shrugged.

When the man reached their table, he bowed awkwardly. 'Good ... day,' he said very slowly, taking time to carefully pronounce each word. 'I ... welcome ... you ... to ... our ... city.'

He bowed again, then turned to walk away. As he took his first step, he reached into his pocket, pulled out a slip of paper, and let it fall to the floor. It was such an obvious act that none of them called it to the man's attention. He kept moving, continuing in his halting gait until he'd left the restaurant, never once turning around to look back.

Paul practically jumped onto the floor to pick up the paper, then unfolded it on the table. Tick and Sofia scooted their chairs around to see the message:

DO NOT READ THIS ALOUD!
I'm a friend of Master George.
Meet me in Tick's room at 9:00.

Don't say a word to me.
We must communicate in writing.
People are listening.

☼

The first thing Sato felt was frigid air, gusting in short bursts of wind that bit through his clothes, pricking his skin like dagger points. Feeling as if he'd just plunged into an icy lake, he gasped for air as he swung off his backpack and searched for the thick down coat within. As he pulled it out and stuffed his arms inside the soft, warm lining, he gaped at the place George had decided to send him.

The highest reaches of an enormous mountain, blanketed in snow.

He stood near the edge of a rocky outcropping that overlooked an infinite expanse of clouds, thin peaks of smaller mountains thrusting through the cottony layer here and there, black stone frosted in white. Above him, the sky was deep and dark and blue, like an ocean hanging impossibly over him. Realising how high up he was, Sato stumbled backwards, falling into the soft snow. The world seemed to sway around him.

He scrambled up and turned his back to the cliff, brushing the snow off before the cold stuff melted and soaked through. To his left, a steep path led up the mountain, the barely visible steps of roughly cut stone glistening with ice. If that was the way he needed to go, it would be a treacherous journey. Other than a sparse bush and a few dead trees, he saw no sign of life anywhere – just endless rock and ice and snow.

Sato took a few steps to the right, hoping to see a more reasonable trail he could follow, but the jutting slice of rock ended in a sheer, knife-edge cliff, as if a recent earthquake had sent a huge chunk of the mountain falling to its splitting, crumbled death far below.

There was only one way to go.

Securing his pack, he started up the ancient stairway. He placed his feet very carefully, bracing them against the small vertical slab of stone marking the next step. Just when he thought he had the hang of it, his left foot slid backwards, throwing his whole body forward;

his chest slammed into a jutting edge of rock. Holding back a cry of pain, he chastised himself and took more care, leaning forward to grip the stairs above him with his hands, as if he were climbing a ladder.

The wind picked up, throwing spurts of snow into his face like cold, rough sand. The sun, though unhindered by clouds above him, failed to provide even a spark of warmth. He had to stop every few minutes to blow warm air into his cupped hands, rubbing them together to create friction. His ears and face grew numb. He looked up, hoping to see signs of life, a building, anything. Nothing.

He kept going, step by frigid step.

Half an hour went by. Sato started to worry that George had made a serious mistake, sent him to an abandoned nowhere by accident.

'George,' he spoke aloud, though the wind seemed to snap his words out of the air and whisk them away. 'If you can hear me through the nanolocator – what's going on? I'm freezing to death!'

Half-hoping he'd be winked away, Sato kept moving up the stairs.

Forty or fifty steps later, he finally saw the end of the staircase – a place where the stone stopped and all was white, a wall of snow and ice reaching for the sky. His heart sank at the thought that he might've reached a dead end.

Legs burning, limbs aching, skin frozen, he reached the uppermost step, which led out onto a small landing that faced a solid wall of dark granite, crystalline icicles hanging from the brief canopy of rock that protected it. In the middle of the wall was an iron door, ridges of rusty bolts lined around its outer edges. On the door was a sign, faded letters barely legible in the awful weather conditions.

Sato took a few steps forward to read the sign, his eyes squinted. They widened when he realised what it said:

END OF THE ROAD INSANE ASYLUM MOUNTAINTOP EXIT
TO BE USED FOR THE EXECUTION OF INMATES ONLY

Cotton Ears

No one said a word, their eyes glancing at the clock every few seconds. In eight minutes, it would be nine o'clock – when they expected the visitor.

Tick sat on the bed, his back resting on a stack of pillows he'd pushed against the wall. In his mind, he'd been picturing the stranger who'd dropped off the note, trying to decide if they'd ever met. There was something vaguely familiar about him, but all Tick could remember was how strange the man acted, sounding out each word and looking about nervously.

Three minutes to go.

'What do you thin–' Paul whispered, but Sofia punched him on the arm, then made a slashing gesture at her neck. Paul winced as he rubbed his shoulder.

They'd been dying to talk about the note since dinner, but paranoia kept their mouths shut – except for the occasional slip-up from Paul. The stranger's message said people were listening, and now Tick couldn't sneeze without wondering what the snoopers might think. If the note was even true in the first place.

A barely discernible click sounded as the big hand on the old-fashioned clock struck nine. All three of them turned their heads towards the room's door, as if expecting the stranger to walk in precisely on time. He didn't.

Several minutes went by with no sign of their visitor. Paul finally got out of his chair and paced the floor, shaking his head and mumbling something under his breath. He stopped at the desk and wrote a few words on the pad of paper provided by the hotel, then tore the piece off and showed it to Sofia. She shrugged, and then Paul brought it over to Tick.

Don't we seem suspicious sitting here and not saying anything?

Tick nodded, but didn't know what else they could do. If people were really spying on them, they'd certainly be alarmed at how silent their prey had become.

I wish the guy would just hurry up and get here, Tick thought.

Paul sat back down in his chair. A few more minutes passed. A shadow crossed over the small slit under the door, catching Tick's attention out of the corner of his eye. He shifted on the bed and put his feet on the floor, leaning forward, expecting to hear a knock.

Nothing.

Tick exchanged questioning looks with Paul and Sofia, then got up and walked over to the door. It didn't have a peephole, so Tick reached forward and slowly pushed down on the lever handle. A loud *click* filled the room like a clap of thunder; he squeezed his eyes shut, not even sure what he was afraid of.

After a few seconds of silence, he jerked the door open and looked into the hallway, ready to slam it shut again at any sign of trouble.

The stranger from the restaurant sat on the red-carpeted floor, his back against the opposite wall. He still wore the dark suit, his shoes so shiny that the hallway light reflected off them and into Tick's eyes. As soon as he saw Tick, he put his right index finger to his lips – a reminder they weren't supposed to talk.

Feeling uneasy, but unsure what else they could do, Tick stepped back and opened the door wide, gesturing with a sweep of his arm that the stranger should come in. The large man – bald head and all – got to his feet and entered the room, giving a quick nod to Paul and Sofia. Tick closed the door as quietly as he could.

The man sat on the bed, waving for the others to come and stand around him. As Tick and his friends obeyed, the stranger pulled out a photograph, a few pieces of paper, and a ballpoint pen. He'd already written one note and handed it to Tick along with the picture. In it, the man stood with Master George in front of the fireplace at the Grand Canyon Realitant complex, both of them with wide smiles; Muffintops perched on the mantle behind Master George's right shoulder.

The message was clear: they could trust the guy.

Paul and Sofia crowded closer as they read the note together:

Your nanolocators done been hijacked. And this hotel is bugged like a bugger.
It's not Master George winking you willy-nilly.
Reginald Chu is behind everything.
You MUST keep passing that sucker's tests.

At first, Tick felt like he was reading Spanish or French or Chinese – the words didn't click inside his brain. Such a monumental statement surely couldn't be said in a quickly scribbled note. He looked at the stranger, knowing his face showed the confusion he felt.

Master George's friend rolled his eyes and wrote another message, hastily scratching the paper with the pen. Then he held it up for them to read:

> You've been under the control of Reginald Chu all
> along. He's testing you. Not Master George.
> It's Chu – it's all been Chu.

Something shuddered in Tick's chest; the room swayed. Losing his balance, he stumbled backwards, falling into the chair where Paul had been sitting earlier.

Everything they'd just been through ... the pain they'd felt in the forest, the riddles, the metaspides, the weird tunnel with its beast? All of it had been orchestrated by *Reginald Chu?* They'd suspected all along it wasn't Master George, but Chu? The man Rutger called the most evil in the universe?

'How–' Sofia said, then snapped her lips closed. Tick felt like he was watching from a distance, the room still spinning. He kept picturing Mr. Chu, his science teacher, appearing in the woods, filthy and acting crazy. Had that really been him? Or had it been *Reginald* Chu from the Fourth Reality? Were they Alterants of each other? Was it possible they were the same person?

When Tick had been a small boy, he'd fallen off a ride at the water park, dozens of feet in the air. If he hadn't landed on the pile of large rafting tubes, he would have smacked into the cement and been one dead kid.

It had taken him weeks to get over that "too close for comfort" feeling.

That was exactly how he felt now. To know they'd come so close to being killed by the metaspides and the tunnel monster scared him. What if they hadn't figured out the name of the pub where they escaped by sitting in that chair? What if they'd left the red square in the glass tube? How would things have turned out if they'd *known* someone so sinister was behind it all?

Tick leaned back in his chair, staring at the stranger on the bed as if the man could read his thoughts, expecting him to answer everything.

The man nodded, seeming to understand the shocking news he'd brought. He scribbled a few sentences on another piece of paper then handed it to Sofia. Tick and Paul leaned over to see:

By the way, I thought you'd done recognised me. It's Sally – ain't my shaved head a beaut? Don't worry, I'll explain purtin' near everything. But you gotta trust me for a minute.

As soon as Tick read it, he knew it was true. The guy sitting on the bed was Sally, head and beard shaved, dressed in disguise. But the thing that made Tick's mouth drop open was the realisation that *Sally* was a Realitant.

'You've gotta be kidding–' Paul whispered. He stopped when Sally shook his head curtly, holding a finger to his lips again.

Sally stood, holding his hands out, palms forward as if to say, *Hold on – give me a second.* Then he reached into the inner pocket of his suit coat and pulled out a small white box – the type in which you'd expect to find a necklace or bracelet, laid out all nice and pretty on a piece of velvet. He knelt down on the floor, placing the box gingerly on the bed, eyeing it like a ticking bomb he needed to disarm.

Paul elbowed Tick, then raised his eyebrows. Tick shrugged and quickly looked back.

Sally reached over and pulled off the top of the box, scooting as far back as he could.

Something shot out of the box and into the air – Tick lost track of it before he could tell what it was. An odd thump filled the air, like the sound of a distant thunderclap. Tick reached up and rubbed his ears; they felt like someone had stuffed cotton balls in them. He heard a faint buzz, like static on the radio.

Sally stood up, folded his arms, then grinned with satisfaction.

'Finally! Dadgum thing actually worked,' he said. 'George ain't never failed before – I reckon one of these days I'll quit doubtin' the old feller. But I didn't wanna whip that sucker out 'til you knew who I was. We can talk now.'

Tick didn't say a word – neither did his friends. The last few minutes had been so strange, so … *weird,* what were they *supposed* to say?

Sally laughed, a deep rumble that Tick swore shook the building. 'You three look as twitterpated as a racoon done found itself fallen in the outhouse bucket. Right diddly-widdly, I ain't never seen such a sight before. What ya'll a-feared of? I had to play dress-up so Chu wouldn't get all suspicious-like. Spies and such about, ya know.'

Still, none of them responded. Tick blinked, then swallowed. Then he blinked again.

'Snap out of it!' Sally roared. 'We ain't got no time to sit here throwin' peepeyes. I got to hurry and gets myself on outta here.'

Sofia was the first one to speak. 'It's just, well, we didn't … we didn't know you were a Realitant.'

'Not to mention the news you just dropped in our laps,' Paul added. 'I think I'm gettin' too old for this stuff.'

'Nonsense,' Sally said, sitting on the bed and crossing his legs. As soon as he did, he winced and put both feet back on the floor. 'Never did get how dem fancy lads like George sit that way. Yipes.'

The static-laced buzzing sound still filled the air; Tick rubbed his ears again. 'Why is it okay to talk now? What was in the box?'

Sally huffed. 'Boy, you think I got da first nary a clue what dat dang thing was? Round dem Realitant parts, I'm known for my brawn and grits-cookin', not much on da brains. Ol' George said pop that sucker open – called it a dang ol' airborne nano whatchamerbucket – and we can talk. I done did it, and here I sit, talkin' my silly head off, and we ain't got nowhere fast.'

Tick took a deep breath before he'd realised it – a sigh of relief. Maybe the world wasn't over after all.

'Sounds like you have a lot to tell us,' Sofia said. Sally nodded. 'Reckon so. Good gravy on raw beef, I ain't got a clue where to git to start yappin' on.'

Tick felt like he understood about one third of what came out of Sally's mouth, but he liked him all the same. 'Just start from the beginning. How'd you find us in that weird place with the metal spiders? And what's going on with Reginald Chu?' Saying the name slammed a fist of reality back into Tick's gut, and his temporary good mood soured.

'All right, den.' Sally shifted on the bed until his back was up against the wall. 'Ya'll git yerselves comfy, and I'll tell ya every last bit I got in dis here noggin. Ain't much, mind ya, but listen up anyhow.'

Sally started talking.

26

NEEDLES

Sato didn't know what else to do – he pounded on the huge metal door of the icy alcove with his fist. A deep, hollow boom echoed down the rocky mountainside. Sato shook his hand, needles of pain vibrating through his cold skin after the impact.

No one answered at first, though Sato hadn't really expected them to. His theory that George might have made a mistake had taken root, entrenching itself deeper into his heart, sickening him. Freezing to death didn't sound like the best way to go.

But it wasn't long before something scraped on the other side of the door, followed by a loud clunk of metal against metal. Sato stepped back as the door slowly swung inwards, the wind blowing wispy trails of snow into the dark interior of the mountain. He braced his feet, held his hands up in defence, not having any idea of what might lunge at him from the gloom.

'What's that?' a raspy voice called out. A pale face appeared, ghoulish with sunken cheeks, like a ghost peeking from beyond the grave. 'What's that, I say?' The man's whitish eyes darted about. Sato was surprised the light from outside wasn't blinding him.

'I'm ...' Then it hit Sato – he had absolutely no idea what to say. 'I ... my name is Sato, and I'm looking for someone.'

'What's that?' the man repeated, stepping forward to reveal his whole body – rail-thin with tattered, filthy clothes hanging on by threads. His eyes still hadn't settled on Sato. 'Lookin' for someone, are ya? What, you one of them Snarkies? Come to help, have you? No help for the Loons – too late for that, I can promise ya.'

The initial shock of seeing an insane asylum on top of a mountain having finally worn off, Sato's hopes lifted. George had sent him to the perfect place to find people who'd gone crazy. Now, if he could just get inside, get a blood sample, and get out. But how would he know if his target patient was *normal* crazy or Reginald-Chu-plague-infected crazy?

Sato felt his courage building. 'I'm looking for someone. I want to visit him. He's one of the people who got sick recently – went insane from the new plague that's been going around.'

'What's that?' the man said, spittle flying from his mouth. 'Plague? There's a plague about?'

'Haven't you had a lot of people brought in recently?' Sato asked, trying to fight off the shivers that racked his body.

'Don't know 'bout brought in.' The man pointed to the treacherous stairs leading down the face of the mountain. 'But an awful lot brought *out,* if ya catch my meanin'.'

Sato turned to look at the stone steps, thinking about the man's words. The sign stated this door was for the execution of inmates – did that mean they threw them off the knife-edged cliff below? Sato felt his stomach twist.

He faced the man again. 'May I *please* come in? I'm freezing to death out here.'

'Right, in ya go,' the poor excuse for a guard replied, stepping back and opening the door until it bumped against the stone wall inside. 'Beats me how ya got here in the first place, but in ya go, nice and toasty. Lots of Loons in here – not much hope of findin' your mate, I can tell ya that. Name's Klink, by the way.'

Sato stepped through the doorway, trying not to show his eagerness too much. 'Nice to meet you, uh, Klink.' Though *toasty* wasn't exactly the word Sato would use to describe the air inside, it sure beat the frigid bite of the outside.

Klink walked down the long, dark tunnel; Sato followed, listening, observing.

'Can't say as I've ever had a stranger knock on that door before,' Klink said. 'Only when the Cleaners come back after droppin' some Loons, that's all. Quite nice to have a visitor after all these years.'

'They throw crazy people off that cliff down there?' Sato asked. 'When they do something bad or what?'

'If they've done somethin' bad, or grown too old, or if they just need more room – whatever tickles them Cleaners' fancy. They ain't too particular when it comes to shovin' off the Loons, ya know.'

They reached the end of the hallway where a small opening led through the stone to a sparsely decorated room: a floor rug, a chair, a filthy mattress. An old kerosene lamp flickered as it burned, somehow making the pathetic place look welcoming.

'Spend most of my days here,' Klink said, looking around with his hands on his hips, proud of his homestead. 'Beats the socks off where I used to live, that's for sure. If anyone ever offers ya to live in a cave full of flying rats, I recommend you say no thanks and move right along.'

'I'll remember that,' Sato half-mumbled.

'Want to sit a spell? Take a blink or two?'

Sato shook his head. 'No, I feel much better now that we're inside. Could you take me to where they keep the inmates locked up? Maybe where they have the more recent ones?'

'Right, come on then,' Klink said, moving along the hall again. They reached a metal grid door, which he slid open, a horrible screech piercing Sato's ears. On the other side, a boxy elevator awaited.

'This lift will take you all the way down to the Loons,' Klink said as he gestured for Sato to enter. 'Down ya go, then.'

Sato, fighting his uneasiness, stepped inside and turned to face Klink just as the man slid the grid door shut. His pale eyes peeked through the slits.

'Best stay on your toes,' Klink said.

'What do you mean?' Sato replied.

Klink reached through a large space in the door – mangled and jagged like it had been ripped out with teeth – and slammed a lever inside the lift towards the floor. The elevator lurched and slowly started going down, the squeaks and squeals of chains and pulleys filling the air.

'Didn't you know?' As Klink's body seemed to move upwards, he called down to Sato just before he was out of sight. 'Ent no one locked up 'round here!'

✸

The trip down the dark elevator shaft was long and cold – especially in light of Klink's pronouncement that the crazies weren't locked up at all. Sato's stomach turned queasy from the jostling and bumping of the steel cage. He saw nothing outside the mesh of metal but black stone, heard nothing but the screech of the lift's mechanics. Impossibly, the seconds stretched into minutes, and he thought Klink surely must have sent him to the middle of the Earth.

Without any hint of slowing down, the elevator jolted to a stop, making Sato's knees buckle. He sprawled across the cold mesh floor, biting his tongue when his chin slammed into the hard surface. He quickly pushed himself back to his feet, rubbing his jaw as he stepped forward to look through the lift door.

Another dimly lit carved passageway led into the distance, no sign of anyone nearby. Having expected someone to greet him – crazy or not – he warily reached out to test the sliding door. It pushed aside easily, groaning as Sato slammed the metal mesh all the way open. The sound of the squeal echoed off the stone walls, and any doubt of his arrival was now wiped away. But still, no one came.

He stepped out of the lift, his eyes focused along the dark tunnel since that seemed to be the only place from which someone could appear. He took another step. Another.

And then he heard a scream.

It started low, an eerie moan that rose in pitch, escalating quickly on the creepy scale to a perfect ten. Sato stopped moving to listen, the hairs on his neck stiff as arrows. The sound was the wail of a lost child mixed with the terrified squeal of an animal in the butchering house. The effect of it bouncing off the walls made it seem like it was coming from every direction at once. Sato felt like getting back into the steel cage of the lift and going back up to safety.

The sound stopped, slicing silent as quickly as if someone had turned off a loud television. Shouts rang out, several voices yelling something incomprehensible – but Sato could clearly hear the anger and the *lunacy* in the voices. Sato's wariness turned into downright terror.

He closed his eyes, breathed, worked to calm himself. His heartbeat slowed; the blood in his veins stopped acting like it was trying to find a way to escape. After a full minute, he opened his eyes and took off his backpack. He rummaged around its contents until he found the packet containing the blood sample kit. There were three syringes in case one of them broke, each with a very long and nasty-looking needle covered with a plastic sheath to prevent unwanted pokes. He'd never been fond of injections, and the sight of the needles made him thankful he'd not be the one getting stuck.

Sato set the syringes on the stone floor, then looked back at the elevator, checking to make sure he knew how it worked. Just inside the cage, the lever Klink had used jutted out of a dented box of rusty steel, slanted towards the ground.

Sato entered the elevator, gripped the lever with both hands, and lifted; he groaned and felt blood rush to his face until the lever finally gave way and snapped up. With a loud clunk the elevator started moving upwards. Sato quickly slammed the switch back down. The steel cage jolted to the floor with a metallic boom.

Some escape route, he thought.

He stepped out of the elevator, slung the backpack onto his shoulders, then very carefully put two of the syringes in his left jeans pocket, making sure not to push down on them. The other he held in his right hand, gripped like a dagger, and removed the protective plastic covering. Having no idea what he was about to get into, he had to be ready for quick action. *Stab, extract, run,* he thought.

His only problem – other than perhaps being mauled to death by a bunch of crazy people – was knowing which of the asylum inmates were infected with Chu's mysterious disease and which were simply crazy. They probably wouldn't be too keen on chit-chatting about it.

Blowing a breath through his lips, Sato walked forwards.

A SAMPLE OF BLOOD

'All righty den,' Sally said after taking a long swallow from his water glass. He set it down on the nightstand, then turned his eyes towards Tick. 'Your turn.'

Sally had made Paul and Sofia summarise in their own words what he'd come to tell them. He said it was to make sure the gist of it got "nailed up in dem there noggins a'yorn." As the weight of Sally's information settled on their shoulders, Tick at least felt some ease in knowing more about what lay behind the craziness of the last few days.

He put his right foot up on his left knee. 'Well, we were supposed to be winked to the Realitant Headquarters at the Grand Canyon for a meeting about the weird stuff Reginald Chu is up to. But before that could happen, Chu tricked us and put a device on our arms that hijacked our nanolocators.'

'Which means what, now?' Sally asked, his eyebrows raised.

'That Reginald Chu controls us now. He can track us and wink us wherever he wants to. And there's not a thing anyone can do about it.'

Sally shook his head in disgust. 'Purtin' near one

of da worst things I reckon a man can do. Matter-fact, breakin' Rule Number 462 bans you from dem there Realitants 'til the day you is deader than a squirrel on a tyre's underbelly.'

'Hey, let Tick finish,' Sofia said. 'We need to make sure we all understand everything you told us.'

'Fair 'nuff,' Sally said.

'Anyway,' Tick continued, 'you said it looks like Chu is testing us and some other people to see who's most worthy to help him in a secret project he's working on. And the project has something to do with a disease or plague that's making people go crazy in some of the Realities.'

Tick paused, not really wanting to say the next part.

'Get on wid it,' Sally prodded.

'Master George wants us to keep going. He wants *us* to be the ones who make it. He wants us to win Chu's contest. It's the only way we can make sure the Realitants get there to stop it – whatever it is.'

After a long pause, Paul said, 'You're the man, Tick. Took Sofia about three hours to say what you just said.'

'Well,' Tick said, 'that's pretty much it, isn't it? We have to keep going, even though it seems like Chu doesn't care if we make it or die trying. Not that much fun to think about, let alone talk about.'

Sofia stood up from her chair and walked to the window, where she parted the curtain just enough to peek out. 'This is so creepy. It was bad enough knowing Master George tracked us last year. Now we've got some power-hungry mad scientist controlling our lives. There has to be a way to get rid of those nanolocators, right?'

'Then you'd be missing the point,' Paul said. 'Which is shocking considering how long you took to talk about it.'

'I'm not missing the point,' Sofia said as she turned back towards the group. 'Even if we could get rid of them, we wouldn't because we need to keep pretending that we're trying to win.'

'Not only that,' Tick said. 'We need Chu to think we don't know he's behind it all.'

'Dang, you kids are plumb smart,' Sally said. 'When I's a youngun like you, I was happier than a crawdaddy at high tide if I could add up my own two feet.'

'I think you're wrong, Tick,' Paul said, ignoring Sally. 'I don't think Chu gives one flip about what we know. He seems like a ruthless dude who doesn't care jack-squat about rules or whatever. All he cares about is who's standing at the end. It doesn't matter how we get there.'

'Maybe,' Tick said. 'But it still seems smarter to play along as much as we can.'

'Say we do make it,' Sofia asked, sitting on the corner of the bed, addressing Sally. 'What are we supposed to do once we get there?'

Sally nodded, pausing a long time before he answered. 'Dat there's a dang ol' good question, miss. I reckon George is tryin' to figger dat one out as we sit here talkin'.'

'What are *you* going to do?' Paul asked.

'I'll be gettin' on back to the homestead,' Sally said, rubbing his hands together. 'Ya'll keep mosin' along on dis here joyride, and I'll come find ya when we's got further word.'

'How are you going to find us? How *did* you find us?' Tick asked.

'I'd reckoned you woulda done asked me dat. Took me forever to find ya the first time 'cuz the signal was weak. But don't you remember me shovin' my finger in ya ear?'

Tick couldn't have forgotten. 'Yeah, what was that for?'

'I put one of dem fancy Earwig Transponder thingamajigs in there. Now George can track ya better and stifle some of dem spyin' devices inside ya.'

Tick reached up and rubbed his ear, then poked his index finger in as deep as it would go. 'You put *what* in my ear?'

'Doncha fret, now,' Sally said. 'Ain't like it's gonna eat your dang ol' brain or nuttin'.'

Tick was about to protest further when someone rapped on the door with a hard and urgent knock. Sofia and Paul jumped to their feet. Sally moved faster than Tick would have believed – running to the door and yanking it open in a matter of two seconds.

No one stood there, but a note had been stuck to the door with a piece of clear tape. Sally ripped it off, read through the words, then walked over and handed it to Tick.

'Read it,' Sally said. 'I'm goin' to look for the rat who left it.' He left the room, marching like he was going off to war.

Tick shot a glance at Paul and Sofia, then read the note to them. '"You people must think I'm an idiot. But I know everything. Everything. The sooner you accept that, the better. The game is on. Win or die."' Tick paused, swallowed. '"Sincerely, Reginald Chu."'

No one said a word for the longest time. Finally, Sofia spoke: 'Looks like you were right, Paul.'

Win or die, Tick thought. *Win or die.*

✸

The sounds grew louder – and more haunting – as Sato made his way down the long tunnel. A man screaming as if going through a horrible surgery without anaesthetic. People arguing, their words impossible to make out. Someone crying. *Lots* of people crying. Mumbling, moaning, retching. Sato couldn't imagine anything worse than being in this place.

The roughly carved walls of the tunnel were dark and shiny, wet with rivulets and flat streams of water sluicing down its sides, disappearing into cracks on the floor. Odd lamps were set into the stone about every thirty feet; filthy glass surrounding a milky light that seemed a mix of old-fashioned wicks and electric sparks. Sato fully expected to see rats scurrying about, but thus far had seen no sign of life.

Just the sounds. The terrible, terrible sounds.

Up ahead, the tunnel made a turn to the right, a somewhat brighter light glowing from that direction. Huddled on the floor was a woman, her face draped in shadow, clutching her legs to her chest, shivering and mumbling the same phrase over and over. Sato couldn't quite make out the words.

His heart pounded as he walked towards the woman, sweat making the syringe clasped in his right hand slippery; he hid it behind his back. Was she infected? Could it be this easy? He stopped a few feet in front of her, thinking about each breath, trying to slow his heart down.

'Excuse me,' he said, his voice breaking on the second word. He cleared his throat. 'Excuse me, I'm looking for someone.'

The woman looked up; Sato took a step backwards. He didn't know what he'd expected to see – someone hideous, scarred, a wart-infested witch, maybe – but the lady sitting in front of him was very pretty. She had perfect skin, and blue eyes that shone like crystals in the pale light. Her dark hair sprawled across her shoulders. White teeth flashed behind her still-moving lips, uttering the indecipherable words repeatedly.

Despite her pleasant looks, she looked sad, tear streaks lining both cheeks.

'Can you help me?' Sato said, fingering the syringe hidden from her sight. He took a step closer.

The woman finally fell silent, pressing her lips together. Then she spoke, her voice soft but firm. 'We're only crazy when he's not in our heads.'

Sato reached for words to reply. The lady's eyes showed no lunacy, no fear, no confusion. She seemed perfectly sane.

'What do you mean?' he finally asked.

'My name is Renee,' she replied, ignoring his question. 'But right now he *is* in my head, and I will do whatever he says.'

'I don't know what you mean,' Sato said, taking a step back.

Renee stood up. Her beauty shone despite tattered, dirty garments. She was short and thin, but held herself with confidence – back straight, shoulders square, chin up.

'Why has George sent you here?' she asked.

Sato took another step backwards, this time bumping into the stone wall across from the woman. 'How ... how do you kno–'

'Stop acting the fool, young man. I know everything. I'm Reginald Chu, and I find it very interesting that you've come here, to this strange place, with a syringe in your hand. *Why?*'

Sato pulled his right hand from behind his back, looking down at it as if ashamed. He didn't know which felt worse right then – his head or his stomach. 'I don't understand. What do you mean you're Reginald Chu?'

'I think I'm the one who doesn't understand,' Renee replied. 'George seems to know so much about my project, yet here you stand, without the slightest clue of the danger you are in. How can you trust such a leader?'

'Nothing you say makes sense.'

'Everything I say makes sense.' Renee crossed the short span of the tunnel, stopping directly in front of Sato. 'Once I have my partner, once Dark Infinity is fully functional, you'll understand. The Realities are about to have a great change, my friend.'

Sato swallowed, trying to build his courage. 'You're crazy, lady. You think Reginald Chu is controlling you somehow. Don't you see how crazy that is? You need help.'

'I told you,' Renee said with a sneer. 'We're not crazy until he leaves our heads.'

'My boss – he thinks he can find a cure for you. If you'll just let me ...' He held the syringe up, raising his eyebrows in question.

'A cure?' Renee backed off two steps, shaking her head. 'A *cure?* Does that man think I'm a toady research assistant at some underfunded university? He thinks he's going to stop me with a *cure?* He'll cure cancer, Parkinson's, diabetes, and regenerate amputated limbs before he'll stop Dark Infinity.'

Confusion swarmed like a pack of bees inside Sato's head. The lady really and truly thought she was Reginald Chu. And it worried Sato that he was sliding towards that same belief as well. 'What *is* Dark Infinity?'

Renee folded her arms. 'As they say in your Reality, that's on a need-to-know basis and you don't need to know. A cure. Ha.' She barked a laugh.

'If you're so confident, why not give me a blood sample? And then I'll leave.'

Renee held out her hand to him. 'Come with me,' she said. 'I want to give you a taste of what Dark Infinity will become. And then I want you to go back and report it to your buffoon of a leader. All the Realitant do-gooders can then have fun dreading the day I take over their lives.'

Sato shook his head. 'Give me a sample first. Then I'll go.'

Renee stared at him for a long minute, her blue eyes seeming to glow. 'You're brave for someone so young. Maybe you should have been included in my special trials. Of course, I need a lot more than bravery – too bad you're not more like your friend Atticus Higginbottom.'

Sato almost fell to the ground at the mention of Tick. This lady had no way, absolutely no way of knowing anything about Tick or the strange ability he'd displayed in the Thirteenth Reality. 'How do you know about him?'

'Come with me.' She beckoned again with her hand.

'The sample first.' Sato wiped sweat from his brow, thinking too late how much weakness the action probably showed. 'You said yourself there's no way George can find a cure.'

'Yes, I did say that. But I'm not an idiot – I won't take chances. This isn't some lame movie from your Hollywood.'

Sato steeled his nerves. 'I'm not going anywhere until you give me a blood sample. You may think you have Reginald Chu inside your head, but I bet he won't be much help in a wrestling match between us.'

Renee laughed, such a pleasant sound in the otherwise dreary place that it disturbed Sato.

'A compromise, then,' she said. Or *Chu* said. 'I'll give you your sample, but you let me carry the vial until we're done. I want – no, I *need* you to report back to George what you see here today.'

'No way,' Sato said. 'I'm not giving you the vial.'

Renee's face creased into a scowl so frightening that Sato would have melted into the stone at his back if he could have. 'You tire me, boy. Do you really think I'm going to let you leave here alive with a sample of my blood? You'll be signing your own death warrant.'

Sato felt his own blood chill. *George will get me out,* he thought. *George will get me out.*

'I'll take my chances,' he said. 'Give me your blood and I'll go with you.'

Renee stuck her arm out. 'Do it, then.'

Sato stepped forward and grabbed her thin arm, leaning over to look at the soft skin in the bend of her elbow. A big vein pulsed, purple in the faint light.

'This might hurt,' he said, not sure why he showed any compassion. 'I've never done this before.'

'Just do it. Nothing you do to me will be worse than when *he* leaves my head.'

As Sato readied the syringe, the needle only an inch from the vein, he looked up at Renee's face. 'Sometimes you talk like you're this Chu guy, and sometimes like yourself. You really are crazy.'

'You wouldn't understand unless you were infected. Stick me.'

Sato held his breath, then jammed the needle into Renee's vein. He quickly pulled back on the syringe pump, relieved to see dark red fluid fill the plastic vial. He finished, pulled out the needle, then replaced the plastic cover. He put the whole thing into his right pocket. He put a bandage on her arm to stop the bleeding.

'Done,' he said, finally taking in a huge breath like he'd just surfaced after diving for oysters.

'That blood will never see the light of day. You understand that, right? The only way you will leave this mountain is by giving it up.'

'Just show me what you wanted to show me.' Half of him wanted to push her down and run for the elevator, but he knew he couldn't. George would desperately need any information he could gather in his quest to find a cure or antidote.

'This way.' She walked towards a branch of the tunnel leading to the right, but paused after a couple of steps and turned towards Sato, her face devoid of expression. 'What you're about to see, you'll never forget. Never. I promise you.'

TRAPPED

With each step down the wet and musty passage of stone, the noises around Sato grew in volume. The screams and wails and shouts and piercing cries for help made him feel as if invisible bugs were crawling across his skin, trying to find a place to burrow towards his heart. His stomach clenched into a tight wad of tissue. He braced himself for the sight ahead, wondering if he'd ever see George or Mothball or Rutger or his other friends again.

They reached a place where a dirty curtain was stretched across the entire width of the hallway, swaying slightly from a breeze behind it. The awful sounds became ear-piercing, no longer muffled by distance.

Sato was now only a few feet away from discovering whatever was wrong with these people.

'Prepare yourself,' Renee said. Then she reached out and yanked the curtain to the side.

For the second time in the last hour, Sato's knees buckled. He fell to the ground, his shins slamming onto the hard stone as he stared at the chaos in front of him.

The passageway opened into a large chamber, tables and chairs scattered about the raggedy carpet, most of them broken or turned upside down. Hundreds of people – horrible, terrified, creepy-looking people – filled the room in a state of utter madness.

Their clothes were torn; bloody scrapes and gashes covered their bodies; big splotches of hair had been ripped from their heads. They attacked each other at random, moving from one to the other without warning. They coughed and spat and snarled and bit anything in sight. They cried one second, laughed the next, then screamed as if their very throats would burst. They climbed the walls until they fell crashing to the floor. They jumped and huddled and kicked and flailed their arms.

It was, without any doubt, the most horrific thing Sato had ever witnessed, and he knew he would spend the rest of his life trying to purge it from his memory.

'What is this?' He had to force the words out, rage clogging his throat. 'What's wrong with them? How could you do this to them?'

Renee knelt on the floor next to him, not taking her eyes off the mayhem before them. 'So you believe me now, do you? You believe that he's inside my head, controlling me, talking to you? That I am Reginald Chu at this moment?'

'I don't care who you are,' Sato said. 'I'll spend the rest of my life making you pay for it.'

Renee tsk-tsked as she shook her head. 'Hard to believe you're only a young man – you speak more like an adult than most men I know.' She shifted until she was sitting comfortably with her legs crossed beneath her. 'But this isn't what I *really* wanted to show you. Let me show you the future.'

Sato finally tore his eyes from the sickening display and looked at Renee. 'What?' he said, throwing all the hatred he could into the word.

Renee didn't return his stare, looking instead at the people around them. 'They're like this because I underestimated the power of Dark Infinity. I can't control it on my own – I need help. I need a partner.'

She pushed herself to her feet and walked forward, seemingly oblivious to the danger she entered. But then, as if spurred by the flip of a switch, every person in the vast room grew silent, freezing in place. After a few seconds, the people – every single one of them – calmly gained their composure and joined Renee in the middle of the chamber, lining up in perfectly straight rows. The formation filled the floor, as ordered and organised as any military group in the world. Not a sound could be heard as they all stood still, each one staring at Sato.

'He is in all of our heads, now,' Renee called out, standing rigid as she spoke. 'We will do his bidding, whatever he asks, until that time he must leave us, and then we will return to the horror that is life without him. The day comes when he will never leave us again.'

Sato slowly got to his feet, nausea and despair threatening to consume him. In the understatement of his young life, he told himself he had seen enough.

'I'm sorry he's doing this to you,' he half-whispered. 'Fight it if you can. I promise we'll try to save you.'

He didn't wait for a response. He turned and ran.

Behind him, he heard the piercing cry of Renee's voice, echoing up and through the air as if she'd used a megaphone. 'He has my blood in his right pocket! Don't let him leave with it!'

And then came the sound of hundreds of people running and screaming in a synchronised cry of pursuit.

☼

'Can you pull him out yet?' Master George asked for the twentieth time in the last ten minutes, pacing the floor of the command room.

'No,' Rutger replied, his eyes riveted to the nano-locator monitor. 'But his heart rate is spiking again – I didn't think it could possibly get higher, but now it's in the danger zone.' In his hands, Rutger held the Barrier Wand, programmed to wink Sato back from the mountaintop.

'Oh dear, oh dear, oh dear,' Master George whispered under his breath.

'Should've gone with 'im, I should,' Mothball said from her chair in the corner. 'Bugger, I should've ruddy gone with 'im.'

Master George stopped, turning towards his tall friend. 'Perhaps, my good Mothball, perhaps. However, we all agreed that this was the perfect opportunity for Sato to snap out of the haze of his past and find himself. If you were there to save him, he might never truly join us.'

'He needs to make it back to the execution cliff,' Rutger said. 'Until then, there's nothing I can do.'

'He'll make it,' Master George said. 'I know it. And when he returns, he'll truly be a Realitant, the shade of his parents' death no longer a crutch to bind him in shadow.'

'Very poetic,' Rutger muttered. 'But the way his heart's racing, we'll need to give him a transplant as soon as he gets back.'

'Just keep that Wand ready, Rutger. Keep it ready.'

✷

Sato gasped for breath as he ran through the dimly lit tunnel; it hadn't seemed so long the first time he'd walked through its winding path. The escalating screams behind him brought horrible images to his mind of what would happen if he were caught. Every muscle in his body begged him to stop, but he kept running, limping slightly from the pain in his shins, especially in his right leg.

Worried the blood-filled syringe in his right pocket might break, he reached in and pulled it out, gripping the plastic cylinder once again like a dagger in his hand. It almost slipped from the sweat on his palm – he shifted it to his left hand while he wiped his fingers dry, then switched back.

He kept running.

He turned a corner and saw the elevator up ahead, its steel cage open and ready for him. He could see the lever mechanism inside the sliding mesh door. He was almost safe.

The hollow echoes of his pursuers bounced through the tunnel like thunder crackling along open plains. Sato heard noises of feet stomping on stone, kicked rocks, heavy breathing, grunts. He heard Renee shout something; he couldn't make out the words, but the intensity of the screams jumped a notch.

Sato looked over his shoulder and saw the pack of crazies only thirty feet behind him and gaining ground. Renee led them, her eyes focused, her horde of followers on her tail, waving their arms, shaking their fists. It was like the villagers chasing Frankenstein's monster – the only things missing were pitchforks and torches.

Sato faced forward again; so close, the elevator was only a few feet away. He reached up, slipped the backpack off his left shoulder, then his right, still running, still holding tight to the blood sample.

He windmilled his left arm and threw the backpack forward. It landed with a thud in the back corner of the elevator just as he crossed the threshold of the cage. He reached out with his free hand and slid the door shut with a squeal and a clank as it landed home. The latch to close it was small and weak – Sato knew it wouldn't last long. He closed it anyway then knelt on the floor and pushed up on the lever with his shoulder, screaming with the effort until the thing finally snapped into position.

With a lurch, the elevator started moving upwards just as Renee and dozens of the screaming mob slammed into the cage, clawing at the steel, screaming and spitting. Hundreds of scabby fingers squirmed through the small openings, some of the crazies climbing onto the elevator, others violently pulling and pushing on the door. Sato scrambled to the far corner, staring at the sickening sight.

The elevator had only gone up a few feet when dozens more of his pursuers crawled beneath it and gripped the floor through the checkered holes, hanging on, pulling towards the ground. The cage slowed to a stop, the weight of the people too great. Sato knew if he could make it to the narrow shaft cut into the stone above, then the psychos clinging to the side would have no choice but to let go or be crushed to death. He jumped to his feet, kicking at the fingers below him, stomping repeatedly in a ridiculous dance, watching in triumph as those he smashed let go and fell to the floor.

The elevator stuttered and paused, screams coming from above as the topmost section entered the main elevator shaft and crushed several of the inmates who still clung to the side. The cage slowed again, and Sato closed his eyes before he could see the gruesome results. He heard the thumps of bodies on the stone below, and the elevator lurched upwards again, regaining its normal speed.

Please, he thought. *Please be over, please let me go home.*

A wrenching click of steel made his eyes pop open just as the door to the cage slid open with a screech. Renee had somehow broken the latch, squeezing her body against the elevator until she could get it open.

She and Sato were alone, having left everyone else below, their wails and cries already dying out with the distance.

'Almost made it, didn't you?' Renee said, her chest heaving with her deep breaths.

Sato reached down and pulled the plastic cover off the blood-filled syringe, then held it out like a knife. 'Stay back,' he said, bending his knees in a crouch. 'There's no way you can win a fight with me.'

'You still don't get it, do you?' she replied. They circled, each staying as far apart from the other as possible in the small cage. 'He's in my head. I'll do whatever he asks.'

'Why are you doing this?' Sato asked.

'I told you, he's in my—'

'Not you!' Sato screamed. 'Reginald Chu! Why are you doing this?!'

'If you have to ask, then you'll never understand why.'

Renee lunged forward, surprising Sato despite his stance. She crashed into him, slamming his back against the side of the cage. On instinct, Sato stuck the needle into her back. She cried out in pain then lashed out at his face, scraping her nails across his right cheek. Sato pulled out the needle and bent his knees, letting his body fall to the floor, Renee landing on top of him.

They rolled and wrestled, Renee punching and clawing like a panicked bear. Sato had the syringe under her, pointed at her face, trying to threaten her because he didn't know what else to do. She grabbed his hand, thrusting the needle away, twisting his wrist so the syringe was heading towards his own skin. He couldn't believe her strength. He groaned with effort, but she kept winning, pushing the needle closer and closer to the soft skin of his lower neck.

He pushed her away with a final burst of exertion; she surprised him by pulling back instead of fighting it. Caught off guard, his grip on the syringe slipped and Renee yanked it free. She twisted backwards and pressed the point of the needle against his leg.

'You ... had ... your ... chance,' she spat out, her face red with exertion and anger as she drove the needle *into* Sato's skin. He felt the prick, the achy slide of the sharp sliver of metal. Then Renee slammed downwards on the plunger of the syringe.

Pain exploded through Sato's body as the needle dug in deeper, as the blood sample rushed into him. He cried out as the syringe emptied, its infected contents now swimming inside his tissue and veins. It felt like millions of tiny bugs squirmed underneath his skin.

'No!' he screamed, a surge of adrenaline giving him the strength to throw Renee off his body completely. '*NO!*'

He scrambled to his feet, unable to stop the tears from flowing as pain racked his body. 'What ... what ... have you done to me?'

'You'll be one of us now,' Renee said, crouched in the corner with a smile on her face.

'No, I won't. Never.'

The elevator slammed to a stop. 'What the devil's goin' on here?'

Sato looked over to see Klink, his eyes moving back and forth between Sato and Renee, surprise and concern on his face.

Sato didn't hesitate. He grabbed his backpack, ran from the lift cage, down the tunnel, and towards the steel door that led outside. He ran.

'Go, then!' Renee called out from behind him. 'It won't matter – you'll be mine anyway. Run and take me to Master George. It'll be fun to have a spy–'

Sato didn't hear the rest. He was through the door, squinting his eyes against the blinding snow, scrambling down the stone stairway, slipping and falling and not caring.

Down the mountain he went.

✿

'I've got him!' Rutger yelled.

He pushed the golden button on top of the Barrier Wand, and Sato appeared in front of them. The boy collapsed to the ground, a terrible mess of blood and dirt and torn clothing, sweat-ice crusted all over him.

'Goodness gracious me!' Master George yelled as he and Mothball reached forward to help Sato. They grabbed him by the arms and pulled him over to a leather chair, plopping his exhausted body onto the cushions.

'What happened?' Mothball asked.

Sato answered, his voice shaky and barely audible. 'Lock ... me ... up. Chain me. Then ... I'll explain.'

'Lock you–' Rutger began.

'Just do it!' Sato snapped, his hand pressed to a wound on his leg. 'Just do it before Chu can control me!'

'What happened?' Master George asked, leaning over to look at the boy. 'Did you get the sample?'

'Yes,' Sato said through a moan of pain. His eyes narrowed, like a wolf on the hunt. 'It's ... *inside* me.'

'Oh, lad. Oh, you poor, poor lad.' Master George paused. Then he straightened, his shoulders square. 'Ready the holding cell, Rutger. And get me some rope.'

PART 3

THE CIRCLE
OF TIME

TICKETS TO FOURTH CITY

'I'm really getting sick of this place,' Paul said.

Tick couldn't have agreed more as he scanned the walls and ceiling of the small restaurant where they had stopped to eat something that was a cross between pizza and toast. Five days had passed since Sally winked back to Master George, and they'd spent every waking hour investigating the town for signs of where they were supposed to be at five o'clock the next afternoon. Though they didn't know what they were looking for, they looked nonetheless.

And, just like this place – one of the last buildings they'd yet to explore – they'd found nothing. No signs, no clues, no Barrier Wands, no magic portals, no further riddles. A big fat zero.

And time was running out. Reginald Chu's riddle had been clear – 5:00 p.m., tomorrow. Maybe they'd finally been stumped.

'Maybe it's a good thing if we don't figure it out,' Paul said. 'Beats going off to have more adventures with a psycho mad genius of the universe.'

'He said, "win or die,"' Sofia said. 'Dying sounds worse to me.'

Tick picked up his last piece of dinner, but then put it back down, his appetite gone. 'Sally said we need to be the ones to win it – so we can put a stop to whatever Chu's doing.'

'Yeah, and I'm sure that'll be a piece of cake,' Paul muttered. 'Hey, Chu dude! We won, but please stop that knuckleheaded horseplay you're up to. Thanks kindly.'

'You want to give up?' Sofia asked. 'Then quit. I'm sure Master George will wink you away if you cry enough.'

'No, Miss Italy, I don't want to quit. Someone has to protect you.' Paul leaned back and rubbed his belly. 'Man, that was pretty good.'

'Come on,' Sofia said as she got up from her chair. 'It's our last night – we'd better get searching.'

☼

They searched until well past dark. They looked on every corner, behind every bush, under every sidewalk bench. They walked the underground pathways of the train stations again. Nothing. Absolutely nothing. Even the trains seemed to avoid them; they'd yet to actually see one despite several trips to the stations.

Tick thought about quitting more than once that night, but the urgency of the dwindling time spurred him on, despite his exhaustion. Finally, a roving policeman told them they needed to get off the streets, that curfew was far past. Sofia complained, but the officer made it clear they'd get one warning and one warning only.

And so they went back to the hotel, back to their beds.

Tick set his watch alarm for 6:00, but he had no idea what he'd do when he woke up. Imagining the glowing monkeys prowling the woods outside his window, he fell asleep.

☼

His alarm had just sounded when he heard someone knock at the door. It was Sofia, dragging a sleepy-eyed Paul behind her.

'We need to get out there,' she said. 'We only have eleven hours left.'

'But what are we going to *do*?' Paul asked. 'We've looked everywhere. There's no point in looking any more. We're just as well off staying here.'

'Well, we have to do something!' Sofia insisted. Tick groaned as he flopped back on his bed. 'I'm with Paul on this one. All we've figured out is that something is supposed to happen at five o'clock. At this point, running around the town makes no more sense than sitting here, holding hands and chanting to the time gods.'

'Chanting to the time gods?' Paul asked. 'Tick, you're losing it.'

Sofia huffed as she took a seat. 'Then *think*. What are we missing?'

No one answered, and they all remained silent for several minutes.

Paul snapped his fingers. 'The last line of the riddle says, "Make sure your feet find air," right? Well, maybe we're supposed to catch a train and go somewhere *else* by five o'clock. Some place called "air" or something like that.'

'Hmm,' Sofia said. 'That's possible. The whole underground railroad system is kind of weird. There must be something about this place, a reason he sent us here – maybe it *is* the train!'

'I'll admit it's better than chanting to the time gods,' Tick said. 'Let's go.'

✷

The streets were surprisingly busy for so early in the morning; most of the people out and about were heading down the stairs that led to the underground railroad.

'These people must all work in another city,' Tick said. 'No wonder they have to leave when the sun comes up.'

'Good thing we're not the only ones awake,' Paul said. 'I didn't want that cop barking at us again.'

They followed the crowd to the ticket counters, old-fashioned brick windows where old men took money and gave out printed slips of paper. Holding some of the local currency given to them by Phillip, they waited their turn.

'Next!' a white-haired man called out, a scowl scrunching up his face like he was having a kidney removed.

Sofia stepped up first. 'We'd like three tickets for … a train.'

Somehow the man's face screwed up even tighter. 'Well, that's real nice to know you have that figured out, missy. How about telling me *where* you want to go?'

'Oh.' Sofia looked back at Tick, who shrugged.

'How many trains are leaving soon?' Paul asked.

'What kind of a fool question is that?' the old man grunted. 'As many as you'd like. As few as you want. Now are you going buy a ticket or not?'

Just when I thought it couldn't get any weirder, Tick thought.

'What are our options?' Sofia asked. 'We're tourists, and just want to do some exploring.'

'Oh, well isn't that just peachy?' the man replied, rolling his eyes under his bushy white brows. 'Good thing you got me, kids. One of the grumpy ticket masters would've sent you walking already.'

Tick could sense that something smart was about to fly out of Sofia's mouth, so he kicked her gently on the calf.

'Please just give us our options,' she said instead.

'From this station, you can go to Martyrtown, Cook Reef, Falcon Bay, or Fourth City. Now choose and be done with it.'

'Okay, please give me just one second, sir,' Sofia said, so gushy polite that Tick was sure the man would kick them out for being smart alecks.

'Did you hear that?' Paul whispered. 'He said Fourth City.'

'That's the number of Chu's Reality!' Tick said.

'Bingo,' Paul said.

'You really think that's it?' Sofia asked, staring at the floor as if deep in thought. She finally nodded to herself and turned towards the old man. 'Three tickets to Fourth City, please.'

'Well, congratulations on making a decision. I hope you have a swell time. That'll be thirty-four yecterns.'

'Oh,' Paul said to the man as Sofia handed over the money. 'Make sure we'll be there by five o'clock.'

The ticket master printed out three tickets from a rickety metallic machine and handed them over the counter. 'Boy, say one more snide remark and I'll have the police boot you out of here. Now go.'

'Sir,' Paul replied, sounding more sincere than Tick had ever heard him before. 'I promise I'm not trying to be difficult – we just don't understand how the trains work here. And we need to be there by five o'clock.'

The man frowned deeper than ever, then looked at each of them in turn. 'You three are just about the strangest kids I've ever seen. You go over to the portal that matches the number on your ticket' – he pointed at a series of large white cubicles – 'step inside, and it'll take you from there.'

'But–' Paul started.

'Go!' The ticket master's face reddened as he pointed towards the booths.

Like three startled mice, they scuttled away. Tick hoped he never had to talk to the man again.

When they were sufficiently far enough away from the old buzzard, Sofia handed out the tickets.

Tick took his ticket. Printed in faded black letters as if the ink were running out in the old guy's machine were the words, "Portal Number Seven. Fourth City. Round Trip."

'Well, let's go,' Paul said. 'Hopefully we'll get there in time to search around.'

The portals – tall, rectangular cubicles, white and shiny – were lined up in order along the sunken line of what Tick had thought were train tracks. He peeked into the ten-foot-deep trench and saw a series of long, metal rods stretching into a dark tunnel at the end of the station.

'Come on,' Paul said, holding open the door. It was made out of the same material as the rest of the small building and fitted to match its shape.

Sofia went in first, then Tick, then Paul, who closed the door behind him.

The inside was a perfect cylinder, completely covered in thick, rubbery padding that was a burnt-orange colour. Along the bottom, a bench protruded from the walls – also covered in soft padding – making a circle for the passengers to sit and stare at each other.

'This is a train?' Tick asked no one in particular.

An uneasy feeling crept into his bones.

'What do we–' Paul began, but was cut off by an electronic woman's voice coming from unseen speakers.

'Please present your tickets,' it said, a soft monotonous tone that made Tick feel sleepy. He clasped his ticket between his thumb and forefinger, holding it up into the air; the others did the same.

'Cleared. State your desired time of departure.'

'As soon as possible,' Sofia said in a loud voice.

'It's not deaf,' Paul whispered, getting an elbow in the gut from Sofia in return.

'Checking departures. One moment, please.' A pause, then: *'Six Forty-Four is acceptable. Please stand on the footrest, backs against the wall.'*

'Huh?' Paul asked.

'Just do it,' Sofia said, climbing on to the bench.

'Three minutes to departure.'

Tick stepped onto the padded bench, surprised at how firmly it held him. He rested his back against the soft wall; Paul and Sofia had done the same, the three of them spaced evenly apart, exchanging worried glances.

'This is weird,' Paul said.

'That about sums it up,' Tick agreed.

'It's obviously okay. All those other people are doing it,' Sofia said. 'We can't expect every Reality to be just like ours.'

'One minute to departure.'

'What do we do – just stand here?' Paul asked.

Sofia rolled her eyes. 'You can do jumping jacks if you want.'

'You're telling me you're not a little scared?'

'I am,' Tick said.

'Maybe a little,' Sofia said.

'Thirty seconds to departure.'

No one said a word after that; Tick counted down inside his head.

'Ten seconds.' A pause. *'Five. Four. Three. Two. One. Departure initiated.'*

The room began to rotate clockwise, slowly at first, but then it picked up speed.

'Oh, no,' Tick said. 'I can't do this – I'll throw up all over you guys.'

They spun faster and faster. Tick felt a pressure on his skin, squeezing his limbs and his torso, like an invisible force pushing him against the curved wall at his back. In a matter of seconds, he'd lost track of their rotation speed, his mind and stomach disorientated, his body sinking into the padding. His thoughts whirled as fast as his body, spinning clockwise in a tight circle.

Something clicked in Tick's mind.

He envisioned the city they'd just left, the layout, the circular road – and the solution to Chu's riddle crystallised in his head, as clear as anything he'd ever known. In that moment, he knew they shouldn't be on the train.

They had to stop. *They had to go back!*

He wanted to say something, but he couldn't. He felt like the world was crushing him. Grunting, he tried to push his arms up into the air. It felt like he had fifty-pound dumbbells in his hands. The second he relaxed, his arms slammed back onto the wall.

Then it got worse.

A horn sounded, coming from everywhere and nowhere at once, and then the room *shifted*. With the spinning and the pressure, it was hard to tell which direction the room was moving, but it seemed to have dropped into a black hole, catapulting forward at a speed that was too much for Tick's mind and body to handle.

He passed out.

FOREST EXIT

'Tick.'

He heard someone say his name, but it sounded hollow, like an echo coming down a long tunnel.

'Tick!'

There it was again. Louder this time. A sharp pain splintered across his mind, and that seemed to do the trick. Groaning, blinking through squinting eyes, he woke up.

'Dude, are you all right?'

Paul. It was Paul.

'Come on. Help him up.'

Sofia.

Tick felt hands grip him by the arms and haul him off the floor, setting him down on a soft bench. Every time he opened his eyes, all he could see were things spinning and rocking back and forth. His mind felt like a pack of termites had been set loose inside for lunch. And the nausea ...

'I gotta throw up,' he whispered.

'Not on me, you don't,' Paul said. 'Hurry, let's get him out of here.'

They grabbed him by the arms again. He heard a

door open, felt refreshing cool air wash over him as they helped him stumble outside the portal.

'There's a garbage can,' he heard Sofia say; they changed directions.

'Hurry,' Tick groaned, trying his best to get his feet under him. A cold line of metal pressed against his neck.

'Go for it,' Paul muttered.

Tick let it all out, then slid to the ground and leaned back against the bin. 'Ah, that feels much better.' He opened his eyes fully and got his first good look at where they'd arrived.

The station looked much like the one they'd left earlier – maybe a little dirtier, less well-kept. Just as many people milled about, though, some leaving portals, some entering them.

'What happened?' he asked.

'You passed out,' Sofia said. 'I think I might have, too, just for a few seconds. When we finally stopped, Paul and I slid down onto the bench, but you crashed straight to the floor.'

'Yeah, man,' Paul said. 'You were out like a light.'

'How long were we in that thing?' Tick asked.

Sofia looked at her watch. 'Only half an hour or so.'

'Worst half-hour of my life,' Paul said.

Tick rubbed his face with both hands, then stood up, wobbling for a second before he felt his legs strengthen and solidify beneath him. 'We have to go back. Now.'

'Go back?' Paul asked. 'Are you crazy?'

'We need to look around,' Sofia said. 'Figure out what Chu wants us to do.'

Tick shook his head, which sent another wave of nausea through his gut. 'No, we got it wrong. We weren't supposed to come here. The trains have nothing to do with the riddle.'

'How do you know?' Paul asked. 'Fourth City – it's the closest we've gotten to anything that makes sense.'

Tick started walking towards the ticket counter. Paul and Sofia followed, but they didn't look happy. 'Our tickets are round trip – does that mean we just get back on Portal Number Seven?'

'Whoa, man,' Paul said, grabbing Tick by the arm. 'Tell us what you're thinking. If we're getting back in that death machine, we need to at least let our brains unscramble for a minute.'

Tick nodded, anxious to leave but knowing Paul was right. He found a bench and they sat down, Tick in the middle.

'All right,' he said. 'Think about everything. The town Chu sent us to is a perfect circle. We counted *twelve* main roads that are basically spokes in the huge wheel of how the place is organised. Even the hotel he set us up in – it's called The Stroke of Midnight Inn. You gettin' it yet?'

'Holy toothpick on a hand grenade,' Paul whispered.

'I don't think I've ever felt as stupid as I feel right now,' Sofia said.

'It never had anything to do with an actual *time*,' Tick continued. 'It was such an easy riddle because he wanted to throw us off track. We were so sure something had to happen at five o'clock today, we never considered that he might be describing a *place*.'

Paul finished for him. 'If we look at the town from a bird's-eye view, it's a big clock. Our hotel is midnight – twelve o'clock. We need to go to the road that represents *five* o'clock.'

'But we already looked there,' Sofia said. 'We scoured that whole town.'

Tick stretched his arms, feeling better already. 'Yeah, but we had so much area to cover, we didn't really have time to study anything in detail. I bet we find something where the five o'clock road hits the outer circle.'

'Ah, man, what if we're too late?' Paul asked. 'If you're right, maybe we didn't have to wait a week. Maybe we should've gone to the place a lot sooner.'

Sofia stood up. 'Maybe it's a double riddle.'

'You're right,' Tick said. 'I bet we have to be at the five o'clock road *by* five o'clock today.'

'Well, then,' Paul said, 'we have plenty of time. Let's go get something to eat.'

'No way,' Tick said. 'You really think it's going to be that easy? Something will try to stop us, I guarantee it.'

'Well, we have to *eat*,' Paul insisted.

'Yeah, but we should get back to Circle City first,' Sofia said. 'The sooner the better.'

All of them slowly turned their heads to look at the spinning nightmare train from which they'd just exited. Tick couldn't think of anything he'd rather *not* do than get back on that thing.

'We have to do it,' Sofia said, as if reading Tick's thoughts.

'I know,' Tick replied.

'Yeah, eating right now would be really stupid,' Paul said. 'I don't want Tick's bacon and eggs on my lap when we get there.'

'Come on,' Sofia said. 'Let's figure out how to get back.'

✦

They had to wait only twenty minutes for Portal Number Seven to open up for the return trip to Circle City. Tick had never felt so nervous about a trip before; butterflies swarmed in his chest like it was mating season. He remembered his mom lecturing him at the amusement park:

'Now, Atticus, you know what the Spinning Dragon does to your poor tummy.'

'One minute to departure,' the nice electronic lady said.

Tick squeezed his eyes shut, pressed his back against the soft padding. *Thirty-minute trip,* he told himself. *It's only thirty minutes.*

The warning for thirty seconds sounded, then ten, then the five-second countdown. When the room started spinning, Tick opened his eyes to look at Paul and Sofia, both of whom were trying to look very calm but failing miserably. This made Tick feel better, and he closed his eyes again.

The portal spun faster and faster, twisting like a tornado, throwing all of his senses into chaos as the invisible force once again pushed him into the padding, pressing against his body. He held his breath, anticipating the explosion of speed – reminding him of how he felt that split-second before the free-fall ride at the Seattle theme park dropped fifteen stories to the ground far below. But this was far worse.

The horn sounded.

Tick tried to scream as the train exploded into instant acceleration, shocking his mind as it bulleted away from Fourth City. He didn't know if any noise escaped his throat. Nothing seemed to be working inside his brain, all of his nerves dead to the world, confused and compressed.

He felt himself sliding away again, moving towards the bliss of unconsciousness. *Do it,* he thought. *Pass out. Anything is better than this.* He faded in and out, feeling like every second lasted an hour. He had no idea how much time had passed when everything suddenly went wrong.

The train jerked, a quick and loud jolt as if they'd hit a cow on the tracks like the steamers in the old days. Then the room shook, rattling up and down, creaks and groans ripping through the air, as if the whole vehicle were about to fall apart. Tick would've thought it impossible, but everything had just got much, much worse. His stomach twisted into a knot of panicked nausea.

His eyes snapped open, but they didn't seem to work. Everything was a blur of colour, images and streaks, flashing and tilting – *vibrating*. He couldn't even make out Paul or Sofia; everything was messed up.

What's happening? he thought. *Maybe it's okay. I passed out last time – maybe this is totally normal.*

But the train shook again, twisted, bounced and rattled. Pain seared through Tick's head like someone had driven a crowbar into the top of his skull and worked it open, wedging the long piece of steel against his brain.

A booming crash sounded through the room, a horrible crunch of metal. The train jolted, and the pressure forcing Tick against the wall abruptly vanished. He fell forward and crashed into Paul. They both fell to the floor, landing on top of a crumpled Sofia.

The next few seconds were complete insanity. The vehicle bounced and twisted and shook, throwing Tick and the others in every direction, slamming them against the curved walls, the floor, into each other. Tick tried to ball up, squeezing his knees against his chest and covering his head with his arms, but it proved impossible. Like a giant gorilla shaking a can of peanuts, the three of them were tossed and jostled about until Tick thought for sure their lives were over.

And then, with one final crash that slammed them all into one padded side of the curved structure, it ended.

Everything stopped, grew still, silent.

The only sounds were the moans coming from the battered humans inside.

'My arm!' Paul screamed out. 'I think I broke my stinking arm!'

'What happened?' Sofia asked, her voice strained and tight.

Portal Number Seven lay on its side. Tick and the others were in a crumpled heap on top of each other, resting on one of the curved, padded sections that used to be vertical. With more groans and moans, they crawled away from each other. A hissing sound came from outside, followed by something that sounded like electric sparks.

Tick sat up, every inch of his body in pain. He looked over at Paul, who cradled his left arm with his right.

'You okay?' Tick said.

Paul looked up, a tear streaking out of his right eye. 'Dude, it hurts, it really, really hurts.'

'You think you broke it?' Sofia asked, rubbing one of her ankles.

'Yeah,' Paul said, his face squeezed into a grimace of pain. 'Ah, man, it kills!' Another tear slid down his cheek. Tick looked away, worried Paul would be embarrassed at being seen crying.

Sofia stood up, wobbling a second before she caught her balance. 'We must have crashed or something. We've gotta get out of here, get Paul to a hospital.'

Tick joined her and together they walked across the curved wall to the door, which was about four feet in the air, sideways. It was twisted slightly, and it took both of them ramming it with their shoulders before it finally popped open and slammed against the crumpled white wall of the portal.

Tick and Sofia made surprised grunts at the same time when they saw where they were.

'What's ... out there?' Paul asked through clenched teeth.

Tick couldn't answer, his eyes glued to the wall of thick, enormous trees beyond the doorway.

'We're in a forest,' Sofia said.

As if the pain had finally sent him over the edge, Paul started laughing.

THE SICKNESS OF SATO

Master George felt his heart breaking in two as he stared at Sato.

The poor lad thrashed in his bindings, twisting his arms and legs, arching his back as he strained against the ropes tied to his ankles and wrists. He lay on a bed in the holding cell, the sheets a jumbled mess from his spasms and fits of lunacy. Deep bruises marked where the ropes touched his skin, yet he didn't stop his fruitless efforts to escape.

He had the illness, the disease. Sato had gone quite insane.

Master George gripped his hands together, wishing so badly he could have just a few seconds of conversation with the *real* Sato, who was locked somewhere inside the mind infected by Chu's mysterious plague. The bravery shown by the boy in entering that mountain insane asylum made Master George so proud it hurt. He also felt again the pains of losing Sato's parents all those years ago; a dreadful death that still made him feel hot, as if the heat from the flying fires of that fateful day had never quite left his skin.

'We're going to make everything right,' Master George said aloud, even though he doubted Sato could hear, let alone understand, his words. 'Rutger and I are working on the antidote every second of the day. And we're getting close, very close. Hang in there, lad, hang in there. Your suffering may be the very key that saves us all.'

Sato stilled, then, letting out an enormous sigh as his body came to rest on the sweaty, crumpled sheets of the bed. Master George leaned forward, terrified he'd made a huge mistake in saying anything.

'He's back in my head,' Sato whispered in a chant-like voice that sent chills up Master George's arms. 'He wants to speak to you.'

'Sato, are you there?' Master George asked. 'Even with him in your head, are you there, listening to me?'

'He wants to speak to you,' Sato repeated.

'I don't care about him, Sato. I want you to know that we're doing everything we can to save you, and that your mission was an enormous success. We *are* going to take care of you.'

Sato slowly turned his head until his eyes – glazed over as if drugged – met with Master George's. 'That's very sweet of you, George. Your softness has always been your greatest weakness.'

Master George sat back in his chair as if slapped, but he quickly regained his composure. 'Am I speaking with you, Reginald? Come to show me how low you've finally sunk, have you?'

'I know what you're doing,' Chu said through Sato's mouth. Perhaps it was the eyes, or perhaps it was the unusual tone of his voice, but somehow it seemed like it really *was* Chu lying there, speaking.

'Quite smart, aren't you?' Master George replied.

A grin appeared on Sato's face, a grin so evil it made him look like a demon. 'Yes, actually. I'm very, very smart, George. Which is why you'll never succeed in creating a cure for Dark Infinity.'

'Who said anything about a cure?'

'Very well, George. Play your games, insult my intelligence. The day is coming, and very soon, when I will have an apprentice strong enough to make Dark Infinity fully functional. Everything will change then. You'd be wise to consider your allegiances – I could use your help as well.'

'What's your plan, Reginald?' Master George asked, knowing he should just walk away but unable to. 'Haven't you enough power? Why must you ruin so many lives? Why can't you use your skills to *better* the Realities? Still not powerful enough to wash away your pathetic loathing of yourself? Quite sad, really.'

Sato's face tightened, reddened, any semblance of a smile gone. 'What I do, I do for the good of all mankind, George. The Realities *need* me, and this is the only way to gain the power necessary to change things. In the end, you and everyone else will thank me.'

Master George leaned forward, elbows on knees, his eyes narrowing. 'That sounds quite familiar, Reginald. I've heard almost the exact same words come out of the mouth of Mistress Jane. The both of you have merely cloaked your evil with good intentions. We will win in the end, I assure you.'

'You have–'

'Silence!' Master George yelled, standing up. 'I will hear no more of your lies!'

He walked out of the holding cell immediately, slamming the door shut with every ounce of strength left in his old body.

✹

'I've never seen such a thick forest before,' Sofia said as they picked their way slowly – very slowly – through the thickly clustered trees. Hoots and howls rang through the air, as if every zoo in the world had released their animals into the woods surrounding them. Pungent smells of rotting foliage, leaves, and bark mixed with the pleasant scents of pine and wildflowers. Tick felt as if all five of his senses were overloaded.

He and Sofia walked alongside Paul, helping him as best they could when he needed an extra hand. Both of his were occupied – one useless because of his broken arm, the other busy holding the bad limb against his body.

'Dude, I know I sound like a sissy,' Paul said through his pain. 'But this is killing me, man. I want my mom.'

'Unless your mom is a doctor,' Sofia said, stooping under a massive, moss-covered limb, 'I don't think she's the one you want right now.'

'Maybe you're right,' Paul replied. He struggled, doubling over to go under the same branch, his rear end and skinny legs the only way to balance himself with no arms to use. 'I want a doctor. *Then* I want my mom.'

'*My* mom would tell me to quit whining and put a bandage on it,' Sofia said. 'Frupey's the only one who'd care in my house.'

Tick faltered for a second, almost tripping Paul, then kept walking as if nothing had happened. Paul's silence showed he must have felt the same way – awkward at yet another sad reference to Sofia's home life.

Despite the approaching noon hour, the forest was dark from the tall canopy of limbs and leaves overhead, everything masked in shadow. As Tick pushed through a thick tangle of brush, scratching his arms and legs, he couldn't help but feel a little desperation at their predicament. They had only a few hours to get back to Circle City, run to the intersection that represented five o'clock, and then find whatever talisman marked their way out of this Reality.

After exiting the crashed Portal Number Seven, they'd seen the huge swath of ruined forest they'd left behind them, a wide slice of knocked-down trees, many of them burning or smoking. Based on the direction of the fiery trail, they could only guess – and hope – that continuing in the direction the Portal *should* have been travelling would lead them to their destination. But with the towering trees and thick undergrowth, it was almost impossible to know if they were walking in a straight line or wandering in circles. Everything about the place looked the same.

'Any guesses on what happened?' Sofia said, practically pushing Paul over a boulder wedged between two trees. His only response was a grunt when he thudded back on the ground.

'A bomb or something,' Tick said. 'It's probably just another part of Chu's game. To see if we'd give up or not make it back on time.'

Paul pushed past an outreaching limb with his shoulder, then let it fly backwards to smack Sofia in the face.

'Hey!' she yelled.

'Sorry,' Paul said, his pain-racked face somehow showing the slightest hint of amusement to Tick. 'No arms, ya know – not much control.'

'How'd you like to have *two* broken arms?' Sofia replied.

'Wouldn't be much worse than now.'

They entered a short break in the trees and found a clearing about twenty feet across, covered in bright green ivy. Rays of sunlight broke through, glistening on the dew-blanketed leaves, still damp hours after dawn. Without discussion, all three of them sat down to take a short rest, each finding a fallen tree or rock on which to sit.

'This is kind of cool,' Paul said, looking around at the border of trees, the green ivy, the cascading sun.

'Looks like something out of a fantasy book,' Tick said.

Paul nodded, then winced as if the small movement had hurt his arm somehow. 'Yeah,' he said through a tight grin. 'Maybe we'll see some elves.'

'Or vicious, man-eating monkeys that glow in the dark,' Sofia added.

Tick sniffed. 'Way to look on the bright side of things.'

'I just thought of something,' Sofia said, ignoring his remark.

'What?' Tick asked.

'Chu wouldn't have any way of knowing we'd take that train today. How could this be part of his plan?'

Tick shrugged. 'We know he's following us, spying on us. With all his freaky techno gadgets, I'm sure he could make a train crash whenever he wanted.'

'I guess.' She didn't sound convinced at all.

Paul stood after a few minutes of silence, his face wrinkling up like an old man's. 'I can't take this much longer. We need to get back.'

'Come on,' Tick said, standing and pointing across the clearing. 'I'm pretty sure we need to go that way.' He walked in that direction, Paul and Sofia right behind him.

✿

'We're getting close on the antidote.' Master George leaned forward, resting his folded hands on the kitchen table. Mothball sat to his left, Rutger to his right, Sally across from him. Muffintops curled on his lap, sound asleep. 'Rutger, why don't you give us a full report?'

The robust little man sat back in his chair, somehow resting one pudgy foot on his other knee – a feat that seemed impossible at first glance. 'This plague is just about as fascinating a thing as I've ever seen. It's completely nanotechnology based, yet it shows qualities of an airborne virus, as well as some bacterial characteristics. It's basically an unprecedented mixture of biological manipulation, microarchitectural nanotech computer processing, and cellular airwave transmissions the likes of which we've never seen.'

Sally slammed his thick-knuckled hands on the table. 'George, what in tarnations is this fool-headed sack of pork-and-beans yappin' about?'

'Fool-headed?' Rutger countered. 'Sally, you couldn't add five plus five using your fingers.'

'So ya admit it, then?' Mothball said.

'What?' Rutger asked.

'That yer a sack of pork-and-beans? Only complained about the fool part, ya did.'

'Ten!' Sally shouted out.

Everyone looked at Sally, who held up his hands, fingers outstretched. 'Five plus five is ten.'

'Well, I *do* apologise,' Rutger said. 'I've vastly underestimated your abilities to perform mathematical functions.'

'Ain't nothin',' Sally replied. 'I ain't never been able to reckon how much food you can stuff down that there gully a'yorn.'

Mothball snorted a laugh, then covered her face as her shoulders shook.

'All right,' Master George said with a huff. 'That's quite enough of this silly bickering. Rutger, I can only speak for myself when I say I had a bit of trouble following your analysis as well, and I've been working with you from the beginning. Please, tell us again, but this time don't try to sound so smart.'

'*Try?* Master George, I–'

'Please, Rutger.'

Rutger shot a nasty look at Sally, then composed himself, taking a deep breath, which resembled a beach ball inflating and deflating on the chair. 'In simpler terms, so *all* of you can understand it – Sato has nano-techs inside his body that can take control of his brain functions – and therefore his whole body. It's a technologically created disease, a virus made completely of artificial materials. However, it spreads just like an airborne virus, and once the plague is inside you, the virus can be controlled from a centrally located command centre, which happens to be inside the Fourth Reality.'

Sally threw his arms up in the air. 'Well, you done cleared it up, han't ya!'

''Tis a robot germ,' Mothball said. 'A wee little robot that makes ya do whatever that ruddy Chu tells ya. Spreads just like the flu, it does.'

Sally looked over at Rutger, raising his eyebrows. 'Now why on mama's grave couldn't you a-said it that simple-like?'

'Because I'm not used to speaking down to your level,' Rutger replied, folding his short, fat arms.

Sally turned to Master George. 'Why ain't *we* caught the sucker if it's liken the flu?'

'Because we've been extra careful,' Master George replied. 'We've worn gloves when we've had to handle Sato. We've fumigated his cell room on a regular basis. We've worn masks when necessary. It's a dangerous disease, dear Sally, but it's not invincible. Not yet, anyway.'

'What about the antidote?' Mothball asked. 'Methinks you've got news, ya do, or we wouldn't be sittin' 'ere tryin' to decide which of these two knuckleheads gots the smaller brain.'

'We're very close to having it solved,' Rutger said. 'Since the whole power of this plague lies in its ability to be controlled from Chu's headquarters, we think we can kill it in one swift stroke. All we have to do is inject our antidote into the home source, whatever that may be.'

'That easy, is it?' Mothball asked.

Master George cleared his throat. 'Easy, Mothball? I'm afraid not. This ... device, this *thing*, that controls those infected with the nanoplague will be well-protected. Ironically, its vulnerability will be the very thing that ensures its invulnerability.'

Sally merely blinked, and Master George had to suppress a smile.

'We can only assume that the device is what Reginald has referred to as Dark Infinity, and there's simply no hope or chance of us ever seeing it in person.'

'Then what you figger we's gonna do?' Sally asked. Master George paused, staring at Sally for a very long moment before finally speaking. 'Our only hope is to get the antidote, once it's completed, to Tick and the others. Then they must win Chu's contest and get on the inside.'

Mothball sniffed. Rutger coughed. Sally scratched his ear.

'Our only hope is for Reginald Chu to summon the very thing that will destroy him.' Master George reached down and stroked the soft fur of his beloved cat, who was still snoozing. 'But how we will do that without losing our dear young friends, I just don't know.'

Monkeying Around

Paul was getting steadily worse. His arm had ballooned to twice its normal size, blue-purple streaks scratched across the tight skin. As bad as it looked, his moans of pain were worse; he sounded as if he were minutes away from dying. Whatever the case, his condition rattled Sofia's nerves.

'It can't be much farther,' she said. 'All that whining is only going to make it hurt more.'

'Thanks for your concern, as usual,' Paul replied, his voice strained. 'Let me break *your* arm – see how you like it.'

Sofia huffed. 'I was in the train too.' She held up her hands, shook them. 'Don't see anything wrong here, do you?'

'It's gotta be up there somewhere,' Tick cut in, trying to prevent an all-out war between his two friends. 'Just keep walking.'

They did. Over huge roots, under branches as thick as three men, through thorn-spiked bushes, past swampy pools of sludge. Scraped and bruised, Tick felt his thin hopes vanishing altogether as trees gave way to nothing but more trees. The forest thickened;

the animal hoots and howls increased in volume; the air darkened with shadows. Nothing gave the slightest hint they were approaching a city or any kind of civilisation whatsoever.

All the while, Paul's grunts and groans made life miserable for everyone – worrying about his condition seemed almost as bad as being in the condition itself.

'Hey, something's up there!' Sofia shouted.

Tick stumbled on a rock hidden under a pile of wet, clumpy leaves. They'd gone so long without anyone speaking that Sofia's words startled him. He grabbed a thick vine, which saved him from hitting the ground, but rubbed a nasty sore spot on his palm as it slid through his fingers.

'What?' Paul asked through a tight breath, the one word taking all his effort.

'A light,' Sofia answered, pointing, then moving in that direction, just slightly off the course they'd been following. 'It's definitely a light – a couple of them. I think it's a building!'

Tick's heart soared, his weary pessimism from just seconds earlier vanishing. 'Let's go!' he shouted, rather pointlessly. Even Paul's step quickened with renewed strength.

The three of them slipped past a thick wall of foliage and rounded a huge oak. Ahead of them, the trees thinned and signs of Circle City were everywhere. Tick could even see a couple of people walking along the great round road bordering the town.

'We did it!' Sofia said, then stepped forward, ready to start running. But something crashed down from the branches above, landing right in front of her. Sofia shrieked and jumped back, almost knocking

Paul to the ground.

Tick stared ahead, his mind battling between fear and curiosity.

A thick, heavily furred animal crouched before them on all four legs, its slimy nostrils sniffing as it bared a mouth full of white fangs. Its body resembled a bear, but its face looked more like a wolf's; yellow eyes glaring from a narrow, elongated face. Drool dripped from its jaws and teeth, a low growl rumbled deep within its chest.

But what caught Tick's attention was how the creature *glowed* – a deep, eerie red that rippled along its fur like small waves on a pond. Each strand of hair shone, as if optical fibres charged with pulsing lava sprouted from the creature's skin.

'The glowing monkeys,' Tick whispered.

'Radioactive demon bears,' Paul replied, a little louder.

The animal took a step forward, its eyes focusing on Paul, then Sofia, then Tick. Its non-stop growl gurgled and grew louder; its mouth opened wider. The thing seemed to have a hundred teeth, all sharp and pointy.

Tick yelped when something crashed to the ground to the right of the animal, then another to its left. Two more creatures, looking as vicious and hungry as the first. But they all stayed where they'd landed, studying the three humans.

'What do we do?' Tick asked, not caring how shaky his voice sounded.

'If we run, they might pounce on us,' Sofia said.

Paul didn't say anything, cradling his swollen arm, his tight face drenched in sweat.

'If we *don't* run, they might pounce on us,' Tick replied.

The lead creature barked, a loud yelp that rang through the air like the sickening, desperate plea of an injured dog. In the distance, something called back, then another, then another – eerie, ringing wails echoing through the thick forest.

How smart are *these things?* Tick wondered as he felt his brief spurt of curiosity quickly igniting into all-out panic. There was nothing they could do – nothing!

Creaking and crashing sounded from behind them, twigs and branches breaking, leaves and foliage swishing as large things moved closer. More of the creatures.

'We have to do something,' Tick said, not bothering to whisper any more. 'Before we're surrounded.'

'Turn and run,' Paul grunted. 'Can you do it?' Sofia asked. 'Got to,' he replied.

'On the count of three,' Tick said, 'turn and go in a wide circle to the left. Head back around towards the city.'

Sofia shook her head. 'Maybe we should split up.'

'No!' Tick said, surprised at how quickly the word came out. 'On the count of three, together.'

'Fine, to the left.'

Heat surged through Tick's veins, his heart skittering. 'One ... two ...'

'Three!' Paul screamed.

They turned in unison and broke into a run, back into the thicker forest, scurrying around a huge tree. The three huge animals yelped their strange barks in response, and Tick could hear the heavy thumps of their footfalls in pursuit.

Sofia pushed into the lead, throwing herself forward through a tangled knot of bushes between two trees. Paul followed her, then Tick. He turned his head to see the first animal barrel around the wide trunk of the oak, slipping in the leaves as it tried to get its footing. Its yellow eyes flared, like two small suns buried in the dark red glow of its huge body.

Tick looked away, throwing his strength into his legs, running, ignoring the branches ripping at his clothes and skin. 'Go, go, go!' he shouted.

They tore through the forest, Sofia dodging and sidestepping, finding the best route, slowly making her way in a wide arc to the left, back towards the city. Paul lumbered as he ran, gripping his hurt arm, leaning forward at a dangerous angle as he pushed ahead. Tick took up the rear, knowing the enormous monsters at his back could rip him to pieces at any second. He could hear their breath, their pounding footsteps, their steady growls.

More sounds entered the fray, crashing and breaking all around them, louder and closer than before. Tick didn't dare look, but it sounded like entire trees had been snapped in two. The ground trembled, as if dozens of the creatures had showed up to join the hunt, flanking them, surrounding them – jumping through the branches *above* them.

'Faster!' he yelled.

The trees thinned again, signs of the city ahead jumping into view. They were only a few seconds from breaking through the forest edge and into the street. Tick suspected something prevented the glowing creatures from entering the town – he had no idea what, but he didn't care; they were almost safe.

They ran on, the deafening cacophony of sounds filling the air like a sonic whirlwind. Splitting wood, cracking, breaking, crashing. The roars and screams of the creatures pursuing them. The thumps of their footsteps. Above it all, a steady rumble shook the ground, as if lightning had struck nearby, thunder splintering the world around them. Tick didn't understand what was happening. Doubt filled him: how had they made it? How had they outrun the beasts?

Sofia broke past the last line of trees, Paul and Tick close behind. They didn't slow or look back, running at a full sprint until they had reached the far side of the wide road encircling the city. Once there, panting and heaving for breaths, hands on knees, Tick turned to make sure they were safe.

Despite his exhaustion, despite his racing heart, despite his need to suck in as much air as possible, his breath caught in his throat. He straightened, eyes widening.

'What ... the ...' Paul managed between gasps of air. 'What ... how ...'

Across the street, past the narrow area of small trees leading to the thicker forest from which they'd just escaped, a huge bulk of mangled wood rose towards the sky, dozens of feet high, countless trees smashed into a coiled mass. It looked like a large section of the woods had been liquefied and squeezed together, *twisted* together, then frozen into a hideous swirl of matter. In several spots, some of the creatures that had chased them were trapped in the wall of wood, as if they'd been sealed in hardened tar right before escaping. One of the animals' legs twitched.

It was just like what they'd seen in the woods by Tick's home, right after the bizarre attack from Mr.

Chu, when a deer had been trapped in the strangled structure of entwined trees.

Tick's mind emptied, void of thoughts. The two incidents had to be connected, but not even a hint of understanding cowered in the darkness of his head. Confused, he thought it must have something to do with Reginald Chu. Breathing heavily, relieved but uneasy, he turned away from the ugliness in the forest and looked at his friends.

'Someone please tell me what just happened,' Paul said, his eyes still glued to the massive lump across the street.

'Wish I could,' Tick said.

'We have the weirdest lives in the universe,' Sofia said.

Paul finally broke his gaze, lifting his broken arm a few inches, testing his injury. With a wince, he lowered his elbow back into the cradle of his other arm. 'I've gotta get to a hospital.'

'We don't have time,' Sofia said.

Paul let out a bitter laugh, but didn't say anything.

'What do you mean?' Tick said. 'We have to find him a doctor.'

Sofia pointed to her watch. 'It's already four-thirty. We only have thirty minutes left.'

'But–'

'Tick,' Paul cut in.

Tick looked at him. Paul's body was covered in sweat, his eyes so bloodshot they looked as if they'd been dipped in red paint. The scowl of pain on his face had created deep lines in his forehead, large cracks that seemed permanent. But somehow, despite everything, Paul smiled – a miserable grimace, but a smile all the same.

'She's right,' he said. 'Broken arm, broken leg, broken head – doesn't matter. Hungry, thirsty, ugly – doesn't matter. We've only got thirty minutes.'

Tick paused, exchanging long glances with both of them. Finally, he nodded.

'Let's go,' he said.

They took off, running along the wide arc of the border street.

Five O'Clock

It took fifteen minutes to find the intersection representing five o'clock. Luckily, their hotel, The Stroke of Midnight Inn, had been two streets down from where they'd exited the forest. Once there, Tick and the others ran with renewed strength, counting the times off as they sprinted towards their destination.

One o'clock. Two o'clock. Three, four, five. Gasping each breath, Tick doubled over to rest, hands on his knees, while he scanned the area for any sign of what they were supposed to do to wink away. They had only ten minutes until the *real* five o'clock.

The thick forest hugged the outside curve of the main street, the line of massive trees looming like ancient wooden towers. Thankfully, there was no sign of any mutant radioactive demon monkey-bears. The road that led from the town square of Circle City to the woods was bordered with various buildings and shops, people bustling about with smiles on their faces but blank looks in their eyes, as if kindness had worn thin and they only wanted to get their next task done. The eerie opera-lady music blared from unseen speakers.

The "T" formed by the two-street intersection was mostly empty, the clean pavement unblemished by potholes or cracks. Tick couldn't see so much as a sewer grate, and wondered why everything about this Reality seemed simple but ... *off* somehow.

I hope I never find out, he thought. *I want out of here.*

Paul zigzagged back and forth as he scanned the street for any sign or clue of a place in which they might need to stand at the appointed time. He clutched his arm and limped as if the pain had travelled through the rest of his body. Sofia searched as well, and Tick joined in. No one said a word, but worry and discouragement hung in the air like wilting clouds. Time was running out. Though confident they were in the right place, Tick didn't know if that was good enough.

```
It does not matter; I do not care.
Just make sure your feet find air.
```

'The word *air* has to be carved somewhere,' Paul said.

'Yeah,' Tick mumbled as he walked awkwardly along, bent over, searching the pavement.

Sofia had stopped, her arms folded. 'I think we're thinking too much. Or maybe not enough.'

Tick looked at his watch. Six minutes. 'What do you mean?'

'I mean, I think all we need to do is jump,' she replied. 'Jump up at five o'clock, and our feet will be in the air.'

Tick stood straight, stretched his back. 'Hmm. Possible,' he said. But something tickled the back of his brain. Something didn't seem right. 'But what if that's not it?'

'Got any better ideas?'

Tick looked at Paul, who was still searching, still wincing with every step. His arm looked like a giant purple slug.

'What do you think?' Tick asked.

Paul answered without stopping his hunt. 'I thought of that, but ... I don't know, I guess there's nothing else to do. Just keep looking, and if we don't find anything by the one-minute mark, we'll stand in the middle of the road and jump at five o'clock.'

'Sounds good,' Tick said, resuming his search. One minute passed. Two. No sign of anything, anywhere. Two minutes left. Nothing.

'Time's almost up,' Sofia said, running towards the exact middle of the intersection. 'Come on, hurry!'

Paul and Tick joined her. One minute to go. Then, like someone had dropped a water balloon on his head, a thought slammed into his mind. *Make sure your feet find air. Make sure your feet find* air!

'Your socks and shoes!' he screamed, reaching down before they could respond and ripping off his right shoe, not bothering to untie it. 'Take off your shoes!' He pulled off his sock and then moved to his left foot.

Neither of them responded or argued – they did as they were told. Paul used his feet to kick off his shoes, then his one good arm to remove his socks. Anyone watching might have thought they'd gone nuts, or had ants crawling along their skin. But in a matter of twenty seconds, the three of them stood barefoot, the pavement warm on their feet, holding their shoes and socks.

'Fifteen seconds,' Sofia whispered through a big breath.

'You're a genius, Tick,' Paul said, his shoes wedged under his armpit.

'Ten seconds,' Sofia said.

'Maybe we should jump just in case,' Paul blurted out.

'Do it,' Tick agreed.

Sofia nodded as she counted the last five seconds. 'Five, four, three, two, one – now!'

Tick had already bent his legs, and jumped into the air on her call.

When he came back down, the world around them had vanished, and his feet landed on something very cold.

☼

'This is weird,' Rutger said as he stared at the Command Centre screen, his eyes glued to the tracking marks of Tick's Earwig Transponder. Master George, Sally, and Mothball stood behind him. They'd all come running when the chime had rung through the building, indicating Tick had winked to another location.

'Weird, indeed,' Master George whispered.

'Whatcha two hanks goin' on 'bout?' Sally bellowed. 'I ain't got nary a clue what that thing a'yorn's tellin' me.' He pointed at the screen.

Rutger answered. 'They just winked to a large plain in Reality Prime – but in the middle of nowhere. The far northern reaches of Canada, it looks like. Nothing for dozens of miles around them.'

'Goodness gracious me,' Master George whispered. 'Chu's tests are getting way out of hand. The poor chaps and Sofia will freeze up there!'

'Mayhaps we need be rescuin' them,' Mothball said. Master George shook his head adamantly. 'Absolutely not. The antidote is as complete as it'll ever get, and we have to get it where it needs to be. Let's just all pray it *works*. Sally.'

The large man jumped, as if he'd been caught daydreaming. 'Yessir?'

'This may be our best chance – our last chance. I want you to wink there right away and give them the antidote.'

Sally's eyes grew wide. 'But ... I'm a-feared of the cold somethin' awful.'

'No matter,' Master George said over his shoulder as he walked briskly away, heading for the testing lab. 'Come on, chop-chop!'

Rutger couldn't help but feel sorry for the big lug of a man. He reached up and tapped Sally on the elbow. 'You'll be fine. Just wink in, wink out. No problem.'

Sally laughed, his booming chortle echoing off the walls of the room. 'You ain't got no thermal undies I could borry, do ya?'

'Hilarious,' Rutger said, hopping down from his chair to follow Master George.

☼

'Ah, dude, it's freezing here!' Paul said. He sat down on the hard ground and started struggling back into his shoes using only one arm. Sofia knelt down and helped him.

Although the bottoms of Tick's feet felt like they stood on ice, he turned in a slow circle, gawking at the new place they'd been winked to. It was a barren, miserable land, flat and grey in every direction, all the way to the horizon. Not a plant or tree or animal in sight. The sun poked through a brief break in a cloud-heavy sky, but it added no colour to the bleakness, no warmth. There was no snow, but everything about the area looked cold and dreary.

Then he saw something that stopped him. A small building – a tiny, leaning wooden hut just a few hundred feet away.

'Just be glad it's not winter,' Sofia said, tying her shoelaces. 'Or we'd have already been frozen.'

Tick snapped out of his daze and sat down, pulling on his first sock. 'I wonder what that little shack is over there.' He pointed.

Paul and Sofia glanced in that direction.

'Looks abandoned,' Paul said. He grimaced as he lay back on his one good elbow, his injured arm resting on his ribs.

Tick finished tying his shoes. 'I wonder where we are.' He stood up, the ground too cold and hard.

Sofia joined him. 'Who knows? Let's go check out that building.'

Paul groaned. 'Couldn't that jerk have sent us somewhere that has a hospital? I'd settle for a place that sells aspirin. But no – he had to send us to Pluto.'

'Come on,' Tick said, offering his hand to help him stand.

Paul shook his head. 'It hurts too much. Got my own way of moving now.' He pushed off with his elbow, then rolled to his knees. After taking a couple of deep breaths, he stumbled to his feet, a little off balance. Tears rimmed the bottom edges of his eyes; one escaped and trickled down his cheek.

Tick quickly looked away, pretending he hadn't

noticed. *Oh, man,* he thought. *He's gonna die on us.*

Sofia wasn't as kind. 'Are you *crying?* I thought you were a lot tougher than that.'

Tick felt a shudder of anger wash through him; he had a sudden urge to punch Sofia in the arm, but quelled it. 'I'd cry too if my arm was broken and I was stuck in the middle of nowhere. Come on.' He started walking towards the small shack.

He didn't look back to see their response, but he heard them following. Paul's feet scraped the ground with every step, sounding like he dragged a dead body behind him.

As they approached the building, Tick noticed it was at least three times as big as he'd originally thought, and farther away. *There's something about a vast land of nothingness that messes up your senses,* he thought.

The building had only one story, its entire structure made from warped, sun-faded wooden boards with thousands of splinters poking out. The two-sided roof peaked in the middle, slanting steeply downwards until it overhung the walls in eaves that almost touched the ground. *To handle all the snow in the winter,* Tick thought. The place had no windows, and its door was a simple slab of wood, the only thing on the shack that had ever been painted. Only a few streaks of dull red had survived the weather. A rusted doorknob hung loosely from the warped door.

'Looks just like Grandma's house,' Paul said. His voice was so tight Tick couldn't tell if he was joking.

'I bet whoever lives here has never heard of Pacini spaghetti,' Sofia said.

Tick was about to respond but stumbled on his first word. They were close enough for him to notice something creepy about the door. The red paint he'd seen wasn't the remnants of an age-old decorating scheme after all.

They were *words,* scrawled across the entire face of the wooden door from top to bottom.

'Look!' he shouted, already sprinting ahead to see what it said.

'What?' Sofia yelled from behind him. Tick ignored them, and soon they ran to catch up.

Tick stopped just a few feet in front of the door. At first, he couldn't make out the words of the message, the writing hasty and messy, some of the paint having run down like blood into the other letters. But there was no mistaking Tick's *name,* and soon everything else became clear.

He tried to speak, but his mouth had dried up and his tongue wouldn't move. He felt like someone had rammed a glob of cotton down his throat with a wooden spoon.

Sofia read the words out loud.

ONLY TWO PEOPLE MAY ENTER THIS DOOR. ATTICUS HIGGINBOTTOM AND MISTRESS JANE.
ALL OTHERS WILL DIE A HORRIBLE DEATH.

DO NOT TEST ME ON THIS.

THE ANTIDOTE

Tick could only stare at the message, the world around him shrinking away. He felt like an entire hour had passed, but he knew it had only been a minute or two since Sofia had read the words aloud.

He could only stare.

'What's that supposed to mean?' Paul said, though his voice sounded to Tick like it came down a long tunnel.

'What do you think, Einstein?' Sofia replied, her tone full of anger. 'Chu wants Tick to go in there, but not us!'

'I know, but what does that *mean?*'

'Looks like ya'll hain't got nuttin' but trouble comin' down dem gullets a'yorn.'

The gruff voice from behind shook Tick out of his stupor. He whirled to see Sally standing there, arms folded, looking like he'd just lost that morning's grits and eggs. Face pale, beard scraggly, eyes bloodshot, the man didn't seem too happy to see them. He was dressed in his usual lumberjack garb – thick green flannel shirt, dusty overalls, big brown work boots. A leather satchel hung loosely over his shoulder.

Paul let out a little yelp at Sally's surprise appearance. 'Sa-Sally? Where'd you come from?'

'Where you think, boy?' He made an unpleasant sucking sound in his throat then spat on the ground. 'Ol' George sent me after you rug rats.'

'How'd you get here?' Sofia asked. 'You can't tell me there's a cemetery nearby.'

Sally turned and pointed at nothing in particular. 'There's a might nice spot of his fancy kyoopy gobbledygook back yonder ways. You three too busy starin' at that big pile of sticks to notice me comin' up on ya.'

Tick shook his head, finally feeling like the world had solidified again around him. *That message on the door, he thought. That message!* 'Why'd Master George send you back to us? I thought we were on our own.'

Sally shrugged his bulky shoulders. 'Still are, I 'spect. Just come to pass on a little somethin', that's all.'

He slid the satchel off his shoulder and down his arm, then opened it up. After a few seconds of rummaging around, he pulled out a shiny silver cylinder, two inches in diameter and six inches long.

'This here whatchamacallit is for you whipsnaps,' he said, holding the small rod out towards Sofia, who stood closest to him.

She shook her head. 'If that's what I think it is, you better give it to Tick. We can't go with him any more.'

Sally's arm dropped to his side, the cylinder gripped in his hand; his eyes squinted in confusion. 'What in the name of Mama's chitlins stew you talkin' 'bout? You ain't done forgot the plan, did ya?'

Tick wanted to say something, but the words stuck in his throat again.

284

'No, we didn't forget the *plan*,' Sofia said with a sneer, then pointed towards the door with the creepy red letters scrawled across it. 'But that stupid door says that only Tick can go through it. If Master George wants him to get close to Chu, looks like he's on his own.'

'You don't know that,' Tick said, forcing the words out through a cough that rubbed the back of his mouth raw. 'Maybe I just need to go in, do something, and come right back out.'

'Doubt it,' Paul muttered.

'Why?' Tick asked.

'I just have a feeling it's done for us, dude. I think Chu wanted you from the beginning because of your freak show back in the Thirteenth – winking us with a broken Barrier Wand and all. We're done – I know it.'

Tick looked at Sofia, pleading with his eyes. 'I think he's right,' she said, frowning.

Sally walked forward until he was close enough to read the message on the door. 'Whoever wrote that nonsense ain't got a bit of learnin' in him, I can tell ya that. I can barely read dem chicken scratches.'

Sofia raised her eyebrows at Tick as if to say, *When did Sally get so smart?*

'Messy or not,' Paul said, 'it doesn't beat around the bush. Only Tick can go in there. If we try, we'll die a, uh, horrible death.'

'That's only half the problem I'm worried about,' Tick said. 'What does Mistress Jane have to do with it? Why just me and her?'

'Reckon you and that no-good tweety-bird's all Chu cares about,' Sally said with a grumble. He spat again.

Tick squeezed his fists at his side, then rubbed them

against his temples. 'I can't do this,' he whispered. 'I can't go in there by myself.' His insides churned with panic, as if internal wires had been crossed, messing up his whole organ system. He felt like a sissy, but the truth of it weighed on him like the chilly air had finally frozen solid around him. *I can't do it,* he thought. *I can't go in there without Paul and Sofia!*

'Ah, now,' Sally said. 'Ain't no time for that. You ain't got nuttin' but brave inside you, boy. Suck it on up, hear?' He held the shiny chrome cylinder out to Tick.

Tick stared at it, not moving a muscle.

Paul walked over and put his one good arm around Tick's shoulders, wincing with the effort. He leaned over and spoke close in Tick's ear. 'You listen to me, bro. No way we're gonna let anything happen to you. You're the one with that transponder thingy in your ear – we'll go back with Sally and keep an eye on every move you make. We won't sleep, won't eat, until we can wink back to get you.'

Tick nodded, then looked at Sofia. She stepped forward and grabbed the silver rod from Sally, then lightly shoved it against Tick's stomach.

'Paul's right,' she said, trying her best to throw compassion into her voice. 'The three of us will wink back to Master George and watch you like a hawk. First sign of trouble and we'll come help you.'

Tick waited a few seconds, then finally took the cylinder from Sofia. It was cool to the touch and slippery in his sweaty hands. 'I don't think you should do that. Follow me *or* come after me, I mean.'

'Why?' Paul asked.

'Well, if Chu wants me alone – or ... with Mistress Jane – then we better do things his way.'

'For a while, maybe,' Sofia said. She looked as if she might say more, but then closed her mouth.

Tick looked at Sally and held up the silver rod. 'What am I supposed to do with this anyway?'

Sally grunted and rummaged through his leather pack again. 'Ain't no way ol' George be lettin' *me* tell ya.' He pulled out a wadded up piece of paper and handed it to Tick. 'Read that, ain't too hard no-how.'

Tick unfolded the paper with shaking hands then read it out loud:

Dear Master Atticus,

You hold in your hands the antidote to Reginald Chu's nanoplague, which is causing people all through the Realities to go insane. We believe the plague can be destroyed by introducing this silver rod and its contents into the mechanism that controls the virus-like nanoparticles. You need simply to smash the antidote against Chu's device - Dark Infinity - and let Rutger's brilliant engineering do the rest of the work.

I need not tell you the incredible amount of danger you are about to undertake. I daresay, I almost feel tempted to abandon the whole thing. But alas, I think you'd agree that we have no choice. The fate of all the Realities may hang in the balance.

Atticus, you must do this thing. You must do it, no matter the cost.

Once we see sign of your success, we will come and rescue you. This, my good man, I swear to you.

Your comrade in arms, Master George

Tick held up the cylinder, studied it closely, ignoring his surge of panic. The odd object had no blemishes, no scratches, no smudges – it was perfectly smooth, perfectly shiny.

'Piece of cake,' he muttered with a pitiful attempt at a laugh. 'Waltz into Chu's house and smash this against something. Piece of cake.'

'Yeah, dude, piece of cake,' Paul said. Tick couldn't help but wish he could trade places with Paul, broken arm and all.

'You heard him,' Sofia said. 'You heard Master George. We'll be watching your every move, and we'll come save you as soon as ...' She trailed off, and Tick wished desperately that no one would say another word.

'I'm going,' he said, pushing the fear away. *Now or never. Just move.* 'I'm going right now. Sally, can I have that bag of yours?'

Sally nodded, then handed over the leather satchel. Tick put the cylinder and the message from Master George inside, zipped it up, then slung it over his shoulder. 'I'm going right now,' he said again.

Without waiting for a response, Tick turned and walked up to the dilapidated wooden door. As he reached down and twisted the loose handle, the others spoke from behind him.

'We'll be watching you, dude,' Paul said.

'You'll be the only thing we care about until we're back together,' Sofia blurted out.

'You be tough chickens, now, ya hear?' Sally shouted.

Tick pushed open the door and stepped inside. As he went through, a cold tingle shot down his back.

BEAUTIFUL BLACK HAIR

The room was completely dark but strangely warm. Tick pulled the door closed behind him, fighting to calm his breath, standing still in the blackness. The floor beneath him was solid, smooth; the air smelled like ... flowers. Like an old lady's perfume. He sniffed, then scratched his nose.

'Hello?' he called out. *Isn't that what they always say in the movies when they walk into a haunted house?* 'Hello?' he repeated. His voice died as soon as it left his mouth, without even an echo.

The entire room abruptly flared with lights; Tick's hand shot up to shield his eyes.

It came from everywhere at once: the walls, floor, and ceiling were made out of a rough material that glowed brightly. Tick turned around to see that the door had disappeared – and nothing looked anything like the inside of an old wooden shack.

Chu had already winked him to a new place.

The room was a perfect circle, thirty feet in diameter, bare of furniture except for several, almost invisible, clear plastic benches curving along the walls. That was it – no decorations, no signs, no light fixtures, nothing.

Just glowing walls and invisible benches.

'Heaven's waiting room,' Tick whispered.

'No, it's not,' a soft voice said from his left.

Tick spun in that direction, stumbling backwards two steps. Ten feet from him stood a tall woman, close to the wall, dressed in a tightly fitted yellow dress. Long, silky black hair hung from her head and framed a pale but perfect face; her red lips pulled tightly into a grim smile. Brilliant green eyes stared through horn-rimmed glasses. Tick was certain he couldn't have missed her before. She had appeared out of nowhere.

'Who ... who are you?' he asked.

The woman ignored him, scanning the room around her with a disgusted look, as if it were full of snakes and lizards and frogs. 'This place is about as far from heaven as you can get in the Realities.' Despite her apparent anger, her voice still gave Tick goosebumps, as if he listened to someone playing the harp.

'Who are you?' he repeated. 'Are you–'

'Yes,' she replied, finally focusing her eyes on him. 'I imagine you saw a message similar to mine. My name is Mistress Jane, as yours must be Atticus Higginbottom.'

She walked over to him, her feet tap-tap-tapping as she did so. She stopped and held out a hand, which he took and shook quickly before letting go, a shudder of nausea trembling in his stomach. Master George's most hated enemy stood inches from him.

Tick cleared his throat. 'I ... I thought you were bald.' He didn't know what else to say, what else to do.

Mistress Jane smiled, though it was empty of humour or kindness. 'Yes, I was bald for a very long time. So very long.' She stared past his shoulder as if remembering something sad from her past. 'And it was quite ... *painful* to grow it back so quickly. Painful, but sweet. That's how the Chi'karda works in the Thirteenth, after all.'

Tick swallowed, fidgeted on his feet. He was so lost and confused and scared. His mind spun; his heart thumped.

Mistress Jane caught his eyes again, then continued. 'So many things have changed, boy. *I've* changed. Do you understand?'

Tick couldn't speak. He slowly shook his head.

Jane nodded. 'Yes, we have a lot to talk about. A lot.' She reached out and took his hand, squeezed it. 'Reginald wanted me to kill you, you know? That was my task.'

'Kill me?' Tick managed to say, almost a squeak.

Jane's eyes closed and opened in a long, drawn out blink. 'Yes, I was supposed to kill you. And I could have, easily – I crashed your spintrain to make Chu think I was at least trying. But I knew you'd survive.' She paused. 'But you and I are going to turn the tables, Atticus.'

'What do you mean?' Tick pulled his hand away from hers.

Jane paused again before answering. 'As dangerous as you and that baboon George may think I am, Mr. Higginbottom, Reginald Chu is far, far worse. *Far* worse. And you and I are going to stop him. Forever.'

✸

Paul stared at the door for a full two minutes after it closed behind Tick, tempted to rip it back open and chase after his friend. But after all they'd been through – after all the things they'd seen Chu do to them – he knew the warning scrawled across the wood was for real.

Finally, he looked away, turned his back to the building. A fresh burst of pain exploded up his arm and into his shoulders, making him cry out before he could stop himself. For the hundredth time that day, tears welled in his eyes.

'Best be gettin' on,' Sally grunted, glancing one last time at the door. 'Better get that little sack of taters Rutger workin' on dat nasty limb a'yorn.' His eyes fell to Paul's swollen arm. 'Dat don't look so good.'

The lumberjack started walking away, making a straight line towards an area that looked just like the miles of dull nothingness in every other direction. 'Come on, rug rats!' he yelled over his shoulder.

Sofia and Paul turned in unison to look at the door one last time.

'Wonder what he's doing now,' Paul said.

Sofia touched Paul's shoulder. 'We'll find him,' she whispered, barely audible. 'Master George'll help us find him.' She nodded, then ran off towards Sally.

Paul followed; every step felt like a sledgehammer against his forearm. *My only hope now is a tiny, fat dude named Rutger. Great.*

They probably walked half a mile before Sally stopped and turned to face the kids behind him. 'Right chere seems 'bout right. Scoot yer buns on over here.'

Paul cradled his arm tightly against his body and stepped as close to Sally as he could. Sofia pressed in from the right until they were all squished together in a small circle.

'Great balls of turtle scat!' Sally bellowed. 'You ain't gotta get so close I can smell yer pits, now do ya!'

Despite the pain, Paul snickered as he backed away a couple of steps. Sofia did the same, but her eyes kept flickering back to the wooden building.

Sally reached into the pocket of his flannel shirt, digging for a few seconds before he pulled it back out again with nothing in his hand. 'Ol' George'll be winkin' us right directly.'

'What did you just do?' Paul asked.

Sally scrunched up his forehead like Paul had just asked him what the colour green looked like. 'Triggered the nanobobbamajig, boy, what else?'

Before Paul could ask another question, he felt a quick chill flash across his shoulders and down his spine. The drab world around him vanished, replaced instantly by a room filled with leather couches and chairs, a warm fire crackling and spitting in a small brick fireplace. Master George stood in front of it, the Barrier Wand clasped in his hands and Muffintops the cat purring at his heels. Rutger perched on a floor pillow, leaning back against one of the sofas, his hands folded and resting on top of his huge belly.

'Quickly,' Master George sputtered, throwing all greetings and formalities out the window. 'Have a seat and tell us everything, and I mean everything!'

'My arm,' Paul said, his voice breaking on the last word. 'My arm,' he repeated. Now that help was so close, the pain seemed to intensify, flaring through his whole body as if more than one bone had been broken.

Master George looked down and noticed the ballooned arm, the skin stretched taut, bruised and bulging. 'My goodness, man! Your arm is hurt!'

Paul said nothing, feebly attempting a smile.

'Rutger,' Master George snapped. 'Take Paul to the

infirmary this instant. Then wink in Doctor Hillenstat from the Second and tell him to deaden the pain, set the bone, cast it – what have you. We'll follow you and have our discussion there. Chop-chop!'

Rutger rolled to his left, got stuck, then grunted as he tried rolling to his right. His body slipped off the pillow, his arms and legs flailing as he tried to find the leverage he needed to stand up. 'Good grief, would someone *give me a hand,* please?'

Mothball entered the room, wiping her hands on her shirt and chewing on something. 'What's this?' she asked. 'There's a ruddy bowling ball loose, there is! Someone snatch it up before it breaks a vase!'

'Oh, go on and make jokes, then,' Rutger said, lying on the floor as his body rolled back and forth. 'Poor Master Paul only has a severely broken arm – no big deal.'

Mothball's face melted into a frown as her eyes fell upon Paul's injury. 'Oh, dear, terribly sorry. Quite nasty that, by the looks of it.'

'Yeah,' was all Paul managed to say. The room had started to pitch and spin in his vision.

'All right, then,' Mothball said as she reached down and yanked Rutger to his feet with a big roar. 'Get the lad the help he needs.'

'Come on, Paul,' Rutger said, swiping at the dust on his round bottom.

Paul nodded and followed him as he heard Master George speaking to the others.

'Sofia, Sally – I need to know everything.'

THE TALE OF MISTRESS JANE

'Let's have a seat,' Mistress Jane said. 'I'm sure Reginald will be here shortly to rant and rave his frustration that we both made it here alive.'

She grabbed Tick's arm again, pulling him towards one of the impossibly clear benches lining the lighted walls. Once there, she let go and sat down, crossing her legs under the tight yellow material of her dress. She flicked her thick black hair across her shoulder then motioned for Tick to sit next to her.

Tick wanted to run. No, he wanted to yell and scream at Jane for the terrible things she'd done, including killing one of Mothball's closest friends, Annika. He wanted to rip her ridiculous glasses off, throw them on the ground, crush them with his shoe, then punch her square between her flaming green eyes. He wanted to –

'Sit down!' she shouted, her voice echoing through the room as though a chorus of Janes had called out the two words.

Tick fell to the bench, his short burst of spirit crushed. He folded his hands in his lap, staring at the glowing floor below his feet.

Jane took a deep breath. 'I'm ... I'm very sorry, Atticus. I should not have spoken to you like that. I apologise.'

Tick closed his eyes for a few seconds, then opened them again. He realised suddenly that the woman sitting next to him was crazy. Crazy and dangerous.

'Now,' Jane said. 'There are a lot of things I need to tell you. I'm sure George has made you think I'm a monster, a cruel and heartless devil who cares nothing for the Realities or their people. Nothing could be further from the truth.'

Tick looked up. 'How can you say that? I saw Annika die – killed by those disgusting monsters *you* created! Then you tried to have them kill me!'

Mistress Jane held up a finger to silence him. 'I want you to be quiet. Do you understand this request?'

'Why should I–'

Jane flicked her finger. Something yanked Tick from the bench and threw him three feet into the air, spinning his body in the middle of the room. He screamed, thrashing his arms and legs. He spun faster, the unseen force gripping him like invisible claws as it wheeled him about, pinching and battering him.

'Stop it!' he yelled. 'Put me down!'

The force vanished in an instant, and he crashed to the floor, one leg bent awkwardly beneath his body. He cried out as he squirmed to the side and pulled it straight. Gasping for breath, he pushed himself to his knees and stared at Jane, his eyes on fire.

'Why would you–'

'*Silence!*' she screamed, cutting him off again as she stood up, her face flushing red. 'You will come over here. You will sit. And you will listen. Do you understand?'

Tick felt as if his old nemesis, Billy "The Goat" Cooper, had just sucker punched him in the stomach three times. Fighting tears, he slowly got to his feet and walked back to the bench. Without looking at Mistress Jane, swearing to himself he would never look her in the eyes again, he sat down.

After a few seconds of silence, Jane sat as well, crossing her legs again.

'Atticus,' she said, almost in a whisper, as if she hadn't spent the last minute torturing him. 'This ... these are the things about me I don't like. My temper, my impatience, my quickness to anger. I've tried very hard in recent weeks to better myself. To improve myself and be kinder to others.'

Tick snorted with all the disgust he could muster. 'Yeah, obviously.'

Mistress Jane paused. 'Think what you will. But know this – if Reginald had challenged me to kill you two months ago, perhaps even one month ago, your body would even now be rotting beneath several feet of earth. I have changed my ways as best I can, but my goal remains the same as it has always been – to save the Realities. I will never waver from it.'

Tick clenched his hands together, still staring at the white floor. 'I don't even know what you're talking about.'

'Reginald needs us, Atticus. He needs someone very powerful to help him with his project. His Dark Infinity project. And the two of us were the only ones he deemed worthy enough for the test – you with your silly riddles and death-defying adventures, and me with the simple task of killing you. Only one winner. Only one apprentice for Chu.'

Tick leaned back against the wall and looked at Jane, already breaking his vow. 'How could he possibly think that killing me would be a challenge for you? That's the dumbest thing I've ever heard.'

Jane smiled, her green eyes flickering with a dark flame. 'Atticus. Boy. You have no idea what you've done these past days. What you're *capable* of doing. Though I don't yet understand it, I have no shame in admitting that *you* have more potential than even I do. And you've done it without the benefit of living in the Thirteenth and soaking in its quantum mutations.'

Tick shook his head and leaned forward, his elbows on his knees, resuming his study of the floor. 'You don't need to talk any more – you've proven that you're crazy ten times already.' From the corner of his eye, he noticed Jane's hands quiver. She folded them together and paused a long time before speaking again.

'I'm going to tell you a story, Atticus,' she said in a calm, quiet voice. 'I want to tell you so you'll understand me. I only ask that you listen without interrupting. Will you do that for me?'

Tick didn't say anything, but he couldn't help feeling a surge of curiosity. He finally nodded.

Mistress Jane began. 'I'm a scientist, Atticus. I have been since my earliest memories, experimenting in the backyard and reading every book in the library on the laws of nature. I have lived it and breathed it, as they say. Twenty years ago I was recruited into the Realitants, in much the same way you were. It didn't take long for me to master the wonders of quantum physics and excel in my assigned missions to study and document the Realities. By my third year, I was the most powerful of all the Realitants, and everyone knew it.'

She paused, as if her pride wanted to ensure Tick realised what she'd said. That she was the best of the best.

Tick didn't move or say a word, and Jane finally continued.

'But then something happened, Atticus. Something tragic that still wakes me in the night, haunting me with visions and memories. I fell in love.'

Tick couldn't help but look up at her. He didn't know what he'd been expecting, but this surprised him.

Jane nodded. 'I won't speak his name to you because your ears aren't worthy to hear it. And please' – she held out a hand and lightly caressed his arm then pulled back – 'I don't mean that as an insult to you. It's just that ... his name is sacred to me, and I've sworn to never say it aloud. I hope you understand.'

'I don't care what his name was,' Tick mumbled under his breath.

Jane's hands shook again, and Tick winced. *Shut up, Tick,* he thought. *Don't say another word or she might twist your head off!*

'He loved the colour yellow.' Jane laughed, a distant, surprisingly light-hearted chuckle that faded as quickly as it began. 'It was strange how much he loved the colour. Yellow shirts were his favourite. He painted the walls of his home yellow. And he always gave me daisies and daffodils. I asked him once why he loved it so much and he told me it was because yellow represented peace. And if anything described the life and purpose of that man, it was peace.'

Tick rolled his eyes, quickly rubbing his face to hide it from Jane.

'I loved him, Atticus. I loved him so much. It hurt me when I had to say goodbye to him and attend to my Realitant missions and assignments. It hurt me when he kissed me goodnight, whenever his hand let go of mine. That's the only way I can truly describe how much he meant to me. I loved him so much, it *hurt*. I would have done anything to take away that pain, to be with him every second of every day. I loved him so much, I almost hated him.'

A ball of sickness grew in Tick's belly. He didn't know why – and he certainly didn't understand all this lovey-dovey stuff Jane was talking about – but something about it made him ill. Something about it was *obsessive*.

'And then it happened,' Jane said. 'The tragedy that would serve as the changing point of my life, the moment that defined my purpose from that day forward.'

After a long pause, Tick asked, 'What happened?' He couldn't help it – he wanted to know.

'He was *murdered*.' She screeched the word, a raw squeal from the back of her throat. 'Killed by inhuman slugs who'd only wanted money. Killed by slime and filth, left in his own blood, suffering as it leaked out drop by drop. Slaughtered like an animal *by* animals, and there was nothing I could do to save him. He was *taken* from me, Atticus. The only person I'd ever truly loved, and he was taken from me.'

Jane took a deep breath, then spoke rapidly as she stared into space, as if in a trance. 'I couldn't accept it, I just couldn't. I knew too much about the possibilities, the endless possibilities of life and the universe. I went to each known Reality, sought out his Alterants. I took them, captured them, tried to love them, tried to train them to love me. But they weren't him, they were different; they were disgusting and filthy and unworthy to bear his countenance. It taught me how disgusting and filthy and unworthy the Realities are – how wretched and *wrong* they are. It's not built right, Atticus, it's not *made* right. It's wrong, it's all wrong! We have to destroy it, fix it, rebuild it!'

Tick scooted away from her. She didn't seem to notice, barely pausing to breathe as she continued blurting out words.

'I devoted my life to him, to his memory, to making things right in the universe. He's out there, floating in the goop of quantum mechanics, waiting for me to find him and bring him back. But first I must remake the Realities, create the Utopia we all believe in. First I must make it right, make it right, make it right, *make it right!*'

She stopped, her chest heaving as she sucked in air. 'I'm sorry ... I'm sorry.'

Tick's eyes were wide, his breath held somewhere inside his chest. He knew for certain he'd never seen someone completely freak out like Jane had just done. Not that he'd doubted it before, but she was now a certified nutso.

Jane pulled at her black hair. 'It's why I cut it off, Atticus. I was ashamed of it. It's black, and I know that *he* always wished it had been blonde, to match his beloved colour. Yellow. Dear, dear yellow ...' She rubbed the dark strands between her fingers. 'But not any more. I've changed. I will change more. The goal is the same, but I've changed how–'

'*What is this nonsense?*'

Tick jumped so hard at the sudden, booming voice that he fell off the bench, his rear end slamming onto the floor. Even Jane sucked in a quick breath as Tick scrambled to his feet, his eyes darting directly to the source of the shout.

An Asian man with black hair stood in the middle of the room, dressed in a dark suit. A man Tick had always considered one of his best friends in the world, teacher or not. But even as he thought it, Tick knew this wasn't his Mr. Chu. This wasn't the kind, funny, humble science instructor of Jackson Middle School in Deer Park, Washington.

No, it was Reginald Chu. The *evil* Reginald Chu.

Tick's Dark Secret

Tick backed against the wall, feeling the edge of the bench cut into the backs of his knees. Though Mistress Jane had obviously been as surprised by Chu's appearance as Tick, she'd recovered, sitting calmly and expressionlessly as she stared at their visitor.

Chu walked forward, his forehead wrinkled and eyes narrowed in anger, his pace brisk. He stopped ten feet in front of them, his eyes never leaving Jane.

'What is this?' he asked, scrunching up his face like he'd just spotted a rotting body. 'I'm trying to find the one person in the Realities worthy enough to help me in the greatest scientific achievement of all time – and you two sit here chit-chatting like old friends. All that's missing are the cups of tea.'

'What did you expect us to do?' Jane asked, her voice calm. 'There's not much here to keep us entertained. I guess we could've wrestled or played tag.' She nudged Tick with an elbow.

Chu folded his hands behind his back, smoothing the anger out of his face. '*Mistress* Jane, I don't care what powers you may think you have, you'll be dead in an instant if I so wish it. Do you understand?'

Tick expected her to get defensive, but she merely nodded.

'I'm very disappointed to see both of you sitting here,' Chu continued. 'I'd expected at least one of you to have the vicious instinct of survival within you, the willingness to win my contest no matter the cost. Only one can win. Only one *will* win. One, or none – I can always scratch the two of you and start all over.'

Tick couldn't take his eyes off Chu. It was unsettling how he looked *exactly* like his teacher back in Deer Park. And to see this mean, nasty personality stuffed inside the image of one of his favourite people in the world was very disturbing.

'Isn't it an even greater accomplishment that we *both* made it?' Jane asked. 'That such bitter enemies could reconcile enough to work together for a common cause?'

'All I see is cowardice,' Chu replied, wrinkling up his nose as if such a notion disgusted him more than anything else. 'If you don't have the strength, will, or ability to kill this young man, then I certainly don't want you by my side.' He shifted his gaze to Tick. 'And you – don't think you've accomplished anything great. Much tougher tests lie ahead.'

Chu paused, looking back and forth between Tick and Jane. 'Still... I need an apprentice, and my patience has run out. Like I said, one or none. You'll both come with me and settle the matter.'

Tick finally found the voice that had been locked in a trap of panic inside him. 'What do you mean? What are you going to do to us?'

Chu laughed, the humourless laugh of a man who just found out he has mere days to live. 'I'm not going to do anything to you. You'll do it to each other.'

'But what—' Tick stopped when Chu held up a hand.

'Don't say another word. You will follow me, both of you. And don't be stupid — I have more weapons hidden in this place than you could count in a week's time. Try anything against me, and you will die. If my sensors detect any spikes in Chi'karda levels within you, you will die. At least until we get to the chamber. Tonight, you'll sleep. I want you well-rested for the morning. Come.'

He turned and walked towards the opposite side of the room, though there was no sign of a door. 'Now!' he shouted.

Mistress Jane stood up and motioned for Tick to come with her after Chu. Heart thumping, Tick fell in line beside her. His head swam with confusion. Both of these people were supposed to be his enemy!

He and Jane stayed twenty feet behind Chu, walking just fast enough to keep the distance consistent. Chu didn't slow when he came within a few paces of the curved wall, and just before he walked right into it, everything went pitch-black for a full three seconds. Tick almost stopped, but Jane grabbed his hand, pulling him along before letting him go.

Lights flickered above them, then ahead of them, flashing as if gaining power before finally shining at full strength. They strode down a long hallway with a carpeted floor of brown-and-black diamonds, the white walls lined with pictures of various instruments and odd scientific experiments — beakers and wires and microscopes and animals in small cages. It gave Tick the creeps.

He looked back and the hallway stretched just as far in that direction as it did before them, as if they'd never been inside the large, round room made of illuminated white material. It surprised him when he realised he *wasn't* surprised. He wondered if anything would seem crazy or magical to him ever again.

Jane reached over and grabbed his wrist. 'Listen to me,' she whispered.

Tick didn't want to trust her, but he nodded anyway, as slightly as he could in case they were being watched.

'When the time is right,' she said, speaking so softly Tick had to strain his ears, 'we'll strike. You and I together. Remember – no matter what you think of me, right here, right now, we have to stop him, or Dark Infinity will make every last Reality an insane asylum.'

'*Strike?*' Tick whispered back. 'What do you expect from *me?* I don't know what you guys think I can do, but I don't have any powers and I can barely lift fifty pounds.'

Jane shook her head in anger. 'Grow up, Atticus. Are you really that dense? Even I've noticed the things you've done the last couple of weeks.'

Tick looked over at her. 'What are you talking about?' He winced; his voice was way too loud.

'Just stay close. Trust me – your abilities will come out. And when they do, I'll channel them against Chu.' Tick almost stumbled. The floor seemed to bounce with ripples as he felt his head swim. 'I don't get what you're–'

Jane held a finger to her lips and picked up the pace. The hallway stretched to infinity before them.

Tick kept walking.

✿

For the first time in a long time, Paul felt like he

might not die of pain after all. Doctor Hillenstat, a wiry old man with a droopy moustache and enormous teeth from the Second Reality, had barely said a word after Rutger had winked him in to work on Paul's arm. Paul had been grateful for the silence, because he'd been in no mood to talk.

The pain worsened before it got better, but once the medicine kicked in and the bone settled in the thin white cast, life became bliss. Despite everything – the near-death experiences and the disappearance of his good friend Tick – Paul felt on top of the world after having suffered for so long.

Now, still lying on the soft bed in the infirmary, he decided he'd better pay attention to the frantic discussions going on between the people sitting in chairs around him – Master George, Rutger, Mothball, Sally, Sofia, and Doctor Hillenstat, who'd insisted on staying around until he was sure Paul was on the mend.

'All right, Sofia,' Master George said after shushing everyone from talking over each other. 'The matter of greatest concern at the moment is this: the odd *melding* of materials you saw on several occasions these past weeks. I want you to take a minute now, think about it very hard, picture it in your mind exactly as it was, and tell us every detail. Can you do that for us?'

Sofia rolled her eyes. 'How many times …' She didn't finish, Master George having given her his gentlemanly stare of death, eyebrows raised. 'Fine, okay.'

'Splendid,' Master George whispered, rubbing his hands together as he leaned forward in his chair.

Sofia took a second before running through it all again. 'The first time it happened was back at Tick's hometown. We were in the woods, and we met that psycho teacher of his, Mr. Chu. He strapped the things on our arms–'

Master George interrupted her. 'I'm certain that was Reginald Chu from the Fourth, not Tick's science instructor. And the thing he put around your arm was a highly illegal device called a nanohijacker. If we ever catch Chu, he'll be punished severely and spend the rest of his days in a Realitant prison.' His face reddened. 'So sorry, please continue.'

'The ... nanohijacker hurt worse than anything I've felt in my entire life,' Sofia said, her face grimacing at the memory. 'We heard loud crashing sounds in the woods, and Chu told us something was coming to get us. Well, the pain made us all pass out and when we woke up, dozens of trees had been smashed together – almost like they'd melted. We even saw a couple of deer in the mess.'

'Hope it wasn't the wee one I saw last year,' Mothball said. 'Sprightly little thing, it was.'

Sofia gave her a confused look then continued. 'In the weird underground place, a bunch of robot things called metaspides attacked us, but they all got melded together, too. There was a big tornado and they turned into one big heap of junk.'

'That was the Industrial Barrens in the Seventh Reality,' Master George said. 'Miserable place. And those metaspides are Chu's security force. I didn't know he'd sent them to the Seventh. We've had trouble with those buggers before. Go on.'

'It happened two more times,' Sofia said. 'In the desert, a huge beast catapulted through the tunnel right before it was going to kill us – and got trapped in a big chunk of melted glass. I think some of the glass might have been created from the super-heated sand. The last time was when we were running from the glowing ... *monkeys* near Circle City and a bunch of trees smashed together again, killing a few of the animals. It looked just like it had back in Deer Park – like the wood had liquefied and twisted together, then solidified into one massive structure. Like it was something from a nightmare.'

Sofia stopped and looked at the floor.

Master George patted her arm and leaned back in his chair. 'Thank you, my dear. Yes, yes, I'm quite certain my suspicions are correct. Quite certain, indeed. I fear our problems are much deeper than we thought. Oh, goodness gracious me.'

'What?' Paul said, his joy and relief from the vanished pain fading at the haunted look that crossed Master George's face. 'How could it possibly be worse? What are you talking about?'

'It's Tick,' Rutger grumbled. 'It's Tick.'

Sofia's head shot up. 'What do you mean, *it's Tick?*'

Master George stood, any sign of the jolly old English gentleman gone, his face set in a stony expression of concern. 'Master Atticus is out of control,' he said. 'He's obviously not even aware of the power that's bursting from him. Tick's inexplicable abilities over the Chi'karda are completely and absolutely out of control. It appears he's *manipulating* matter on the quantum level – destroying it, reshaping it, restructuring it. It seems to be triggered when he is frightened or angry. I cannot stress enough the danger of such a thing.'

Paul felt like someone had just ripped his brain out, stomped on it, then shoved it back in his skull.

'You mean *Tick* did all that weird stuff with the trees ... and the glass ...?'

'Quite right, Master Paul, quite right. Now imagine an out-of-control Atticus in the vicinity of Chu and his Dark Infinity device.' Master George brought a hand to his chin and shuddered. 'My fellow Realitants, we now have a new number-one priority. Tick must be stopped at all costs, or he might trigger a chain reaction that could destroy every last Reality. We need to bring him back here, where we can figure things out.'

He paused. 'Again, I can't stress it enough: Atticus Higginbottom must be stopped.'

Part 4

The New
Mistress Jane

A TIME FOR SLUMBER

Tick was exhausted by the time Chu stopped and turned to face them. The hallway continued on for as far as Tick could see, but Chu opened a hidden passage to his right by placing the palm of his hand on a square section of a metal wall. A hissing noise sounded as the panel slid to the right and disappeared, revealing a long corridor with doors spaced at regular intervals on either side – maybe forty in all. The doors were made of wood but had no handles.

'It's late,' Chu said, motioning the two of them to step into the new hallway. 'You'll both be confined to a cell for the night, where I expect you to get sufficient rest for tomorrow's events. Much will be decided when the sun rises, and before it sets, one of you will be dead. Or both. Think on that as you sleep.'

Tick fought the sudden urge to push Chu out of the way and run. Oddly, he wanted Mistress Jane to yell at Chu, to use her powers against the creepy man. With a lump in his throat, Tick realised that the woman Master George had deemed the most evil to ever live had become his ally and his only hope. It sickened him, and he didn't know how he could ever sleep.

'I could use a good night's rest,' Jane said, stepping into the corridor as she ran a hand through her black hair. 'Which one is my room?'

Chu made a quick gesture and a door on either side popped open, swinging outwards. The hallway was narrow enough for him to reach out and grab both doors, holding them open. 'The lady to my right, the boy to my left. You'll find food, a shower, fresh clothes – everything you need. But *rest* is your priority. In you go.'

Tick looked at Mistress Jane, but she didn't return his glance. She simply nodded to Chu and entered her room. Chu slammed the door closed; it sealed with a hiss.

'In, boy,' he said.

From somewhere within him, courage swelled in Tick's chest. 'You won't win. The Realitants know everything, and they'll be coming for you.'

Chu glanced at the leather satchel slung over Tick's shoulder, his eyes lingering.

Stupid! Tick thought. *You shouldn't have said anything!*

'*In,* boy,' Chu repeated.

This time, Tick kept his mouth shut and quickly entered the room. He'd barely crossed the threshold when the door slammed shut behind him.

✿

'It's very late,' Master George said, walking at such a brisk pace down the dark hallway that Paul had to jog to keep up with him and the others. 'But before we slumber, I must show you one last thing. Tomorrow is perhaps the biggest day any of us will ever face – and I want you to know exactly what's at stake.'

He paused in front of a steel door with a heavy bolt thrust through its lock. He reached out and slid a small, two-inch peephole open, the scrape of metal piercing the air.

'I want each of you to look in here, for as long as you can stand it. Then we will speak one last time before we say goodnight.'

Master George stepped aside and gestured for Sofia to go first.

As she peeked through the small slot, Paul saw her body go rigid, her hands clenched into tight fists. She finally looked away after several seconds.

'Why didn't you tell us?' she yelled, looking accusingly at everyone in turn. 'What's wrong with him?'

Paul pushed past her and looked through the hole in the door. His breath caught when he saw Sato, his arms and legs strapped to a bed in several places. Despite the number of constraints, he still thrashed about madly, ropes of veins bulging under his skin, his face red from the effort. Dark bruises and scrapes marked where he fought against the straps.

His lips moved as he screamed something, spit flying, but a wall of glass between the door and the bed trapped the sound in and Paul couldn't hear a word. Paul didn't know if he'd ever seen something so heartbreaking. He finally stepped back, wondering if the image would ever leave his mind.

'What's wrong with him?' he whispered.

'Yeah, what's wrong with him?!' Sofia shouted.

Master George took a deep breath. 'Sato was infected with the Dark Infinity plague – the very thing Tick has been sent to destroy with the antidote. You need to know that Sato displayed a supreme effort of sacrifice and courage to bring us the sample we required. But even more important, you need to know there are thousands, perhaps millions, who are in the same state as this poor boy.'

Paul and Sofia locked eyes, not saying a word, but sharing the horror of what they'd just seen.

Sato, Paul thought. *Oh, man, Sato.*

'As you can see,' Master George said, 'we have a lot of problems on our hands. We have sent in as our only hope a boy who has a power that could destroy everything around him if he loses control. We have a plague of insanity sweeping through the Realities. And it all could come to a head tomorrow.'

'So what do we need to do?' Sofia said, not so much a question as a statement.

'Yeah,' Paul said to show his support.

Rutger answered. 'Tonight, we get some sleep – everyone needs rest. Plus, we're still waiting for some of the others to arrive.'

'The others?' Paul asked.

Master George stepped forward and took a look through the peephole at Sato. After a long moment, he turned and faced the group, his face solemn.

'Tomorrow, we send an army of Realitants to the Fourth Reality.'

☼

Tick lay in the small bed, the covers pulled up to his chin, staring at the ceiling he couldn't see because of the darkness. Full of delicious food, freshly showered, dressed in a nice set of flannel pyjamas, he kept his eyes open, staring at the blackness hanging above him like the void of deep space.

Tears trickled down his temples, into his hair and ears. Never, not once in his entire life, had he felt so utterly alone. He finally squeezed his eyes shut, sending another surge of wetness across his skin. He concentrated, picturing each member of his family one by one. His dad, hooting and running in place as his guy scored a touchdown in Football 3000. His mom, baking cookies, tasting dough on her finger. Lisa, talking on the phone, sticking her tongue out. Kayla, her eyes glued to a Winnie the Pooh cartoon on TV.

Then he thought of Sofia. And Paul. Sato. Mothball and Rutger. Master George and Sally.

And then the image of Mr. Chu popped in his head. Not the evil one, not the one who looked at him like he was nothing but rubbish. The Mr. Chu in his mind was the good and kind one, the one who loved science like a kid loves sweets. The man who'd devoted his life to helping students gain an understanding of the world and how it works, to help prepare them for life. To plant a seed in future doctors, engineers, chemists, biologists.

What happened to you? Tick thought. *What did ...* he *do to you?*

Despite everything, Tick felt a little better. No matter what happened tomorrow, he would always have his friends and family in his heart and mind. And then a thought hit him: he should stop feeling sorry for himself – those people he'd just been thinking of *needed* him. Though he had no idea what to expect when morning came, he had to face it and do whatever it took to win. Everything depended on Tick.

Finally, the events of the day caught up to him. To think he'd awakened that morning in a place called Circle City, hoping to figure out a clue that seemed so silly now. Could this really have been only one day? It had to be the longest day of his life. And he felt it.

As exhaustion pulled him into sleep, he had one last coherent thought.

Tomorrow, I'm going to win.

WEAPONRY

For some odd reason, Paul was dreaming he'd just been sworn in as President of the United States, but everyone in the huge crowd booed and threw rotten tomatoes at him. One hit him square in the face, wet and gooey.

He woke up to see yellow eyes and the flicker of a tongue. Muffintops had been sent to get him out of bed.

'Get off me, you furry rat,' he said, pushing the cat aside. He groaned as he pulled himself to a sitting position – his casted arm almost felt stronger than the other one – and swung his legs to the floor. Muffintops glared at him, her yellow eyes regarding him with distaste.

'Sorry, dude,' Paul said, reaching down to pet her. 'I'm grumpy when I wake up.' He looked at his watch: 5:00 a.m. 'Ah, man, what's up with that? Muffins, go tell the old man I'm not ready to get up.'

The cat hissed and clawed at Paul's foot.

'Holy lumps of stew,' Paul whispered. 'You are one smart kitty. Fine, I'll get up. Go scratch Sofia's face for a while.'

They'd slept in a room similar to the one in the Bermuda Triangle complex – plain cots and blankets, no decorations. Mothball, Rutger, and Sally had slept there as well, but they were already out of bed and gone. While eating a scrumptious meal of pork chops and mashed potatoes the night before, Master George had told them he couldn't wait to move the main operations back to the ocean, but they still needed more time to make repairs and rebuild after Mistress Jane's attack back in May.

Paul stretched and yawned, then laughed when he heard Sofia yelling at the cat. He quickly ran to get in the shower before Sofia claimed it.

☼

After breakfast, Master George summoned everyone to the meeting hall, where Paul was shocked to see dozens of people he'd never met before. He and Sofia took a seat while scanning the room, gaping at the strange visitors.

Tall people and short people, skinny people and muscled people. The clothing varied – everything from a large dude with a fancy robe containing every colour possible to a slender woman with pale skin and red hair dressed head-to-toe in black. There was a guy with a turban, a woman with a baseball cap, another woman with a hat the size of a sombrero but decorated with tiny stuffed animals. Quite a few of the strangers wore what Paul considered normal clothes – jeans, flannel shirts, golf shirts, casual blouses, T-shirts – but the ones who didn't stood out like huge chunks of coal in a bowl of vanilla ice cream.

A tall man with night-dark skin had eyes so blue they seemed to pulse and glow. He wore a one-piece suit with shreds of cloth hanging off like mummy wrappings. A woman sat three chairs down from him with bleached-blonde hair, her face painted in the fanciest make-up job Paul had ever seen – bright red lips, purple eyeshadow, lines of blue streaking across her temple like coloured wrinkles. She'd drawn a star on one cheek and a crescent moon on the other. Next to her was a man almost as short as Rutger but not nearly so fat, wearing a white shirt, white trousers, and white socks and shoes.

'Who are these people?' Sofia whispered to Paul.

'Other Realitants, I guess,' he replied.

Sofia tapped the cast that covered his forearm from just below his elbow to his wrist. 'How's that broken bone of yours?'

'Feels great, actually.' He held up his arm and punched the air a couple of times. 'Especially compared to how I felt yesterday. Can't wait to whack Chu upside the head with this puppy.'

'You think Master George will let you go?'

Paul glared at her. 'I'd like to see him stop me.'

Sofia rolled her eyes. 'Ooh, you're such a tough guy.'

'Tougher than you,' Paul muttered, but flinched backwards when Sofia made a fist to punch him. 'Calm it, girl! You're the boss, you're the boss.'

Sofia folded her arms and pouted. 'We shouldn't be acting like idiots. Tick's in all kinds of trouble, I know it.'

Paul felt his heart sink to the floor. 'Yeah,' was all he could get out. The room felt as if a dark cloud had formed on the ceiling, dimming everything to a dull grey.

'Can I sit next to ya knuckleheads?'

Paul looked up to see Sally. 'Sure.'

He and Sofia scooted over, letting him have the aisle seat.

'Thank ya much,' Sally said with a grunt as he plopped down. 'Gonna be one heckuva day, ain't it?'

'Guess so,' Paul said.

'What's the plan?' Sofia asked.

Before Sally could reply, a door opened and Master George came marching through, Mothball and Rutger close behind. Both of them carried wooden boxes.

Master George stepped up to the small podium while his two assistants set their boxes down. Mothball's was the size of two coffins and looked like it weighed a thousand pounds. Rutger's was as small as a shoebox, but sweat poured down his red face and he sucked in two dramatic breaths when he dropped his box on the floor with a loud clonk.

Master George gave him a stern look, then turned towards the audience. 'Good morning to you all, and thank you so much for being here. Coming on such extreme short notice mustn't have been easy, I'm sure. But a dreadful time has come upon us, and we must act quickly. We will need everyone in this room, without exception.'

He took a breath, then folded his hands together on top of the podium. 'You were all briefed on the circumstances in our message to you, but I want to stress the most important issues of the day. The Dark Infinity plague is wreaking havoc among the Realities as we speak, but we're very close to a solution. Realitant Second Class Atticus Higginbottom is armed with a powerful antidote that will shatter the source device and send out a cure through the quantum Chi'karda waves Chu has been using to control those he has infected. Thanks to Rutger's tireless work, I have no doubt it will be a success.'

Several people in the room clapped, and Rutger did his best to bow, though it looked like a beach ball trying to bend in the middle.

'But unfortunately,' Master George continued, 'we have an even bigger problem. Master Atticus has a power over Chi'karda that is extraordinary – far greater than we'd first thought and far more complex and difficult to grasp. It's out of control, and the potential for disaster is extreme. It is vital that we find him, stop him, and bring him back here for a comprehensive study. I must say, as much as I admire the boy, he's frightened the dickens out of me, and I don't know what to think of it.'

The man in the colourful robe raised his hand, and Master George pointed to him. 'So what ye thinking on the plan? How do we make sure we flush out the plague and save the boy from killing us all?'

Master George nodded. 'Yes, Master Hallenhafer, how indeed? Though we haven't had much time to prepare, we do have a plan. Rutger?'

The short fat man cleared his throat. 'Tick's ear transponder confirms what we've guessed – he's been taken to the heart of Reginald Chu's business palace in the Fourth Reality. No doubt the Dark Infinity device is located there in his research and development chamber underground. We've had spies in the Chu complex for many years, saving them for the day we'd need them most. Today is that day.'

'Sha people!' the dark-skinned man in the mummy suit shouted. 'Sha to do such a linka?'

Paul exchanged a look with Sofia, having no idea

what the guy was talking about.

'Yeah,' a brown-haired woman said, dressed in a T-shirt and blue jeans. 'What good are a few spies against Chu and all his weapons?'

Rutger held up his pudgy hands. 'You're right, you're right. Our spies may only be good for opening a door here, smashing a window there, perhaps rearranging some schedules of workers if they can. No, we're not saying we're going to enter the heart of Chu's lair because of a few spies. But they *will* help.'

'Then what's the plan?' Sofia yelled out, surprising Paul.

Rutger looked at her, then scanned the full audience. 'We'll have to, I mean, all of *you* will have to *fight* your way in.'

A small roar sounded from the crowd as everyone started talking at once. A couple of people stood up, shouting at Rutger.

Master George slammed a hand against the podium, sending a sharp crack of thunder echoing across the room, silencing the Realitants.

'Please, good people,' Master George said. 'Don't get in a tizzy before you've heard the entire plan. Many of us have spent our entire summer working on developing our weapons programme, and we've come up with some dandies, I assure you.'

Paul looked at Sofia. 'Weapons? Sweet!'

Rutger spoke next. 'In these boxes are samples of our latest inventions, most of them based on items taken from the Fourth. We have enough to equip an army of thirty-two Realitants, and we think that will be enough to get us to Tick and the Dark Infinity device. And, if I may be so bold as to express my professional opinion, these things are going to kick some serious ... um ... er ...'

'Booty!' Paul shouted.

'Exactly!' Rutger pointed at Paul, grinning. 'Now, shall we begin?' He plopped down onto his knees and opened the small shoebox. He reached in and pulled out a tiny, dark ball, about the size of a marble. He held it up between his thumb and forefinger. 'This, my friends, is called a Static Rager, and it's not something you'd want to use for playing catch with little nephew Tommy.'

'Unless you be wantin' little Tommy to be eaten by a forty-ton ball of dirt,' Mothball added. 'Nasty buggers, those are. Could've used 'em on the Bugaboo soldiers.'

Paul leaned over to Sofia. 'Now *this* is what I'm talking about!'

Mothball pulled a silver device from her bigger box. It was several inches thick, cylindrical, about two-and-a-half feet long, and had several tubes running down the sides, all coming together in a tapered point at the front. Two straps of cloth hung from it.

'This 'ere's a Sonic Hurricaner,' she said, hefting it up for everyone to get a good look. 'Call 'em Shurrics for short. Makes the old Sound Slicer look like a BB gun, it does. Come on, 'ave a look.'

'Yes, yes,' Master George said. 'Come up, gather round. We have much more to show you and not enough time. Demonstrations will take place at the canyon bottom shortly. Departure for the Fourth is in three hours. Chop-chop!' He waved his arm towards Mothball and Rutger's boxes.

Paul was the first one to get there.

A Thin Sheet of Plastic

Tick's eyes snapped open.

He shot into a sitting position, wondering what had woken him. Had it been a noise? Did something touch him? He scanned the small room but saw nothing out of place – except for the lamp shining brightly on the dresser. That was it. Someone had turned the light on.

Man, he thought. *My brain must still be asleep.*

A tiny closet offered the only hiding place, and it was barely large enough to fit a little kid. He kicked off his blankets and walked over to the closet, then ripped the door open. Nothing but a pile of his old clothes and a few fresh shirts and trousers.

Sighing, he stumbled backwards and flopped onto the bed. *Chu created something that controls people's minds in other Realities,* he thought. *Making a lamp turn on to wake me up is nothing.*

After another minute, he stood, rubbed his eyes and stretched, then started undressing to put on some of the fresh clothes in the closet. As he slipped into a long-sleeved grey shirt and black trousers that were as comfortable as tracksuit bottoms, he felt an icy chill in his chest. He had absolutely no idea what to expect or what to do.

He put on his own trainers, slung the leather satchel over his shoulder, and stepped up to the door. There was no handle, just a dull slab of smooth beige material. He reached out, but before his hand made contact, the door clicked and moved, swinging out into the narrow hall. Pale lights in the hall revealed that Mistress Jane's door was also open; her room was dark.

Tick wanted to say something, ask for help, run. He expected someone to come for him, to summon him to Chu. But as far as he could tell, the whole place was deserted.

He stepped out of his room, then peeked around the door. The main door leading into the long hallway was open. It was dark out there, too – darker than it had been last night. He walked into the hall and glanced in both directions. Small emergency lights cast pale semicircles of red that didn't even reach the floor – anything could be hiding in the shadows.

What's going on? he thought.

He started walking to the right, sliding the tips of his fingers along the wall. He heard a faint buzzing from the lights; the air smelled like plastic and computer machinery. He'd only made it a hundred steps or so when a shadow formed ahead of him, the figure of a person leaning against the wall.

'Who's there?' Tick asked.

'It's me,' a female voice whispered.

Mistress Jane.

Surprisingly, Tick felt a wave of relief splash over him. 'What are you doing? What are we supposed to do?'

Jane pushed herself away from the wall and walked towards Tick, stopping beneath one of the emergency lights. It cast an eerie red glow on her black hair and down her face, creased with angled shadows under her eyes and nose and mouth. Tick pushed away the thought that she looked like she was covered in blood.

'What are we supposed to *do?*' she repeated. 'We're supposed to kill each other.'

Tick felt a chill at the simplicity of the statement, but he knew she was right. 'That's it? He's just going to wait around until we follow his orders and fight to the death?'

'Looks like it,' Jane said. She held out a piece of paper. 'This was taped to the front of both of our doors – looks like you missed yours.'

Tick took the note from her; the paper had an odd roughness to it. Jane tucked a strand of black hair behind her ear, staring at the floor. Tick's gaze lingered on her for a second – and he thought for the first time that she was one of the prettiest women he'd ever seen. He snapped his eyes away, focusing on the note in his hands.

She's evil, Tick, he told himself. *Evil people aren't supposed to be pretty.*

He could barely see the paper so he held it up closer to the light. To his surprise, he saw it wasn't paper at all, but rather an extremely thin piece of plastic. Electronic, glowing green letters scrawled across its face one by one, just like someone typing a message on a computer screen:

There are no instructions. No rules. Nothing is forbidden. When only one of you remains, please walk to the end of the hallway outside your dormitory. Go to the right. You have until noon, or you both die.

'We have three hours,' Jane said when Tick looked up from the note.

☼

'Someone's done lumped you over the 'ead with a teapot, they 'ave,' Mothball said, glaring down at Paul with her thin arms folded. 'You've got a ruddy broken arm.'

'I don't care,' Paul said. He flexed his fingers while moving his arm up and down. 'It's set. It feels fine. I'm going.'

They stood with Rutger and Sofia next to the armoury door; the other Realitants going to the Fourth had already received all they needed.

'Now's not a time for false bravery,' Rutger said. 'This makes your trip to steal the Barrier Wand from Mistress Jane look like a nice stroll down a country lane. This is serious business, and it's highly doubtful everyone will return alive – if anyone does.'

Paul opened his mouth then closed it, swallowing a sudden lump in his throat. He looked over at Sofia. 'You're going, right?'

'Of course I am,' she replied, looking awfully bored considering what was about to happen.

Paul turned back to Mothball and Rutger. 'Then I'm going too.'

Mothball surprised him with her booming laugh. 'So be it, then. Won't be me goin' to tell yer mum you've been sliced to bits by one of Chu's nasties. Come on.'

She stooped to enter the room; Rutger waved Paul and Sofia through before he followed.

The armoury was large but cramped with several aisles of metal-grid shelves rising from floor to ceiling, packed with an odd assortment of menacing objects. Some looked like guns, but most resembled trinkets and gadgets from a futuristic toy store: metal shafts with glass spheres attached to one end; awkward chunks of machinery with no rhyme or reason, like 3D puzzles; cool watches with all kinds of dials and switches, but no timepiece; countless small devices that gave no clue as to their purpose.

'Where was all this stuff when we went to the Thirteenth?' Sofia asked.

'Most of it's junk,' Mothball replied. 'Experiments and such that couldn't hurt a fly on a toad paddie. Sound Slicers were our best bet then.'

'Over here,' Rutger called from a couple of aisles down.

Paul almost stumbled over Sofia as they both hurried towards Rutger. The short man pointed up to a shelf holding the same large cylindrical objects Mothball had shown them earlier, with several tubes that tapered to a point on the end, straps hanging off both sides.

'Those are the Shurrics,' Rutger said. 'Sonic Hurricaners. Grab two of them, Paul.'

Paul reached out – the shelf was at his eye level – and pulled two of the weapons down. They were much lighter than he'd expected, and he handed one to Sofia before examining his own.

'The two straps go around your shoulders and across your back,' Rutger explained. 'It keeps the wide end flat against your chest while you activate the trigger mechanism in your hand.' He pointed to a small plastic rod jutting from the bottom of the Shurric with a red button in the middle, just like a joystick. 'It'll leave your other hand free to throw nasty horrible things at the enemy. This way.'

He walked farther down the same aisle then turned left, where several large black boxes lined the bottom shelf. 'Those little marbles are the Static Ragers. We just call them Ragers for short since Stragers is hard to say and sounds really stupid.'

'What do they do?' Paul asked.

'You won't believe it until you see it,' Rutger said with a huge smile of pride on his fat face. 'They have static electricity compacted inside them under extreme pressure. After you squeeze the suckers with your fist, you have five seconds to throw them. Once unleashed, the Rager uses the lightning-strong static inside to gather hundreds of pounds of materials to it – dirt and rocks and plants, whatever – like the world's worst snowball as it rolls, growing larger and larger until it smashes into something.'

'Nasty little things,' Mothball muttered. She pointed at Rutger. 'This little ball of lard just about smushed me into a hotcake, he did, testin' the buggers. Not much can stop 'em once they get movin' and such.'

'How many times do I have to apologise!' Rutger said with a frown. 'It wasn't my fault you decided to relieve yourself in the weeds, now was it?'

Mothball's face reddened, something Paul was sure he'd never seen before.

'What else do you have?' Sofia asked.

Rutger shook his head. 'That's it, I'm afraid, at

least for you two. Some of the others have more ... *specialised* weapons, prototypes and such.'

'Ah, dude, why can't I have one of those?' Paul asked. 'Specialised weapons are my speciality.' He grinned.

Mothball swatted Paul on the shoulder. 'Zip it. You're lucky you're goin' at all.'

'Before you leave,' Rutger said, 'we'll make sure the Shurrics get strapped on properly and give you a sturdy bag for your Ragers. But it's time to go down to the canyon floor – Master George wants everyone to test things out before leaving, which gives us just over an hour.'

He started pushing past Paul to head out of the room, but stopped and looked up at Sofia. 'Ah, I almost forgot. Master George has something very special he wants to give you. I have to admit I was surprised at his choice, but he said he felt strongly that you should be the one entrusted to use it.'

Sofia's raised eyebrows, creased forehead, and greedy grin made her look half-shocked and half-thrilled. 'What is it?'

Rutger exchanged a long look with Mothball, neither of them showing much expression or saying a word.

Finally, Rutger said, 'On second thought, we better let Master George explain it to you. Come on, let's go down the elevator to the canyon floor.'

A Cloud of Stars

'Do you trust me, Atticus?'

Tick looked at Mistress Jane, almost expecting her to laugh and say she was kidding. They'd been standing in silence for at least ten minutes since reading the Note of Doom. 'What kind of stupid question is that? You're a traitor, and you really seem to like hurting and killing people. No, I don't trust you.'

Jane scowled, the pale red light making her look like a devil. 'Fair enough. Then answer this – do you trust Reginald Chu?'

That made Tick think. 'Well, no. He's as bad as you.'

'Listen to me,' Jane said. 'I know I can't convince you I'm a fairy godmother who loves to make cookies and play hide-and-seek with children. But you're a smart boy. Think about our situation. No matter the troubles between us – between me and the Realitants – we have a bigger problem, right here, right now. We have to stop Chu before he causes every last person in the Realities to go insane. And I need your help.'

Tick threw his arms up in frustration. 'Need my help? You keep saying that. Yeah, somehow I winked people out of the Thirteenth and–' He stopped, not wanting to tell her about how last spring he'd made the burned letter from Master George reappear. 'But it was probably just a freak thing and will never happen again. Plus, what good will that do us? You want me to wink you somewhere like I'm some kind of human Barrier Wand?'

Mistress Jane grabbed her black hair that lay over her shoulder and gripped it in her fist like a ponytail. 'Atticus, you're either a brilliant actor or not quite as wise as I thought.'

'What are you talking about?'

Jane reached out and poked him in the chest. 'Your whole body *exudes* Chi'karda. It practically glows on your skin. You're like a supercharged battery just waiting to unleash your power. I've never seen anything like it, and you can't tell me you don't feel it.'

Tick suddenly felt very ill, and all he could do was shake his head.

'I visited some of the places Chu sent you to – after you were gone. Back when I was still deciding whether or not to kill you as he'd challenged me to do. How could you have done those terrible things and *not* realise you'd done it?'

'I have no idea what–'

'Please!' Jane shouted. 'The twisted trees, the melted glass with a huge creature stuck in the middle – what do you think did that? A stiff hot wind? It was you!'

Tick felt too weak to stand any more. He slid down the wall as his knees bent. His rear end thumped onto the hard floor. 'What do you ... I don't ... you're nuts. That's not possible.'

Jane crouched down until her face was level with his, reddish-green eyes shining through her glasses.

'You really had no idea, did you? It was *you,* Atticus, it was you. Extreme amounts of Chi'karda are flowing through you like pulsing electricity, and you have no control over it.'

Tick found he couldn't speak, his throat constricted. But he shook his head. Emotions swirled inside him – anger, confusion, disbelief. Panic. He'd done all those things? He didn't want to have some kind of weird power over Chi'karda, he didn't want the pressure, he didn't want to be *here.*

He felt hot, as if his heart pumped out boiling water. His mind *burned.*

Then everything seemed to go crazy at once.

A loud bang echoed down the hallway; the walls and floor shook as if a thousand pounds of dynamite had just been detonated below them. Mistress Jane cried out and fell backwards, slamming her head against the wall. Tick sprawled across the floor, rolling as if the whole building had been tilted on its side. The floor gave way beneath him, dropping with another loud boom. Tick plummeted several feet and landed awkwardly on his arm. As he twisted it out from under his body, he looked up in time to see a wave ripple down the hallway like a massive mole burrowing its way underground.

As the ripple disappeared into the darkness, the building shook again, but this time constant and steady, rocking back and forth, an earthquake. Tick scooted back against the wall, looking around, not knowing what to do.

Jane got up on her hands and knees, shaking her head as she bounced up and down with the moving floor.

'What's happening?' Tick yelled.

Jane didn't answer, crawling towards him as best she could, getting back up each time she fell. A huge lurch sent her rocketing forward. She crashed into Tick and grabbed his arms to steady herself.

'What's happening?' Tick repeated.

Jane shifted until she was side by side with him, her back against the wall. She put her left arm around his shoulder and grabbed his hand with her right. She tilted his head towards her and started whispering in his ear, caressing his hair like a mother trying to console her child.

'Listen to me, Atticus, listen to me. Take a deep breath. Calm yourself. I promise you I won't let anything hurt you. Calm yourself, *breathe*.' She pulled his head down onto her shoulder. 'Everything's okay, everything's okay. Close your eyes, breathe – everything's going to be okay.'

Everything was a blur to Tick, shaking and rattling. He did as Jane told him, closing his eyes, sucking in deep breaths, surprised at the calm warmth that spread through him despite the chaos. Jane continued to stroke his hair, whispering words of safety in his ears.

As quickly as it had begun, the shaking stopped and all was silent except a creak or two as the building settled. Tick heard himself breathing, felt his chest rising and falling, felt the comforting touch of Jane. The thought repulsed him, but he didn't move.

'Open your eyes,' Jane said, gently pushing his head off her shoulder.

Tick did, and gasped at what he saw in front of him.

A misty mass of bright orange sparkles floated in the air, a condensed cloud several feet wide, hovering and pulsating slightly as if it breathed. His eyes hurt, but he couldn't look away. It seemed as if he'd been transported to deep space, viewing a nebula or a swirling galaxy.

'What ... what is that?' he whispered.

Jane's voice was soft. 'It's your Chi'karda, Atticus. I told you I could channel it if you would only unleash it for me. I can't say I understand what's happening, but it seems that when you get angry or afraid, power bursts from you, completely out of control and dangerous. If I hadn't been able to calm you, I'm not sure I would've been able to harness it and form it before us. Now, don't worry, I'm about to do something. Trust me.'

The cloud moved towards Tick, the shining particles dancing in the air, darting back and forth as they surrounded him, dissipating into the darkness. He felt a surge of warmth, like walking out of a freezer into the hot desert sunshine. For a few seconds, all he could see was light, a million bright stars, swirling around him. And then it was gone.

'It's flowed back into you,' Jane whispered, her voice loud in the silence. 'You may never see it in that form again, but now you know what sleeps inside you. I don't want to be your enemy the day you figure out how to control it.'

Tick's mind spun in countless directions, too confused and overwhelmed to grasp what had just happened or even formulate a question. 'I don't get it,' he said.

Jane stood up. 'Neither do I, and I suspect Master George is clueless as well.' She held out a hand. 'Come on.'

Tick took it and let her pull him up. 'I'm a freak.'

Jane shook her head. 'No, you're not. If you're a freak, then so am I.'

Tick thought of all the things he could've said to that, but he stopped himself. Jane had probably just saved his life. 'What now? Looks like we're not gonna try to kill each other, I guess.'

Jane looked down the hallway in the direction they'd been ordered to go once things were settled. 'No, we're not. And we're not waiting until noon, either. Come on.' She grabbed his hand and pulled him along as she started walking.

'Wait!' Tick called out, snapping his hand back. He searched around until he spotted the leather satchel holding the antidote. He ran over and picked it up, then joined Jane again, still marching down the hallway. 'Okay, what are we going to do?'

Jane paused before answering. 'You and I are going to stop Chu. Right now.'

SOFIA'S TASK

Sofia stood by the small cave leading to the elevator shaft, leaning back against the warm stone of the dusty canyon wall. Master George had asked her to wait there until he could speak to her. At the moment he was explaining to Paul how to use the Sonic Hurricaner – the Shurric. Sofia had picked it up easily and destroyed three huge boulders in quick succession.

The Static Ragers fascinated her, though. She watched as a Realitant woman threw one along the ground with a quick jerk of her arm. A sharp crack filled the air, then a low rumble of thunder as the Rager rolled forward, gaining speed and size with every passing second. Everything in its path – dirt, mud, rocks, bushes – compacted together in a huge chunky sphere, snowballing as it rolled. When the Rager finally smashed into a test boulder, both objects exploded in a spectacular display of earthy fireworks.

Awesome, Sofia thought. She couldn't wait to hurl one at Chu himself.

Master George was walking towards her, shouting at the Realitants scattered around the riverside. 'Everyone! Back up we go. We can't spare another second!'

As the two dozen or so people gathered their weapons and headed for the elevator, Master George touched Sofia lightly on the arm, leading her out of earshot of the others.

'We must talk before you go,' he said in a low voice.

'Rutger told me you had something special you wanted me to do.'

Master George nodded, his mouth pursed with worry. 'Indeed, my good Sofia, indeed.'

When he didn't say anything more, Sofia said, 'Well?'

'Ah, yes, sorry.' He pulled a tiny silver pen out of his pocket and held it up for her to see. It had no distinguishing features other than a clicker at the top and a small black clasp on the side for attaching it to a shirt pocket or notebook. 'I felt I must trust *you* with this. Please take it – but don't push the button.'

Sofia took it from his hand and held it with only the tips of two fingers, as if its surface might contain some poison. 'What is it?'

'Well, it's most certainly not a pen. Won't write a single letter, I assure you.'

'I figured that much.'

Master George looked troubled, his mouth opening and closing several times before he finally explained. 'We expect things to be quite ... chaotic once you get to Chu's industrial palace. Though you must do your part to fight whatever forces Chu might throw at you, I must ask you to consider that your second priority.'

'And the first?'

'Yes, yes, it's difficult to say. Sofia, I need you to run through the chaos, get past Chu's forces, and enter the main complex at all costs. Our spies will do their best to ensure the locking mechanisms and seals are sabotaged when I give the signal. I need you to get in, locate Chu's research and development laboratories, which is where I expect Master Atticus to be, and *find* our troubled friend.'

'Why? What am I supposed to do?'

'I'm afraid Tick may lose control of his powers when he confronts whatever Chu has planned for him. I fear it will be worse, far worse than anything that has happened during your adventures these past days. He may do irreparable damage – damage that could grow and trigger chain reactions, doing very nasty things to matter both there and in the other Realities if it seeps through the borders.'

Sofia felt a knot tighten in her stomach even before Master George said the next part.

'You need to find him, Sofia. You need to place the tip of that pen against his neck and push the button. It will traumatise his system terribly, sending him into a coma, but it will also block his body from his mind, his emotions, his anger and fear. That should cut him off from the massive surge of Chi'karda that I expect. But I promise you, Sofia, it will not kill him.'

Sofia felt a cyclone of emotions storm inside her – pride at being chosen for a special mission, fear of doing it, concern for Tick and his out-of-control powers, sadness that she'd have to inject him with something horrible. Though she felt it in her nature to argue, to push back, she didn't. Master George was right. He *had* to be right.

'Okay,' she said, feeling like she should say more but unable to find the words.

Master George nodded with a satisfied look, then reached out and squeezed her shoulder. 'I debated this within my heart for many hours, Sofia, as well as with Rutger and Mothball. But in the end, I knew it had to be you. It must be you. I know you will succeed, as surely as I know Muffintops is up there' – he pointed to the complex above – 'hissing at every Realitant who steps off the elevator who isn't me.'

Sofia smiled, then looked at the dangerous pen.

Finally, she slid it into her pocket.

'Let's go up now,' Master George said. 'It's time to send you off.'

☼

It made Tick's stomach turn to see the warped and twisted walls of the hallway. Some of the panels had melted completely into globs of metallic goo on the floor. *I did that,* he thought. *How is that possible?* He tried as best he could to stop looking and stared straight ahead at the never-ending corridor stretching before them.

He gripped the strap of his satchel. *I have to tell her. I have to.*

'Um, Mistress Jane?'

She'd been quiet while they'd been walking. She looked over at him. 'Yes? Sorry, just planning things out in my mind.'

'I need to tell you something.'

Her eyebrows shot up, appearing above the rim of her glasses. 'Oh?'

'There's something in this bag. Something I'm supposed to use against the Dark Infinity thing. An ... antidote.'

Jane stopped, turned towards him. 'An *antidote?* How did ...' She trailed off, as if not sure what to ask.

'Master George got a sample from one of the infected people. Then he and Rutger figured out what to do. He said if I smash it against the device that's sending out the nanowaves or whatever you call the stuff that's controlling people's minds, it'll work its magic and destroy it. Somehow send the cure out to everyone. No clue how it works, but that's what I was told.'

'Hmm.' Jane started walking again. Tick fell in line beside her. 'Well, I guess that will make our task easier. But only a little – the hard part will be getting to Dark Infinity in the first place. There's no telling how Chu's going to react when he sees us both still alive, or what weapons he'll use against us. Prepare yourself – I'm going to need every ounce of your ... *abilities.*'

☼

Sofia stood next to Paul, both of them in the long, single-file line of Realitants about to be sent to the Fourth Reality. Mothball was with them; she said she wouldn't miss it if she had only one arm and leg. Rutger stood still and silent by the podium, looking somberly at the floor, while Master George paced back and forth, doing his best to give a pep talk.

'I needn't say much,' he said, his hands clasped behind his back. 'I know that all of you know the dire nature of the task ahead of you. Not only do we have a nanoplague running rampant through the Realities, but one of our own is on the verge of a catastrophic breakdown that could shatter the very substance of the Realities. Not to mention our dear friend, Sato, who is suffering so much in our own home. For them, for your families, for the people of your world and others, I ask you to do this thing.'

He stopped pacing and turned to face the group. 'I

do not ask it lightly. But I also ask that you do not *take* it lightly. I send you with my utmost confidence in your abilities and in your strengths. I send you in the good graces of Chi'karda itself. May it be strong within you on this terrible, terrible day.'

He paused for a long moment, the room completely still. Then he turned and pulled his Barrier Wand off a shelf under the podium, its golden, cylindrical surface shining, the seven dials and switches preset and ready to go.

Rutger spoke. 'Though it would be easier if you were all touching it, we have too many people for that, so it's been programmed accordingly. We've checked and rechecked all of your nanolocators, and replaced the hijacked ones inside Paul and Sofia. We'll be watching you closely.'

Sofia closed her eyes and breathed deeply, trying to quell the sickening swarm of butterflies in her stomach. The tranquiliser pen in her pocket bulged, feeling twenty times bigger than it should be and weighing a hundred pounds. She fingered the strap of her bag holding the Ragers, and tightened her grip on the handle of the Shurric, its straps slung over both shoulders.

I'm ready, she thought. *I can do this.*

'Are you scared?' Paul whispered.

'No,' she replied, hating how shaky her voice sounded when it came out.

'Me too.'

Master George held the Wand up high, then lowered it back to his eye level, holding his right index finger above the trigger on top. 'My friends, we very much look forward to your safe return.'

He pushed the button.

43

THE DILEMMA OF THE DOORS

Tick and Jane walked another twenty minutes before the long hallway finally came to an end. Large double doors marked an entrance to whatever lay beyond, heavily bolted slabs of steel with no handles or windows. A large blank square decorated one of the doors, black as pitch.

'What now?' Tick asked.

'I guess we knock,' Jane responded. She stepped up and slammed the palm of her hand against the steel several times; the muted thumps barely registered through the thick doors.

The black square ignited with colours, swirling like mixed paint until the image of Reginald Chu's head solidified, but in 3D. His face jutted from the flat surface, every detail of his features perfectly clear. It was almost indistinguishable from the real thing, and Tick felt the sudden urge to reach out and smack it.

'You're trying my patience, both of you,' he said, the slight electronic static in his voice the only indication that what they saw before them was artificial. 'I'm almost ready to pull the plug on this sad experiment and start anew. If neither of you have the guts to conquer the other, then you're of no use to me.'

'What's beyond these doors?' Jane asked coolly.

Chu's recreated eyes glared at her. 'You know how to find the answer to that question. I gave you a simple task. I watched your act of compassion when the boy lost control again – and Atticus, I assure you, it was an *act*. She knows she can't harm you, even though you don't know what you're doing or how to ignite the power within you. But if she struck, my guess is that you would win – albeit with some serious collateral damage to my facilities. That's why I put you in the underground tunnel connecting Chu Industries to the Winking Yard at Bale's Square.'

'But we're *here* now, Reginald,' Jane said, as though speaking to a child. 'I think I know what's beyond these doors. Aren't you afraid of what the boy and I can do now?'

Tick didn't like how things were going. Not at all. Was it true what Chu had said about Jane? And how could they sit there and talk about him like he was just a tool, an object, a dangerous weapon?

'I'm not afraid at all, Jane,' Chu said. 'There is zero risk of Chi'karda levels spiking from you or the boy. Go ahead and try.'

Jane's face whitened, the smirk vanishing from her face. Tick had no idea what she was doing, but a vein at her temple bulged and her fists tightened. 'What did you do?' she asked, her voice tight.

Chu almost smiled, but it was more of a grimace. 'Your mutated powers gained in the Thirteenth will never – and I mean *never* – come close to matching what I can do with technology. I've conquered the science of Chi'karda. You've merely captured a fleeting anomaly that will squeak its way out in the natural order of things. You should've done what I asked, Jane. You should have *done* what I *asked*. It's too late for you now.'

Tick couldn't take it any more, as scared and nervous as he was. 'Would you two just shut up!' he yelled. 'I'm a couple of weeks short of fourteen – but I feel like I'm the only one around here who doesn't act like a snot-nosed brat trying to pick a fight.'

Jane stared, unable to hide the shock at his outburst; Chu's face remained stoic. Tick felt like his mind had split in two – one side telling him to zip it, the other reminding him that Master George and the Realitants were relying on him to find and destroy Dark Infinity. And there was only one way to do it.

'I'll do it,' Tick continued. 'I *want* to be your apprentice, so tell me what to do.'

'I already have,' Chu said, his bizarre magical face turning to face him. 'You have until noon to destroy Mistress Jane. If you do, you'll be allowed through the doors and we will begin our work together. If not, you will die. Both of you.'

Tick looked at Jane, who returned his stare. *How could I possibly hurt her? I don't even know where to start. But I can't let Master George down!* He fingered the strap of the satchel on his shoulder.

He looked down at his watch. 'We still have an hour.'

'True,' Chu said.

'Then leave us alone.'

Chu laughed a mirthless chuckle. 'If it makes you feel

better, I'll remove myself from the Imager. But don't worry – I'll still be watching.' His face disappeared and the screen returned to blackness.

'Atticus, I'm sorry,' Jane whispered. 'I've never heard of a technology that blocks someone from Chi'karda. Somehow he's kept that a secret – a formidable task, trust me.'

'I don't get how it works,' Tick said. 'Normally, can't you just fill up with Chi'karda and do all kinds of magical stuff? Like a wizard?'

Jane rolled her eyes. 'Something like that. Perhaps all I need is a pointy hat with stars and moons sewn on it.'

'And right now you can't do anything?'

Jane shook her head, squeezed her fists again. 'It's gone, completely. I can't feel it, can't grasp it, can't do anything. It feels like my soul has been ripped from my body.'

'I don't feel any different,' Tick said.

'That's because you've never controlled it or understood it. You couldn't even tell when you'd used it before – which I still find hard to believe.'

Tick looked at the floor. 'I might've felt something. A ... a burning.'

'Well, it doesn't matter now. We need to make a decision.'

Tick knew what she was going to say. 'He's watching us, you know. I doubt it will count if one of us *volunteers* to die.'

'That's not what I had in mind.' She gave him a creepy look – a blank stare, her eyes glazed.

Tick took a step backwards before he realised what he was doing.

'I have no choice,' she said, taking one step towards him. 'But … it's for the best. Best for the Realities. I'm the only one who has a chance.'

'What are you doing?' he asked, his back hitting the wall of the hallway.

Tears glistened in her eyes. One escaped and spilled down her cheek. 'I'm sorry, Atticus. I'm so sorry. I have no choice but to kill you.'

44

Fingers on Neck

Sofia's breath stuck in her throat as she stared up at the humongous structure that was Chu's headquarters.

It rose from the ground like a mountain – with a pointed peak and everything – as tall as any building she'd ever seen, stretching to her left and right until it disappeared in a slew of other offices and complexes. There were no straight lines on the structure, nothing flat, nothing symmetrical. Countless odd-shaped windows were scattered across the building's surface, most of them with lights shining through, but others were filled with dark shadows. Chu's headquarters towered over her and the other Realitants like a natural formation, a man-made mountain of glistening black stone.

Spanning the several hundred yards between them and the building was a broad expanse of grass and trees. A nice park complete with little streams, bridges, benches, and sidewalks that couldn't possibly contrast any more with the massive thing that kept it half in shadow.

'That is one cool building,' Paul said beside her.

Both of them were armed with Master George's strange weapons. The bulky body of the Shurrics were strapped on and pressed against their chests, joystick triggers clasped in their hands. Paul was using his broken arm for that, since all he needed was a finger to push the button. Each carried a leather bag tightly against their left sides, directly under their arm, with a small opening for retrieving the Static Ragers.

'Yeah, it's cool,' Sofia said. 'I can't wait to see it crash to the ground.'

The Realitants stood in a rough formation, in lines of eight, all facing the mammoth mountain of black glass. Mothball was in front, her head tilted back as she gaped at the top of Chu's palace so far above. She finally turned to face them.

'Done with speeches, we are,' she said, fingering her Shurric. 'Master George got us quite nice and inspired, he did. Are we ready for a bit of battle? Ready to go in there and stop the monster named Chu once and for all?'

Several Realitants shouted their agreement.

'We all know the plan,' Mothball continued. 'Get inside and make our way to the studies. Third lower level, section eight. Seen the map, you 'ave.'

Sofia felt a cold pit in her gut, her nerves jittery. An emptiness floated somewhere inside her; she knew what she had to do. *If* she could actually find Tick.

'I 'spect Chu'll be sendin' nasties after us before long,' Mothball said. 'Better get a move on.'

Her last word still hung in the air when a great boom rolled across the park, shaking the leaves on the trees. Mothball turned around sharply and Sofia rose on her tiptoes to see what had happened. Another boom shot out, then another. Several more in rapid-fire succession. Soon they were almost indistinguishable from each other.

Sofia saw holes had opened up along the front of the mountain building, big circles that were black on black, barely visible. Silvery balls shot out of them, one after the other. After a very short flight, the things landed on the grass and started ... *changing*. They reformed and reshaped themselves, twitching as objects twirled and spun on their bodies, long appendages protruding out and reaching for the ground. There were dozens of them. No, hundreds.

'Uh-oh,' Paul said beside her.

As soon as he said it, Sofia realised what the things were.

Metaspides.

☼

Tick had to keep reminding himself to breathe.

A long, long moment passed, he and Jane staring at each other. Her eyes flickered away now and then, as if turmoil raged inside her as she thought about what she should do. Tick tried to think of his own options. *Run* seemed like a good one, but he couldn't move, as if his feet were riveted to the floor. Then Jane's eyes refocused on him, like she'd departed her own body for a few minutes and had finally returned.

She slowly walked forward, arms coming up, outstretched and reaching for Tick, her fingers curved like claws. Tick was so baffled by her sudden change, and the almost laughable Frankenstein gait she'd chosen, that at first he didn't react. When she came within a foot, though, he snapped out of it and dodged to his right, ready to run.

With shocking speed, Jane spun and kicked her right leg out, smacking him in both shins. Tick lost his balance and dove towards the ground, just getting his hands beneath him before he crunched his nose. He started scrambling, but Jane was on top of him, grabbing both his shoulders from behind. With a jerk of her surprisingly strong arms, she flopped him over and onto his back, gripping his torso with her legs like a vice.

She clutched his face with both hands and leaned forward, putting her mouth flush against his ear, her breath hot. She whispered so low Tick could barely hear her.

'*Listen* to me. I don't think Chu can stop the Chi'karda in you – it's too strong. But I need to draw it out. *Listen* to me. I'm going to strangle you, do you understand? I'm going to kill you unless you fight back. It's the only way, Atticus. Do you hear me? I will not stop until you die or until you let the Chi'karda explode out of you and it saves us both. *Listen* to me. I ... am ... going ... to ... kill ... you. For your own good.'

Jane pulled her face away, staring down at him with her green eyes aflame. She put both of her hands around his neck, squeezing. Panic flared inside Tick. He kicked out with his legs, beat on her arms with his fists, but she didn't budge.

'Let go of me!' he tried to yell, a guttural croak that barely came out.

Jane squeezed tighter. 'Look at me, Chu!' she bellowed out, lunacy glazing her eyes. 'I obeyed! I will be your apprentice!'

As pain enveloped him, as his breath left his body – squeezed from him – Tick thought distantly that he couldn't tell her intentions. *Is she really going to kill me? Is she acting? Would she really* kill *me?*

Her fingers closed tighter, gripping his skin, pinching the tendons and nerves. Tighter still. Tick struggled, kicking, beating her arms, thrashing beneath her. She squeezed even harder. Tick couldn't breathe, couldn't find air.

'He's almost dead!' Jane yelled. 'Chu! I've won your test!'

Tick's eyes bulged and he felt his face puffing up. He heard the choking sounds torn from his own throat. Black stars formed above him, swirling in the air, growing bigger until they blackened his vision. Darkness fell upon him, complete.

Images flashed across his mind's eye almost too fast to register: his family, Sofia, Paul, the library back home, Master George, snow, school, Mr. Chu at the chalkboard, the Barrier Wand, the Grand Canyon, Rutger, Mothball …

I don't want to die!

Something snapped inside Tick's mind. He felt it – he *heard* it, like a branch cracked by a bolt of lightning. Heat surged through him, first warm then hot, pulsing through his veins, as if his blood had combusted into lava, *burning* him.

A piercing scream rocked the air. He realised it had come from him just as the blackness swept away, replaced by Jane's face, hovering above him as she kept trying to strangle him.

Tick screamed again.

Jane flew off him, catapulting across the hallway and slamming into the wall. An unseen force pinned her arms and legs flat as her head thrashed back and forth. The ground shook as Tick struggled for breath, gasping in air, fighting to get his arms and legs under him. Sounds of bending and breaking filled the air. He looked up to see the metal panels of the walls warping and cracking, bubbling and melting. Tremors rocked the floor, ripples surging back and forth like waves on water, crashing into each other as large cracks rent the hard material.

Jane hadn't moved, still pinned to the wall. The chaotic sounds of destruction hurt Tick's ears. Everything had gone crazy; he couldn't take it. Somewhere inside him, he knew it was coming from him, that it was all his fault. *I'm a freak. I'm a freak!* Knowing he had this power only made it worse, panicked him further, sent his mind and thoughts reeling.

I'm going crazy, he thought. *I can't do this. I can't control it! What have I done?*

Chu. Reginald Chu. This was all his fault. Everything was his fault.

Tick glared at the massive double doors, the black square still blank. The world around him rocked back and forth, things breaking and crashing and melting. The heat within him intensified. He felt certain his organs were about to burn, fry to a crisp, leaving him dead.

Tick threw all of his anger and pain at the doors.

At Chu.

With a terrible squeal, the doors wrenched to the sides, crunching into a mass of twisted steel, leaving a gaping, smoking hole behind. Tick caught movement out of the corner of his eye – Jane falling to the floor in a crumpled heap.

I can't do this, Tick thought. *I can't do this!*

Screaming, he got to his feet and ran through the twisted and broken doorway.

THE SHOWER OF GOLD

A sea of metaspides littered the park outside Chu's artificial mountain, crawling along the ground with their creepy, jointed legs. Sofia found it hard to believe they were *machines* because they seemed so alive. They swarmed together in a tight pack, heading straight for the Realitants.

'Ready yourselves!' Mothball roared.

Sally stood a few people down from Sofia. He lifted his left hand into the air and shouted something completely unintelligible. But he looked ready to fight.

A small tremor abruptly shook the ground, making Sofia stumble backwards a step. The Realitants looked around in confusion, Mothball in particular. Sofia looked up at the black mountain; it shook as well. in the distance, she heard the sounds of breaking glass and twisting metal.

'Need be keepin' our focus!' Mothball shouted. 'Master Tick must be goin' about 'is business. On the count of three – we charge! *One!*'

Sofia nudged Paul in the arm with her elbow. 'For Tick and Sato,' she said, not caring if her voice betrayed how scared she felt.

357

'Two!'

Paul nodded without breaking his focused stare. 'For Tick and Sato.'

'Three!'

Sofia sprinted forward before anyone else, her body acting before her mind could talk her out of it. Pumping her fist in the air, she screamed out one word, louder than she'd ever shouted anything in her life, almost ripping her throat raw.

'REEEEAAAAALITAAAAAANTS!'

The thunder of footsteps and echoing calls of her rallying cry sounded from behind her.

Sofia ran straight for the closing pack of metaspides.

☼

The world shook.

Tick felt as if his mind was detached from his body. He rotated in a circle, staring at the huge open chamber he'd run into. He saw a vast open space with an artificial sky above him, complete with stars and a moon. Half-completed machines and menacing structures covered the hundreds of square yards of floor space. Workers hung on for dear life as scaffolding fell apart beneath them. Large holograms of floor plans and complicated designs hung throughout the chamber like see-through kites, countless lifts constantly moving between them, hovering and flying as if by magic.

Tick saw it all, but still felt his mind slipping away from him, out of control, on the edge of insanity. He staggered back and forth, the ground shaking and cracking.

To his right stood a huge tower made of gold that rose at least ten stories into the air. Near the top, partially obscured by a metal-grid catwalk, two words were stamped into the shiny metal.

Dark Infinity.

At the bottom of the tower, a panel of gold slid to the side, revealing a bright interior. A man appeared, then ran straight for Tick.

Don't come near me, Tick thought. *Stay away!*

But then he saw it was Chu, and the anger and fear that had subsided flared anew.

'How!' Chu screamed, still running for Tick. 'How could you possibly have done this?'

His words were distant, as if spoken through a wall. Splitting pain hammered in Tick's skull. He squeezed his hands into fists to stop them from trembling. Pressure mounted in his chest and it became difficult to breathe. He could feel heat scorching him from the inside out.

He felt that strange separation from his body. He knew he was losing control, completely – but he couldn't do anything to stop it. The chamber shook, the tremors increasing in magnitude. He stared at Chu and Dark Infinity and from the corner of his eye he saw things falling. Metallic crashes filled the air.

Chu stopped, his eyes darting around the complex. 'How ... what ... stop this! Stop this right now!'

Tick could barely hear him. As if reaching through a bucket of mud, he grasped for and found a tiny glimmer of sanity in his mind. He'd been sent here for a purpose – to destroy Chu's plague. He held on to that one thought, forced his hand to steady, and reached inside the leather satchel at his side for the silvery cylinder that held the antidote to Dark Infinity. All he found was something hard and jagged, dusty and rough. Confused, he pulled it out and held it up to his eyes, squinting to see it through the blur of the chaos swimming around him.

It was a big rock. Frantic, he dug in the satchel again. Nothing. The bag was empty.

The antidote was gone.

☼

Sofia did as she'd been instructed and threw a Rager towards the army of metaspides, never stopping her sprint. The little ball hit the ground and spun forwards, ripping along with increasing speed as the static electricity erupted from it, gathering massive amounts of grass and dirt and rock. The weapon quickly grew into an earth-made bomb, a gigantic bowling ball of nature ready to destroy something. Sofia watched with elation as it crashed into the front line of the spidery robots and smashed a dozen of them into metal shards.

To her left and right, other Ragers hit the metaspides, wiping out the first wave of their enemy. As soon as the dust settled, Sofia started firing her Shurric, pushing the trigger repeatedly as she swept the nozzle back and forth, pointing it at anything shiny and silver. With each shot, a muted clap of thunder shook the air, rolling forward in an invisible tidal wave until it slammed into its target. Metaspides flew through the air as if ropes yanked them backwards, dozens of them catapulting towards the black mountain as more and more injections thumped from the Realitants.

Sofia kept running, reaching into her bag and grabbing another Rager. She spotted a thick cluster of robots and threw it in that direction, then ran after it.

As soon as the massive ball of dirt and rock smashed another line of metaspides, she went in, firing.

She was almost starting to have fun.

✦

Despite the whole world shaking around them, Chu laughed – a bitter, empty chortle. The man reached into his pocket and pulled out the silvery cylinder containing the antidote. He held it up above his head.

'Looking for this?' he shouted. 'How many times are you people going to mistake me for an idiot?'

Tick ignored him, focusing his eyes on the shiny object, his heart sinking. If only he–

The antidote suddenly shot out of Chu's hand and flew through the air, turning end over end before it slammed into Tick's palm and stuck there, even before he closed his fingers around it. His breath caught in his throat as he stared at his hand in disbelief.

Chu couldn't hide the shock on his face, his eyes wide, his lower lip quivering. 'How is this possible?' he whispered, too low to hear but his lips making the words obvious to Tick. The man's eyes shifted from the antidote to Tick's face.

'Listen to me!' Chu yelled, holding his hands palm out as if approaching someone about to jump from a bridge. 'You don't understand! Dark Infinity is a giant Barrier Wand. It's powerful enough to control and shape the Realities. It's the greatest achievement in history! All I need is your help – and we can use it for good. You have to trust me. Give me a chance. Stop this madness!'

Tick stumbled about as the earthquake got worse, things crashing everywhere, the massive golden cylinder of Dark Infinity pitching dangerously from side to side. The black specks returned, swimming in front of Tick's eyes, but this time mixed with flashing colours, blinding lights. He felt as if his heart was a furnace, burning him from within.

'Atticus!' A female voice, barely audible, came from his right. 'Atticus, you have to stop! You don't understand what you're doing!'

Jane. It was Mistress Jane. But he couldn't see her.

The chamber shook and spun.

Tick screamed and threw the silver antidote in the general direction of Dark Infinity, the cylinder blurry and bouncing in his vision. He heard an ear-splitting crack, then the bubbling sound of sizzling acid eating at metal. His vision darkened until he could barely see. He fell to his knees, screaming, and grabbed his head with both hands, squeezing his eyes shut.

Then, though he would have thought it impossible, everything got worse. The pain, the sounds, the shaking, the spinning, the flashing lights. Tick didn't think he could survive another second.

A booming crack rocked the air, and his eyes snapped open. His vision cleared in time to see that Dark Infinity had exploded into countless tiny golden pieces, flying and swirling through the air like snowflakes in a blizzard. A sparkling tornado. It sounded like millions of killer bees swarming.

'Atticus!' Jane yelled again, somewhere closer to him. 'You have to *stop!*'

Tick knew he wasn't thinking straight. His mind was a chaotic soup of jumbled memories and thoughts. He glanced to his right and saw Jane running for him;. Chu had disappeared. A small part of his brain knew she was coming to help him, but all his eyes saw at that moment was the woman who had tried to kill him, to choke him to death in the hallway. The horrendous fear and rage he'd felt when he'd been so close to death returned full force.

He didn't know exactly what he did, but he knew he couldn't stop it. The swarming specks of metal that had been Dark Infinity flew at Mistress Jane, like flies descending on a feast, surrounding her in a blur of sparkling gold. The metallic tornado consumed her body, obscuring her from sight.

Somewhere deep inside of him, Tick knew he'd just done something terrible.

I didn't mean to, he thought. *I didn't mean to!*

In answer, Jane's screams erupted through the air.

THE DRAG RACE

Paul threw a Rager at the only remaining metaspide close to him, watching with glee as it steamrolled into a massive ball of earth and wiped the machine out, sparks flying as pieces of crumpled metal flew in all directions.

'Yeah, ba–'

A hard claw grabbed his ankle from behind and lifted, slamming his body to the ground. Paul tried to scream but there was no breath left in his body. He looked up to see a metaspide staring down at him with glowing robotic eyes. He wanted to say something – spit, yell for help – but he could only open and close his mouth, fighting to get air back in his lungs.

Scissoring metal blades came out of a hidden compartment, snipping on its hinges as it moved towards Paul's face. But then the spider paused; its body rotated upwards, as if it had spotted something behind them. Paul heard the glorious shouts of Mothball charging in to save him, when the metaspide took off on its spindly legs in the other direction, dragging Paul with it.

Paul's body finally let him suck in a huge gulp of fresh air. It was enough for him to shriek with pain as rocks and dirt scraped his back, ripping his clothes. He kicked with his free foot, tried to slow the metaspide down by clawing at the ground, but to no avail. A burst of pain exploded inside him when his casted arm smacked a stray piece of one of the creature's destroyed buddies.

'Mothball!' he shouted, trying without success to turn his head back to see if she was close. He kicked at the metaspide's body and legs, but it kept running, dragging him like a sack of rubbish.

✺

Enough of this ruddy nonsense, Mothball thought as she ran after Paul.

She lifted her Shurric, aiming more carefully than she'd ever done in her fighting life.

'Keep your legs down!' she shouted, still running, still aiming.

She pulled the trigger.

✺

Paul came to a sudden stop, watching in disbelief as the body of the metaspide catapulted away from him and landed fifty feet away with a mechanical spurt of buzzes and sparks.

The thing's claw was still attached to Paul's ankle, the arm of it ending in a shredded clump of coppery wires. Paul reached down and easily separated the clawed metal fingers, then threw it far as he could.

Mothball ran up, towering over him as she sucked in gasps of air. 'Ain't the first time I saved your life,' she said.

Paul stood, wincing at the stings on his back from the cuts and scrapes. He didn't want to think about what his skin must look like. 'You used your *Shurric*!'

'That I did,' Mothball replied, calmly.

'You could've smashed me, too, ya know.'

'Reckon you're right.'

'Or the spider could've ripped my leg off when it went bye-bye.'

'Reckon you're right.'

Paul shook his head. 'Well, thanks for saving me.' He scanned the dusty area around them. Not a single working metaspide was in sight, and he heard the muted thump of a Shurric in the distance and a couple of Ragers wreaking their havoc somewhere.

It's almost over, he thought. *We wiped them clean out!*

The ground shook worse than before, swiping away his extremely brief elation.

'Need to gather the others, we do,' Mothball said. 'Meet me at the entrance to Chu's mountain.' She took off running without waiting for a reply.

Paul thought of Sofia. He turned in a circle, searching for her.

He ran in a stumble towards the dark shape of the mountain, the haze making it look even more sinister than before. The quaking ground was making him sick. He shouted Sofia's name, mad at himself for getting separated. As the dust settled, he finally caught a glimpse of her near the huge glass doors marking the entrance to Chu's palace. From the looks of it, the doors had been mostly obliterated by a Rager, jagged shards of glass littering the ground.

'Sofia!' he shouted again, running towards her. She spotted him and stared for a long moment, then turned her back to him. The earthquake made it appear as if she were jumping up and down.

'Sofia!' he called, but she ignored him, her attention focused on the gaping hole leading to Chu's palace.

What is she doing?

Without so much as a glance back at him, Sofia sprinted for the destroyed glass doors, disappearing into the darkness beyond.

What...

'Follow her!' he heard Mothball roar from a distance. 'Everyone! We gotta get to Tick!'

Paul ran forward, but only made it two steps when the earthquake doubled in intensity, knocking him to the ground. He looked up just in time to see a huge section of the mountainous building crack and fall, exploding when it hit the ground, the sound of its crash splintering through the air.

'No!' he shouted.

The entrance was completely blocked off.

PACINI

Sophia ran, her Shurric at the ready for anything that jumped out at her.

The building shook horribly around her; she heard a crash of breaking glass far behind. Around her, the walls and floor bent and rippled; chunks fell from the ceiling. Every step took her full concentration and balance to make sure she didn't fall down.

Tick is doing this, she thought. *I don't know how or why, but Tick is doing this.*

She pictured in her mind the map Master George had shown them – third lower level, section eight. Her legs already exhausted, she somehow kept going, winding her way through hall after hall, down staircases, through more halls. With every turn, she saw people running, heading in the opposite direction, fleeing the destruction.

She kept going forward.

✿

Tick was lost.

The blackness killing his vision was complete now, which only escalated the sheer panic that surged through him, competing with the intense heat that still burned. He stumbled about, waving his arms, calling for help. Jane's screams still rocked the air, though they'd grown deeper, guttural, filled with gurgles and raw shrieks.

What did I do? he thought. *What did I do to her?*

And where had Chu gone?

All around him, the sounds of destruction penetrated the darkness of his sight, scaring him. Huge *things* crashed nearby; it was a wonder he hadn't been crushed yet by a falling object. He wanted to shrink to the ground and curl into a ball until it was all over. But he couldn't. He had to run. He had to get away.

He kept stumbling forward, searching for something, someone, anything.

☼

When Sofia saw the big metal doors, she knew she'd arrived. Without pausing, she threw a Rager forward, then readied her Shurric. The Rager pulled the metal and plastic from the floor and ceiling as it rolled along, growing bigger and bigger. It crashed into the doors, bending them with a metallic squeal, but not breaking them open. Sofia fired repeatedly with the Shurric, its invisible thumps of sonic energy enough to finish the job. The doors parted to let her through.

She scrambled into a chamber as big as a football stadium, chaos reigning as things crashed and burned all around her. Most of the people had already fled, but she heard the skin-crawling screams of a woman in the distance.

'Tick!' Sofia shouted, getting no answer.

She ran forward, scanning her eyes left and right. *Tick – where are you?*

'Tick!' she yelled when she spotted him, sprinting towards her friend.

He looked terrible, sweaty and cut up, wandering around like a drunk man, feeling at the air with shaking hands, staring with blank eyes. His mouth opened and closed, but no sound came out. Every step he took sent a ripple surging through the floor away from him, like a stone dropped in water. Chunks of the ceiling fell and were whipped away just before crushing his body, as if a host of guardian angels hovered above him, protecting him.

'Tick!' she yelled again, but he didn't respond. He looked so awful, so … *crazy,* she could hardly believe it was the same boy she knew.

Sofia kept running, looking above to dodge falling objects, winding her way back and forth towards Tick. A few remaining workers pushed past her in the opposite direction, fleeing. A thick man with a spotty beard crashed into her, knocking her to the ground. Sofia screamed something rude in Italian as she scrambled to get back up.

She caught a flash out of the corner of her eye, looking up just in time to see a spinning rod of metal right before it slammed into her shoulder. She fell again, and a boxy contraption plummeted from the sky, landed on its corner, then fell over to pin her legs to the floor. She pushed at the smashed box with both hands, but couldn't move it off her feet.

The sounds of destruction intensified – crashing, banging, exploding, breaking. Objects of all sizes fell from the false sky like the world's worst hailstorm, smashing to pieces all around her. The volume of noise pierced her ears, threatening to break her eardrums.

Sofia saw the long rod of metal that had smacked her shoulder nearby. She squirmed awkwardly until she could reach it; she grabbed it, pulled it close. The rod was twisted and curved like a crowbar. Wedging one end under the clunky, destroyed box that used to be part of who-knew-what awful invention of Chu's empire, she pushed on the other end of the lever with both arms, gathering every ounce of strength left inside her. At first nothing moved, but she let out a scream of effort, throwing every part of her into getting that stupid thing off–

The metal box toppled over with a sound lost in the symphony of destruction filling the gigantic chamber. Sofia got to her feet, ignoring the throbs of pain lancing through her legs. Half-limping, half-running, she went after Tick. He was so close, still spinning in circles, stumbling, shouting things Sofia didn't understand. He looked like a man who'd lost his mind. Falling objects from the ceiling were deflected at the last minute as though a shield protected him from harm. Sofia ran on, zigzagging and stumbling herself.

She reached Tick, tackling him to the ground. 'Tick, what's wrong with you?'

'It burns!' he screamed. 'Someone help me! I can't control it! Someone *help me!*'

Sofia didn't think he even knew she was there. She fumbled in her pocket, panic making her hands shake. She felt around, grasped the silver pen, pulled it out.

'My brain is splitting!' Tick screamed, thrashing around, hitting her.

Sofia didn't know exactly what the pen would do

to him, or if it would hurt, or how long it would affect him. She didn't know anything for sure. But she had to do it.

'Tick, I'm sorry,' she whispered.

She jabbed the end of the pen into Tick's neck and pushed the button. A quick hiss sounded as Tick's head jerked and hit the floor. His body went limp.

Everything went still – the shaking, the crashing, the ripping, the bending.

Everything stopped.

The only sound was a woman still screaming in the distance.

Out of the Rubble

Paul grunted as he moved another chunk of black glass off the pile.

'Isn't there another way in?' he asked.

'Ain't nary a one that ain't blocked!' Sally shouted, lifting a piece the size of a large suitcase. He threw it and Paul watched it split into several pieces upon landing.

Then Paul noticed the silence. 'Hey ... *hey!*' he shouted.

Everyone else stopped working, looking about.

'It's ruddy well stopped, it 'as,' Mothball said, a crooked-toothed grin breaking across her face.

Paul ran away from the pile, craning his neck to look up at the mountain as he got farther away. Though full of cracks and missing pieces, the building wasn't shaking or falling apart any more. The ground wasn't trembling. The air had grown still and silent, the dust already settling to the ground.

'Sofia did it,' Mothball said, waving Paul back over to help. 'Come on, gotta clear this pile. Gotta find 'er and Master Tick.'

Encouraged for the first time in a while, Paul sprinted back and started sorting through the rubble with renewed vigour, knowing his hurt arm would be some kind of sore tomorrow. Piece after piece, chunk after chunk, the Realitants worked together until a shaft of light escaped from within. They'd found a way through.

'We did it!' Paul shouted, grabbing more pieces. Soon they had a hole big enough for them to enter the damaged building.

Mothball went first, then Sally, then Paul and the other Realitants. They regrouped inside, sweeping their weapons back and forth in case of an attack. There wasn't a sign of anyone or anything dangerous, only dust and debris.

'Come on, let's–' Paul started to say, then stopped when he saw movement up ahead in the hallway. He couldn't make it out at first – it looked like an injured animal crawling along, slide-and-stop, slide-and-stop.

But then the dust settled and the figures came into the light. Everything became clear.

It was Sofia, her back to them, dragging Tick's battered body down the broken hallway.

⚙

Somehow, Jane finally stopped screaming.

She lay on the floor, her mind trying to shut down in order to avoid the sheer agony of her pain. It filled every inch of her, every organ, every cell, every molecule. Her nerves bristled with it. The slightest movement of her ragged breathing sent fresh pinpricks shooting across her skin, *through* her skin, into her blood and muscles and bone. She hurt, she ached, she stung. The pain consumed her. The only thing that kept her from weeping was the promise of even more pain.

I tried to help him, she thought. *I was only trying to help him. How?* How *could he have done this to me?*

Her eyes had been closed for a long time, the prospect of seeing the damage to her body too horrific. But finally, she allowed her eyelids to slide up. The movement sent a new wave of agony across her face and through her head, as if needles had pierced her skull. But she kept her eyes open.

She did not, however, have the courage to move anything else. She saw only what she could from her current position, crumpled like a rag doll. But it was enough to let her know her life was over.

Shards of gold, small but jagged, covered every inch of her body, jutting from the skin at all kinds of angles. Blood was everywhere, seeping from the wounds. Her body was like a sea of red, a million tiny golden icebergs breaking the surface. Most of the shards appeared to be *fused* to her skin, impossible to remove. She could only imagine what her face must look like. A beast. A hideous beast.

A bit of the old Jane returned to her then. The one who'd been courageous and strong, unwilling to break under any task or trial. The one who'd fought on, no matter what.

Realities help me, I can do this. I will do this.

Bracing herself, Jane counted silently to three, readying her mind and soul for what she was about to do. Then, as quickly and as efficiently as she could, she pushed her arms below her and stood up.

The blood-curdling scream that erupted from her was inhuman – the terrified shriek of tortured demons. The sound tore through the air, filled the world around her, pierced her own ears until they bled. It

375

seemed impossible that she didn't faint from the pain that had ruptured inside of her like the detonation of a nuclear bomb.

She stood still, enduring. Eventually, the pain lessened. Barely, but enough so that she had the awkward sensation of bliss, a warm calm.

All things are relative, she thought.

Then, a very strange thing occurred to her. She didn't understand it, didn't know how the thought formed in her mind or where it came from. Perhaps it had been something Reginald had said in the moments before he ran away, something he'd told the boy about Dark Infinity. No matter – she'd figure it out later. But regardless of *how* she knew, she *did* know.

She had changed forever. In the midst of all the horror, perhaps there was a silver lining after all. Yes, she knew. She *knew*.

Mistress Jane had no Barrier Wand within her reach. No one in her Reality had a Wand to pull her away from this place. No one, anywhere, had a lock on her nanolocator besides those who could do nothing about it. Yet, despite all that, Jane winked herself away, away from the Fourth Reality and back to the Thirteenth.

She did it by *thinking* it.

Yes, she had changed forever.

AN UNFORTUNATE MEETING

Tick looked dead.

He lay flat on his back, his head cradled in Sofia's lap as every last Realitant stood in a group around them, staring down solemnly as if it were a funeral. Tick's face was pale, scratches and welts marring almost every inch of him. His clothes were ripped, bloodied, even melted in some places, attached to the skin. But he was breathing, marked by the slight rise and fall of his chest.

Man, Paul thought. *When that dude wakes up, he's gonna hurt something awful.*

They were gathered in an open grassy area of the ruined park, ignoring the hundreds of people who had evacuated Chu's mountain building. Most of them stood in silent huddles, staring back at the black structure, probably in shock at how close they'd come to dying.

'Gonna be just fine, he will,' Mothball announced, kneeling next to Tick. 'Sofia 'ere may ruddy well win a medal from the old man for this.'

The crowd of Realitants broke into applause as Sally bellowed a long-winded cheer that echoed across the park but made absolutely no sense. Paul thought he caught the words *rabbit* and *raccoon dog*. Sofia showed no reaction to anything, staring at a blank spot in front of her.

Mothball reached across Tick and grabbed him around the torso, lifting him up with a heavy grunt. His body flopped over her shoulder with no sign of life, his arms and legs dangling.

'Come on,' she said. 'Chi'karda spot's only a 'undred yards up yonder.' She nodded her head in the direction away from the destruction.

As the others started following Mothball, Paul reached down and offered Sofia a hand. 'Let's go, Miss Italy. Tick's gonna be fine, thanks to you. You can beg me for forgiveness later.'

Sofia took his hand and pulled herself to her feet. 'Forgiveness for what? Killing more spiders than you did?'

'*No*. For not telling me you had a super-secret mission to put Tick in a coma.'

'Oh. Yeah. Sorry that Master George thinks I'm better than you.'

Paul sighed. 'You're forgiven.'

A shout from behind turned both their heads. A dark-haired man, his clothes ripped to shreds, his body battered and bloody, was limping along as fast as he could, yelling something unintelligible. Sofia recognised him before Paul did.

'It's Chu!' she yelled. 'Mothball! That's Reginald Chu!'

Mothball turned and ran back towards them, Tick still slung over her shoulder. 'Right, you are. Reginald

Chu! Sally! Grab the monster!'

Sally had barely taken a step before an even louder shout came from a cluster of trees to their right. *Another* dark-haired man bolted from the shadows, his fist raised in the air, screaming obscenities that made Paul wince. Then, in disbelief, he saw who it was. Paul looked back at the other man.

Two Reginald Chus were running straight for them.

'Whoa,' he whispered.

'Oh, no,' Mothball said, standing right next to Paul. 'Oh, no!' she said louder. Then she screamed at the top of her lungs. 'Run! Everyone *run!*'

Without waiting for a response, the tall lady sprinted for their Chi'karda launching point, Tick bouncing up and down on her shoulder, the other Realitants right behind her.

It took Paul a second to break his stare from the impossible sight of two identical men coming towards them – one limping, the other moving at full speed. Both seemed oblivious of the other, each wanting to reach the Realitants and unaware of his twin.

'Come on!' Sofia yelled, grabbing Paul by the arm and pulling him as they ran after Mothball. 'I think I know–'

An ear-piercing noise cut her off just as a surge of blinding light flashed behind them. A terribly loud boom rattled the air, the sound of a million amplified horns going off at once. Paul had heard that sound before.

He'd barely had the thought when a rush of tornado-force wind hit them, knocking him and Sofia flat on the ground. The wind passed over them, a solid wave of air that was almost visible as it tore at trees and bushes and benches, travelling outwards in a wide arc.

It knocked over the other fleeing Realitants and kept moving along its destructive path.

All was still for a single moment. Then the ground started violently shaking, far worse than before. Trees crashed to the ground. Sounds of breaking glass and bending metal filled the air as the mountainous palace of Chu started collapsing all over again.

'Tick!' Paul yelled over the deafening noise. 'He must've woke up!'

'No!' Sofia shouted back. 'I think it has something to do with Chu meeting his Alterant.'

Paul risked a glance over his shoulder and saw that only one Chu remained – the injured one. He limped towards them, struggling all the worse because of the earthquake.

Sally suddenly bolted past Paul and Sofia, running for the man. Like picking up a bag of sticks, Sally grabbed Chu and flopped him over his shoulder just like Mothball had done with Tick. He ran back towards them, stumbling left and right as the ground shook.

'Get up! Get up!' Sofia shouted, pulling on Paul's good arm.

He obeyed and ran after her, his mind twisting in a million different directions.

The earthquake worsened, throwing Sofia to the ground. Paul helped her up and they kept running, losing one step for every two they made forward. Sally caught up with them, moving as if Chu weighed only ten pounds.

Eventually, the Realitants gathered in the designated spot, every last one of them staring back towards Chu Industries in awe and fear. Mothball still held Tick, and she was shouting something over and over.

'Wink us out, George! Wink us out! Ruddy wink us out!'

Sounds of splitting and cracking and shattering glass rocked the air. A thunderous roar ripped across the ground, and Paul felt his heart wedge itself in his throat.

Chu's palace collapsed towards the ground, the whole thing at once. Paul threw his hands over his ears. The sounds of destruction were louder than anything he'd ever heard before as an entire building of metal and glass exploded nearby. He watched as a massive cloud of black dust rolled out of the falling ruins, billowing out and rushing towards them at an alarming speed.

'Now, Master George!' Mothball roared, barely audible over the sounds of the mountain collapsing. *'Now!'*

Like a fleet of starships zipping into hyperspace, the Realltants winked away in quick succession. Paul actually *tasted* the choking dust and saw the suffocating darkness before he felt the familiar tingle and was winked to safety.

MUCH TO DISCUSS

No one did any celebrating.

After getting safely back to headquarters and undergoing full debriefings, most of the Realitants said their goodbyes and winked back to their home Realities. Paul and Sofia stuck to Tick's side. Except for the rise and fall of his chest, he seemed as dead as a corpse. Paul couldn't think of much to say as they followed Mothball to the infirmary, where Doctor Hillenstat hooked Tick up to several monitoring machines; an IV dripped a clear liquid into his veins. Rutger watched from the side, scrutinising the doctor's every move as if waiting for him to make a mistake.

'How long will he be out?' Sofia asked. 'Is he gonna be okay?'

Hillenstat frowned. 'An hour. A day. A week. No telling.'

'But will he be *okay?*' Paul said.

The doctor felt Tick's forehead. 'Yes, he's fine for now. But in the long run?' He shrugged. 'I think I'll let Master George be the judge of that.'

Sofia huffed. 'Aren't doctors supposed to make you feel better?'

Hillenstat smiled through his droopy mustache, the first time Paul had ever seen him do it. 'Doctors are supposed to be honest. Now, I'll go and get Master George and you can bother *him* with your questions. I need a nap.'

He wiped his hands together as if wiping away crumbs from dinner, gave one last look at Tick, then walked out of the infirmary.

Sofia looked at Rutger. 'Nice guy you got there. I'm glad I'm not sick.'

Rutger ignored them, looking over at a machine that monitored Tick's vitals, but Mothball spoke up. 'Best doc in the Realities, he is. A bit snippy, though.'

Master George walked in, Sally lumbering along behind him. They both pulled up chairs to the bed and sat down so the whole group was in a circle, looking solemnly at the comatose Tick.

'So what's the deal?' Paul asked.

'Yeah, what's wrong with him?' Sofia added.

Master George cleared his throat, not breaking his gaze from Tick's face. 'Yes, yes, a very good question, my young friends. I certainly didn't expect things to go in this direction with the lad. Troubling, I tell you. Very troubling indeed.'

He paused, and after a few moments of tense silence, Sofia threw her hands into the air, palms up. 'Well?'

'Show some respect,' Rutger growled.

'No, no,' Master George said, throwing a quick glance in Rutger's direction. 'We've seen a lot this past day, and answers are deserved. If everyone would give me a moment, I'll do my best to tell you what we know.'

He took a deep breath, then began. 'First of all, Sato is recovering nicely. The lunacy left him as soon as the trouble started with Tick in the Fourth – the antidote obviously found its target during all that chaos. But Sato's very battered and bruised from the abuse he gave himself while under the control of Dark Infinity. I'd encourage you all to visit him. He's back in his normal quarters – quite a relief, actually. It was very hard to see him locked up like that.'

Master George pointed at Tick. 'As for our young sleeping lad, here … goodness gracious me, what a turn of events. I believe I may have found a connection that explains what is happening.'

Paul noticed everyone in the room leaned forward just a little, himself included.

'Entropy,' Master George announced, looking around to see the reaction.

Paul squinted his eyes as if that would make his brain work better. 'You used that word in the weird spinner movie you sent us.'

'Quite right. It refers to the rule of nature that all things move towards eventual destruction. Entropy *accelerates* when a branched Reality begins fragmenting. The nuclear force holding matter together weakens, and things begin to break apart and dissolve – but at a pace millions of times faster than nature's course. A fragmented Reality can be gone – completely gone – in a matter of weeks or months.'

'What does that have to do with Tick?' Paul asked.

The skin around Master George's eyes seemed to melt, sinking into a worried frown. 'I fear that Master Atticus has no control whatsoever of the inexplicable amounts of Chi'karda stored within him. Where it comes from, and why it's there, I've yet to determine. But I do know what it's doing. It's unleashing itself on objects that frighten or threaten Tick. And when it does ...'

He paused, as if expecting someone to call him crazy if he continued. 'Well, it's *fragmenting* them. Tick is doing, on a very small scale, exactly what happens to a fragmented Reality. He's a catalyst – triggering a heightened state of entropy that dissolves the matter around him. But because it's so out of control, the matter slams back together, the quantum forces regaining their strength and forming the monstrosities you've seen along your latest journeys.'

'Whoa,' Paul whispered.

Sofia tried to sort it out. 'So basically, if Tick freaks out, he can destroy and reform things, trapping whatever gets in his path.'

Master George nodded. 'Yes, and depending on how far along the entropy develops – how much matter is destroyed before it reforms – the objects may retain some of their old qualities and characteristics.'

'We thought it was something Chu had done,' Sofia said. 'The trees by Tick's house, the spiders, the glass tunnel exploding and melting – all of it. We thought it was all part of the test.'

Paul looked down at Tick's sleeping face. 'Remind me not to make him mad.'

Master George sighed. 'I'm afraid Tick's life will have to move in a new direction. He'll have to stay at home, be monitored, watched over. We'll need an extraordinary amount of help from his parents – and we'll have to find ways of ensuring he doesn't have another ... episode. At least until we sort things out.'

'What about us?' Paul asked. 'We can help. We can stay with him.'

Master George shook his head. 'No, no, Master Paul. I need you and Sofia to return to your homes right away and pick up on the rest of the school year. With Dark Infinity destroyed, I believe things will be quiet for a while, and I need both of you to live your normal lives for a bit.'

Paul felt his stomach squeeze into a knot. Nothing, absolutely nothing, sounded worse than going back home and living a "normal" life.

'But,' he said, searching for arguments, 'we're Realitants. Why do we–'

Master George held up a hand. 'All in its appointed time, lad. For now, you must go to school, learn, experience growing up. I promise it won't be long before we wink you in for further training or to help with whatever obstacle presents itself to deter our mission.'

'What happened to Mistress Jane?' Rutger asked.

Master George looked at him sharply, then glanced away as if trying to hide his alarm at the question. 'That, I don't know. We can only hope she's ...' He didn't need to finish.

'Maybe when Sato's well enough–' Rutger began, but was cut off by Mothball.

'Pipe it for now, little man. One worry at a time.'

Master George stood up. 'Paul and Sofia, I need the two of you to prepare to return home. I'll send several specially prepared science books with you so that you can study beyond those things you'll learn in normal schooling. I need a little more time with Tick, and I need him to help me resolve the matter of' – he pointed a thumb over his shoulder in the direction of the holding cell – 'our captive, Reginald Chu. Tick may be the only one who'll be able to tell *which* Chu it is.'

Paul stood as well, trying to ignore the hurt growing inside him. He really didn't want to say goodbye to everyone. 'Yeah, what's the deal with the Chu thing? What happened back there?'

Master George stared at him, his face serious. 'Two Alterants *met*, lad, face to face. Such a thing is a disaster – a complete disaster, always.'

'Why? What happens?' Paul asked.

'One survives, while the other is thrown into ...' Master George looked about nervously. 'Well, we don't know for sure. But Reginald himself always called it the Nonex, and it's something I hope to never encounter. Whenever Alterants meet like that, it causes a terrible disturbance in Chi'karda and the Realities. I wouldn't be surprised if an entirely *new* Reality, perhaps even solid enough to be a main branch, was formed from this. Dreadful, really.'

Paul rubbed his eyes and temples. 'My head hurts.'

'Yes, yes, off you go,' Master George said, shooing them away from Tick. 'It's time for you to go home. Rutger, please fetch my Barrier Wand.'

51

AWAKENING

Tick didn't know how much time passed between the instant he grew aware of himself and the moment he opened his eyes. An hour maybe. Possibly two.

It was the pain that kept him hiding in his own darkness. Terrible, terrible pain, right in the middle of his skull, as if he'd spent the last week lending his head out as a neighbourhood speed bump.

But he finally slid his eyelids open, scared the light would only make it worse but having no choice.

Master George sat in a chair to his left, leaning over him with a huge smile on his ruddy, puffy face. Sato sat to Tick's right, his face swollen but somehow cheerful – for him, anyway.

Tick started to get up, but only made it an inch before thumps of pain slammed his brain like hard fists.

'Now, now, Tick,' Master George said, placing a hand on Tick's arm. 'Let's not be hasty. You've been through quite an ordeal.'

Tick had squeezed his eyes shut again, but forced them open. 'What ... what happened? Chu was there ... and Mistress Jane ... and a huge Barrier Wand–'

Master George patted his arm. 'Yes, yes, we know much of what happened, thanks to Sofia. Though I'm quite anxious to debrief you about what happened from the time you left your two friends to the time Sofia knocked you senseless. Quite anxious indeed.'

'Tick,' Sato said, almost a whisper.

Tick tilted his head to the right, raised his eyebrows. 'Yeah?'

'You've made me very unhappy. As soon as you're better, I'm going to punch you in the ear.'

'Huh?'

Tick could only remember Sato smiling once during the few times they'd been together, but something close to a grin broke across the boy's face.

'Twice, now, you have saved me,' Sato said. 'You're making me look bad.'

'I saved you?' Tick asked, then looked at Master George. 'The antidote hit the thing? It worked? Last I remember, the whole place was about to fall down.'

'Atticus,' Master George said. 'You're in no condition right now to learn the things you need to about what happened in Chu's black mountain. Just know that you're safe and Dark Infinity is destroyed, as are the nanoplague bugs it was controlling. Though things did get a bit hairy, it's all worked out in the end.'

'Well, what about—'

Master George shushed him, then held up a thick, messy binder stuffed with papers, some folded, others ripped. 'It's all been documented here for you to read while you recover. I'll also be sending you home with a big stack of Realitant textbooks and manuals. Now that you're a Realitant First Class, you can begin further study.'

'First Class?'

'That's right, old chap.' Master George held out a card, similar to the one Tick had been given in May, but dark red this time. Tick saw the words printed on it:

ATTICUS HIGGINBOTTOM
REALITANT FIRST CLASS

'I've already sent Rutger and Mothball ahead to have a very long discussion with your parents,' Master George said after he placed the card in Tick's left hand.

'I'm afraid you'll need to be schooled at home now, and watched very closely—'

'What?' Tick tried to sit up again, but this time Sato pushed him back, gently. Pain throbbed through Tick's head.

Master George continued speaking. 'No need to worry, good man, no need to worry. As you're well aware, you have an uncanny link to Chi'karda, and it appears capable of spinning completely out of control. But we'll all keep a close eye on you, and if anything troubling happens again, we'll wink you straight in and take care of it. It'll be quite simple, really, considering you'll have plenty of Chi'karda surrounding you wherever you go.'

Tick groaned, so confused at the swirl of emotions inside him he didn't know if he felt sad, angry, hopeless, or happy. But suddenly, all he wanted in the world was to go home and see his family.

'Just wink me back,' he said. 'Please. We can figure it out later. Just send me home.'

'An extraordinary idea, Master Tick! Exactly what I had in mind. Paul and Sofia have long since gone, and it's your turn. Don't worry' – Tick's mouth had opened at the mention of his friends – 'they said they'd have emails waiting for you by the time you arrived in Deer Park. Muffintops, Sato, and I will miss you greatly, but I'm sure our next reunion will happen very soon.'

Tick nodded, the pain in his head making him feel nauseated. 'Where's your Barrier Wand? Can you wink me from here?'

Master George bit his lip. 'Well ... yes, yes, we can, but I need you to do one thing for me first.'

'What?'

Master George looked across the bed. 'Sato?'

Sato stood and walked out of the room, slightly limping. His arms were severely bruised, especially around his wrists.

A long minute passed. Muffintops wandered into the room and jumped up onto Tick's chest, purring as she settled into a comfy position, staring at him with her glowing eyes.

'You be good, cat,' Tick said, wincing at how stupid it sounded. 'Take care of the old man.'

A sound at the door took Tick's attention away. Sato had returned and right behind him, looking even more dishevelled and bruised than Sato or Tick, was Reginald Chu.

Tick sucked in a gasp of air, bolted into a sitting position, and squirmed backwards until he hit the wall. Muffintops shrieked and jumped to the floor. Master George stood, trying to grab Tick's arm.

'Calm yourself!' the old man said. 'Master Atticus, calm yourself!'

Tick ignored the pain that exploded inside him.He noticed handcuffs on Chu's wrists, but that meant nothing. Nothing! The man had more tricks up his sleeve than–

'Tick.' Chu said it, softly, calmly.

Tick ignored him, glaring back and forth between Master George and Sato. 'How could you just let him walk around here?'

'Tick,' Chu repeated. 'Please. *Please,* look at me.'

Finally, still breathing heavily, Tick did. An inexplicable warmth spread through him, and then a realisation hit him. 'What did you call me?' he whispered.

'Tick,' Chu said, acting as if he hadn't heard. 'Please tell these people who I am. I don't know anything about what's going on, or this other Reginald Chu they keep talking about. It's me, Tick – please, tell them!'

Thoughts churned inside Tick's mind. He remembered back in the woods by his house when Mr. Chu had appeared, looking haggard and desperate, acting like he wanted to help them. Something had seemed wrong then, something had been off. And now Tick knew what it was.

'That's my science teacher,' he finally said, feeling so calm it seemed the pain had been cut in half. 'That's Mr. Chu, not ... Reginald Chu. Or ... you know who I mean. This isn't the bad guy.'

Master George gave a knowing look to Sato, the slightest hint of a smile creasing his face. 'I suspected as much, but wanted to be certain. Sorry to spring it on you like that, but I didn't want any chance of your having preconceptions.'

'How do you know for sure?' Sato asked. 'Because he called me Tick. The evil Chu, back in Deer Park, kept calling me Atticus. My science teacher has called me Tick since the first day I met him. Never once has he called me Atticus. I can't believe I didn't think about that back then.'

'No matter,' Master George said. 'I seriously doubted this could be the Reginald from the Fourth, but we had to be certain. Sato, please free the man.'

Mr. Chu sighed, his shoulders sagging in relief as Sato took off the handcuffs.

'I'm sure the two of you will have much to discuss as you get caught up on things,' Master George said. 'Mr. Chu, I hope you'll serve as a tutor to our young friend back in Reality Prime, help him grasp the complexities of the science that is so closely linked to his welfare.'

Mr. Chu didn't look much happier than he had when he'd first entered the room, but he tried his best to smile. 'I think Tick has a lot to teach me first.' He walked over and took Tick's hand, and squeezed it hard as he shook it. 'I'll be expecting a full report, you hear me? And it'd better be good to explain everything I just went through. I think I'll be avoiding dark streets and alleys for a while.'

'Deal,' Tick said. 'As long as you give *me* a full report too. I don't even know why you're *here*.'

Mr. Chu laughed, his face finally winning a victory and looking genuinely pleased, like the teacher Tick had always known. 'Yeah, me neither.'

'Very well, then,' Master George said. 'Sato, please take Mr. Chu and debrief him one last time. I'd also like to speak to him before we send him on his way.'

'Follow me,' Sato said curtly, standing at the door. Mr. Chu patted Tick on the shoulder. 'Real pleasant people you associate with, Tick. Can't wait to spend some more quality time with your friend Sato here.'

'Could be worse – could be Billy "The Goat" Cooper.'

'Good point. See ya back in Deer Park. Take care, okay?'

'You, too.'

Mr. Chu hesitated, sharing a long look with Tick, then left with Sato, who closed the door behind him.

'Right, then,' Master George said, clapping his hands together. 'Atticus, I'll put all of your study materials, this binder, and your other belongings in a suitcase of sorts and wink it straight to your room. I'm quite good at that by now. I promise not to destroy any more walls. As for you – your parents are waiting for you to appear in the forest near your home. Near the heavy Chi'karda spot we've used in the past.'

Tick blinked. 'Right now?'

The old man nodded. 'Right now.'

Despite everything, a laugh croaked out of Tick's parched throat. 'Sweet. I'm ready.'

Master George's face grew serious. He came closer and sat back down in his chair, leaning in towards Tick. 'Atticus, my dear young friend. I just don't know what to think. There has to be some secret about you we've yet to discover, some ... well, *something,* anyway. Your abilities and influence over Chi'karda are just mind-boggling, and there *has* to be an explanation. I give you my word, we'll not rest until we figure it out.'

'I know what it is,' Tick whispered. 'I'm a freak. Mistress Jane only tried to help me because she wanted my freak-boy powers.'

Master George's face reddened, his lips trembling. Then he composed himself before speaking again.

'Listen to me, young man, and listen to me well. Though I fully expect to discover something uncanny about you and your relationship to Chi'karda, I also know this: a large part of it has to do with *you*, and the kind of person you are.'

'What do you mean?'

Master George leaned forward even more. 'You, my friend, have an incredible amount of conviction. Courage. A sincerity of belief and principle. All of those things that make up the very essence of the power of Chi'karda. In other words, a considerable portion of your extraordinary gift comes from the simple fact that you very much want to do good. And for that, I'm proud to call you my friend.'

Tick wasn't sure what he felt at that moment, but he knew if he tried to talk, it would come out sounding like a frog.

'And now,' Master George said, patting Tick's hand, 'off you go. I suspect your parents are quite anxious to have you home.'

ONE WEEK LATER

'Touchdown!'

Tick's dad leapt off the couch, dropping his game controller onto the floor as he started doing a horrific dance, waving one arm about like an elephant's trunk as he shimmied back and forth.

'Tippy-toe left, tippy-toe right,' Dad sang. 'Our team's the best, we're outta sight!'

'Dad,' Tick groaned, not too happy about losing once again in Football 3000 – in overtime, no less. The awful victory dance only made it worse, and the old man didn't show signs of stopping any time soon, shaking his larger-than-usual rear end from side to side.

'Watermelon, watermelon, watermelon rind! Look at the scoreboard and see who's behind!'

'Dad, the neighbours might be watching through the window. Please stop.'

'Two, four, six, eight ... okay, that's enough.' Dad flopped back onto the couch, breathing deeply as if he'd just run a six-minute mile. 'Whew, all that celebratin' can really wear a man out. I wish you'd win more often and make it easier on me.'

'Hilarious. One more game?'

Dad leaned over to pick up the controller. 'You sure enjoy punishment, don't you?'

Just then, Tick's mom walked in, and without saying a word, she sat next to her husband. Tick felt his heart drop when he saw the look on her face, like she'd just been told she had cancer or lost a child.

'Mom, what's wrong?' Tick asked, feeling the controller slip out of his hands.

She didn't answer for a moment, staring at the floor. Finally, she looked up, her eyes haunted. 'Atticus, I can't take it any more. I have to tell you something. I told your dad several months ago – when he broke the news to me that you'd gone off to be recruited by the Realitants.'

'Honey–' Dad began, but cut off at a sharp look from Mom. 'Well, I guess he does deserve to know.' He glanced over at Tick. 'Don't worry – it's pretty neat, actually.'

'Neat,' Mom said in a deadpan voice. 'Once again, Edgar, you've summed things up so eloquently.' She reached over and squeezed Dad's hand. 'Which is why I love you.'

'What are you guys talking about?' Tick asked, much louder than he'd meant to.

'Watch your tone, young man,' Mom said as she folded her hands in her lap. 'It's just that, well, I feel so bad for not telling you before. I think it might have helped you a little, helped you feel more confident. But then again, if I'd known before you winked away that first time, I might have locked you up in a dog kennel.'

'Uh ... sweetie?' Dad said. 'Maybe you should actually tell him what you're talking about.'

Mom looked at Tick for several seconds without saying anything. Then, surprising him, she smiled. 'I think the best way to tell you is to show you.'

As Tick watched, he felt like the laws of gravity had just intensified, pressing him into his seat.

Through the neck of her red blouse, his mom pulled something out that was attached to a golden chain. A pendant. A Barrier Wand pendant, exactly like the one dangling against Tick's chest. He reached up and touched it through his shirt, his eyes stuck on the pendant in his mom's hand. His mouth opened, but no words came out.

'Now before you fall apart,' she said, gripping her pendant in her fist, 'hear me out. I only kept this from you and your dad because I was under strict orders from Master George. He wanted to wait until you were old enough to accept it. Well, I think it's high time – especially now that he's sending Mothball and Rutger to us like ordinary mailmen.'

'Mothball's a woman,' Tick whispered, and somewhere deep down inside, he knew it was exactly the kind of ridiculous statement that pops out of someone who is in complete shock.

'Sorry,' Mom said. 'Mail *persons*. Anyway, yes, I was a Realitant recruit many years ago and earned my pendant. Back then, it was all about science – none of the dangerous things that are happening now. In fact, I left the group right after' – she paused, touching her lips as if holding back tears – 'right after I met your dad. I wanted a normal family life, and Master George let me leave on amicable terms. I should have known that one day he'd go after one of my children.'

'I can't believe it,' Tick said.

His mom folded her arms defiantly. 'Well, why *not?* I know more about science and quantum physics than most people, thank you very much. And now that all of this is out, I can tell you one more thing. I expect you to hit those books Master George sent with a passion, and I'll be on top of you every step of the way, quizzing and pushing. You've got a lot to learn, son. A lot.'

'How did I end up with all these smart people?' Dad asked to no one in particular.

'Hush, Edgar,' Mom whispered, patting him on the knee.

Dad looked at Tick. 'I love when she says that.'

Tick stood up, surprised he could do so – everything seemed to spin around him. 'You've got ... to be ... *kidding* me.'

'Now, look here—' his mom began.

'No, Mom, that's not what I mean.'

'Then what *do* you mean?' Her eyebrows shot up when Tick laughed out loud.

'It's just ... that's the coolest thing I've ever heard. *My mom* was a Realitant.' He took a seat again on the couch. 'I guess it's finally official where I got my brains from.' He paused. 'Uh, no offence, Dad.'

☼

Later that night, Tick sat in front of the fireplace, staring into the flickering flames. Autumn had settled in on Deer Park, making everything cool and crisp. Dad was too stubborn to turn the heater on just yet, so Tick warmed himself before heading up to bed.

As he sat there, almost in a daze, fingering the Barrier Wand pendant through his shirt, his thoughts spun. He'd be fourteen years old in a couple of weeks

– hard to believe. How different his life had become in just one year. Not only was he a member of a group that studied and worked to protect alternate realities, he had some freaky power that was completely out of control. He'd been pulled from school to be taught full-time by his mom, with weekly lessons with Mr. Chu, and was monitored constantly for any signs of Chi'karda trouble. It wouldn't be proper to cause an earthquake and destroy half the town of Deer Park.

And always, always, there was the threat of a call for help from Master George. Who knew what waited on the other side of the horizon?

My mom was a Realitant, he thought. *Holy–*

A tap on his shoulder interrupted his thoughts. He turned to see Kayla, holding a teddy bear in one hand, a red-and-black scarf in the other. Her curly blonde hair brushed the shoulders of her pink pyjamas.

'Well, what are *you* doing?' he asked, reaching out to ruffle her hair.

'This nasty old scarf was in my closet. Mommy said you lost your other ones.'

Tick looked at the dusty scarf clutched in her hand. He had to admit he'd thought about the missing scarf and his birthmark a few times in the last few weeks. It still made him uncomfortable to think people might be gawking at the ugly red thing on his neck. But for all that, he realised he never cared about it much when it was just Paul and Sofia around.

Kayla held out the scarf. 'Want it?'

Tick took the scarf, then ran it through his hands, staring at the oh-so-familiar pattern of red and black. 'Kayla, if I let you do something, do you *promise* not to tell Mom and Dad?'

'Will I get in trouble?'

'*No* – but I don't want you to tell them. Don't worry – this isn't a bad thing. It's a really good thing, actually. But we don't want them to worry, now do we?'

Kayla shook her head.

'I want you to throw this into the fire.'

Her eyes lit up, almost as bright as the flames. She looked for all the world like he'd just offered her a lifetime pass to Disneyland. Burning things had always been the one no-no of which she was notoriously guilty.

'Really?' she asked, licking her lips.

'Really. But just this once, okay? You'd better not burn anything else. Promise?'

She nodded her head. 'I promise.'

Tick handed her the scarf and scooted out of the way. 'Go for it.'

Kayla wadded up the cloth into a ball, then stepped close to the fireplace. She looked one last time at Tick, as if she thought the opportunity had to be too good to be true. When he just nodded encouragingly, she turned back and threw the scarf into the fire. It took a second to catch, but then smoke billowed up as the flames began to eat away at the material. They both watched as it burned to ashes.

Tick stood up and gave her a hug. 'Good job. You're the best pyro I've ever met.'

'What's a pie-row?'

'Nothing. You better get up to bed or Mom will take that teddy bear away.'

''Kay. Goodnight.' She turned and ran out of the room, shuffling along with her tiny footsteps.

Tick watched her go, then thought of the stack of Realitant and science books sitting on his desk upstairs. 'I've got a lot of work to do,' he said aloud to no one but himself.

He reached down and turned off the fire, then headed for his room.

YELLOW AND RED

Frazier Gunn hadn't spoken to Mistress Jane for more than two months.

As he stood in the dark stone corridor outside her room, he suddenly wished he had another two months. This summons had been unexpected, and he felt the uncomfortable sweat of fear slicking his palms. Everyone in the castle knew something horrible had happened to Jane; they'd all heard the screams coming from her chambers, often long into the night.

She'd gone through no fewer than eleven servants – only half of them surviving to tell about it, though it did Frazier little good, since they all had sworn a vow of silence, on penalty of death.

Frazier steeled himself, wiped his hands on his trousers, and knocked on the door.

On the third thunk, the door swung open violently, slamming against the stone wall on the other side.

'Enter, Frazier.'

It was a voice he barely recognised. Raw and scratchy – *weak,* as if Jane had swallowed a glass of lava, scorching her throat and vocal chords.

'Enter,' she repeated.

Frazier couldn't see where she was in the room.

He stepped across the threshold, then closed the door. The only light in the room was a fire, burning hotly with several fresh logs, spitting and cracking. With a shudder, he remembered back to Jane's flying cinder display, and he hoped there'd be no repeat tonight.

'You called for me?' Frazier asked the darkness.

A figure stepped out of the shadows behind a deep wardrobe in the corner between the bed and a large open window, where curtains fluttered in the breeze. Though Frazier could not yet see any details, he knew it was his boss. But she appeared to have something draped over her head.

'It's good to see you again, Mistress Jane,' he said, fighting to keep his voice steady.

'My dear Frazier,' she said, her voice the sound of rocks rubbing on sandpaper. 'You will never know how very good it is to see *you.*'

For the first time, Frazier realised there was a slight hollowness to her voice, as if it were muffled by something over her mouth. Subtle, but there all the same.

'That means a lot to me,' he finally said. And he meant it.

'I've often been ... cruel to you,' Jane said, taking a step forward. Though she was still mostly in shadow, Frazier could see that she wore a long, flowing robe, its hood pulled up over her head. Something glinted off her face, a flickering reflection from the fire.

Must be her glasses, Frazier thought.

'You've only ever done that which needed to be done,' he said. 'I know I'll have my reward some day, when we make the Realities as they were meant to be.'

'Frazier,' she whispered.

'Yes, Mistress Jane?'

'I want you to know that I love you as if you were my own brother. I promise never to be cruel to you again.'

Frazier felt a strange mixture of elation and sick fear. 'The feeling is mutual.' His hands were sweating even worse than before. So was his face.

'That makes me happy, Frazier. Very, very happy.' Mistress Jane stepped out into the full light of the fire, and a puff of sharp air escaped Frazier's lips before he could stop it. He took a step backwards, cursing himself silently as soon as he did.

The floor-length robe that draped over her head and shoulders and body was a brilliant yellow, glowing like molten gold in the flickering light of the flames. Where her face should have been, a red mask floated, bright as fresh blood. Though it sparkled like shiny metal, its surface moved and flowed, creating subtle facial expressions, alternating between anger, sadness, excitement, confusion, joy, pain. Small holes, as dark as the deepest depths of the ocean, made up her eyes, and somehow Frazier knew she was looking at him through the mask.

'Mistress Jane ...' was all he could get out.

The flowing, red metal mask solidified into a stark expression of rage, eyebrows slanted up from the nose like a big V.

'*He* did this to me, Frazier,' she said, her raspy voice bitter and tight. 'I tried so hard to make him see – to work with him, to *help* him. But in the end, he looked at me and threw all of his powers against me. He *hurt* me, Frazier. I will always be in pain now.'

'Who?' Frazier asked. 'Who did this to you? What ...'
He almost asked her what was hidden beneath the
yellow robe, but he knew better.

She turned her red mask to look at the fire as
she continued speaking. 'But perhaps it was for the
best. I've been reminded of my life's duty. I've been
reminded how cold and cruel the Realities can be.
I've been reminded of the goals I set so many years
ago. And I've been reminded of what kind of person
it takes to accomplish ... what we *need* to accomplish.'

'Yes, Mistress Jane,' he answered fervently. 'I'll be
by your side. Always.'

'If I ever falter again, Frazier – if I ever doubt myself
or doubt the things I need to do and the way in which
I need to do them, I want you to do me a favour.'

'Anything.'

'I want you to say two words to me. Two words. It'll
be all the reminder I ever need.'

'What words, Mistress?' Frazier asked.

Jane looked back in his direction, the darkness of
her eyeholes boring into him out of the shiny red
mask of liquid metal. And then she told him.

'Atticus Higginbottom.'

A Glossary of People, Places, and All Things Important

Atticus Higginbottom – A Realitant from the state of Washington in Reality Prime. Also known as Tick.

Alterant – Different versions of the same person existing in different Realities. It is extremely dangerous for Alterants to meet one another.

Annika – A spy for the Realitants who was killed by a pack of fangen.

Barf Scarf – The red-and-black scarf that Tick wears to hide the ugly birthmark on his neck.

Barrier Wand – The device used to wink people and things between Realities and between heavily concentrated places of Chi'karda within the same Reality. Works very easily with inanimate objects, and can place them almost anywhere. Humans must be in a place with concentrated Chi'karda (like a cemetery) and have a nanolocator that transmits their location to the Wand in order to be transported. Useless without a Chi'karda Drive, which channels and magnifies the mysterious power.

Benson – A servant of Reginald Chu in the Fourth Reality.

Bermuda Triangle – The most concentrated area of Chi'karda in each Reality. Still unknown as to why.

Billy "The Goat" Cooper – Tick's biggest nemesis at Jackson Middle School.

Chi'karda – The mysterious force that controls quantum physics. The scientific embodiment of conviction and choice, which in reality rules the universe. Responsible for creating the different Realities.

Chi'karda Drive – The invention that revolutionised the universe, the drive is able to harness, magnify, and control Chi'karda. It has long been believed that travel between Realities is impossible without it.

Chu Industries – The company that practically rules the world of the Fourth Reality. Known for countless inventions and technologies, including many that are malicious in nature.

Command Centre – Master George's headquarters in the Bermuda Triangle, where Chi'karda levels are monitored and to where his many nanolocators report various types of information. Heavily damaged by the forces of Mistress Jane and currently under repair.

Darkin Project (Dark Infinity) – A menacing, giant device created by Reginald Chu of the Fourth Reality. May be the source of a plague of insanity sweeping the Realities.

Earwig Transponder – An insect-like device inserted into the ear that can scramble listening devices and help track its host.

Edgar Higginbottom – Tick's father.

Entropy – The law of nature that states all things move towards destruction. Related to fragmentation.

Fangen – The sickening abomination of a creature created by Mistress Jane, utilising the mutated version of Chi'karda found in the Thirteenth Reality. Formed from a variety of no fewer than twelve different animals, the short and stocky fangen are bred to kill first and ask questions later. They can also fly.

Fragmentation – What happens to a Reality when it begins losing Chi'karda levels on a vast scale due to entropy. It can no longer maintain itself as a major alternate version of the world, and will eventually disintegrate into nothing.

Frazier Gunn – A loyal servant of Mistress Jane.

Frupey – Nickname for Fruppenschneiger, Sofia's butler.

Gnat Rat – A malicious invention of Chu Industries in the Fourth Reality. Releases dozens of mechanical hornets that are programmed to attack a certain individual based on a nanolocator, DNA, or blood type.

Grand Canyon – A satellite location of the Realitants. Second only to the Bermuda Triangle in Chi'karda levels. Still unknown as to why.

Grinder Beast – An enormous, rhinoceros-like creature with dozens of legs. Found in the Tenth Reality.

Hans Schtiggenschlubberheimer – The man who started the scientific revolution in the Fourth Reality in the early Twentieth Century. In a matter of decades, he helped catapult the Fourth far beyond the other Realities in terms of technology.

Haunce, The – A mystery of the Realities that Master George has yet to explain.

Henry – A boy from the Industrial Barrens of the Seventh Reality.

Hillenstat – A Realitant doctor from the Second Reality.

Jimmy "The Voice" Porter – A Realitant from the Twelfth Reality. He has no tongue.

Katrina Kay – A Realitant from the Ninth Reality.

Kayla Higginbottom – Tick's little sister.

Klink – Guard of the Execution Exit at the End of the Road Insane Asylum.

Kyoopy – Nickname used by the Realitants for quantum physics.

Lemon Fortress – Mistress Jane's castle in the Thirteenth Reality.

Lisa Higginbottom – Tick's older sister.

Lorena Higginbottom – Tick's mother.

Mabel Ruth Gertrude Higginbottom Fredrickson – Tick's great-aunt in Alaska.

Master George – The current leader of the Realitants.

Metaspide – A vicious robotic creature from the Fourth Reality that resembles a spider. Chu's security force.

Mistress Jane – A former Realitant and ruler of the Thirteenth Reality. Has an uncanny power over Chi'karda.

Mothball – A Realitant from the Fifth Reality.

Ms. Sears – Tick's favourite librarian.

Muffintops – Master George's cat.

Multiverse – An old term used by Reality Prime scientists to explain the theory that quantum physics had created multiple versions of the universe.

Nancy Zeppelin – A Realitant from Wisconsin in Reality Prime.

Nanolocator – A microscopic electronic device that can crawl into a person's skin and forever provide information on their whereabouts, including Chi'karda levels.

Nonex – When Alterants meet, one disappears and enters the Nonex. A complete mystery to the Realitants.

Norbert Johnson – A post office worker in Alaska who helped Tick and his dad escape an attack by Frazier Gunn.

Paul Rogers – A Realitant from Florida in Reality Prime.

Phillip – Owner and operator of The Stroke of Midnight Inn in the Sixth Reality.

Pick – Master George's nickname for a major decision in which Chi'karda levels spike considerably. Some Picks have been known to create or destroy entire Realities.

Priscilla Persephone – A Realitant from the Seventh Reality.

Quantum Physics – The science that studies the physical world of the extremely small. Most scholars are baffled by its properties and at a loss to explain them. Theories abound. Only a few know the truth: that a completely different power rules this realm, which in turn rules the universe – Chi'karda.

Quinton Hallenhaffer – A Realitant from the Second Reality.

Ragers (Static Ragers) – An advanced weapon that harnesses extreme amounts of static electricity. When unleashed, it collects matter in a ball that can shatter whatever gets in its way.

Realitants – An organisation sworn to discover and chart all known Realities. Founded in the 1970s by a group of scientists from the Fourth Reality, who then used Barrier Wands to recruit other quantum physicists from other Realities.

Realities – A separate and complete version of the world, of which there may be an infinite number. The most stable and strongest is called Reality Prime. So far, twelve major branches of Reality Prime have been discovered. Realities are created and destroyed by enormous fluctuations in Chi'karda levels. Examples:

Fourth – Much more technologically advanced than the other Realities due to the remarkable vision and work of Hans Schtiggenschlubberheimer.

Fifth – Quirks in evolution led to a very tall human race.

Eighth – The world is covered in water due to much higher temperatures caused by a star fusion anomaly triggered in another galaxy by an alien race.

Eleventh – Quirks in evolution and diet led to a short and robust human race.

Thirteenth – Somehow a mutated and very powerful version of Chi'karda exists here.

Reginald Chu – Tick's science teacher in Reality Prime. His Alterant is from the Fourth Reality and founded Chu Industries and turned it into a worldwide empire.

Renee – An inmate at the End of the Road Insane Asylum.

Ripple Quake – A violent geological disaster caused by a massive disturbance in Chi'karda.

Rutger – A Realitant from the Eleventh Reality.

Sally T. Jones – A Realitant from the Tenth Reality.

Sato – A Realitant from Japan in Reality Prime.

Shockpulse – An injection of highly concentrated electromagnetic nanobots that seek out and destroy the tiny components of a nanolocator, rendering it useless.

Shurric – Short for Sonic Hurricaner, a more powerful version of the Sound Slicer. Shoots out a heavily concentrated force of sound waves almost too low for the human ear to register but powerful enough to destroy just about anything in its direct path.

Slinkbeast – A vicious creature that lives in the Mountains of Sorrow in the Twelfth Reality.

Snooper Bug – A hideous crossbreed of birds and insects created by the mutated power of the Chi'karda in the Thirteenth Reality. Can detect any known weapon or poison and can kill with one quick strike of its needle-nosed beak. Pets of Mistress Jane.

Sofia Pacini – A Realitant from Italy in Reality Prime.

Soulikens – A mystery of the Realities that Master George has yet to explain.

Sound Slicer – A small weapon outdated by the much more powerful Shurric.

Spinner – A special device that shoots out a circular plane of laser, displaying video images on its surface.

Tick – Nickname for Atticus Higginbottom.

Tingle Wraith – A collection of microscopic animals from the Second Reality, called spilphens, that can form together into a cloud while rubbing against each other to make a horrible sound called the Death Siren.

William Schmidt – A Realitant from the Third Reality.

Windbike – An invention of Chu Industries, this vehicle is a motorcycle that can fly, consuming hydrogen out of the air for its fuel. Based on an extremely complex gravity-manipulation theorem first proposed by Reginald Chu.

Winking – The act of travelling between or within Realities by use of a Barrier Wand. Causes a slight tingle to the skin on one's shoulders and back.

ACKNOWLEDGMENTS

Somehow we made it to Book two, so there must be a lot of people to thank.

I'm extremely grateful to my agent, Michael Bourret. He has single-handedly taken my career to an entirely new level. If it weren't for him, I'd never be doing what I love for a living. Thanks, Michael, and I look forward to more great things to come.

Just like last time, I owe a lot to Chris Schoebinger, Lisa Mangum, and everyone else at Shadow Mountain. It just baffles me how much hard work goes into getting a book in the hands of readers. Thank you all very, very much.

Thanks to Bryan Beus for his awesome artwork. You are one talented dude, and I'm honoured to be partnered with you.

Thanks to those who read the manuscript and provided valuable feedback: My wife, Lynette, of course – she's always first. J. Scott Savage, friend, fellow author, and constant lunch partner. LuAnn Staheli and her incredible middle school class. Danyelle Ferguson, a very talented and up-and-coming writer. Heather Moore, good friend and brilliant editor, and her son, Kaelin. And probably others. If I forgot you, please forgive me and call me for a free dinner.

Thanks to Lisa Guerrero, a cancer research scientist from Chicago, for her services as a consultant and science genius. She's way smart, yo. Like, really, really smart.

Once again, thanks to the dude who invented football. I could never thank you enough. Oh, and I also really appreciate the guy who invented Tiger Woods.

Thanks to the cow that provided a very juicy steak at Hamilton's in Logan, Utah, in February of 2008. You will be missed.

Thanks to the mother of Christopher Nolan for going through the pain of birthing him. I never thought I would say this, but Christopher is now tied with Peter Jackson as my favourite directors. You are both geniuses.

Last but never least, thank you to my readers. You're what it's all about. I look forward to sharing stories with you for a very long time.